CHRONICLES OF THE
SENTINELS
CHAMPIONS

Jon Wasik

This one's for me. I know, strange, right? Call it stubbornness or stout determination, but I believe in this book, in this *trilogy*. Shoving through self-doubts and doubters alike, I completed this trilogy because I couldn't let myself fail.

Also by Jon Wasik

The Sword of Dragons
Rise of the Forgotten – The Sword of Dragons Book 1
The Orc War Campaigns – A Sword of Dragons Story
Burning Skies – The Sword of Dragons Book 2
Secrets of the Cronal – The Sword of Dragons Book 3

Chronicles of the Sentinels
Legacy
Retribution
Champions

ACKNOWLEDGMENTS

This trilogy has been a passion project of mine for a long time, and I owe some amazing people for helping me bring it to light!

First and foremost, a shout out to my wife, Beck, for their endless and undying support, encouragement, and help. Beck was one of my first beta readers for Chronicles of the Sentinels, and helped me ensure I did the LGBT+ community justice throughout the entire trilogy. In fact, every part of this crazy creative endeavor? They've been there for me with ideas, feedback, encouragement, and love. I know it's a cliché to say this, but I truly am beyond fortunate to have someone like Beck as a part of my life!

Thank you to Wayne Adams from VtW Productions for always supporting my writing.

Thank you to Jen Immer and Sean Carter for helping me with cultural terminology.

Thank you to all of my Facebook, Instagram, and blog followers for enduring my social media ineptness! I struggle with it to this day, but you all are incredibly supportive!

And as always, to the Welts family for their constant support. Especially my best friend of over 20 years, Nick. You've endured beta reads, story ideas, frustrations, and celebrations with me. Thanks for always being there for me!

A NOTE FROM THE AUTHOR:

Chronicles of the Sentinels contains a diverse cast – representation and inclusion are important to me, and as it happens, is an important part of the story told in this trilogy.

It is my sincere hope that what I have written is respectful and accurate, and I've had a lot of help in ensuring I've done so. However, I am still human and will inevitably make mistakes. I hope you enjoy the story you're about to read, but if I have portrayed anything inaccurately, I would love to hear from you!

You can contact me through my website, http://jonwasik.com

CHARACTER REFRESHER

When last we left our intrepid heroes, after struggling to protect their families from Nabu, the demigod struck at their heart in a bid to find the enchanted dagger Imhullu. The Denver Sentinel tower now lies in ruin in the streets of Denver, Nabu has Imhullu in-hand, and the President of the United States of America, under Nabu's influence, has declared all Sentinels enemies of the state, forcing the Denver Sentinels to flee for their lives.

Christopher Tatsu - The hero of our journey, Chris is a young college graduate who, after a fateful party invitation, discovered that not only was magic real, he himself is able to use it. More than that, he has discovered that he is a descendant of the first Sentinel, Tattannu, and is fated to destroy Nabu and Marduk, but at a terribly vague cost – everything. Fearing that he will be forced to sacrifice his own life in the endeavor, Chris has opted not to act on his feelings for Alycia.

Typical fatalist hero, right?

Still, he's the biggest repository of geek and pop culture quotes west of the Mississippi, so that counts for something, doesn't it?

Emmanuelle (Emmi) Dubois – Another hero in this journey of heroes, Emmi discovered at the beginning of all of this that she can shapeshift into just about any creature on Earth. Unfortunately, shortly after that, she was captured by Nabu and forced to endure something no one should ever have to endure. Emmi has struggled ever since to control her rage and hatred, fueling a rage-form bear that she nearly lost control. With some time and effort on her part, she has mastered her rage.

Now Emmi is on the run with the rest of the Denver Sentinels.

Alycia Taylor – An enchanter and conjurer, before becoming a Sentinel, Alycia had no idea her father commanded the Denver-based Sentinels, and only knew that Nabu supposedly murdered her mother, Mia. Her mother survived, in actuality, and was under Nabu's control for almost two decades. While Chris managed to cleanse Mia of Nabu's control, Alycia still doesn't trust her mother. Worse still, her father, gravely injured when Sentinel Tower literally fell, was left behind. Now, Alycia feels alone and isolated, but has spent the past three months, while on the run with the others, honing her skills and crafting additional enchanted items for the team.

Thomas Taylor – Commander of the Denver Sentinels, Tom spent the past two decades bent on recapturing Nabu and avenging his wife's death. Except she's not dead. She serves Nabu. Or served. It's complicated. Anyway, Tom was gravely injured during the death-defying escape from Sentinel Tower, and was left behind in the hospital when the rest of the Sentinels fled. As a result, once he was healthy enough, he was remanded into the custody of the Federal Bureau of Investigation, and is now a prisoner.

Shara – Second-in-command of the Denver Sentinels, Shara is *not* an elf. She just looks like one, with pointed ears, blue hair, and purple eyes. Like Emmi, Shara is a shapeshifter, who was stranded on Earth during World War II, and was subsequently rescued by the Sentinels. Having served with them ever since, and with Tom out of commission, she now acts as commander while the Sentinels hide from Nabu and the United States Government.

Mia Taylor – Mia was long-thought dead at the hands of Nabu, but in reality, under Nabu's magical influence, she helped Nabu escape from a Sentinel prison in Adelaide, Australia. Mia served as Nabu's trusted lieutenant ever since, until she was recaptured by the Sentinels three months ago, and subsequently cleansed of Nabu's influence by Chris. Now she tries to prove herself to the Sentinels and, more importantly for her, to her daughter, and make up for the atrocities she committed for Nabu.

Eric Taylor – Alycia's estranged brother, he was used by Mia to bait Tom and the other Sentinels to the Melbourne Airport in order to further Nabu's goals of sowing international chaos. Eric was particularly miffed that Tom and Alycia never told him that his mother was alive, and still hasn't forgiven them.

When the Sentinels were declared America's Most Wanted, he decided he didn't need to run and hide with the others. However, since he was in the United States illegally, without a passport or record of entry, he is stuck, and so has remained in Abby's care.

Babbar Nurin – A gnome who has willingly hidden himself on Earth, along with his companion dragon Nina. Babbar was a dealer of magical artifacts until he was captured by Shara just before the Barrier cracked. Since then, he has offered his and Nina's help in staying one step ahead of Nabu. Like the Sentinels, he is on the run and hiding from Nabu and the United States Government.

Ninazu – Better known as Nina, she is a tiny, foot-long dragon who loves bottle caps (seriously, she hordes them like gold,) and can create portals to anywhere if fed a copper coin (real copper coins, not those U.S. pennies.) Strangely enough, Nina was able to use her magic even when the Barrier was at full strength. Stranger still, Nabu is terrified of her, and used a cheap-shot sniper attack to incapacitate her at Sentinel Tower. Nina has since recovered, and is helping the Sentinels escape and elude federal agents.

Abigail Turner – The heart and soul of the Denver Sentinels, Abby is their 'gal behind the computer,' an expert white-hat (or maybe gray-hat) hacker and computer genius. When the Sentinels were declared enemies of the state, Abby used her l33t hacker skills to create a false identity for herself and Eric, and went into hiding. Since then, she's supplied the Sentinels with information where possible, while keeping an eye on the news feeds for anything hinting at Nabu's next move.

Tiana Jones – One of the elite members of the Sentinels, Tiana is a talented pilot, able to fly both fixed-wing aircraft and helicopters. She is also the best sharpshooter on the team. Unfortunately, there hasn't been much call for piloting since the Sentinels have been on the run. Nevertheless, Tiana's skills with a weapon have helped ensure the Sentinels' continued freedom.

Marisol Rodriguez – Usually one of two American Sentinels on night shift, Marisol joined the Sentinels specifically because of her fascination with magic, and her desire to see more of it. Like the other Sentinels, she is on the run from the U.S. Government.

Benson – A former member of the Denver Sentinels who occasionally trains new recruits. He trained Chris, Alycia, and Emmi in the mountains west of Denver.

He's a bit of a prick.

The Collector – A mysterious 'person of interest' with a southern drawl, not much is known about the Collector, and other than the fact that no one knows what he looks like, he can change accents on the fly, and is a collector of both magical artifacts and information. He is believed to have served Nabu, and tried to capture Chris and his friends during their one and only encounter.

Nabu – The half-human 'son' of the Babylonian god Marduk, Nabu's original human body was destroyed by Chris in Babylon. Since then, Nabu has inhabited the body of a young Scottish woman, consuming her soul in the process. Nabu has used her powers and influence to assault the Sentinels at every turn and has reclaimed the enchanted dagger Imhullu, with plans to use it to destroy Marduk. Odd, if you ask anyone, since Nabu is literally part of her father, but she's grown to like being independent, and intends to keep it that way at any cost. She was last seen controlling the President of the United States and setting scientists and enchanters on a mission to adapt Imhullu to a more nefarious use.

Marduk – *The* villain of the series, even if he hasn't actually been encountered yet, Marduk was known as a Babylonian god. In truth, Marduk is an infernal, a sort of anti-god, who was imprisoned by a celestial eons ago. He intends to regain enough strength through consuming human souls to break free of his otherworldly prison and enslave humanity, ensuring a steady supply of human souls for the rest of eternity. There's even talk of him using 8 billion human souls to fuel a Universe-wide war against all celestials.

He likes to dream big.

CHAPTER 1

When a federal agent slaps handcuffs on a person's wrists, it doesn't matter if it's part of 'the plan,' it still makes one nervous.

The icy grip of fear and the slow burn of doubt crept into Christopher Tatsu's thoughts as the cold steel clacked against his wrists, and the agent facing Chris in a local café gave him a scornful smirk.

Chris resisted the urge to gulp, every vein in his body rushing with teeth-chattering anxiety. He faced the agent and his partner, a younger woman who vaguely reminded him of Agent Scully, with as much composure as he could muster.

Searching for something to ease his fears, he took a page from Alycia's book and quipped, "A little old-fashioned, isn't it?" He jangled the chain between his cuffs. "I thought you guys used plastic ties or something like that these days."

Narrowing his eyes, the agent remarked in a gruff, bass voice, "You've watched too much TV, kid. And besides, we know how to contain freaks like you now. Just try and use your magic in these." Gruffly, he hoisted Chris's hands up, and pointed to a small etching on each cuff.

Chris was supposed to be surprised, and the agent searched his eyes for the look that might satisfy him. The truth was, Chris and the other Sentinels knew about the enchantments used to secure magic-wielding prisoners. After all, they had not been idle in the three months since the tower collapsed in Denver, and while hiding and surviving had been their primary goal during that time, gathering information had been a close second.

The café they stood in was a popular local haunt in Springfield, Virginia, and was carefully chosen as the place to 'give himself up.' It was very lively with a lunch-rush crowd, and most of the two-dozen tables were occupied.

Of course, as far as anyone else knew, Chris wasn't giving up, he just didn't have a choice, not when surrounded by heavily armed federal agents. The two arresting him weren't wearing suits and ties like the famous X-Files agents. Instead, they wore tactical gear with automatic weapons, and the girl in particular had her gun pointed at Chris's chest.

As did the twenty other agents crammed around him in the coffee shop, having rushed in moments ago, disturbing the peaceful gathering of caffeine-deprived customers consumed in their day-to-day. Chris was sure the shattered front windows of the store were particularly vexing to the owner, who stood behind the counter gaping at the movie-like scene playing out before him.

Chris had entered the coffee shop only ten minutes ago, wearing disheveled, smelly clothes like he'd been on the run for three months (which he had,) and had used his credit card to buy lunch and a latte. A mistake he hadn't made in all this time, but a calculated one made now to draw in the federal 'Magic Hunters.'

The agent in front of him yanked on his cuffs and forcefully pulled him toward the exit. "H-hey," he protested. "Don't you have to read me my Miranda Rights or something?"

The girl looked disdainfully at him. "Scum like you doesn't get rights," she remarked in a low, cold tone.

A young man, probably around Chris's age, gaped at her words as they passed by, and he started to stand up to protest. Chris looked him in the eye, and shook his head. That wouldn't help. Not only would it probably land the guy in jail along with Chris, but it would be counter-productive to the plan.

Besides, he wasn't technically alone. Nearby, the pointy-eared second in command of the U.S. Sentinels watched along-side the team's sharpshooter, Tiana, ready to help Chris if things took a turn for the worst.

It was their backup if Chris's plan failed, which as plans go, he wasn't sure was the wisest course of action.

When the agents yanked him outside, the chill winter air sent shivers along his spine. A long stream of well-armed men and women followed, and it took every bit of self-control he had not to look towards a nearby, taller building, where his friends watched.

Them and Nina. A tiny little dragon capable not just of cloaking herself, but of concealing others when asked to. Otherwise the two helicopters orbiting around the coffee shop would have spotted the Sentinels. Of course, no one, not even Babbar, knew that Nina could hide others. When the gnome had asked his dragon why she hadn't mentioned it before, she had chortled a response that drew an indignant stare from Babbar. "I never asked you before? Really? That's your excuse?!"

So far, so good, Chris thought as the agents led him into the street. Surprisingly, they didn't throw him into the back seat of a hopelessly outdated sedan. Instead, they yanked him up the ramp into the bowels of an Armored Personnel Carrier, the kind military and S.W.A.T. used, and Chris barely ducked in time before smacking his head on the low entrance and ceiling.

The agent hauling Chris along stopped, bodily turned him sideways, and shoved him into a seat before sitting across from him. The girl sat one seat over, and two more well-armed and armored agents joined them before the back hatch rose up with a mechanical whine and sealed them in.

With no windows and poor lighting inside, Chris felt more trapped than ever.

The APC's engine rumbled to life, shaking Chris to the core, before the driver shifted into gear and they trundled off. Chris looked at the agent that had arrested him carefully, while he stared with narrowed eyes back at Chris. The girl obviously hated magic users, but did he? *More than likely,* Chris grimaced.

Still…

Raising his cuffed hands up and jangling the chain, he started to say something, but everyone raised their guns at him at once, as if he were the most dangerous person on the planet.

"Hey, easy, *easy,*" he froze. "I can't do anything with these on, right?"

"We've learned not to take chances with your kind," the girl growled at him. He knew there was a story in there somewhere, a reason behind her revulsion towards him, but now wasn't the time to ask.

"But they work, don't they?" he asked, lowering his hands very,

very slowly.

Raising a curious eyebrow, the arresting agent asked, "You haven't tried magic yet?" He carefully lowered his rifle and narrowed his eyes again. "I know who you are, I know that you're one of the most dangerous magic users out there."

That was true. Unlike most people on Earth who had suddenly found themselves capable of using magic six months ago, Chris had the souls of millions of ancestors powering his magic. As time went on, his control over that power, and the amount he seemed to be able to wield at any given time, grew. In fact, since those long-forgotten days at a training camp in the mountains, Chris's powers had easily doubled, if not tripled, and he'd picked up a trick or two since then.

But nothing, not even his abilities, could realistically contend with the agents' boss. Even if the agent didn't know it.

"So where'd you get them?" Chris asked, eyes darting to his cuffs. "As far as I know, magic is the only thing that can stop magic, and I know an enchantment when I see one." It helped that one of his best friends, Alycia Taylor, was an enchanter. He'd seen her work her magic often enough. Continuing on, Chris added, "Odd that you hate magic, yet you employ it to stop magic users."

Before the guy could say anything, the girl venomously replied, "How else are we supposed to deal with your kind?"

"My kind?" Chris asked with a frown. "We're still human."

"That's debatable," she sneered. How many different angry expressions did she have in her repertoire?

"Wilson," the guy barked at her. "That's enough!"

Her cheeks burned, but she clamped her mouth shut. Chris wanted to antagonize her more, to insult her for the way she treated him, but he somehow resisted, his insides rushing with that base-level fight-or-flight instinct, with the fight aspect growing stronger by the minute.

But he could do neither, and he didn't want to do either. He had to let them take him to lockdown. To a specially created prison, hastily erected in Washington, D.C. for magic users.

Where Thomas Taylor was being held.

They hadn't left Tom behind by choice. But when the President had declared all Sentinels as America's Most Wanted, Tom was still recovering from surgery after being pierced in the torso by a chunk of their former base in downtown Denver. There was no way the

Sentinels could have moved their commander safely.

So they ran. They left Tom behind and they ran and hid, and for three months, they'd kept one step ahead of the hunters.

Barely.

Speaking of hunters. "So you have an enchanter making special cuffs for you, but what about the Sniffers?" Chris asked. "Why didn't you bring one of them?" Sniffers was what he and the other Sentinels started calling those who could use magic to find other magic users.

Before recent times, Chris had assumed there were only a handful of types of magic out there, and he expected most magic users to be like him, Alycia, or his other best friend Emmi. That is, those capable of arcane magic, those who could enchant and conjure, or those who could shapeshift.

Turns out there was a *lot* more types of magic than that.

"We did," the arresting agent snuffed. "They're still at the coffee shop looking for your friends that you no doubt brought along." He leaned forward menacingly, and added with a sinister whisper, "I know you're not stupid enough to use your credit card. You're up to something, kid, you and your traitorous rat pack."

Chris frowned and mouthed, 'rat pack?'

Leaning back against his seat, no doubt as uncomfortable as Chris's, the agent sighed. "Even if we don't, we have ways of persuading you."

Calculating that the guy, whose name Chris dearly hoped to learn soon, was far more reasonable than the Wilson girl, Chris narrowed his eyes and said, "You mean *she* does."

Not Wilson.

Nor anyone else present.

Nabu.

Formerly the half-human son of Marduk, Chris's nemesis occupied a woman's body that the demigod had forcefully taken after Chris and the Sentinels had destroyed the original form.

The Sentinels knew that Nabu was in D.C. as well, at least some of the time. Worse, she had worked her way into the White House, and now controlled the President, whether through magic, lies, or a combination thereof.

Nabu was the limiting factor in Chris's plan. By now she would know that Chris had been arrested and was on his way to the holding facility.

The arresting agent didn't react to Chris's question, and they rode along in silence. He knew who Chris meant, but he must not have asked too many questions about her.

Chris had to be careful not to reveal just how much he knew, but he wanted to push the agent a little harder, to maybe open the door just enough to make him curious.

"What name does she go by? Nancy? Nikki?" Chris shrugged. "I know her as Nabu. You want to talk about a dangerously powerful magic user, you need to look at her."

"The President's chief adviser on magic doesn't have power herself," Wilson scowled at him, the muzzle of her weapon rising.

"But how does she know so much?" Chris asked with a frown. "Until six months ago, only the Sentinels knew anything about magic, so how does she know so much?"

"She used to be one of you," the arresting agent opened his eyes. "Said so herself."

"Ah," he nodded, already aware of that particular lie. "How convenient. So she no doubt tells you that's why she has no past records. She was 'hidden' in the secret organization."

"And was smart enough to come forward when we needed the most help," the agent nodded.

"Tell me," Chris frowned, "why only her? I mean, why is she the only Sentinel with no past?" He looked at Wilson, whose glare never wavered, and then back at the arresting agent. "Last I checked, none of us have had our records erased from history. I was put on the Sentinel payroll before you started hunting us. I had taxes taken out while I worked for them. My existence wasn't kept secret, my identity wasn't washed away. So why was hers?"

Wilson didn't take the bait, but for the first time since they'd started talking, she looked away.

The other agent, however. He hid it well, but Chris saw it in his eyes.

Curiosity.

Doubt.

Then the agent's face slackened for a second, before it widened into a smile as he pressed his finger against his ear, where Chris surmised a radio earpiece was pushed in.

"Hah!" Wilson sneered at Chris. "Chalk one up for the good

guys."

A wide emptiness grew within Chris, and he felt his face slack down into a grimace.

And it was the arresting agent who delivered the bad news. "We found your friend by the coffee shop. Soon enough, we'll have them in custody."

Wilson shrugged. "Or a body bag."

Shit, Chris thought. *Shara, Tiana!*

This wasn't part of the plan.

CHAPTER 2

The rest of the ride passed by in silence, with Chris nervously working his hands. It took him several minutes to realize that the agent had said 'friend,' not friends, so maybe that meant they were only on to one of them. It also answered the uncertain question he had asked before they implemented the plan – does Nina's cloak hide them from sniffers? *Apparently not…*

A perpetual grin was affixed on Wilson's face, and she glanced at Chris now and again, reveling in his worry. Part of him wanted to press her, to find out why she hated magic users so much, but his anxiety was too high now, and he needed to pull himself together. Even if one or more team members were captured, the plan could still work.

It all revolved around him, Emmi, and Alycia. And the fact that the agents had only searched him for weapons.

After what felt like an age, the lumbering, rough-riding APC ground to a halt. Then started moving, and a few seconds later, ground to a halt again. *Must have been the gate,* Chris thought.

The back hatch popped open and harsh sunlight beamed into the cabin. Wilson stooped up and pointed the muzzle of her weapon at Chris, and nodded towards the hatch as it whined down into a ramp. "Move it."

The other agents, whom Chris decided needed names to keep straight in his head, preceded him out, and as he straightened up, he decided on the perfect names for them. The two he'd had no interaction with would be Sleepy and Dopey. The arresting agent he decided was Bashful, since he'd never given Chris his name even when arresting him. And Wilson behind him would forever be known as Happy, for the irony. Plus, he didn't feel like she was worthy of the name Grumpy, since that was one he'd given to one of the first Sentinels he'd ever met, and who was now dead, thanks to Nabu.

Stepping out into the early winter sun, which was already sailing towards the western horizon, Chris squinted against the brightness, and looked upon the infamous 'Magic Asylum,' as the news had taken to calling it. Formerly one of the surviving buildings of St. Elizabeth's Medical Asylum, the building now surrounded by a barbed-wire fence was a five-story red-bricked structure, with windows barred over (which appeared to be a newly-added feature, based on the pristine shine on the stainless steel bars,) and was surrounded by armed guards.

Whatever the building had been before, it was now solely a prison and interrogation center for those gifted with magic in the Washington, D.C. area.

And it was where Tom had been held ever since he'd recovered enough in the hospital.

Tom's presence was a baited trap. Nabu knew that Chris, Shara and the other Sentinels would come for him, and that's why Tom was here, despite having no magical affinity himself. Because it was the only place in the world that might be able to hold Chris.

But the Sentinels had done their homework. As Wilson, a.k.a. Happy, gruffly shoved his shoulder towards the reinforced steel front door, Chris took stock of what he could see. He tried to settle his nerves by confirming what Emmi had found in her shapeshifted reconnaissance jaunts.

It was impossible to see the tiny enchantment etchings in the bars on the windows, but as he passed through the steel doors, he glimpsed etchings in the doorframe. They weren't the Norse runes that Alycia used, but rather looked similar to Egyptian hieroglyphs. He wondered if, in years to come, that would aid in tracing enchantments to their enchanters – it didn't matter so much what language or form you used when enchanting something, but rather it was an enchanter's intent that made a difference, and using a consistent form or language aided in focusing on intent.

These doors, for instance, when sealed shut would be able to withstand magic attacks. Theoretically, anyway. Whether or not they'd been tested was anyone's guess.

Inside, the old age of the building was far more apparent. The federal agents that occupied it had hastily repurposed it, and as such, they hadn't repaired much. Some weird aqua-blue paint was peeling off of the walls in droves, and he saw more drywall than he did paint. The floors, at least on the bottom floor, were concrete and not well maintained, forcing Chris to watch his step so that he didn't trip on pockmarks.

They ferried him into a hastily-erected cubicle ten feet by ten, where a woman waited next to a laptop set upon a plastic desk, horribly clashing with the spooky worn-antique look of the rest of the interior.

Happy and Bashful pushed Chris into the chair in front of the desk, while the woman, a forty-something officer decked out in tactical gear (and shifting uncomfortably in it) pulled out a plastic fold-up kit and opened it up. To Chris's surprise, it looked like an ink pad, and a second later, she pulled out two thick, square cards with squared lines on it.

It took him several seconds of watching her fill out information on each to realize what they were.

"Uh…" he frowned. "I thought fingerprinting was done electronically?" He glanced at the scanner in confusion.

The woman's eyes darted up at him, a crisp, icy blue color with hints of crow's feet at the corners. "We do," she nodded. "However we learned very quickly that magic and technology do not always work well together." Her eyes darted at his handcuffs. "Even if that magic is suppressed."

Chris could understand that. In the days leading up to the fall of the Barrier, he had experienced numerous unexplainable electric shocks that often wreaked havoc on electronics, but ever since he'd learned to better control his powers, that hadn't happened again.

Unfortunately, most 'awakened' people around the globe hadn't received the training Chris had. No doubt most magic users had no idea how to control their powers.

Except maybe those working under Nabu's direction. Chris glanced again at the engravings in the handcuffs.

The woman, whom Chris decided, in keeping with the Seven Dwarfs naming convention, would be called Doc, glanced at Bashful. "Name?"

"Christopher Tatsu," Bashful replied confidently.

The woman's eyebrow arched, and her icy stare turned to him again. "How unusual. Even for a Japanese-American."

The burn of ire lit within, memories of his last conversation with his father flashing through his mind's eye. Bubbling and boiling up, the old wound never having time to heal, he set his jaw tightly and kept his mouth shut.

Her arched eyebrow rose just a millimeter higher, and then she set back to filling out the information on the cards. Chris drew in a deep breath on a four count, held it for seven, and then slowly exhaled, using the ever-familiar breathing techniques that Emmi and Shara had taught him to help push the rage down and regain control of himself.

Calm was needed to successfully pull this off.

After the awkward exercise of rolling his fingers across cardstock while wearing handcuffs, and failing to fully clean the ink off of his fingertips with the strange, orange-smelling soapy goop, he was led by Bashful and Happy to what had no doubt once been a double-occupied patient's room, now setup similar to an interrogation room, with a fold-up table in the middle and a single fold-up chair on either side.

The agents sat him so that he faced the door, and then told him to stay put.

Something skittered against his leg and down onto the floor, and he saw a flash of a small, gray, fluffy critter.

As the agents reached the door, Chris called out, "What, no water?"

They paused only a moment to glare at him, while the gray flash skittered around behind them and out the door. Without another word, the agents left, slamming the steel door shut behind them.

Another part of the plan gone right, Chris thought with a smile while easing back into the uncomfortable chair. *Now all I have to do is hurry up...and wait.* His shoulders slouched. Waiting was the hard part.

It was in Emmi's hands, for the moment.

Waiting had become the name of the game over the past three months. Waiting interspersed by moments of terror when sniffers found them and they had to relocate. Waiting interspersed by occasional intelligence-gathering missions.

And then more waiting.

Chris stood up and paced around the room anxiously, fiddling with the cuffs and resisting the urge to try to look inward. Even if the handcuffs would let him touch his magical core, he would find no comfort there.

The last time he had heard anything from Tattannu, he had said Chris would have to sacrifice everything. Since then, the ancient Babylonian man had been conspicuously absent. No matter how much Chris called to him when he meditated, no matter how much yelling into the void, his ancient ancestor never answered, never appeared, and never clarified. Naomi was his only spiritual contact in dreams now, and she didn't know the answers to Chris's questions.

That left Chris to his own thoughts. To his own reasoning.

Sacrifice everything.

Including myself.

In order to defeat Nabu and Marduk, he would have to sacrifice himself.

Without Tattannu to clarify or refute that thought, his mind spiraled and reeled against it, against the idea of giving up everyone and everything, of giving up a life he had never really been able to live.

Frustrated, Chris clenched his hands into tight fists and pulled against the cuff chain, the slim metal bands pressing deeply into his skin and threatening to break the surface.

"Dammit," he spat out, and looked around the room more. He had to focus on the task at hand, and with his blood boiling, he would miss important details. Like the camera in the corner left of the door.

He blinked at it, and frowned. It wasn't a normal security camera. Rather it looked like a GoPro. *This place really was hastily put together. Do they have GoPro's in every room?*

Imagining a flurry of agents streaming into every electronic store and buying up every GoPro or wireless camera they could, it made him chuckle, and his bemusement helped take the edge off of his frustration.

Relaxing his arms, he sunk down into his chair and slouched, heaving out a sigh. Could he meditate without magic?

Worth a shot.

Sitting up straight, Chris did his best to clasp his hands together around the handcuffs, and he began repeating the breathing exercise from earlier, over and over again until his frustration started melting away.

Don't touch the core, he reminded himself. *Not yet.*

With his thoughts returning to the mission, he was able to leave the past behind him, and the future ahead. An old Star Wars quote passed through his mind, and he heard a Jedi Master's voice say, "Keep your thoughts here and now where they belong."

Time passed a little more quickly, but he was left alone longer than he thought he would be. His thoughts drifted to Bashful's statement that they had caught up with one of his companions, and he wondered who it was. His crush on Shara had faded, but he still cared for her, and his early visions of her made him feel a stronger connection to her. He wanted her to be safe, but he also had grown to care for Tiana as well. That quirky, sometimes cocky smile, her lame jokes, and lately she had taken to giving a mock, two-fingered salute whenever someone asked her to do something.

And Nina. The little dragon. Babbar, their gnome companion, would never forgive Chris if something happened to Nina. *I wouldn't forgive myself,* he thought. She had been gravely wounded by Nabu in Denver, but thankfully the little dragon healed fast, and within two days, she was able to use a portal to help them flee agents on the outskirts of Denver.

The clang of the door unlocking startled Chris out of his thoughts. Through the little window on the door, he saw Bashful's face. Chris glanced behind himself outside, and it was still daylight out, but his grumbling stomach told him it was approaching dinner time already.

The door swung open, and Bashful stepped in and closed it behind him. Chris noted that no one outside clicked the lock closed. Was that because Bashful was afraid of Chris?

The agent wasn't in tactical gear anymore, but he wore what Chris recognized as BDUs, or Battle Dress Uniforms, which weren't really combat gear so much as just loose-fitting, camouflaged clothes.

"Well, Mr. Tatsu," Bashful gave him a fake smile. "It seems I've caught you in a lie."

Chris arched his eyebrow up. Nothing about the agent's statement indicated he knew about Emmi, so what was he talking about?

When Chris said nothing, Bashful sauntered over to the table and rested his hands on the back of the other chair. He leaned forward and bore into Chris's eyes with an accusatory glare. "You claimed that your organization doesn't hide the past of its members, yet you employ one off the record, one who has no record to speak of, that we can find."

Chris frowned. Even Shara had an official identity in U.S. records. She even paid her taxes, which she had grumbled about after the President had turned against the Sentinels. Unless they found Babbar, but he wasn't supposed to be involved in the operation and shouldn't have been anywhere nearby yet.

Genuinely perplexed, Chris asked, "What the hell are you talking about?"

Bashful waved his hand behind him, and the door swung open again. Happy shoved someone else in ahead of her, and Bashful stepped aside to let Chris see who they had captured.

It was a complete stranger. A face Chris had never seen before. The person had features both feminine and masculine, especially in their face with a square jaw, but narrowed eyebrows. They were shorter than Chris and slightly more diminutive in stature, with a short pixie-type haircut, dark hair dyed a deep, almost-black blue, and a loose, forest-green button-up shirt and black jeans, torn at the knees. Their eyes were a deep, dark brown, their skin a light tan.

The person waved sheepishly at Chris, their hands cuffed in enchanted bracelets. "Hi," the person said, their voice somewhere between a tenor and an alto.

"Umm," Chris frowned. "Hi? Who are you?"

Bashful's expression faltered, but Happy's turned scornful. Again. "Oh nice try, Tatsu," she grumbled.

Chris blinked at the agents, and then focused again upon the newcomer. "Look, I may not have met any of the Sentinels stationed at satellite outposts throughout the U.S., but I've no idea who this person is."

The newcomer's eyes darted at Bashful. "I told you. I'm not a Sentinel."

"And yet you just happened to be watching the coffee shop from the roof across the street," Happy spat out. "Give me a break."

"Maybe if you give us your real name," Bashful countered, "we can believe you."

"Ash *is* my name, jackass," the newcomer replied. "Ash Patel."

"And all of the Ash Patels on record look nothing like you, and you aren't carrying ID," Bashful loomed over the newcomer. "There's also not a single Ash Patel registered as a magic user, so either way, you're a criminal."

Ash narrowed their eyes at Bashful. "Look, Agent Callous," they growled at him. *Is that really his name?* "You can take your registration and shove it up your ass, okay?"

Bashful glowered at Ash, and Happy decided to wrench their cuffs up, eliciting a sharp, surprised yelp of pain from Ash. "Watch your tongue, you little witch," Happy ordered.

"And my name is Agent Simpson," Bashful countered.

It took a heartbeat to dawn on Chris, but the moment he realized that, like him, Ash had given Simpson a nickname, he cracked a grin.

"What are you smiling about?" Happy scornfully asked.

"Oh nothing," Chris shrugged, suppressing a chuckle. "I thought his name was Agent Bashful, is all." All three of them stared at Chris quizzically, and his grin faded. "Which I suppose, out of context, makes no sense to anyone…"

Shaking his head, Bashful looked upon Ash again, and folded his arms thoughtfully. "You know, since you two *apparently* don't know each other, I think we'll leave you to get to know one another."

Happy's eyes grew wide. "Sir?"

"Let her go," Bashful ordered.

"Them," Ash interjected.

With a frown, Bashful asked, "Excuse me?"

"I'm not a her," Ash narrowed their eyes at him. "Nor a him."

Bashful and Happy exchanged bemused looks. "Riiiight."

Instead of immediately letting Ash go, Happy shoved them forward, and forced them to sit in the chair across from Chris. "Enjoy your reunion," She remarked. "Oh, I mean, enjoy meeting for the first time."

Happy and Bashful turned to leave, and Chris's mind raced to come up with another remark to distract them, especially when he noticed movement low to the ground near the door. But Ash was faster. "Do you think you sound clever?" Happy halted and turned around, her face radiating heat. "You need to work on your sarcasm, Agent Bumble."

Happy surged towards Ash, but Bashful grabbed her shoulder. "Hey, let it go," he ordered. "Come on."

Reluctantly, she relented and allowed Bashful to lead her out. The steel door slammed shut behind them, and a second later, the lock clicked.

Leaving Chris with a complete stranger. "So, uh," he shrugged helplessly at them. "Wanna play Twenty Questions?"

CHAPTER 3

A deep frown furrowed Ash's brow, their dark eyebrows just a shade lighter than their dyed hair. "Twenty Questions?"

Chris's self-approving grin faltered. "Sorry. Bad joke."

His cell-mate's frown shifted into a grin. "I've heard worse." The grin widened. "Bashful?"

"Seven Dwarfs reference," Chris replied, waving his hand dismissively. "He never gave me his name, so I assumed-"

"That he's shy," Ash snorted in laughter. "I like it!" And then the laughter died, and their eyes dimmed sullenly. "Dammit."

With the other agent's nickname on the tip of his tongue, hoping to get another snorting laugh from his new cellmate, Chris was caught off guard by the sudden change in attitude. "What?"

Averting their eyes from Chris, Ash shook their head. "Nothing, just..." Gritting their teeth, Ash drew in a deep breath, held it apprehensively, and then exhaled slowly. "I wanted to hate you."

Blinking away his surprise, Chris asked, "Hate me? But, we've never met."

"I know," Ash nodded, eyes searching for anything to look at but Chris. "I've been looking for you, though. I..." And then they noticed the GoPro in the corner near the door. "Oh. Maybe we shouldn't talk too much. I mean..."

He followed Ash's eyes, and then felt something tug on the hem of his pants. Grinning, he slid the chair away from the table, giving him a better view beneath. There, sitting on its haunches, was a teeny tiny gray mouse, no bigger than Chris's middle finger from nose to tail-tip, and it stared up at Chris with unnaturally blazing-blue eyes. It tugged again on the hem of his pants.

"Found him?" he asked the mouse. From here the camera wouldn't be able to see the tiny creature, but no doubt anyone watching would be wondering what the heck he was talking about. Or whom he was talking to. The little mouse nodded emphatically.

"Beg your pardon?" Ash asked.

He looked at his cellmate again, and sighed, before he looked again at the GoPro. And then, taking a page from Luke Skywalker's book, he gave a casual salute to the camera, and then stared at Ash silently. Ash's frown deepened, and then they started to look uncomfortable, but he hoped, *willed* Ash not to squirm or make any sudden movements for the next few seconds.

Finally, when he felt like enough time had passed, he gave the camera another salute.

The signal to Abby.

Ash glanced at the camera, and then asked, "What the hell are you doing?"

Giving Abigail Turner, the U.S. Sentinel's resident computer expert, another few seconds to switch the camera feed to a loop, he glanced at the tiny mouse before he stood up. "Look, I'm sorry to cut this short, but I didn't plan on anyone else being here. Having said that..."

The mouse scurried to Chris's left, out from beneath the table, and then the strangest thing happened – a blue glow engulfed the mouse, and without warning, it grew rapidly to about five and a half feet tall, all without triggering the normal pressure sensation in Chris's body that magic usually did. A side effect of the magic-suppressing handcuffs, no doubt.

A second later, and his best friend in the world, Emmanuelle Dubois, stood next to him. Almost as tall as Chris, her bright red hair, having grown longer in the interceding months, was pulled back into a short ponytail, and her electric blue eyes darted between Ash and Chris. She wore a dirty black t-shirt and yoga pants with a series of runs worn in at the knees, a sign of the hard times she and the rest of the Sentinels had endured. Emmi's most noticeable feature was her facial scar, two purple marks starting on the right side of her forehead and raking down to her cheek, the inner-most scratch having cleaved her eyebrow in the middle. There were three claw marks on her stomach as well, but she never wore anything that revealed that anymore, especially not since winter had set in.

Ash blundered in panic, bolting up and sending their chair tumbling and half-folding behind them. "Woh, what the shit?!" Ash squeaked.

And then Chris tensed and stared at the door, craning his neck to look around Ash. He waited cautiously, as did Emmi. Ash's face paled, and they turned slowly towards the door, probably half-expecting someone to barge in at that very moment.

No one came. Abby had their backs.

Heaving out a breath he hadn't realized he'd been holding, Chris smiled at Emmi. "Am I glad to see you."

She gave him a weary smile. "Yeah. I overheard in the…vehicle? Car? Van?"

"A.P.C.," he corrected her.

"Yeah, heard about them finding someone else near the shop…"

Chris nodded at his cellmate. "It was them, apparently. Ash, this is Emmi."

Ash blinked in shock at the newcomer, while Emmi frowned. "Friend of yours?" she asked.

"Not that I know of," Chris replied. "But there's no time. I need to get out of these cuffs. Give me just a second."

He closed his eyes and drew in a long, deep breath, getting ready to hold it for a few beats and trying to look inward, at his core of magic that, for the moment, proved elusive.

"How exactly are you going to do that?" Ash asked.

Catching his breath, Chris opened his eyes. He thought about explaining to his cellmate, but given their earlier banter, he grinned and shrugged. "Magic."

Closing his eyes again, Chris began to center himself once more, drawing in a breath, and…

"Magic won't work with those cuffs on," Ash interrupted again.

Sighing, Chris nodded, "Normally, no. But I'm special. Now let me focus."

Beginning again, Chris sought out the golden core of energy deep inside of him, a sign of…

"Because of Tattannu?"

Chris grit his teeth, and opened his eyes, ready to snap at his cellmate. And then he stopped short when Ash's words registered.

Gaping, Emmi asked, "How the *hell* do you know that name?"

Glancing at Emmi, Ash met Chris's gaze a second later, and he saw a spark inside of them that he recognized. A rage that mirrored the one he'd felt so very often over the past six months. Shrugging in a curt manner, Ash said, "Magic."

Pursing his lips together, Chris sighed. "Well, whatever your reasoning, I need to focus. We'll..." He hesitated, and exchanged an uncertain squint with Emmi. "I suppose we can talk later..."

With an annoyed glance, Emmi asked, "How'd I know you were going to say that?" Chris looked at her with faux-innocence. "You know we can't take her with us."

"Them," Ash corrected. "Not her."

Emmi blinked at Ash, and nodded. "Sorry. Them."

Truthfully, no, they couldn't, or *shouldn't*. But Ash knew Tattannu's name. Was that because they worked with Nabu, and were some sort of strange plant by the bad guys? Or was there more to their story?

Insatiable curiosity and an absolute need to get answers nagged at Chris. He hadn't heard from Tattannu in so long.

Narrowing his eyes, Chris sighed impatiently. "Alright, ten words or less," he said. "How do you know the name Tattannu."

Ash's eyes darted back and forth between Emmi and Chris, before they clenched their jaw. "Because," Ash finally said. Hesitating another agonizingly annoying second, they added, "He comes to me in my dreams."

That was the last thing Chris expected to hear, and the surprise slammed into his chest like a hammer. He even staggered backwards a step. "He...what?!"

Nodding, Ash repeated, "He comes to me in my dreams. Almost every night."

Gawking wide-eyed at his cellmate, Chris felt his mouth opening and closing like a landed fish, unable to fully comprehend.

Tattannu was visiting Ash. Another person. When Chris was expected to destroy humanity's greatest enemy, following a plan laid down four thousand years ago by Tattannu, the ghostly, magic-powered ancestor was visiting someone *else* and was ignoring Chris?!

Drawing in a breath to say something to Emmi, she held up a hand, her face mirroring his earlier shock. "No, I get it," she nodded. "They're coming with us. Fine."

He clamped his mouth shut and nodded, and then looked at Ash.

"Give me just one second," he spoke barely above a whisper, his insides twisting and turning.

The shock and anger he felt would make this harder, but he'd practiced it all day yesterday, and he knew it would work as long as he found his center and *focused*.

Repeating the earlier exercises, Chris closed his eyes and drew in a deep breath, and exhaled slowly, imagining his frustrations leaving his body through his breath. It only worked marginally.

After repeating the exercise several more times, he could practically feel Emmi's impatience and worry. He felt it too, and that only made matters worse. It wouldn't be long before someone watching the cell's camera feed would realize the video was on a loop.

The enchantment on the handcuffs worked like a veil. Comparing his metaphysical self to his real self, the cuffs prevented him from touching or seeing his core. Except his core was powered by millions of souls, and through the darkness, if he focused just enough...

There! A faint flicker of golden light. A soft warmth washing over his face. In his mind's eye, he saw the spark of life, of power. Chris reached towards it, feeling resistance, but he pushed as hard as he could, heedless of any harm it could possibly bring to him. One of their contacts that had provided them with intel on the prison had provided them with about a dozen of the enchanted cuffs, and Chris had done this same exercise three times yesterday.

So the pain he felt wasn't a surprise, but he sucked in air in agony none-the-less. A dull sensation on his real senses told him Emmi's hand was on his shoulder, squeezing sympathetically.

He couldn't stop. Tom's life was on the line, and more than that, they needed the commander's guidance. They were lost without him, and even Shara didn't know where to go next or how to keep the fight against Nabu alive.

The shadows of the veil weren't like cloth, but instead clung to his metaphysical hand like a thick, goopy, web-encrusted substance. Chris pushed his hand through, wondering if, minus the heat, this was what it was like fighting against hot tar. Something wrenched at his hands, a force trying desperately to push him back to the other side, to separate him from his inner being.

Just a little further, that was all he needed. His core didn't like being separated from his body. It needed connection, it needed *him*.

Finally, the winking light flickered, and a bolt of golden electricity lanced out and touched his hand, igniting the inky black substance into glowing orange embers, a wave of flame spreading out from Chris and unraveling the closed-in tapestry. The spark of light flared into its normal radiance, leaving before him a golden sphere with an inner point of light, bolts of energy playing about the inner sphere like the old-school plasma balls.

In the waking world, the handcuffs grew orange-hot, and then suddenly clicked open, dropping onto the floor with sizzling effect, and leaving behind raw skin, burned only on the surface, just like with the practice cuffs.

Chris was free. And his growing powers were ready to spring them from jail.

Opening his eyes, he looked directly at Ash, who gaped back at him.

With a satisfied grin, he looked at Emmi. "I aim to misbehave."

Emmi blinked once, twice, frowned. The epic moment was lost. "You…What?"

Before Chris could say anything, Ash asked, "Did you just quote Firefly?"

CHAPTER 4

At least someone gets my references, Chris thought, suddenly wishing Alycia were here beside him. "Alright, let's go," he started around the table.

Ash's bemused look faltered, and they held up their handcuffed hands. "Any chance you could do the same thing for me?"

Chris faltered, stopping just on the side of the table, and glanced at Emmi. She shook her head, almost imperceptibly.

But the truth of the matter was that they would have an easier time with Ash's help. Not to mention it should be easier for him to burn out the enchantment on someone else's handcuffs.

"Alright," he nodded, eliciting a scowl from Emmi that Ash noticed.

"Hey, I happen to be pretty powerful myself," Ash grumbled at Emmi.

"That doesn't make me feel any better," Emmi retorted.

"Yeah, well..."

"Hey," Chris barked. "Enough, you two, we don't have time! Emmi, trust me. Ash..." He paused and narrowed his eyes at them. "You've just seen how powerful I am. So don't even think of trying to betray us."

Giving him an incredulous look, Ash shook their head and defended, "That wasn't my plan! I just..." Faltering, they shook their head. "You know what? Never mind. Just get me out of these things, alright?"

Glad that they understood the urgency of the situation, Chris stepped up to Ash and wrapped his hands around their cuffs.

Instantly he felt the thrumming power of the enchantment, pulsing against his core. It felt so different when it wasn't blocking his powers.

Closing his eyes, Chris let out a slow, measured breath, and extended his inner being outward. Instantly the veil presented itself, but since he already had his powers, he didn't have to endure the pain of pushing through it. Instead, he assaulted it with his energy, washing away the black, oozy substance with his soul.

Ash hissed in pain, and Chris felt the heat of the cuffs a moment later. He yanked his hands back, just as the cuffs popped open and fell to sizzle on the floor, leaving behind red burn marks on Ash's wrists. "Sorry," he winced sympathetically.

And then he felt their power. It radiated outward in a great wave, stronger, more measured than anything he had felt from another human being. Without realizing what he was doing, Chris reached towards his cellmate, fingers closing in on their hand, and…

Emmi's hands interceded, blocking their connection. She was breathing heavily, as was Chris and Ash.

"What the hell was that?" Emmi asked with widened eyes. "I…I *felt* that. You two…"

Chris and Ash locked eyes, and for the second time today, he felt a connection to them. But it was more than just a common rage.

It was a common power.

Tattannu visited Ash. Did that mean…?

"Holy shit," he whispered. "You're a descendant of Tattannu."

Drawing their lips into a thin line, Ash nodded. "Yeah, I guess I am. So he tells me, anyway."

Feeling his stomach cinch in an unfamiliar emotion, Chris withdrew his hands. Was it jealousy? Annoyance? Fear? Some strange combination there-of?

Shaking his head, he sighed and stepped past Ash, hoping to hide whatever expressions his face betrayed. "We'll figure it out later. Come on." His voice wavered, and while Ash might not know him in the least, Emmi would have heard it. She always heard the nuances in his voice. When he glanced at her, he saw the knowing look in her eyes.

Turning to the task at hand, he pressed his nose against the security glass on the door and tried to look down both ways of the hallway. His field of view was limited, and the lighting was relatively poor, but as far as he could see, there was no one out there.

To ensure the next part of their mission went well, he decided to reach out with his core, to search for the hint of anyone else nearby. Physical touch always helped him sense a person's soul easier, but he knew that if he tried, if he cleared his mind, he could feel others.

Except that Ash's presence was blinding, even with them behind him rather than in front. It overwhelmed his senses so much that he couldn't even feel Emmi's magic core.

Sighing, he knew that they couldn't very well stay where they were.

"Alright, stand back," he cautioned the others, while taking a single step back from the door. He summoned his power into the palm of his left hand, holding it up and away from his face, and focused it into a plasma-like energy. Except he didn't create a plasma ball, one of the first powers he had ever learned. Instead, he repeated an exercise from the roof of the damaged building across the street from the former Sentinel Tower, when an I-beam had blocked the rooftop door.

A jet of superheated plasma blinked into existence, extending a good four inches from his palm and into a defined point. Just as had happened before, he could feel the heat radiating towards his face, but the base of the plasma jet on his hand felt no warmer than a heating pad set to low.

The next part would be hard, since he had no protection for his eyes. He turned the jet towards the steel door handle, and pushed up against it, narrowing his eyes to the barest of slits as the metal flared. Through the window, he saw sparks flare out the other side. *Shit, if someone sees that…*

Impatient, he pressed his hand closer, allowing the bulk of the energy to be directed into the handle. A second later, it was completely melted, molten metal slopping down onto the floor and sending up a stream of smoke. The acrid scent of ozone stung at his nose, and his eyes watered from it.

Cinching off the flow of magic, the plasma jet died, and the door eased opened just a little bit. He had worried that heating up the door would have expanded it too much and it wouldn't have opened for them, so he heaved a sigh in relief.

Emmi was next to him in a heartbeat, just as she pulled a tranquilizer gun from a holster on her thigh.

"Wait, what?!" Ash gawked at the weapon. "How…weren't you

really small or something a second ago? Where were you keeping that?"

"I've learned not to ask," Chris interjected, winking at Emmi, who in return rolled her eyes. *Yes,* he thought. *First eye-roll of the day by my doing!*

He eased the door open, noticing it groaned a little more than before, and that made him wince. He peeked his head out the door, looking one way and then the other in rapid succession, and sighed in relief. They'd gotten out without anyone noticing.

Yet.

Dropping his voice down to a loud whisper, he waved Emmi forward, "Lead the way."

Holding her pistol-sized tranq gun ahead of her in a perfect stance, she eased out the door and took her turn looking down both ways, and then darted left, surprisingly silent on the concrete floor. *Bloody cat,* Chris thought before he waved for Ash to follow him, and then jogged along after Emmi. He ensured a constant connection to his inner core, ready to strike anyone who got in their way.

He had no desire to hurt anyone who was just here to do their job, and he thought he had refined his magic attacks enough to stun and not kill, but this wasn't exactly Star Trek, either. People were going to get hurt.

But even more will die if we don't stop Nabu, he reminded himself.

A summer of training combined with being on the run throughout autumn left Chris in well-enough physical condition, and by the time they reached the end of the long hallway, he felt his heart rate elevated, but his breathing was measured and steady. Ash was out of breath by the time they caught up with the group.

"Gods, I'm out of shape," they huffed.

Chris blinked, frowned at Ash. "Gods?"

Ash heaved in a breath, and then bent over, resting their hands on their knees and sucking in air. Their reference to multiple gods was interesting, but Chris knew there would be a *lot* more conversation later.

Right now, the trio stood in front of Tom's cell door, the last door on the left before the hallway intersected with another hall on the back side of the building. Emmi peaked through the security glass, and then stepped aside to let Chris look in.

Just as Emmi described, the room looked more like a traditional prison cell, except instead of a metal bed, the cot was one of those wooden fold-up types with a canvas-like 'bed' that Chris knew from recent experience was harder than a rock. To the left was a toilet, the front of it just barely visible behind a hospital curtain for some level of modesty. Tom lay on his back on the cot, his eyes closed and his hands clasped behind his head. He wore an orange jumpsuit like any prisoner might, but his sleeves were rolled up, showing off his well-defined arm muscles. His grizzled face sported a growing gray and white beard, a sign that they hadn't let him shave at all since they'd taken him from the hospital.

Yet all in all, he looked healthy. His scars were hidden by his jumpsuit, but to be pierced like he had been, Chris could only imagine the recovery he had gone through.

Looking around for a hint of a patrol or anyone else that might see them, Chris nodded in satisfaction, and ignited another plasma jet from his hand. As before, he squinted just as he pushed his hand against the steel handle, and a bright flash dazzled his vision. Sparks flew into Tom's room, and he saw their commander bolt up out of his cot, pressing his back against the wall just underneath the window.

The handle melted apart in seconds, and the door groaned open. Chris pushed it in, and stepped through with a flourish, planting his hands on his hips. "Hello, there!" he said through a grin.

Tom stared at him dumb-founded, his jaw slack and his brown eyes wide.

When he didn't move or say anything, Chris felt his cockiness fade. "Uh, don't worry. I know, I know, I'm a little short for a stormtrooper."

Still no reply. Emmi shoved her way in past Chris. "Ignore him, Tom," she grumbled, rolling her eyes again at Chris. "He's just being stupid and-"

"GUARDS!"

Tom's shout startled Chris and Emmi, sending a surge of fresh adrenaline through his system. "Tom?!"

"GUARDS, THEY'RE HERE!" Tom waved at the camera.

Shouts echoed down the hallway, and on instinct, Chris grabbed Ash's shirt and yanked them inside before they could be seen, and then slammed the door shut.

"Dammit, Tom," Chris reeled on the commander. "What the hell are you---urk!"

Tom surged forward and grabbed Chris's arm, yanking him around and wrapping his other arm around Chris's throat while twisting Chris's wrist and elbow painfully.

"Tom!" Emmi shouted.

A combination of his nerves already being on edge and training made Chris act without thinking. He pulsed magic down the length of his arm, raising his hairs on edge and sending an electric-like shock into Tom that made him spasm, which unfortunately meant twisting Chris's arm harder for a split second before his grip vanished and Chris was able to tear himself out of the commander's hold.

Spinning around, Chris prepared what he hoped would be a stunning energy beam, but the next thing he saw was a fist coming straight at him, smashing into his face and sending him sprawling, while stars exploded in his vision.

A second later, as he shook his head to clear the stars away, Emmi's tranq gun clattered onto the ground next to him. He tried to look at the pair, and even through his swimming vision, he could see that Tom had targeted her next, and they were engaged in hand-to-hand. Emmi was no slouch, having taken yoga and tai chi before their training in the mountains, but Tom was an experienced combatant.

Emmi tried to grab Tom's arm when he threw a punch at her, but he must have anticipated her moves and he used the opportunity to grasp her and then slam his body into her, sending her stumbling backwards and into the door.

Chris clamored for the tranq gun, hoping Emmi hadn't already discharged it, but before he could bring the weapon to bear, he felt a pulse of magic, and saw a golden light slam into Tom's body, flinging him hard against the back wall with a "WHUF!"

The blast had come from Ash.

Their powers were arcane!

More than that, their power somehow felt *connected* with Chris's, *and* they had met Tattannu.

With his head spinning over the implications, Chris almost missed his opportunity. Tom wasn't out cold, though he looked somewhat stunned, and if he attacked again, Ash might use too much power to subdue him.

Bringing the tranq gun to bear, Chris pulled the trigger, heard the hiss and thump and felt the recoil, and a dart embedded itself in Tom's chest. The deranged commander grunted, grasped at the dart, and then glared at Chris.

"You'll never win," he growled groggily. "You'll...never..."

He slumped down onto his rump, and his eyes rolled back into his skull before his eyelids fluttered closed.

Chris gawked at the commander as he slouched further, all tension in the older man's muscles going out. Chris glanced at Emmi, who stared first at Tom, and then at Ash.

Ash reached out a hand to Emmi and helped her up, and looked ready to do the same for Chris, but then hesitated, looking first at Chris's hand with uncertainty, and then their own. Emmi brushed her backside off, and then helped Chris up.

"What...what *was* that?" Emmi asked. "I mean, *all* of it, Tom, and Ash, your powers."

Shrugging helplessly, Ash turned towards the door, and then frowned. "People are coming."

An idea struck Chris in a heartbeat, and he rushed past Ash and turned on a weaker form of his plasma torch, hoping he got the strength of it right. Just as an armed guard appeared in front of the door, Chris shoved his foot up against the bottom of it, and then pressed his plasma jet up to the door jam and slowly drew it upwards.

The guard shouted at him and shoved against the door, threatening to break Chris's fresh, poor-man's weld, but the door held. Emmi shoved up against the door next to him to help hold it closed.

Shouting some more, the guard stepped back and raised his service weapon, what looked like a military issued MP5. Chris smirked at the guard, and the guard must have realized why, as he lowered his weapon. A 9mm weapon, even an automatic, would never breach a steel door or a bullet-proof window.

That didn't mean they'd have unlimited time. Before long, someone would come along with a breach charge.

Once he'd sealed about half of the door jam, Chris stopped fueling magic into his palm and let the jet die, before he turned around and looked at the outer wall. Shrugging at Emmi, he said, "Well, this next part was part of our plan anyway." He stepped forward and looked up at the camera, another GoPro-like device hanging in the corner. "Abby, if you're still watching, tell the others we need extraction now." He glanced out the window, and frowned. "Shit, what side of the building are we on?"

"North," Emmi replied.

"Thanks." He nodded at the camera, and gave it another fake salute.

Emmi touched her hand to an ear piece that Chris hadn't seen yet, but knew about, and then shook her head. "Still can't get a radio signal in here, but obviously she's in their system."

And then a crackling sound startled them, followed quickly by Abby's sing-song, perpetually up-beat voice calling out, *"Don't worry, guys, I'm still with you!"*

Chris's head whipped around, until he noticed a white circle with multiple small holes embedded in the ceiling – the speaker for a PA system.

"Abby!" he cried out in relief.

"Heyooooo," Abby replied cheerily. Then her voice dipped to the most somber tone he'd ever heard from her. *"What's going on with Tom?"*

That was a good question, but Chris had a suspicion. Knowing that they'd have to drag Tom out of the way anyway, he stepped over to the commander's limp form and knelt down to place a hand on Tom's chest. Closing his eyes, Chris focused on expanding out away from his core, to try to sense Tom's.

Next to his core, he saw a smaller sphere, a soft shade of orange and without a single tendril of energy – Tom's soul. But it was tainted. A black, oily substance swam around and intermixed atop Tom's soul, suppressing and perverting his very being. Just like Chris had felt atop Sentinel tower, except it was stronger, more like what he'd felt from Mia's core.

Nabu had infected Tom, taken control of his spirit and made him worship the demigod.

It took next to no time to cleanse a soul, as Chris had found out on the fly three months ago, but it *did* take considerable energy, and he didn't want to risk doing it just now. Besides which, Tom wasn't about to wake up either way, so Chris decided to save his energy.

"Nabu has taken hold of him," Chris announced, releasing the commander's chest and then grabbing him by the arm. "But I'll be able to cleanse him later. Emmi, help me move him away from the wall."

Emmi stooped down and grabbed Tom's other arm, and then together, they awkwardly dragged him away, his shoes screeching across the painted concrete floor.

Muffled voices echoed from the hallway, and Chris looked to find another face staring inward, pounding on the door. It was Happy, her expression decidedly pissed.

"Abby, how we coming with backup?" Chris asked.

"They're ready when you are," she replied. *"I told them about Tom, but the plan's the same."*

"More or less," Chris agreed, and then looked at the door. Happy backed away, letting another guard in, and a loud clunk resonated on the door.

A breach charge had been placed.

Eyes going wide, Chris said, "Time's up!" He turned towards the outer wall, and brought his hands together, drawing power from the millions of souls to form a basketball-sized plasma ball. And then he released it, blasting the outer wall into tiny shards of brick and rending apart rebar.

With a grin stretching across his face, Chris thought, *I always wondered what it'd be like to break out of prison.*

CHAPTER 5

Without another word, Chris and Emmi hoisted the surprisingly heavy Sentinel commander up and wrapped their arms around his torso, and then moved towards the hole in the wall.

"Alright, Ash," Chris grunted. "Get busy living, or get busy-"

His quote was interrupted by a second massive explosion from ahead, the base of the barbed-wire fence blasting apart in a shower of mud and grass, opening up a hole. *Just in time,* Chris thought.

He and Emmi rushed outside, trying not to trip on debris as they went, and he was ever so thankful, as he hefted Tom's dead weight, that the prison cells had all been on the first floor.

And then, just as they left, Happy and the guards detonated the breach charge, flinging the steel door inward. The concussion reverberated against Chris and nearly sent him sprawling to the ground, but when he heard Ash cry out, he knew that his cellmate was not so lucky.

From the breached fence, a white van, back windows painted black with yellow smiley faces, slid into the courtyard, with Alycia hanging out of the passenger window, her gloved hand glowing blue. The driver, whom Chris immediately saw was Shara, spun the wheel around rapidly and gunned the engine, allowing the van's tires to spin and swing the van around to face backwards.

Of course, the prison was heavily guarded, and while the guards from the breached door streamed into the room with guns raised, those guarding the grounds shouted and responded instantly. In seconds, a hail of gunfire would rain down upon them.

But that's why they had Alycia.

Emmi likewise had gloves on her hands, courtesy of Alycia, but these weren't the same ones Alycia had made for them just before the Adelaide Airport encounter. Raising her hand up, Emmi did the 'Spider-Man Maneuver,' drawing in her middle and ring finger and leaving the other digits spread out, and pressed on an enchantment symbol on the glove.

A translucent sphere of blue-white light sprang to life, surrounding them all.

Except Ash, Chris realized with a start. He tried to crane his neck around, and found them sprawled on the ground just at the edge of the hole in the wall.

Gunfire roared from the room, automatic weapons mixed with semi-automatic pistols. The rounds slammed into Emmi's shield, harmless to them, but sending potentially deadly ricochets back towards Ash.

"Shit," he shook his head. "I've gotta grab Ash!"

"What?!" Emmi gawked. Chris extracted himself from Tom, and the commander immediately sagged, Emmi unable to hold his full weight. "Hey, stop! What are you doing?"

As Chris turned away, he felt the pulse of magic from further towards the fence. Alycia must have gotten out of the van and summoned her own protective wall, just as they planned, giving everyone inside, including Shara, Marisol, Tiana, Babbar, and Nina, time to come streaming out the back of the van. More gunfire roared from around the compound.

He ran to the edge of Emmi's shield and stopped short of crossing the threshold, knowing that once he was on the other side, he couldn't get back in unless Emmi moved closer to him.

A crowd of five people were in Tom's room, including Happy and Bashful, who were already reloading their pistols with fresh magazines. The automatic weapons ran out of ammo a second later, blessing the immediate area with a modicum of silence.

Shaking his head at Bashful specifically, Chris yelled out, "I'm sorry! I'd hoped no one would get hurt."

Drawing power into his hands again, Chris thrust his palms outside of the shield and unleashed two small, low-powered beams of arcane energy at the guards. Bashful dove to the ground, but Chris's beams connected with the other four and slammed them against the walls, and sent Happy sliding through the door and into the hallway beyond.

Not waiting around for anyone else to attack, Chris bolted out from Emmi's shield, and reached for Ash, who was just beginning to stir blearily. "Uhh," they moaned. "I...wuh...?"

Chris touched Ash's hand.

A flash of light blinded him.

Images swam before him, blurring in and out of focus like a camera lens struggling to keep up with an ever-changing scene.

Images of the past. The hangar at Centennial Airport. The unknown man that Nabu had stabbed with Imhullu, his face pale, his hair and eyes dark brown. The dagger plunged into his chest, releasing his soul and channeling it through the dagger.

He saw next the battle in Sentinel Tower, moments before Nabu slammed Chris out a window and down onto the street. The eager, hungry look in Nabu's eyes as she demanded that Tom hand over the dagger.

Images of the present flickered before him. He saw Alycia, clear as day, both hands raised and glowing bright blue with the effort of maintaining her shield.

Nina stooped on Babbar's shoulder as he stood next to Alycia, armed with a tranq gun but not using it. No one could fire through the shields, and until recently, no one had been able to pass outside of one of Alycia's shields unless she dispelled it first. Thankfully she had refined her barrier spells enough that they could at least leave their protection without dispelling them.

The image shifted to a hotel room with a kitchen and a small, square dining table. Sat at it was his father, hair a little grayer, his face a little harder. He stooped over the table, forehead resting in his hands. Tears streamed down his eyes, slamming an uncomfortable feeling of surprise and regret into Chris's gut.

Then he saw familiar surroundings.

Nabu hovered above the prison, raining destruction down upon them all. At first her magic deflected off of Alycia's shield, laying waste to the prison, but then it breached Alycia's shield and...

Yanking his hand back, Chris brought himself back to reality. Ash blinked up at him, and shakily said, "We gotta go."

He gulped, nodded. Their time was out. Nabu was on the way.

Ash helped themselves up, and then turned back towards the hole in the wall. Their eyes widened, and before Chris could see what was wrong, Ash unleashed a blast of arcane magic, catching Bashful in the shoulder just as he scrambled up, and sent him spinning through the air to land with a painful-sounding crunch on the ground.

Someone shouted from the left, "There, shoot them!"

Without thinking, Chris darted between Ash and the guards that had just rounded the prison building and spotted them, and focused his plasma field outward. A dense energy field surrounded Chris, blindingly bright and hot enough to singe the gravel beneath his feet. The guards opened fire on him, but were interrupted by a sudden, deafening screech, and their fire stopped instantly.

Allowing the energy to dispel, Chris turned and saw Shara, shapeshifted into her beautiful, white-gold gryphon form, standing over the guards.

As weapons fire died down, Chris looked around in awe. Alycia had lowered her shield, and most of the guards were now unconscious or hiding behind cover, or worse.

But the Sentinels weren't out of the woods yet.

"Nabu's coming," he shouted, rushing back over to Tom and helping Emmi lift him up again. Urging Emmi onward with him, he added, "Babbar, Nina, we've gotta go, *now!*"

The gnome didn't have to be told twice, and he, along with the other Sentinels nearby, rushed towards Chris, while Shara half-ran, half-flew over to them, landing with a vibrating thud on the ground. Just as she shapeshifted back into her normal, blue-haired, pointy-eared self, Alycia recast her shield spell, barely in time to intercept gunfire.

"What about the van?" Marisol asked while everyone gathered around Chris, Emmi and Tom.

It was too late. A pressure wave of magic resonated against his soul, and a resounding bang echoed across the sky, worse than a sonic boom. A bright flash of white light appeared above them, and when it faded a second later, a lithe, red-headed woman hovered fifty feet above them, her eyes glowing.

Nabu spotted them instantly.

The image from the future flashed through Chris's mind, and he knew what came next.

I can't let that happen.

Noting a sudden and distinct lag in gunfire, Chris ordered, "Alycia, shield down!"

She gaped at him, but if Benson, the man who had trained them in the mountains, had taught them one thing, it was to act.

The shield fell just as Chris released Tom and brought his wrists together, palms outward and facing Nabu, whose eyes widened.

The instant he summoned his powers, he felt a similar intense surge beside him. A massive, two-foot-wide beam of energy leapt from his palms, at the same time that another one appeared from beside him. Nabu, in her arrogance, summoned a shield instead of dodging the attacks. Against just Chris, she had proven a match in the past.

Against Chris *and* Ash, her shield fell in moments, and the blast threw her backwards, shooting up out of the sky like a rocket.

"Babbar, now!" he shouted the moment that he and Ash ceased their attack.

The gnome was ready, and he flipped a pure-copper coin to the tiny foot-long dragon on his shoulder, who chomped down on it hungrily.

Chris glanced behind him at Tom's cell. There he saw Bashful holding onto the edge of the hole in the wall, his right shoulder hanging loose from its socket. But he wasn't looking at Chris or his companions. Bashful's eyes were instead fixed on the sky where Nabu had been seconds before.

Blinding red light engulfed Chris's vision. White noise drowned all sound. Copper on the tip of his tongue. A portal engulfed the team, and whisked them away from the carnage.

CHAPTER 6

The light and noise cleared, and in an instant, the Sentinels found themselves in a dingy, run-down, decaying factory in Detroit. Their arrival was jarring, but by now, Chris and the other Sentinels had grown accustomed to it.

Ash, on the other hand, fell on their backside, wide eyed and heaving deep breaths.

"What..." They shook their head, looking at the strange and motley crew before them. "The hell." Ash gulped. "Was that?!"

Emmi started losing her balance against Tom's weight, and Alycia rushed forward, yelling "Dad!" just as she got her arms under him and helped steady Emmi.

"He'll be fine," Chris assured her, before turning his attention back to Ash. "And *that* was your first portal trip. Congrats." He held out a hand to help his former cellmate up, but then hesitated. Would their powers surge every time they touched?

Ash didn't look any more eager to relive the experience than Chris.

"Help me get him to a mattress," Emmi growled at Alycia. Together, they dragged Tom towards an area in the middle of the wide-open, airy, abandoned factory. It wasn't their first choice of hiding places, but Shara had known about it from an encounter with a monster last year.

The outside wall was made mostly of rectangular window panes, most of which were broken, along with steel frames and brick bases. The smashed panes allowed frigid air and snow to blow in, broken only by a roaring fire built up in the middle of the wide-open area.

The floor was completely covered in dirt so thick that Chris had no idea whether it was concrete or something else beneath. Any equipment once contained in the factory was long-gone, leaving empty space interspersed by steel pillars holding up the tall, corrugated metal roof.

No one would think to look for them here. At least, that was their hope.

Mattresses scrounged from who knew where lay between two pillars on one side, their designated sleeping area, and while the mattresses were old, dirty, lumpy, and somewhat gross-looking, it was better than sleeping in the dirt or mud. Emmi and Alycia eased Tom onto one, but he was so heavy and they struggled so much that they lay him down face-first. Shara helped them roll him over onto his back, and then she checked his pulse.

"He's fine," she announced, to the cheers of others.

Marisol, a Hispanic woman only seven years older than Chris, clasped him on the shoulder. "Good job, kiddo," she grinned at Chris. "That was a good plan!"

"Despite Nabu showing up earlier than expected," Tiana nodded while checking her weapon, a rather large and powerful sniper rifle. She hadn't been with the Sentinels after the tower fell in Denver, but they had linked up with her when the President had declared all Sentinels enemies of the state. Like Chris and the others, her life was now completely upended, her bank accounts seized, her apartment under constant surveillance.

"Now," Shara stood up from beside Tom and looked at Ash. "Someone wanna tell me who…" She paused and frowned, looking down for a second, and then she gave everyone a sheepish look. Pressing at her right ear, where a radio link no doubt was, Shara quickly said, "We're all fine, Abby, we made it back to the factory." A pause, "I know, I know, I'm sorry, love! Tom's still unconscious, but alive."

Marisol suddenly snorted in laughter, and he caught chuckles from some of the others. It was obvious that Chris and Ash were the only two without radios, and they'd missed some comical remark from their I.T. expert.

With a weary voice, Shara sighed. "Yes, dear, I will." Another pause, followed by another round of chuckles. "Hey, that's not fair!"

Guessing it was another round of flirting, Chris couldn't help but grin and looked at Ash, who merely looked around in confusion. Shaking his head, Chris said, "Lover's quarrel."

"I heard that," Shara stated. The conversation with Abby was apparently finished, and she stalked over to Chris and Ash. "Now spill it. Who exactly are you?"

Chris started to reply for Ash, but they interrupted him, "My name is Ash Patel."

Raising a blue eyebrow, Shara's violet eyes bore into Ash, searching their face.

"Ash was arrested after I was," Chris stated. "And there's…" He hesitated and looked at Ash again. Without even realizing it, he had tapered off his connection to his core, and as a result, the overwhelming sense of power from Ash was difficult to detect. "There's something about them. You mentioned Tattannu earlier," he nodded at Ash.

"Yeah, he comes to me in my dreams," they nodded in reply. "He…he said that I'm one of his descendants."

Shara's face slackened into shock. She stared at Ash thoughtfully for a second, her eyes darting around as if she sought some piece of data to pull out of thin air. Slowly, carefully, as if afraid to give away too much information, Shara asked, "And what exactly has Tattannu told you?"

Ash's face flushed, and they looked down at their feet, brushing at the dirt with their toe somewhat bashfully. "It, uh…kinda sounds ridiculous when you say it out loud. But, I, uh, apparently am connected to a powerful source of magic. Souls, he said," Ash looked at Chris. "Souls of all of our ancestors from all of the lines. Millions of souls."

A twinge panged at his stomach, and Chris felt his hands involuntarily curl up into fists. "I thought…" He shook his head, his mouth going dry. Clearing his throat, he said, "I thought I was the only one meant to wield that power. I thought…"

His face burned, his chest heaved, his heart raced. Chris suddenly felt like the world was falling apart on him. This was his mission. Not because he was special, but because he had been there, at the dismantling of the Barrier. *He* had made the choice, not Ash, not anyone else.

Ash continued on, "Tattannu told me about the family line. About how it diverged during generations of exile, migrating east and spreading throughout Asia. My ancestors ended up in India. Tattannu told me about you," they nodded at Chris, and he looked into their dark eyes, seeing a depth to them that rivaled his own. Ash wasn't much older than he was, he wagered. "Told me that your line ended up in Japan. He-" Ash's voice faltered and cracked, and their eyes sank back to their feet. Wrapping their arms around themselves, Ash looked off to the right with mournful eyes. "He told me you were there when Nabu cracked the Barrier. When they sacrificed...killed..." Tears welled up in Ash's eyes. "When they *murdered...*"

The visions from earlier returned to the forefront of Chris's thoughts. Something nagged in his mind. Why would he and Ash touching have conjured up images from the hangar incident? What did it have to do with anything?

Then the answer came to him. "The man Nabu murdered," Chris said softly. "Did you..."

Though Ash didn't meet his gaze, they nodded curtly, sniffling and pawing away tears. "He was my cousin. On my mother's side."

'I wanted to hate you.' It was one of the first things Ash had said to him.

"Do-" His voice cracked and stuck. Clearing it, he asked, "Do you blame me for his death?"

Sniffling, their expression turned darker, anger fueling their next words. "I don't know. What Tattannu told me was that *you* were Nabu's target that night. You and your friends," Ash waved vaguely at the Sentinels. "But Nabu picked David instead." Shaking their head, Ash added, "Claire – his girlfriend, she said Nabu picked him out at random. Just pointed into the crowd, and one of his sycophants grabbed him and brought him over and just...just..."

Chris nodded understanding. The images had been seared into his memory. The first murder he had ever witnessed. *If only it had been my last.*

Suddenly his stomach tumbled when he realized who the 'sycophant' had been. He looked around, searching for Alycia's mother Mia, but she wasn't there. Alycia's brother, Eric, had stayed behind in Denver when the Sentinels first ran, unwilling to be caught up in all of this with 'their lot.' Unfortunately for him, Nabu still considered him a target, and now he was in hiding with Abby.

"Hey, uh, where's Mia?" Chris asked Shara with a frown.

"I'm here," an Australian accent matching Alycia's called from Chris's right. She had just walked in from outside, still wearing her leather jacket and black jeans from Adelaide, though they were as worn down as the clothes everyone else wore. Her hair was pulled back into a loose ponytail again, like it often was nowadays, but she looked more gaunt than those earlier days, like she was eating less and less. "I just needed to use the dunny. Or, you know, a corner away from prying eyes."

Chris's eyes darted to Ash, but they seemed no more surprised to see yet another face, and there was absolutely no recognition in their eyes. That was good news, at least for now.

Mia's eyes fell upon Tom's unconscious form, with Alycia knelt next to him, and her face slackened. "You did it!" She broke into a run, rushing past everyone and sliding in the dirt onto her knees. "Tom!" She lightly tapped his cheek, and then looked up at Alycia. "What's wrong with him?"

"He's fine, Mum," Alycia reassured, her voice still somewhat stony and expressionless when talking to Mia. "Chris just needs to, uh," she frowned and looked over at him. "Deprogram him?"

"Cleanse him," Chris replied, and started walking towards them. "He's...*infected* again. Just like you were," he nodded at Mia, intentionally saying it loud enough for Ash to hear as well. "I need to clear the stain away before he wakes up."

Behind him, he heard Shara say to Ash, "We'll talk a bit more later, but I have to ask you to stay in sight at all times until we know whether we can trust you."

"Right," Ash replied sullenly. "Fine..."

By all rights, they shouldn't have stopped. Ash deserved their attention, and with the Sentinels on the run, it was a danger to have Ash around without knowing if they could be trusted. On the other hand, Chris knew Alycia and Mia wouldn't accept any delay in cleansing Tom, even if the commander might not wake up for hours.

More than that, Chris felt like he owed them. He owed Alycia. For the heartache he'd given her, and the heartache yet to come.

With Alycia on one side of Tom and Mia on the other, he walked around above Tom and knelt down, placing the commander's head within easy reach. "Alright. This'll only be the second time I've ever done this, so it might be a good idea to stand back-"

"Not gonna happen," Mia shook her head adamantly, grabbing

Tom's hand and grasping tightly. "I won't abandon him again." She looked at Alycia, who avoided her mother's gaze. "I won't abandon either of you again."

Ever since Mia's cleansing in the Sentinel Tower, the older woman had struggled with herself, with all of the atrocities she had committed under Nabu's control. The worst of it was abandoning Tom and Alycia.

But Alycia, even knowing it had all been Nabu's fault, struggled to accept it. Especially knowing that Nabu's powers had been severely limited when Mia had joined him. Magic influence couldn't shoulder the entire blame, as far as Alycia was concerned.

Chris looked to his friend, his crush, the one woman he wished he could have made happy in this life, trying desperately to catch her eye. She blinked, turned her golden-brown eyes upon him, and sighed. "I'm not leaving either. Besides, you'll protect me, yeah?"

Smiling weakly, he nodded once. "As best as I can." He almost said always, but knew that would be a lie.

Drawing in a deep breath and shoving those feelings of regret and hopelessness down, Chris closed his eyes and exhaled slowly, centering himself and reaching for his golden core. When he felt confident, he reached out in the waking world and touched Tom's temples with his fingertips.

In his mind's eye, he saw a tendril of light reach out from his own core and connect with Tom's small, faded, tainted orange sphere. Vaguely he was aware of the other spheres surrounding him, of the other souls within reach. To his left, he felt the familiar warmth and saw the pale blue light of Alycia's core. It had steadily grown stronger, brighter, more powerful over the past few months.

To his right was Mia's core, orange like Tom's, but brighter. Stronger. Powerful. He had deduced in the tower that Mia could use some form of magic. Yet in the past three months, her abilities hadn't manifested in any way. No accidental casting, nothing.

Chris felt more than heard the other Sentinels surrounding him, but their cores, even Emmi and Shara's green cores, were overshadowed by the more distant, but brilliant golden light of Ash. They hadn't come closer, but even from this far away, he sensed their presence, felt his power trying to reach out to connect with theirs. He would have likened it to two ends of magnets trying to connect, but rejected that analogy all at once, when he realized how similar their powers were.

Realizing he'd allowed his mind to wander, Chris once again fixated on Tom's core. The stain hadn't changed one iota. Even from far away, Nabu could maintain her hold on infected people.

But Chris had the cure.

Surrounding them all was a vague, hazy gray field, with humanoid shadows moving about. One of those shadows stepped forward, coalescing into a familiar figure. Dark, long hair, dark eyes, the teenage form of his sister Naomi.

Against the flaring light cast from Chris and Ash's cores, her figure seemed more defined than ever before, a sharp clarity that he hadn't realized her visage had been missing before.

"Hello, Chris," her sing-song voice said to him, a soft smile brightening her face. "Need a hand?"

He reached for her, and she for him, until their fingers touched. He drew her closer and clasped their fingers together, and then turned again to Tom's core. "Last time I only succeeded because you and others helped me," he nodded. "I can't do this alone, can I?"

A light chuckle escaped his sister. "You're never alone, Chris. You should know that by now."

With his own wane smile, he nodded. "Good point. Alright, let's do this."

Drawing in another deep breath, he turned inward at first. Emotion was the key, that much he remembered. Cleansing the taint of Nabu's hatred and malice required something pure, something that would charge his soul in a way that negated Nabu.

Last time, he had focused on Alycia, on his feelings for her. He tried to do so again, but immediately he faltered. His feelings for her only brought him pain and fear. Regret and sorrow.

'Everything.' That had been Tattannu's words to him when he asked what would be required to destroy Nabu and Marduk.

Chris would have to sacrifice everything.

It didn't matter that he loved Alycia. In due time, he would have to say goodbye to her.

"Chris," Naomi cautioned.

Her voice shook him out of the abyss for a moment, but it did little to shake the cold ache he felt in his heart, or to dispel the emptiness gnawing away at his stomach.

The connection to Tom didn't falter, but there was no pulse of light, no cleansing energy.

Tom was still infected.

"Stop," Naomi insisted. He blinked his eyes open and looked at her, his mouth hanging open, unsaid words on the tip of his tongue. "No, stop it," she shook her head. "You're sinking into self-blame and depression, stop it!"

The hopelessness was almost instantly replaced by annoyance. "Then make Tattannu talk to me."

"I can't!" she practically shouted, tearing her hand from his grip. Stepping away, she shook her head and spoke out into the mists beyond. "I can't call him, I can't find him when he's not here."

"Try looking over there," he pointed at Ash's bright core. "He must think I don't have the courage to do it."

Spinning around to gape at him, and then following his finger towards Ash, Naomi shook her head. "Is that what you think? Is that why I'm feeling waves of fury coming off of you?"

"He said I have to sacrifice everything!" Chris shouted back at her. "*Everything,* as if I haven't lost enough! But finally, when I've resigned myself to my fate, suddenly there's Ash, with powers like mine, and Tattannu whispering in their ear. He must think I won't go through with it. Well," he waved towards Alycia's core, "I'm prepared. I've distanced myself, I've not given in to my feelings. What more does he want? I've come this far, I've lost you, Mom, Dad…" He faltered upon mentioning his father.

Naomi gave him a skeptical look. "You're mad about losing Dad?"

"Well, no," he shook his head. The vision he'd seen of his father, alone in a hotel room in tears, passed through his mind. Guilt wove into his heart.

Mom's death was my fault, he thought, gritting his teeth and turning away from his sister. *Nabu went after them because of me…*

Sucking in a breath, even though he knew none of this was happening in the physical realm, he cried out, "If I don't go through with it, none of those sacrifices will mean anything." He spun around and faced his sister. "Including yours."

She pursed her lips and folded her arms, her eyes averting from his. "Maybe so," she nodded. "But right now, you can't even cure Tom. How do you intend to destroy Nabu or Marduk if you can't even cleanse one person?"

He clamped his mouth shut, and then looked upon Tom's soul. "I guess I can't. Maybe it's a good thing Ash is here after all." His eyes wandered over to their blinding, golden core. "Maybe Tattannu knows I'm not strong enough."

His words hung in the darkness, weighing him down and opening up a void in his chest. He knew it was true, the moment the words had left his ethereal mouth. He wasn't strong enough.

Christopher Tatsu was too broken to save the world.

Naomi stood still, her gaze fixed upon her brother, but he wouldn't meet her eyes. He couldn't.

"You know that's not what I meant," Naomi soothed. "I didn't…"

"No," he shook his head, and then forced himself to look into her eyes one more time. "No it's okay. I know you didn't. It's me." He nodded, forcing down a lump in his throat. "I'm sorry."

She started to say something, but he broke the connection, broke out of his meditation, and released his hands from Tom. Opening his eyes, he saw hopeful looks upon Alycia and Mia's faces. Those looks died as his expression turned grim.

"I…" His voice caught again. Clearing it, he shook his head and averted his eyes from theirs, turning instead to look upon Tom's unconscious form. "It didn't work."

A beat.

Mia asked, "What do you mean it didn't work?" There was an accusatory tone in her voice.

"I mean I failed," he clarified hotly. "I couldn't do it."

Out of the corner of his eye, he saw Alycia's eyes darting between him and her father. "You mean…did Nabu change how she infects them or something?"

Pushing up onto his feet, he shook his head, but still refused to look into Alycia's eyes. He couldn't bear to. "No," he added. "I mean *I* failed."

Turning, he stalked away from them, past Tiana and Emmi, snatching up his heavy jacket from his mattress as he headed outside.

All he wanted now was to be alone. *It's what I deserve.*

CHAPTER 7

"Get back in there and save my father!"

Alycia's voice shook with every over-enunciated word. She hovered over Chris, who had come outside and found a sunny patch of frozen Earth to sit on. Snow blanketed Michigan already, the lake effect in full swing, burying everything around the abandoned factory in white. He was on the back side of the factory, an open lot with several closed garage-style doors for loading and unloading.

His heart ached upon seeing her eyes red and puffy, tears streaming down her face while her breath came out in puffs of mist. She had pulled her hair out of its customary ponytail and it sprawled along her shoulders.

But for all that he wanted to make her feel better, he knew he couldn't.

"I wish I knew how," he spoke sullenly, averting his eyes from hers, no longer able to bear seeing the pain she felt. "I can't do what I did in the tower again."

Planting her hands on her hips, she asked, "Why?" There was a note of accusation in her voice. "Why not? Your powers have grown stronger, not weaker! We've all seen it, we've seen the things you can do now!"

Gulping, he nodded, and looked over at her boots. "I know," he nodded. Still, he couldn't bear to meet her eyes again, so he studied her shoelaces instead. "But this isn't about power. It's about..." His voice faded, and he shook his head. Butterflies stirred up inside of his gut, and he tried desperately to squash each one down. Now wasn't the time to talk about how he felt. Now wasn't the time to admit he'd fallen in love with Alycia.

He had to save her from further pain.

Alycia fell to her knees, heedless of the cold and wet, sinking into the snow with a crunch. She tried to catch Chris's eye, but he turned away from her.

She shouted, "God dammit, will ya just tell me what's going on?"

Chris winced at her volume, and felt a shiver overcome him. He thought about how to answer her question without giving away too much, mulling it over while his eyes darted over the crystalline reflection from the snow.

"It takes…emotion," he shuddered. "Specific emotions. But every time I think about…*what* makes those feelings within me, I'm overcome by the wrong thoughts and feelings. Grief." He finally forced himself to look at her, into her reddened eyes, deep into her beautiful, no, *gorgeous* soul. "Regret. Loss. I can't conjure what's needed to break Nabu's hold over him." Turning away from her confused and pained expression, he trembled. "Not anymore."

Silence fell upon them for a long time after that. He'd come out here to be alone, but he was afraid now that she'd leave without another word. That she'd never talk to him again. For whatever time he had left on Earth, he wasn't prepared for that.

After some time of watching the shadows lengthen, he was startled by her voice, soft and measured. "What emotions do you need to feel?"

Something tightened inside his chest, and his breath caught.

Stuttering just a little, he replied, "Well, I, uh…positive emotions. Good emotions." He tried to look into her eyes again, but was too afraid too. "Happy feelings."

Out of the corner of his eye, he saw her raise a querying eyebrow. "Chris…?"

The cold on his backside from sitting in the snow finally started to get to him, so he quickly stood up and walked forward, brushing off his pants as he went. "I…" He paused, stopping halfway through his footsteps.

Alycia followed along behind him, and then rested a hand on his shoulder, urging him to turn to face her. When he refused, her grip became more insistent. The butterflies moved up from his stomach and into his chest, fluttering about like mad and setting his heart racing. His cheeks flushed, but he hoped they already looked that way from the cold.

Chris finally took a deep breath and met her gaze, their eyes becoming absorbed in each other's, staring, gazing, wondering and searching. All at once, he wanted to tell her everything and nothing, hoping she would confirm her love for him, and terrified that she would.

He was stuck in a loop, and he wondered if he could ever break himself out of it.

After another eternity of gazing upon one another, Alycia's face hardened. "Why can't you say it?"

Faltering, Chris stumbled over his words. "I, uh, what? Say what?"

"That you love me!"

His thundering heart halted for just a split second, his mind turning blank along with his sudden lack of a pulse. Eternity swirled around him as he took in her words and tried to think of an appropriate response.

When he didn't reply right away, she sighed in frustration. "Hell with it," she shook her head, and then grabbed him by the jacket and yanked him in to plant a kiss right on his lips. The world exploded in sensation, lips tingling, heart fluttering, face flushing. It was as if light and color became sharper than ever, and for the first time ever, he felt his chest explode in delight and glory!

The shock had hardened his lips, but as the moment blissfully drew on, surprise was replaced by desire. Chris wrapped his arms around her, drew her in closer, wanting to hold every part of her all at once, never wanting to lose this moment, this feeling. Her warmth, her touch. They didn't part for an age, and an age was never long enough for a first kiss.

As the age ended and they parted lips, Alycia and Chris held close to one another, staring into each other's eyes again, lingering in the moment for as long as they possibly could. He wished it could last. He wished they could be together forever.

He wished that wishes came true.

"Alycia…" How could he tell her? How could he say it without ruining the moment he'd imagined for four years? Four long, agonizing years of self-doubt, of thinking she could *never* love him. Of seeing hints and signs of those feelings from her, but believing it was just his imagination. Now, to have confirmation that it was true, that she *did* want him, he didn't know what to think.

But the most maddening part was that he knew it wouldn't last.

Not unless he found a way to defeat Marduk without sacrificing himself.

Her eyebrows rose up. "Mhm?"

"I…don't think…this is…a good idea." Each beat was more painful than the last, each word more difficult to tear out of himself than ever before.

Her soft, loving gaze faltered, her features hardening. "You what? Wuh…why?" Her grip on his jacket loosened. "Dammit, don't do this to me, Chris." His heart panged with guilt, and he loosened his arms around her waist. "You do love me, yeah?" He didn't reply, but it seemed like he didn't need to. She could always see right through him, he realized. Not just now, but always.

She's always known, and she's waited for me to figure myself out, he thought. *Until now, when she's lost all patience and made the first move.* He stared in amazement into her beautiful, golden-brown eyes. *She's braver* and *smarter than I am.*

When he didn't answer her question right away, her expression drew down into a heartbreaking expression, and he just couldn't stand it. "Yes," he whispered, afraid to say it any louder. "I do."

The heartbreak halted, and then hastened into a look of confusion. "Then what's the deal?"

Chris's face drooped, and he sighed, staring downward, at nothing and everything all at once. A breeze blew through the area, sending fresh shivers throughout his body. A chilling reminder of his fall from Sentinel tower, the ache in his arm reminding him of the broken bones he'd endured.

"Tattannu," he started. "The last time I heard his voice was in the hospital. I asked him what I would have to sacrifice to defeat Marduk." Drawing in a shuddering breath, he forced himself to look into her eyes and finish, "He said 'everything.'" A frown crept down Alycia's face while she processed his words. Forcing down a hard lump in his throat, Chris nodded. "I think…" He stopped, trying desperately to control the timbre of his voice. "Alycia, the souls within me, linked to me. I am their instrument. I am their Champion. And all magic has a price."

She nodded. "I remember Shara told us that."

He tilted his head down. "Exactly. I think…" His voice caught again, and he cleared it. That was quickly becoming an annoying occurrence. Alycia must have known what he was about to say, but they were both terrified of hearing it said out loud. He trudged on anyway, and finally managed to tell her, "I think I'm going to have to sacrifice myself."

Chris watched her for her reaction, forced himself to look even though he knew it would hurt. He owed her that much. The edges of her mouth creased downward, the realization taking hold of her features. Her hands, still loosely clinging to his jacket, tightened, grasping as if she could hold him here, in this life, through sheer physical will.

"No," she whispered, shaking her head. Fresh tears welled in her eyes. "Not you. I can't…"

Releasing her waist, he clasped her hands in his and held on tight. He couldn't imagine the devastation she felt, but he knew how horribly it hurt him just to see her look this way.

"If there's no other way, then I must do it," he insisted. "Nabu, Marduk, they're a threat because of the choice *I* made. Magic is back because *I* destroyed the Barrier. It's my job. My task. My purpose."

"I don't care," she whispered with a high-pitched squeak at the end. He felt her hands trembling, or was she shivering from the cold?

"Alycia, this is why we can't," he shook with the words. "Why I can't. Why we *shouldn't*."

"No," she shook her head rapidly. "Dammit, *no!* Don't give me that bullshit excuse." He recoiled against her outburst. She drew in a sharp breath, coughed against the cold, and held his jacket even tighter. "I don't go for the tragic hero crap, remember? That's such a lame trope."

He couldn't help but laugh, the tension in his arms and chest easing just a little, but that laughter acted like the release of a floodgate. His tears streamed down all at once, no longer held back by willpower.

"Dammit, I don't want to hurt you anymore than…"

"Stop!" Her brief smile instantly turned to annoyance, to frustration. "I mean it."

Letting go of her, he flailed his hands outwards. "We'd have so little time together, and all it would bring you is pain in the end!"

"Even if that were true," she drew him closer, bringing them nose-to-nose. "Even if you were supposed to die tomorrow, that doesn't mean we shouldn't finally admit our feelings to one another. Actually, scratch that - *because* of that, we should!"

Grasping her shoulders, he tried to shake his head, but she finally let go of his jacket just so she could grasp his face, tight enough to stop him from moving his head. "I mean it, dammit. If all we have is tomorrow, then we damn well better make today worth it. Worth it *all.* Otherwise what are we fighting for, eh? What's the point of it all if we can't enjoy living?

"And besides," she managed a half-cocked grin. "You assume I'll *let* you die. You ought to know by now, I'm as stubborn as a pelican."

He blinked at the reference, but the wry grin that drew across her face helped him to realize she was making up the phrase to get a laugh out of him. A deep chuckle escaped him, and he lowered his head until their foreheads touched. "Dammit, don't make me laugh when I'm trying to be…"

"A tragic buffoon?"

"Yeah, that."

"Well, don't be that way," she insisted, and then pulled her head away so that they could look into one another's eyes again. "Don't go. Don't let them take you. Because I…" Alycia paused, and smiled. "I love you, Christopher Tatsu. And there isn't a god or devil above or below who will take you away from me, do you hear?" His heart swelled, his chest expanding at the wellspring within. "I love you and I'll *never* let you go again."

Chris drew her in and clung tightly to her, willing the moment to last forever. She slid her hands around his chest and grasped up by his neck, near-crushing him in her embrace.

The words were there. He wanted to say them, even against all of the fear and the future anguish and pain. Something inside of him broke down, something that had held him back for years. A feeling that he didn't deserve such a wonderful companion. He never would.

But she had proven him wrong.

"I love you too," he whispered into her ear.

Deep inside, he felt his core flourish, grow stronger, brighter, more powerful.

Unleashing everything he needed.

"Besides," she added, and he could feel her smile against his cheek. "We have a lot of talented and powerful friends back in there, yeah? I'll bet if you tell them, then we can all figure something out together."

It was hope. And he wasn't sure yet if he was ready to feel hope. Was there a chance he could come out of this alive?

Alycia squeezed him tighter, and he knew then that there *had* to be. He couldn't break her heart.

"We'll get through this," she added. "Together."

He nodded, sniffling against both the cold and his tears. "Right. Together."

"Now go," she whispered, and then pulled away, renewed tears in her eyes, fueled not by remorse or fear or sorrow, but by blissful, giddy happiness. "Save my Dad, yeah? And then we can both watch him react to us kissing."

An uncontrolled laughter seized him at that, and it was all he could do to keep his chest bursting from delight.

CHAPTER 8

Ash tried to beat him to it.

When Chris and Alycia walked inside, shivering against the blowing snow, they saw their companions all gathered around Tom's unconscious form again, except this time, their eyes were fixed upon Ash, who knelt at Tom's head.

"What's going on?" Alycia asked Chris, who in turn shook his head and led her in a jog towards the group.

Ash's presence was still too blinding for Chris to feel any surge or pulse of magic, but their hands touched Tom's temples, and as Chris and Alycia rounded and their friends parted to let them in, he saw that Ash's eyes were closed, their face screwed up in concentration.

"Hey," he impulsively said. "What's going on?"

Before anyone could answer, Ash huffed and opened their eyes, glaring up at Chris. "If folks would let me concentrate," they said, "I'm trying to clear up the stain on his soul."

Chris's chest contracted. "You...can do that?"

They stared back at Chris with a blank face, and then Ash sheepishly shrugged. "I don't know, but they all told me you'd done it before. I figure why not give it a go?"

The sour sensation of jealousy and fear of being one-upped overtook Chris, and before he could stop himself, he folded his arms and asked, "Do you even know how?"

Arching a dark eyebrow at him, Ash asked, "Do you?"

The burn of embarrassment replaced his jealousy, and he let his mouth fall open in an unvoiced retort. He glanced at Alycia, then across at Emmi, and finally at Shara. "I do," he announced, turning again upon Ash. "I just had to, uh…" His eyes darted towards Alycia, and then back. "Had to work some things out."

It felt too new to tell them what had just happened outside. For one thing, his face still felt raw from the cold, but more than that, he had never really, truly had a girlfriend before. A part of him wanted to savor that fact, keep it between them for even just a few minutes. But another part, a part screaming with joy, decided differently, and he reached for Alycia's hand just as she reached for his.

In the comical sort of way you sometimes see in movies, everyone's eyes drew down to that hand hold, and a pregnant silence fell upon the group, broken only by the occasional snap or crackle of the nearby fire.

A wry grin lifted the corners of Emmi's mouth, and she whispered just a little too loudly, "It's about goddamn time."

Ash's cheeks grew a shade darker, and they withdrew their hands from Tom's temples. "Well alright, then," they spoke indignantly. "If you're so damned special, show us all how it's done."

A prideful scorn soured his stomach, and when he realized that all eyes were on him, a tinge of fear added itself to the spectrum. What if he failed again? Alycia squeezed his hand, and when he looked at her, he thought, *What if I fail her again?*

He heard Ash stand, and turned his eyes to them, and then down upon Tom.

What if I fail them all?

Alycia's words mere minutes ago echoed in his thoughts. 'We have a lot of talented and powerful friends.' Could they count Ash among them? Was Ash their ally? Or an enemy?

The answer to his problems came to him a second later.

"Together," he looked at Ash.

They blinked once, twice, frowned. "Excuse me?"

"You and I," he nodded. "If we work together, we'll have a better chance at cleansing his soul."

Alycia's grip cinched hard on his hand, and it was all he could do not to wince. He faced her, saw her wide-eyed terror, and she shook her head. "Are you crazy?" she asked. "We don't know them yet!"

A good point, that made Chris wonder how Ash convinced the others to let them try. With a frown, he looked at Shara, their commander in Tom's absence. Her violet eyes darted back and forth between Chris and Alycia, and then settled on Mia.

When they all looked at Mia, she kept her gaze upon Alycia, and said, "Unless they're a recent recruit, Ash was never a part of Nabu's group. Believe me, I knew *every single* cultist."

Frowning, Chris looked at Tom, but it was Alycia who pointed out, "Nabu recruited Dad since then. She could have infected Ash too, for all we know, or Ash could even be a completely willing servant."

"I serve no one," Ash hissed, taking a step towards Alycia. At first Chris had the instinct to step between them, but then he felt Alycia surge forward and had to hold *her* back.

"We don't know you," Alycia barked.

"I saw Ash attack the guards," Tiana volunteered, "the ones in the cell. Would Nabu's servant help us escape?"

"Nabu has a tenacity for long-term plotting," Babbar pointed out while he absently stroked thin air next to his shoulder. Nina must have been 'cloaked' there. "It is conceivable that Ash is a plant."

"But to what end?" Shara asked. Chris wasn't surprised that she argued against Babbar's point. "With Nabu's power, all she needs is to know where we are and attack with all of her powers. For that matter, if Ash were a plant, we should be surrounded right now by Federal agents."

"STOP TALKING LIKE I'M NOT HERE!"

Ash's outraged scream halted the argument, and everyone gaped at them. Chris felt the tinge of guilt inside again, realizing what they had done. Talking around someone who was present like they weren't in the room? *I've endure that far too often from my father.*

"Ash is right," he blurted out. He gritted his teeth, and then let go of Alycia's hand so that he could step up next to their new companion. "You're right. I'm sorry."

Anger burned in Ash's eyes, and they tore into Chris's soul, almost like a soul gaze. Their power flared intensely, fueled by Ash's frustrations. *No, not just frustrations,* Chris realized, feeling a tenuous connection growing with the other's golden sphere of light. *Rage. Fury. All the words that convey unfathomable anger, yet fall short of describing it.*

Ash was like him, in more ways than one. And he recognized the raw, boiling rage he saw within their eyes, just like when he had found out that Nabu had killed his sister. And from when Nabu's golem had murdered his mother.

The question was, how to convince the others? For that matter, how to be sure himself?

By going through with my earlier thought.

"You and I can work together on this," he glanced at Tom. "But I'll admit up front, my reasoning is two-fold. First, if our souls are truly linked as Tattannu's descendants, we can bring twice the power down upon the stain tarnishing his soul." The voices of the others, including Alycia's, began to object, but he held up a hand. "The second reason," he spoke louder, and then waited for everyone to stop and listen. "The second reason," he repeated, and looked intently at Ash, "is to get a good look at your soul, better than that connection we shared at the prison. If there's a stain from Nabu upon your soul, I'll see it. You won't be able to hide it from me."

He sounded more confident than he felt, but that was part of what he needed to do to sell this. To ensure Ash feared him if they were indeed an agent, and to reassure the others that Chris would be alright, and could protect Tom from Ash if necessary.

Ash regarded him coolly. Would they be okay with that sort of invasion of privacy?

Their expression softened, and they looked down for a second, before frowning at Chris. "You know it'll go both ways. If you can see all that I am, then I'll be able to see all that you are."

He hadn't thought of that, but he nodded. "I guess that's only fair, isn't it?"

A wry grin stretched across Ash's face. "Yeah, I suppose so."

Nodding, Chris looked around at the others, until his gaze settled upon Alycia's worried expression. He drew closer to her and held both of her hands in his. "I'll be okay," he insisted.

"But it's a risk…" she started to say, and then stopped before she looked at her father. "But I guess that's what we do. That's what we *have* to do, if we want to beat Nabu."

He nodded. "Exactly."

After a moment of gritting her teeth, she closed her eyes and sighed. "Fine." Then she looked him in the eyes and said, "But be careful."

At first he simply nodded again, but then he thought of the perfect movie quote for the moment. With a sarcastic grin, he said, "Hey. It's me!"

Rolling her eyes but still cracking the widest smile he'd seen her give him in months, she nodded. "Alright, Solo." He smiled triumphantly, but then her smile faded. "Just bring my dad back, yeah?"

Feeling his own grin falter, he nodded. "I will."

Knowing that there was at least one other person's permission he needed, Chris squeezed Alycia's hands one more time, and then he turned to Shara, the current commander in lieu of Tom. "With your permission?"

She arched an eyebrow at him, and he tried desperately not to see a Vulcan in that instant. Shara nodded. "Do it."

Letting out a breath he hadn't realized he'd been holding, he turned to Ash and nodded. "Let's go."

He stepped over to Tom's side opposite of Ash, and together, they knelt down next to the Sentinel commander.

It occurred to him that Ash hadn't been given the same training that Shara had given them, so he asked, "Do you know how to find your core at-will?"

Ash frowned in response, their eyes darting around, until their features hardened. "You mean enter the soul realm?"

Chris cocked his head to one side. "Soul realm?" He felt his face crease up into a grin. "I like that. Yes, do you know how to do that at will?"

"Of course I..." Ash's heated retort died, and they sighed. A second later, they said in a much softer tone, "Yes. Tattannu taught me."

The burn of jealousy ached in his chest again, but for now Chris pushed it aside. The time for reckoning with Tattannu would come soon enough.

Chris let out an exasperated sigh. "Alright," he whispered. "We can do this." Looking at Ash, he started, "On three." They hovered their hands above Tom's shoulders, Chris on the commander's left, Ash on the right. He drew in a deep breath, held it for a second, and then exhaled slowly, focusing on releasing his stresses and worries on his breath. "One...two...three."

They touched Tom's shoulder, and Chris closed his eyes.

At first, Chris was blinded by the surging, sun-like golden core hovering inches away from his. He could neither see nor feel Tom's diminutive soul. However, there was a link. A physical link to Tom that he *knew* was there, so he turned his attention to that link, averting his spectral eyes from Ash's resonating soul.

Finally, the tether to Tom appeared, and he clung to that link, and crawled along it, centimeter by centimeter. The spark of life within Tom grew sharper the more that Chris tried to focus on it, until at last, the blinding, deafening, overwhelming sense of Ash's soul no longer obscured it.

The taint of oily darkness swilled around Tom's soul, blotting out the core now and again, sickening Chris just by its sight, let alone how it made him feel.

Waves of exhaustion overwhelmed Chris, and his focus upon Tom's core wavered for a second. *That* was a new sensation when in the soul realm, and he shook his head, trying to clear his thoughts and fight off the weariness.

What's wrong? Why's this happening?

And then he knew, as he looked over towards the blinding, bright light of Ash.

He wasn't just having to focus, he was having to *fight* against an overwhelming light. They were twin powers out of sync with one another, two waves interfering with one another.

If they were to work together… "Ash," he said, though he wasn't sure if he spoke in the soul realm, reality, or both. "We have to sync up. We have to learn to attune ourselves to work together. Otherwise we're fighting each other."

Ash didn't verbally reply, but he sensed an answer through their link, an affirmation, an acknowledgement, with only a bit of uncertainty. How would they do it? How could they? How do you adjust the frequency and amplitude of your own soul?

"You're already linked," Naomi's voice startled him from the ether. "Use that engineering degree to figure it out, Chris."

He wanted to give his sister a smirk, but she was right. It was magic, but that didn't mean the principles of engineering and physics couldn't be applied.

They were already so close, and if he was right, their cores already shared a common source of power, a link to not just Tattannu, but millions upon millions of others.

So what caused their dissonance?

The answer came to him almost immediately. *Emotion.*

They were afraid of each other. Or at the very least, Chris was afraid of Ash. Of what they represented.

"I'm afraid," he voiced it aloud. With a whisper, he repeated, "I'm afraid…"

"So am I," Ash's voice floated to him from afar.

"Of what?" he asked.

"Of you," Ash replied, their voice shaking. "Of myself. Of my future. My past. What all of this means. But more than anything, I'm afraid of you."

At first, that admission surprised Chris. Why would they be afraid of him? But then he realized, and voiced aloud, the thought that, "I'm afraid of you, too. That your powers, your link to the Tattannu line, will take away my destiny. My role. I'm afraid I'm meant to fail." He hung his head. "I'm afraid that you're here because I'm not good enough."

The flickering and flashing of Ash's soul appeared to ease, but he knew now that it was more than that. It wasn't that they blinded each other or overpowered each other.

It's that they were linked when they didn't want to be.

He still didn't want to link to Ash. Chris was still scared.

But so was Ash, and *that* was the link they needed, the common ground to begin to calm the storm.

As Ash's soul appeared to settle into a steady, glowing thrum, he saw them standing next to their soul, more diminutive than in-person. Their fear was personified. Chris wondered if he, too, looked a mirror of his inner turmoil and fear to Ash. He had only ever seen the spiritual manifestation of the dead before now, and there were certainly no mirrors within the soul realm.

Ash's soul form looked away from Chris, and they hugged themselves.

If he looked hard enough, however, he could see the glowing line of light passing between his core and Ash's core, and a stronger line between their respective cores and Tom's dimmer, tainted core.

Seeing Ash like that, he suddenly knew he had no reason to be afraid. Not of Ash, at any rate. *They're just like me,* he thought. Their core looked almost identical to his. And as he walked around the soul realm to get a better view of all three at once, a strange vibration became apparent whenever both his and Ash's were visible at the same time. Instinctually, he knew why, as quantum physics lessons dawned upon him and he began to understand the nature of their link.

They each had their unique, self-contained souls, but each was enhanced and linked to the greater whole of the millions of Tattannu's descendants. It was like a magic version of the double-slit experiment. Two individual results that really came from one source.

Two answers to the same equation.

Ash isn't a threat to my goals, he thought, staring at their core, which looked so much like his own. *Ash is part of the equation.*

Within the soul realm, Chris walked across the empty void to stand next to them, and gently touched their shoulder. It felt strange, nothing like touching his sister's shoulder, which felt real and solid in this realm. Ash's shoulder felt cold, soft, almost unreal, the opposite of what he'd expect from interacting with another living being.

After a moment of him standing beside Ash, they worked up the courage to look into his eyes.

"We have nothing to fear from one another," he said.

They smiled weakly, and he knew without Ash having to say a word that they didn't quite believe him. That was fine, for the moment. They had synced up enough that he felt confident in their next task.

"Look," he pointed at Tom's soft, orange core. "We must let go of our fears, let go of our apprehension. Accept who we are, *what* we are, and find within ourselves the power to free others."

"How can we free others if we can't free ourselves?" Ash asked.

Thinking back to Naomi's words to him when he cleansed his friends in the tower, he said, "That's why it's so important to accept ourselves as we are."

Ash's self-hug appeared to tighten, and they looked away. "Yeah, that's not so easy for me."

He recognized that reaction, those words. More than once, he'd seen the look in Ash's face in the mirror. "Because your family doesn't accept you as you are?"

Favoring him with a shocked look, Ash's jaw hung open. "How...?"

"My father rejected me," he explained. "My mother was caught in the middle, I think. Wanting to love her child, but wanting to honor her husband, who despised his second-born child. I wanted to feel. I wanted to be my own person. I loved to play, to laugh. Fanciful stories like Lord of the Rings drew me in. But he was a man of science. Of math. I took up engineering to try to appease him, but in the end…" He closed his eyes and shook his head. "In the end, he blamed…"

Shuddering, Chris shook his head. "I've come to realize that I will never be accepted by him, but that's never what mattered." Looking to Ash intently, he nodded. "I had to learn to accept myself. Actually, I'm *still* working on that. But one thing is for certain – I am where I should be. This is where I'm supposed to be. This is who I am meant to be. An arcane caster, standing between Marduk and humanity." Tilting his head back just a little, Chris narrowed his eyes and asked, "Do you know who you are meant to be?"

"I…don't know," Ash shook their head. "I don't know where I belong. I've never belonged before. I mean," they blushed and looked down. "That sounded stupid."

"I think I know what you mean," he nodded, "even if I can't relate, I can empathize."

Ash nodded, and looked at him. "For entirely different reasons, my parents rejected me, too. My cousin…the one Nabu murdered. He was the only person in my entire family, on *both* sides, who accepted me. He was the only one who stopped using my dead name. Actually," they shuddered and hung their head lower, "he was the only one who still talked to me after I…"

The deep, dark emptiness that threatened to swallow Ash up resonated through their link, and Chris felt his stomach open into the void. It threatened to take him with, to force him to see his father's face again, the blame he had leveled upon Chris in the hospital…

"Hey," he shook himself out of it, and then squeezed Ash's shoulder. "That emotion, not the pain and anguish of loss, but the love of your cousin. That's the key. That's what we need to save Tom. Later, we can use those other feelings to get our revenge on Nabu, but for now, focus your thoughts on your cousin and how much he cared about you."

Their eyes turned up to look at Chris's. "Do you really think I can do this?"

He nodded. "I do."

Frowning, Ash asked, "How? How can you possibly know I'm strong enough or good enough?"

Grinning, he looked over at their core. "I can literally see your soul, Ash. I know the strength you have now, and I know that, even with the help of Tattannu and his descendants, you wouldn't be here if you weren't strong enough."

A hint of a smile drew open Ash's face, and they beamed at Chris. Something happened then, and the weak beam of light between Chris's core and Ash's doubled in intensity, casting them both in a golden glow of warmth.

He could feel Ash's heart turning from sadness and remorse to warmth and kindness. He could *feel* their attitude change, even if only for a moment, and a moment was all they really needed.

Turning back to Tom's core, Chris nodded. "Send that feeling outwards, along the link to Tom's soul. If we both do so, we should be able to unravel the darkness within Tom without even getting help from the other souls."

Ash nodded, and together, they closed the distance to Tom's core. They reached out for it, and at the same time, they gently touched the outer shell. The darkness within writhed and convulsed as waves of energy passed into Tom's soul.

A blinding flash followed, until there was nothing left but the warm, sunset-orange sphere, pulsing quietly in time with Tom's heartbeat.

CHAPTER 9

Opening his eyes, Chris expected Tom to have woken up, but even magic couldn't counter copious amounts of tranquilizer. The Sentinel commander remained as motionless as ever, and seemed no different on the outside.

Ash opened their eyes and looked expectantly at Tom, and then over to Chris. "We did it."

He nodded, wanting to smile, but feeling solemn about what he had learned about his counterpart. "Indeed." Pushing up onto his feet, he held out his hand for Ash. They stared apprehensively at it, and then gingerly took hold of it. There was a brief golden spark, a discharge of magical static, but otherwise nothing else happened, and Chris helped Ash stand.

"Welcome to the team," he nodded, and then turned to Alycia. Surprisingly, Mia stood next to her, having moved closer while Chris and Ash worked, and the two held hands. "Tom'll be okay when he wakes up," Chris explained. "Nabu's control has been removed."

They both let out relieved breaths, and then Mia opened her free arm up, beckoning Chris forward. He blinked in surprise, and then stepped into her embrace, which was joined an instant later by Alycia.

"Thank you," Mia half-sobbed. "Thank you for restoring my family." Over his shoulder, she added, "To you as well, Ash."

Mia's hug tightened, crushing the air from Chris, before she let go. It was easy to forget just how strong she was under the worn and torn clothes she wore, but she was well-built, and stronger than Chris by at least double. Alycia caressed his cheek and smiled brightly at him. "I told you," she spoke quietly, and winked.

With cheeks warming, he returned the smile, and then looked down at Alycia's hand in her mothers. With a scarlet blush, Alycia released Mia's hand quickly, and turned to Shara. "Well then. What now?"

Looking as relieved as everyone else, and sharing a tight hug with Tiana, Shara turned her gaze upon Chris and sighed, tension in her shoulders deflating. "Now we breathe," she replied. "We regroup." Turning to Ash and letting go of Tiana, Shara added, "and we find out more about you."

"I'll go into town and get us some food," Mia volunteered.

"I'll go with," Marisol automatically volunteered. That was no surprise – Marisol still didn't trust Mia. "Keep the chica company and see if our mysterious contact made another drop."

Mia shot Marisol a weary glare, but assented, and together, the two of them donned heavy jackets and set out.

Tiana sauntered over to the fire, shivering and pulling her jacket closer, and threw on a couple of quartered logs. Chris and the others took that as a silent cue, and everyone gathered around the warming blaze, with Alycia on Chris's right, Emmi on his left, Shara directly across from him, and Tiana and Babbar bracketing them. Ash stayed out in the peripheral at first, shivering against the cold, flurried breeze that blew through the factory, until Shara motioned them to come over, and then Ash stepped up to Emmi's left.

The blaze was hot enough that Chris instantly warmed up, and he unzipped his jacket and sighed contentedly. The familiar smell of a campfire soothed him to his bones, and he inhaled deeply.

"Well then," Shara began, and glanced at Ash. "Formal introductions. My name is Shara, second in command of the United States Sentinels. This is Tiana Jones, our pilot and sharpshooter."

Tiana shrugged. "Not much call for piloting these days." Chris grimaced sympathetically.

"You've met Chris Tatsu," Shara motioned to him, "And Emmi Dubois. To Chris's right is Alycia Taylor." Ash nodded and waved to each person Shara introduced, and then silence fell upon the group.

Babbar cleared his throat exceedingly noisily.

"Oh," Shara glanced towards him. "And this little fungus is Babbar."

"Oye, manners!" Babbar planted his hands on his hips.

A chortling noise emanated from thin air on his shoulder, and Nina appeared a second later, her emerald scales shining bright in the firelight, and her red lizard-like eyes flashing at Shara indignantly.

"I'm so sorry," Shara said to the mini-dragon, genuine sincerity in her voice. "And this cute little girl is Nina."

Ash stared at Shara, Babbar, and Nina, blinking slowly, deliberately, as if trying to clear something from their eyes.

After a protracted silence, Ash said, "So, let me get this straight. Not only is magic real, but now Earth has an elf, a dwarf, and a dragon?"

"Hey!" Babbar growled.

"I'm not an elf," Shara added indignantly.

"And I'm no dwarf," Babbar grumbled, consciously rubbing at his large nose. "I'm a gnome, thank you very much."

Remorse drew down Ash's features, and they held up their hands disarmingly. "Okay, okay, I'm sorry. I didn't know. You're a gnome. And if you're not an elf, then…"

Shara sighed and considered the question. "Well as Chris once pointed out, I'm an extra-terrestrial."

"Oh," Ash frowned. "But not a Vulcan."

Chris pretended to scratch his face to cover the grin that crossed his expressions. Shara looked impatiently at Ash. "No, I'm not any fictional creature. I just…look, my species is called sinéliar in our language, and no, I have no idea what it would translate to in English." Chris gaped at Shara, never having heard her actually say what her species called itself. "But instead of thinking of me as an alien or a fantasy creature, just think of me as a person, and we'll get along just fine."

A light smile shone upon Ash's face. "I think I can appreciate that." That comment drew the gaze of all present, and Ash's grin faded to a shy grimace. "My name is Ash Patel," they finally stated. "But you won't find me under that name in any records."

"Because you haven't had an official name change yet?" Alycia asked.

Ash nodded. "Exactly. If it's important to you to look up who I really am, I can…"

A dreadful look crossed Ash's face, and after a few seconds, Shara shook her head. "I think we're fine knowing you as Ash. We don't have to look up your dead name."

Flashing Shara a bright and appreciative smile, Ash nodded. "Thank you."

"But we do need to know your story," Emmi insisted. "Regarding magic and how you know about Nabu and Tattannu."

"Yeah, I know," Ash nodded. "It started when I'm guessing it started for all of you. I lived in Denver with my cousin. He…" Their voice caught. "From what Tattannu has told me, and from what the police told me, he was in the hangar when Nabu made her…or his…*their* first move. They used some special dagger to sacrifice him, and that released his soul into the realm of magic and damaged some mystical barrier that blocked magic on Earth."

Ash swallowed hard, and looked down. "I felt it. Not just the sudden surge of magic in Denver, which felt like an adrenaline rush in the middle of my shift at work, but I felt David die. It was so strange, I just broke down crying at work, and couldn't explain to my coworkers or customers why. They let me go early for the day, and I raced home, but I knew David was at a party with his girlfriend." Ash's voice grew very quiet, almost a whisper, barely audible above the crackling fire. "A few hours later, the police showed up."

A massive lump formed in Chris's throat, and he tried to force it down, but it stubbornly refused. Visions of the hospitals where Naomi and his mother were taken popped into his memories. The desperate, sullen look on his father's face. Chris remembered just how horrified and empty he felt when he learned that his sister was gone and would never come back.

Naomi…

After a long, silent minute passed, Ash cleared their throat and continued on. "The, uh…well, all hell broke loose after that. The blizzard, strange occurrences all over the world. I was getting these weird-ass static shocks left and right." Chris exchanged knowing looks with Emmi and Alycia. "And our…our neighbor started blasting his music again, thumping against the walls, and it just pissed me off. The next thing I knew, a golden ball of light flew out of my hand and blew a hole in the wall between our apartments. The dipshit neighbor was stoned off his ass and thought it was the coolest thing ever to happen, but I was horrified, and I ran."

Hugging themselves, Ash shook their head and continued, "Technically I was never on the lease, so the landlord never knew who to blame or go after. I spent a few nights in my car. Shattered a window with another unintended blast of magic. Then…" Pausing, Ash looked at Chris specifically, their eyes flickering in the firelight. "Everything changed. The Barrier fell, and all of the weird stuff going on inside of me settled down. I felt different. Stronger. I can't explain it beyond just a feeling. And then that night, Tattannu came to me for the first time. Along with countless others."

Chris frowned, thinking back to what happened after the Barrier fell. He recalled specifically not seeing Tattannu or even his sister after falling unconscious at the end of their battle with Nabu at Babylon. Was this why?

"I found myself atop some pyramid-like structure," Ash continued. "In ancient times, middle of the desert. A golden sphere of light in the middle that apparently was an amalgamation of my soul and the souls of millions of others from history…" Pausing, Ash looked sheepishly around the fire. "You all already know about this?"

"Kind of," Chris nodded. "I found myself in the same place when I touched the Dragonstone and was about to dismantle the Barrier. I thought I was alone. I thought I was supposed to *be* alone in this."

Timidly, Ash's eyes darted to Chris, then away, then at him again. "I don't think I was supposed to be part of it, either. Tattannu said the one who dismantled the Barrier was meant to join with all of those souls. But something apparently happened when Nabu killed my cousin. Even though my cousin wasn't part of the Tattannu line, the fact that the same family blood ran through his veins and mine linked our souls, and something happened when his soul was destroyed. An unintentional side effect…"

Ash's eyes fell downward, a terrible look of sadness pulling down at their features. "I…don't belong."

Chris arched an eyebrow up, felt his insides swirl. So it wasn't that Tattannu didn't believe in him. It wasn't that Ash was meant to succeed where Chris had failed.

His fears had all been for naught.

Nina chortled and made a sound that was a cross between a meow and a growl. Babbar looked at her curiously, and then said, "Apparently Nina disagrees."

Stunned eyes from every member present fell upon the duo. "She does?" Ash asked, a measure of guarded hope in their voice.

Nina continued to gr-meowl. Babbar translated, "There is a difference between fate and destiny, and it was always your destiny to be part of this. From here, it is up to you to find a path forward, to choose what to do with the gifts you have been given. But she believes you belong here." Nina gaped at Babbar and nipped at his ear. "What? I summarized. You're too wordy, you know." Nina growled in response.

Covering another grin with a faux-face-scratch, Chris cleared his throat, and then looked at Ash. "So that settles it," he said, trying not to let the relief he felt enter his voice. "If you wish, you're welcome to stay with us."

"It might be the best thing to do," Shara added. "Nabu knows your face now. Chances are high you'll be added to that most-wanted list."

Ash shrugged. "I've got nowhere else to go. My cousin's girlfriend took me in for a time, until the President signed that new law into effect about registration, and she saw me cast magic. I had to run then, and I've lived in my car ever since."

"How'd you end up in D.C.?" Emmi asked, doubt still in her voice.

"Tattannu told me a week ago you'd be there."

Chris and Emmi exchanged shocked looks. "We didn't even know we'd be there until yesterday," he explained when Ash gave them a quizzical look. It wasn't entirely surprising, given the prophetic dreams Chris used to have, but it did aggravate him. Curling his fingers up into tight fists, he shook his head. "Why the hell is he talking to you, but not me?"

Shrugging helplessly, Ash replied, "I dunno. Maybe he somehow got stuck with me?"

It was a thought that had never occurred to Chris, and he forced his hands to relax. For all he knew, Ash was right. To say that the dual nature of their connection was unprecedented was like saying the year 2020 was a minor inconvenience. Magic was tumultuous when unstable, and the disparaging resonance between him and Ash had been a major disruption.

"Maybe now that we've managed to sync our, um," Chris frowned, "magic frequencies, or whatever it is we just did, he'll be able to talk to me again."

"Is that what happened?" Alycia asked.

"We felt some pretty crazy things happening when you two first touched Tom," Emmi explained. "Anyone with magic power felt it. Even..."

Chris glanced at Shara, and then at Alycia. He had told them all, without Mia's knowledge, about the power he'd felt in her back in the Sentinel tower. Yet to this day, Mia had not shown any hint of powers. It was for precisely that reason that Marisol and Emmi still didn't trust her, and part of why Alycia still kept her distance from her mother.

"She looked as disturbed as we felt," Alycia acknowledged. "But I'm starting to wonder if she really doesn't know."

Chris looked again at Shara. "And you say that the color of her soul doesn't indicate a power?"

"Colors change," Shara nodded. "You've noted it yourself that my shade of green is different from Emmi's, and given time, they could diverge even more, and we'd both still be effective shapeshifters." Shrugging, she said, "Long story short, I still haven't a clue what her powers might be."

Letting out a defeated sigh, Chris nodded. "Alright. Well, what do we do now?"

"Rest," Shara immediately replied. "Today was exhausting. We need to rest so we can be prepared for whatever comes next."

It was a good point, and a good plan. Tom was still asleep, and until Mia and Marisol got back, there wouldn't be much else to do. But tomorrow? That might be another story altogether.

They'd made a move against Nabu, for the first time in months.

Nabu wasn't likely to let them get away with it.

CHAPTER 10

Contrary to Chris's paranoia, evening came quietly. Tom still hadn't woken by the time Marisol and Mia returned with supplies and, thankfully, more firewood pre-bundled from the stores.

Shara took the opportunity to offer some basic training to Ash, who graciously took advantage and set to meditation. Chris, Emmi and Alycia sat on their mattresses and sleeping bags while Alycia took out a sewing kit and worked on a new enchantment for her jacket. With the ancient enchanting book that Shara had given her now lost in the destroyed Sentinel tower, she had turned to coming up with her own symbols to represent her intended enchantments, consisting most often of emojis or something meme-related.

Once, last month, Chris had asked Alycia why she didn't do something more complicated or artistic, as he'd known her to do in the past. She merely shrugged and said, "This is more entertaining for me," as she sewed a flaming smiley face into her gloves. Chris secretly believed it was meant to be Calcifer from *Howl's Moving Castle*, but Alycia never confirmed nor denied it.

Hoping that his recent connection to Ash would unlock something, Chris decided to try meditating. Drawing his legs under him into a pretzel fashion, he closed his eyes, drew in his relaxing breaths, and entered the soul realm.

Naomi was the one who greeted him, smiling as always and embracing him in a warm hug.

"That was a good thing you did," she told Chris. "You could have saved Tom yourself, but by including Ash, I think you've helped them overcome a significant personal hurdle."

Favoring Naomi with an easy smile, he turned to his golden core, and saw the hint of a tether leading off from it. Following its line, he could see Ash's core far in the distance, hazy but still present. Their connection still existed, even when they were physically a good hundred feet apart.

Was he now forever linked to their newest companion?

Looking around in the surrounding gray haze, Chris searched the shifting humanoid shadows. "Tattannu still hasn't come back?"

Naomi grimaced and shook her head. "No."

Unable to help himself, Chris let out a frustrated sigh. "This is getting ridiculous. We still have no guidance, no clue as to what his final words to me meant. How the hell do I end Nabu?"

When he looked at Naomi, her eyes were downturned, and she held her left elbow with her right hand, a nervous antic she used to employ when something bothered her.

"Naomi?"

For a moment, she didn't reply, and a twisting fear gripped Chris's stomach. Finally, she looked up at him, her eyes haunting in the golden glow. "I...feel something," she said, her voice almost a whisper. "Like something is coming. All paths are coming together. I can almost..." Her gaze shifted to the golden core. "...See it."

He turned his gaze upon their shared center as well, and shortly after, looked upon the hazy link to Ash. *All paths are coming together.*

When he looked upon his sister again, she stared back. "I think the answers you seek are coming soon. I can *feel* it."

Clamping his mouth shut, Chris nodded. His throat felt dry, and an ache of fear crept up inside.

He asked the only thing he could think to ask in that moment. "Was it a mistake to kiss Alycia?"

Naomi blinked in surprise, her hardened features softening. "No," she soothed. "It's never a mistake to give in to your heart, Chris."

A broad smile stretched across his face. Before he could say anything else, something in the waking world demanded his attention, an insistent voice calling his name. Naomi waved a quick goodbye, and then Chris came to.

It was Emmi, shaking him awake and calling his name. When Chris opened his eyes, Alycia was no longer next to him, but instead was next to Tom, whom she and Mia were helping to sit up.

Chris scrambled to his feet with Emmi's help, and they hurried over along with the rest of the Sentinels.

"Hey there," Shara knelt down at his feet. "Welcome back."

Blinking sleep from his eyes, Tom stared sullenly at Shara, and then at his daughter. "Aly," he whispered. "I'm so sorry…"

Without another word, Alycia threw her arms around her father and grasped him tight enough that the commander winced before he returned the embrace. "I'm just glad you're back, Dad."

After an eternity of them holding one another, Alycia finally let go and slouched backwards onto her knees. Then Tom's eyes turned to his other side. To his wife.

"Mia," he said, his voice uncertain. "Are you…"

Smiling, eyes furtively glancing at their daughter, Mia nodded. "I'm here, my…my dear." She motioned to the gathered team, and continued, "Thanks to all of these fine people, especially Chris and," she nodded at the newcomer, "Ash, we're both fine."

Tom blinked, eyes darting around before settling on the only unfamiliar face. "You. You were in my cell with Chris."

Ash nodded. "That'd be me."

Then realization seemed to dawn on Tom's face. "Mia," he turned back to his wife. "You mean…"

"Young Chris over there cleared Nabu's hold over me," she smiled weakly. "So, yes. I'm back. And I am so sorry for the hell I put you through." A tear slid down her cheek, followed by another. Her voice wavered, and then broke, "I'm so sorry that I hurt you…"

Without another word, Tom drew her into a tight hug, shushing amidst her sobs. Mia gripped Tom's shirt into fistfuls of fabric, clinging to him, as if afraid to lose him all over again.

Alycia's face drew down into a deep grimace, and she stood up and hugged herself, staring at the scene with uncertainty in her eyes. Chris stepped closer to her and drew her into his arms, and she rested her head on his shoulder.

It should have been a private moment for Tom and Mia, for Alycia as well, but there was no such thing as privacy in this place. Not really. The trio needed time together, time to reunite, and time for Alycia to learn to trust her mother again.

Time they just didn't have.

When Mia's sobs lessened, the two Taylors parted just enough to rest foreheads against one another. "We'll make up all of that lost time together someday, I promise," he told her. "When all of this is over."

It was an unspoken cue that Mia must have recognized from days long past, and she nodded before she stood up, and then held a hand down to Tom to help him stand. He was a little unsteady on his feet at first, but managed to keep upright.

Looking at the troupe surrounding him, his face hardened into the normal look of determination that Chris had missed more than he realized over the past three months.

"Thank you, all of you," he said. Settling his gaze on Ash for just a second, he then looked at Shara and said, "I think I have a lot of catching up to do."

Over the next several hours, Shara and the others, gathered around the fire, filled Tom in on all that had happened since Sentinel Tower, calling up Abby on their burner phone so that she could chime in as well. Marisol and Mia had brought back fresh packages of hotdogs, and the group set to using sticks to cook them over the fire. It wasn't the best dinner, and by now Chris had grown completely sick of them, but having any food in his belly was better than nothing.

Once they caught up to the events that took place after rescuing Tom, it was Chris's turn to brief the commander on what he and Ash had done, and he summarized who Ash was and why they were there.

With relatively full stomachs, the Sentinels and guests sat around the fire, watching as Tom contemplated everything he had learned. The sun had set long ago, leaving only their fire to cast flickering, eerie orange light upon the gathering.

Drawing in a deep breath, Tom shook his head. "As grateful as I am that you all came after me," he finally started, "your best bet would have been to leave me there."

Chris felt startled, and saw similar looks upon everyone else's face. "Sir?" Shara asked.

"Nabu wanted to trap you all," he said, and then settled his gaze upon Chris. "But especially you. She wants you. She *needs* you. I didn't learn much while I was captive, but when she came to my cell and did...whatever it was she did to me," he shook his head, "she made it clear that capturing you would be my priority."

With an amused smirk, Chris said, "Good thing I didn't give you the chance to."

Pushing his eyebrows up, Tom shrugged. "It could easily have turned out differently."

"True," Shara interjected before Chris could say anything else, "but we had to know if our informant was trustworthy."

"So you committed the entire team to it?" He asked with an accusing glare. "Come on, Shara, you should know better."

"It was my plan," Chris stated defiantly, an adrenaline surge setting his hands to shaking. "We had info on the facility, on their enchantments and counter enchantments, and I knew that we had to work together."

"Like I said, you should have left me there," he glowered at Chris. "We're all that stands between Nabu and Marduk's return right now, no one else knows exactly what the threat is. Your choice to save me was an unnecessary risk."

Feeling the sour taste of indignation, Chris clenched his hands into fists. "Yeah, maybe you're right. I guess we should have just left your ass back there to rot. I'm sure once Nabu realized we weren't going to fall for the trap, she'd just let you go, right? Oh, no, she would have *killed* you."

"Better me than you," Tom countered, fury boiling into his voice.

"Dad!" Alycia interjected. "What the hell?"

"Stay out of this, Aly," he replied, slicing his hand through the air.

That was exactly the wrong thing to say. "God dammit, Dad, I won't! Not now, not ever!" Alycia stood up defiantly, glaring down her father. "We saved your ass, and the best you can do is lecture us? What sort of ungrateful crock of shit is that?"

Blinking rapidly in surprise, Tom was on his feet a second later. "I thanked you before," he defended, sounding more irritated than repentant, "but that doesn't change the fact that-"

"That we needed you," Alycia interrupted. "That we needed someone with a history of seeing the bigger picture. Chris stepped up, saw what we needed, and spurred us into action! He led us to victory!"

"Well then what the hell do you need me for?" Tom flailed his arms around. "If he's such a good leader..."

"That's what this is about?" Alycia shrieked.

"No, it's about saving humanity," he countered. "And that isn't gonna happen if you keep-"

"ENOUGH!" Chris's roaring voice surprised even himself. At some point he'd risen to his feet, but he couldn't remember when, and all he could hear once silence fell upon the group was his pounding heart, and all he could feel was the pulsing vein in his temple. "Christ, we've enough on our plates, and you want to start lobbing accusations around? Should Ash and I take another look at your soul, make sure you're not still tainted and trying to sabotage us all?"

Tom's eyes opened wide, the whites overly visible even in the low firelight. "What did you just say, you little...?"

"Tom!" Shara's lecturing tone cut him off, and for that matter, prevented Chris from interrupting. "We brought you back for your leadership, not your self-righteousness."

Somehow, those words appeared to slam into Tom like a lead weight. He staggered back, gaping at Shara. "Self-righteousness?" he echoed.

"Yeah, and don't give me that look," Shara folded her arms defiantly. "Don't act like I've wounded your pride or some stupid shit like that. You've always been a good leader, but you never take a loss well, and you *always* have to act high and mighty to cover your embarrassment. Now's not the time for that, and you know it."

The murderous look in Tom's eyes had Chris waiting for another outraged explosion from him. The commander's knuckles cracked from how tightly his fists clenched, and the tendons in his neck bulged out.

But Shara's words must have been the right ones. The bulging neck softened, and he took three deep breaths before relaxing his hands. The effect was surprising, and it caught Chris off-guard, his own anger fizzling.

After another few moments passed, Tom sighed and nodded, his chest deflating like his rage had been hot air. "You're right," he conceded, his voice low and more remorseful than Chris had ever heard it. Turning to Chris, he drew in a breath, held it, and said, "I'm sorry, Chris."

Vaguely, Chris became aware that his jaw hung open. Clamping it shut, he sought for something to say, and quite lamely, ended up just saying, "Okay."

Alycia shot him a look that said, 'that's the best you can do?!'

Tom clasped his hands together behind the small of his back and began to pace around the fire. Chris and Alycia remained on their feet and watched, while all others remained seated, most of them looking too scared to say or do anything else.

After half of a circuit around the group, Tom finally said, "You've all done admirably on your own."

"But it isn't enough," Shara looked up to him as he passed by her. "Just being on the run all the time isn't getting us any closer to stopping Nabu."

Tom nodded. "Agreed. Still, better to be alive and able to fight than to not."

Chris felt his temper flare, feeling like that was another jab at his plan to rescue Tom, but he kept his mouth shut.

The commander stopped short just as he started passing Ash, and he looked down at the newest fugitive amongst them. His eyes darted back and forth between Ash and Chris, and then he glanced at Alycia, then at Mia, before gazing into the fire. Ash looked decidedly uncomfortable having the largest person present loitering behind them, and they shifted nervously.

"Family is the answer," Tom mused.

Uncertain looks were exchanged amongst the gathering.

"Come again?" Tiana asked.

"Family, blood," Tom nodded insistently before resuming his pacing. "You're both descendants of Tattannu," he motioned to Chris and Ash. "You're both somehow connected to the millions of souls of his descendants, and those souls are somehow part of the long-term plan to defeat Marduk."

The commander stopped again, half a dozen feet between him and Chris, and they stared back at one another. "So what?" Chris asked. "That's nothing new."

"Right," Tom nodded. "Nothing new. Even with Ash here, it hasn't changed the fact that a descendant of Tattannu has more power than any other magic-wielding human. I think the answer is in the family line. Maybe." Sighing in frustration, Tom wiped his hand down his face, and then scratched at his beard. "We need more info, that's the truth of the matter."

More info, Chris thought. *About family. About blood. About souls.*

He thought of the images that had flashed before him. The dagger, the Dragonstone…why had his and Ash's shared vision shown them those things?

"Abby," he blurted out.

"Hey, you remembered I'm here!" her modulated voice came through the speakerphone.

"Yeah, sorry," Chris nodded. "Do you still have a way to get into the Sentinel databases across the world?"

A pause followed, before she replied, *"If I'm careful, yeah. Why?"*

"Because I have a theory," he replied, and looked directly at Ash. "Tom is right, family is important. Family *tradition* is important. My father hated that I didn't follow tradition, and I know my grandfather on my father's side lectured *my father* over the name they chose for me. I have this memory of sitting down with my ojiisan as a child, and him explaining to me the importance of carrying on family tradition, even after living in the United States for so many generations. But I was defiant." He frowned and shook his head. "I was always defiant of family tradition."

After a few moments of silence, Tom folded his arms in front of himself again and said, "I assume there's a point to all of this?"

Chris blinked, and felt his cheeks grow warm in embarrassment. "The point is that you're right." Tom blinked in surprise at Chris's admission. "The family line."

There was a pause as everyone thought about it. They heard the click-click-clicking of rapid-fire keyboard work over the speaker, and then Abby said, *"If you're referring to family legacies, the first census in Japan was reportedly in the sixth century. In India, it was-"*

"Not genealogy," Chris shook his head. "History. Myths. Legends. Family stories."

Another pause followed. *"What do you want me to look for?"*

"Look for anything in the Sentinel archives, both physical and digital, that might relate to family history," Chris stated. "Especially if the name Tatsu or Patel appear in it, *especially* if both appear. More importantly, look for anything that either references the Dragonstone or Imhullu, or anything that looks like or represents them."

A soft whistle echoed out of the speaker. *"That's a tall order."*

With a smile on his face, Tom nodded. "I think I see where Chris is going with this, and I think he's right. And I have every confidence in your abilities, Abby."

"Aww, shucks, boss," Abby replied. *"I missed you too."*

CHAPTER 11

With little more to do, the Sentinels and their guests settled into tending the fire. Shara continued to teach Ash about mindful presence and controlling their powers, while Alycia spent time with her father and mother.

Chris tried to respect their private conversation, but every now and then, he caught snippets. At one point, Tom stopped Mia from another string of apologies and said, "I understand now. When she's in your head, it's like everything has a clarity to it that you never thought possible. Like every uncertainty in the world doesn't matter, because Nabu will sort it out, if only you're loyal enough, *good* enough to be worthy."

Listening from the other side of the fire, Chris looked down, ashamed to have overheard Tom, and embarrassed by how much he wished for that kind of clarity.

Emmi, sitting beside him, must have read his expression the way only she could, and she elbowed him. "Hey," she started, and then stopped.

Arching a curious eyebrow, Chris replied, "Hey yourself."

A light smile touched her lips, and Emmi leaned over and rested her head on his shoulder. "It's gonna be okay, you know."

As well as she knew him, Chris knew Emmi just as well, and he caught the hint of fear in her voice. She reached over and clutched onto his jacket, affirming his suspicion.

Lightly touching her hand, he nodded, and leaned his head against hers. "Yeah," he managed to croak through a tight throat.

After a few more hours, Tom ordered everyone to bed,

volunteering to take the first watch. Not wanting to sweat through the night, Chris took his jacket and boots off, shivering like mad, until he could slither into his sleeping bag. It was still freezing inside of it, but weeks of being on the run had taught him that within ten or fifteen minutes, he'd be warm enough, even with the Earth trying to suck all the warmth out of him.

Alycia shuffled into her bag next to him, and then sighed in annoyance, before turning to him. From his perspective, her eyes were in shadows, unlit by the flickering firelight, but he knew she was staring at him.

"Too bad we don't have a double," she whispered to him.

The moment he realized what she meant, he felt his cheeks warm against the biting cold. His chest suddenly ached, and all he wanted to do was wrap his arms around her. That was the true irony of their situation – they finally had admitted their feelings to one another, but couldn't spend even a single evening alone together. Not yet, anyway.

Maybe never.

Banishing those thoughts, he tried to scooch his bag closer to hers, and she giggled. If it weren't the middle of winter, he would have unzipped his side enough to hold her hand or even just lay his arm over her, but the last thing he wanted was to wake up freezing, or worse, endure the bitter, painful sting of frostbite.

So they did the best they could, leaning up against each other through the bags, and falling asleep listening to each other's breathing.

When he entered the soul realm, he immediately noticed Alycia's familiar lightning-blue core hovering next to his larger, brighter golden core, with an almost-invisible tether of light between them.

"I'm happy for you," Naomi's soft, bright voice startled him. She came up next to him and stared at the linked souls. "More than ever, you deserve happiness."

It was a cheesy, corny line, but he sighed contentedly, while trying desperately to shove down the fears he felt, to the very bottom of his gut, where they belonged. *Don't ruin my moment,* he lectured himself.

Chris spent the rest of the night telling Naomi all about their rescue of Tom, unsure how much she had witnessed through his eyes. Whether or not she already knew the details, Chris's sister listened patiently, a warm smile upon her face as they paced patiently around the linked souls.

Bitter annoyance still struck at Chris, and though he could sense Ash's presence, there was still no sign of Tattannu, so that when he woke up the next morning, he felt a mix of happiness over spending an evening with his sister and fear about the unknown days ahead.

When he opened his eyes, however, he was greeted by the beautiful sight of Alycia, her gorgeous face mere inches from his. It was a very, *very* cold morning, and every time she exhaled, he saw a little puff of her breath in the frigid air.

Low voices caught his attention, and he lifted his head just enough to see Tom, Mia, and Shara warming themselves by the fire.

When he looked back at Alycia, her golden-brown eyes were open, staring at him, sending butterflies all through his chest.

Before he knew what he was doing, he leaned closer and kissed her. She sucked in air in surprise at first, but then she pushed into the kiss, until they broke away and gazed into one another's eyes. "Good morning, beautiful," he whispered.

She smiled, but a gagging sound from behind Chris startled him, and he turned in surprise – only to see Emmi sitting up in her bag, mock-gagging. "Ugh," she glared at him. "Could you get any cheesier, Chris? Wait, let me turn into a cat, I'll leave a hairball in your sleeping bag."

He glared at his friend, but the remarks had elicited a soft giggle from Alycia, and that killed his sour disposition.

"Shut it," he tried to sound angry, but the grin stretching across his face failed to make that happen. "You're just jealous."

"Oh my," Emmi's eyes widened. "Did you hear that, Aly? He thinks I want to kiss you."

"Wait, you don't?" Alycia mocked surprise.

"Oye, do you mind?" Babbar's voice asked. "It's too early to listen to a gaggle of giggling girls."

More chuckles followed, but then Babbar's words registered on Chris. "Did you just call me a girl?"

A middle finger appeared out of Babbar's sleeping bag.

Laughing despite himself, Chris looked back to Alycia, and allowed himself just a few more minutes to lose himself in her eyes.

With a resigned sigh, she asked, "Shall we?"

Bracing themselves for the cold, they unzipped their bags at the same time and got out of bed, immediately convulsing into shivers.

Chris threw on his jacket, and then hastily pulled on his boots and laced them as rapidly as his freezing fingers could. Alycia did likewise, and murmured something like, "I miss Denver." He sympathized. Sure, it got cold in Denver, sometimes even below zero once or twice a year, but the old joke about Denver's rapidly-changing weather was absolutely true, and usually a few days later, people were outside again in light jackets or even just t-shirts.

Michigan's winter weather just plain sucked.

Emmi grumbled and tore herself out of bed, just getting her jacket on as Chris and Alycia joined the others by the fire. It didn't feel as warm as he'd like, and he almost went over to the wood pile to throw another log on, but then he noticed that the pile was perilously low.

"Well hell," he grumbled. "We'll need to run into town again this morning."

"Yeah," Tom nodded. "Was waiting for more people to wake up. We'll need a couple volunteers."

"Chris and I will go," Alycia quickly stated. Too quickly, actually, and the stink eye that both Tom and Mia gave them unsettled Chris's stomach. "That is…"

Tom and Mia exchanged concerned looks, though Chris thought he caught a hint of amusement in their expressions. "I don't know," Mia said slowly. "Maybe you two need a chaperone."

"Mum!" Alycia protested, folding her arms over her stomach. "I'm a bloody adult."

Eyes wide, Mia replied, "With that language, I certainly hope you are."

"I'll go with," a soft voice startled them all. It wasn't Emmi's, who had just joined them, but rather it was Ash's voice, just as they were getting out from beneath several layers of raggedy blankets, since there hadn't been another sleeping bag to lend the newcomer. "I've never been up this far north before," Ash added, as if that explained their decision to volunteer.

Chris looked at Alycia and saw her expression dip into disappointment. He was surprised at first by her volunteering them, but now he understood – it could have been a mini-date, their first ever.

Tom, Mia, and Shara looked to one another, and then, after Shara shrugged, Tom nodded his assent. "Alright. Maybe pick up some coffee, yeah? I'm dying for even just a black cup of joe."

The thought of a nice, hot latte warmed Chris's gullet, and he smiled. "Alright. Any requests for breakfast?"

As Ash rushed up to the fire and set themselves to warming, Tom nodded. "Bagels probably wouldn't go amiss, and we can try to toast them over the fire."

Chris nodded, but then realized why Ash had sped over. "Wait, you don't have a jacket."

Sounding hopeful, Alycia said, "Aww, darn, I guess that means you can't go with after all. We don't want you getting frostbite…"

"They can borrow mine," Emmi volunteered, already pulling her parka off. The glare Alycia gave Emmi sent shivers down Chris's spine, but Emmi simply smiled and handed her jacket to Ash, who gratefully accepted it.

"What do we have left for cash?" Emmi asked. "Maybe while they're out, Ash can get their own jacket."

Everyone had pooled whatever cash they had from the start, but it hadn't been enough to get them through the first month of being on the run, and the Sentinels had been forced to stoop to petty theft now and again. Chris wasn't proud of it, not at all, but it was Emmi and Shara who had done most of the stealing, using their shapeshifting to take cash where they could. Both had been adamant about heading into rich areas to do so, and Emmi joked, after returning one day as a fox, that she was the cartoon Robin Hood, stealing from the rich to give to the poor Sentinels.

The fact that she made a pop-culture reference at all had shocked Chris.

After looking through their cash reserves and Alycia taking charge of the money for this trip, the trio set out. A fresh blanket of snow lay upon everything as they slid through one of the many available exits, and Chris grimaced. With no one around the abandoned factory, it would make it easier for anyone to track them back, if they picked up a tail. *We'll just have to watch for such a tail,* he thought.

At first, he and Alycia tried to hold hands, but without gloves, the cold nipped at their fingers and knuckles, and they were forced to shove their hands into their jacket pockets. Then, with an expression that screamed 'ah hah!' Alycia shoved her hand into Chris's jacket pocket and clutched his hand in hers. Ash studiously ignored them.

The trio headed north-west along Hastings Street, bound for Grand Boulevard where they knew a coffee shop and a gas station were relatively close, and they could get some essentials, including pre-cut bundles of firewood. Finding a jacket for Ash, however, would be a real challenge, as they didn't know where any clothing stores were.

Whereas the sidewalk next to their abandoned factory was unkempt and un-shoveled, the next block over was better maintained, though Chris still had no idea what the relatively large paved lot on the left was for. On the right they passed by a long stretch of stacks of...*something*. There were rows upon rows and stacks upon stacks of multi-colored, metal grids, almost like it was a storage facility for scaffolding. Chris, Alycia and Emmi had spent too many hours pondering over what the place actually was, a vein effort to pass the hours of boredom. The sidewalk sloped down to graffiti-covered brick and cinderblock walls, blocking their view of any other buildings on the lot while they passed underneath a bridge between a large factory building and another lot, eventually letting out to what looked like an abandoned warehouse, based on the shape it was in, except for the cars parked around it and evidence of foot traffic on the sidewalk.

Basically, everything looked old or abandoned in this part of town, and their walk towards Grand Boulevard was interesting once, and ultimately beyond boring every subsequent time.

"Why is everything so...run down?" Ash asked, their question directed at no one in particular as they passed into an area next to an open field.

"I don't know," Chris shrugged. "But that may be part of why we haven't been found by Nabu or the sniffers yet."

Despite trudging in ankle-deep snow, the trio made it to Grand Boulevard in just over ten minutes, and after a left turn, found themselves walking along a brick building, intent on the local coffee shop they had found on accident a week after arriving. The buildings on this side of the street were made of brick, pressing up against the sidewalk, and pressed together to give no sort of easement between them, and the coffee shop was in the red-brick building in the exact center of the block.

The sidewalk was well shoveled here, and there was no way to see how busy the store had been. Strangely, like many of the stores in this part of town, there was no sign or label indicating that a coffee shop was inside, just a number above the door.

Inside was fairly cozy, despite the concrete floor and brick wall. Directly ahead of the entrance was a wood-faced counter, behind which the on-duty baristas, both of whom Chris recognized from earlier visits, worked. Off to the right were a few wooden tables, a long bench, and bar seats set up against the outer brick wall beneath the row of windows. It was especially bright inside today, thanks to the glaring reflection from the snow outside.

There were a handful of patrons inside, and Chris did a cursory glance over them before stepping up to the cash register, with Alycia and Ash on either side.

And then he did a double-take at the patron seated at a table in the furthest corner.

Even seated, he was obviously very tall, and had a clean-shaven head. There was no way to know how long he'd been seated there, but he still wore his wool tweed overcoat, which given how chilly it often was in the coffee shop, wasn't entirely strange. And the patron had blazing blue eyes, which had honed in on Chris the moment he had entered the store.

More than that, he looked familiar. Chris couldn't tell from where, but he *knew* he had seen the man before.

Alycia asked what was wrong, and then followed his line of sight.

Her hand gripped his forearm tightly. "Oh God. Chris…I know that face. I know *him!*"

"Yeah, he looks familiar," Chris nodded. "But from where?"

With a frown, Ash commented, "He seems to know you two…"

Then the man stood up and headed purposefully towards them, abandoning a laptop at the table. Chris felt the familiar rush of adrenaline surge through him, and he instinctually touched his golden core. One of the baristas welcomed them, but he ignored her and focused only on the familiar man.

"The Collector's place," Alycia said, and suddenly the familiarity struck home. "He was one of the goons that tried to grab us at the Collector's place."

Way back in the beginning of all of this, when they had first met Babbar and Nina, a portal had taken them to meet the Collector, only to be ambushed by the Collector's 'goons,' as Alycia called them.

Now that he knew where to place the face, Chris had a distinct memory of looking at it over the barrel of an assault rifle.

Holding his arms up disarmingly, the man spoke in a distinctly southern drawl, "G'morning. Terrible weather, isn't it? Spring here is beautiful, but winters can be brutal." He nodded at the barista. "I'd love to buy your coffees for you."

Chris blinked. Looked back at Alycia, and then looked at the man again.

That first part was the code phrase that their informant had left for them, or so Chris had been told by Shara.

"You?!" Alycia asked incredulously, having come to the same conclusion as Chris.

"Actually, no," the man shook his head. "My employer would." The man motioned for the laptop. "He would very much like to speak with you this morning."

CHAPTER 12

Chris blinked in surprise. As did Alycia. Ash's head snapped back and forth between the two sides.

The barista cleared her throat. "Is there anything I can tempt you with?" she asked cautiously.

The question barely registered on Chris. Some automated part of his brain answered for him, "Medium vanilla latte, hot." He stared another moment at the Collector's representative and added, "Extra shot."

"You got it," the barista said brightly, in what was probably her attempt to lighten the mood between potentially problematic customers. "And for either of you?" she asked Alycia and Ash.

"Uh," Alycia said intelligently. "Chai tea latte, hot. No wait! Do you have peppermint mochas?"

"We certainly do," the barista grinned.

"Yeah, let's do that," Alycia nodded, holding her stomach. "Large. I could use the peppermint…"

Ash, completely unaware of the significance of who the man was, sauntered over to the counter and glanced over the menu placard to their left. "Umm, just a medium black coffee, please. Room for cream."

"Got it." The barista looked at the Collector's representative. "Sir?"

"Another black for me," he said, and reached into his jacket pocket. Chris and Alycia both tensed, and it was all Chris could do not to visibly radiate magic. No one else in the coffee shop knew that he was an unregistered magic user.

Rolling his eyes, the man said, "Relax," and pulled out his wallet. He eased past Chris to the counter and paid with cash, telling the barista to keep the change. "When your coffee's ready, please join me over by the laptop," he motioned towards his table. "My employer is already waiting."

As he walked away, Chris and Alycia looked at each other wide-eyed. "How…"

"So, who is this 'Collector' person?" Ash asked, louder than they should have.

Chris motioned his hands downwards to indicate Ash should lower their voice, and then drew the others in closer to whisper. "He's supposed to be one of Nabu's…umm…"

"Henchmen," Alycia volunteered.

"Henchmen?!" Ash hissed. "What is he, a supervillain or something?"

Chris and Alycia shrugged simultaneously. "I mean, magic is real," Chris quipped, shrugging. "So why not?"

"Well other than a supervillain, who is he?" Ash inquired.

"We don't know," Alycia replied. "We've only spoken to him, we've never met him. But he tried to ambush us back before the Barrier fell, and set us up to be ambushed by my mum."

"By…your mom?" Ash's frown deepened. "I thought your mom was on our side."

"She is now," Alycia nodded.

"Mia was one of the first persons I cleansed," Chris added. "Before that, she'd been a devoted servant of Nabu for, well…*years.*"

Rolling their eyes, Ash said, "Great," and then went to the counter when a barista called out Ash's drink order, along with the Collector's henchman's drink. While Ash stirred in some cream, Chris glanced at the table. The man had put a wireless earbud in his ear and was talking quietly to the screen. Was the Collector on a video call with him? Would they finally see his face if they went over there?

"Chris," Alycia said, frowning towards the laptop. "If he was truly our enemy…well, he knows where to find us. Why isn't this place swarming with feds? Or at least sniffers?"

"Good question," Chris nodded, and then looked into her eyes. "You're thinking we should hear what he has to say?"

"Well if the Collector really is our informant," she nodded, "then he gave us the intel we needed to save my dad, so…yeah."

Something twisted in his stomach, a distrust of the second person ever to try to kill Chris creating a burning suspicion in him that the Collector would never just suddenly turn altruistic. Babbar had taken them to the Collector to try to find out more about the dagger Imhullu and what Nabu's plans might be. They had meant to pretend to be sellers of rare artifacts, but the Collector immediately knew who they really were, and tried to apprehend them. Thankfully, he hadn't counted on Chris's powers or Nina's fast portal work.

Somehow, Chris doubted they could get the drop on the Collector so easily again.

When Ash rejoined them, Chris sighed and nodded. "The Collector seems to collect information as much as he does artifacts. Maybe I can find out something from him that'll help us defeat Nabu, even if that isn't his intention." Unspoken annoyance burned in Chris when he thought, *Wouldn't that be ironic – I get the info I need to save humanity from the Collector instead of from Tattannu.*

The baristas called out Chris and Alycia's drinks, so they grabbed them, while Chris grabbed the fourth, black coffee, and they walked over to the table.

As he set the coffee down, the man nodded, but didn't smile. "Thank you kindly. My name is Samuel Carol, by the way. I apologize, I didn't say so earlier."

Chris nodded, and as he took a seat across from Samuel, he said, "I take it you know who we are."

"You and the young lady, yes," Samuel said. "But I don't know you," he looked at Ash.

"They're with us," Chris insisted while Alycia took the seat next to Chris. Ash looked at the only available seat left, next to Samuel, and instead elected to stand behind and between Chris and Alycia.

"Alright," Samuel said. He pulled up a laptop bag from between the seats and rummaged around inside of it, while Chris nursed his hot drink, letting it warm up his cold hands. After a minute, Samuel withdrew three more wireless earbuds, and set to turning them on and syncing them to his computer. Curious, Chris tried to peek over, knowing that most computers only had a single bluetooth interface. How was Samuel syncing more than one device? The laptop didn't have a brand logo on it, strangely enough, so Chris had no idea who the manufacturer was.

After finishing, Samuel put the earbuds down and slid them across the table to Chris and the others, and nodded. "Please put those on. My employer is ready for you."

Chris eyed Samuel suspiciously, and then the earbuds. Finally, he took a sip of his latte, enjoying the blissful taste of vanilla, before finally taking one of the buds and putting it on. Ash and Alycia followed suit.

Then, Chris held his breath and waited to finally see who the Collector was. He watched as Samuel grasped the laptop's corners, lifted it, and rotated it around…

Only to be greeted by the generic Skype logo.

No photo.

No identity.

The caller ID said 'Boss.' Simple as that.

He sighed in disappointment.

"Howdy, Sentinels," a southern drawl he'd not heard in six months spoke. Whereas Samuel's voice was deep, the Collector's was more baritone. However, as Chris had learned six months ago, the Collector's accent was intentionally learned, and he could slip in and out of various accents with apparent ease. His voice had a tonality that made Chris think the gentleman was older, but beyond that, there was nothing else to identify him by.

Chris stared at the screen, watching the Skype logo light up when the Collector spoke, and found himself at a loss for words.

"Um," Alycia came to the rescue. "H-hello."

"Ah, Miss Taylor," the Collector replied in a congenial tone. *"It gives me pleasure to see you and Mister Tatsu alive and well. That is, except for your clothes and hair. Looks like you all could use a stay at a five-star hotel."*

A skeptical look drew across Chris's face. "Are you serious? Small talk?"

"Well, now, I'm just tryin' to be polite," the Collector replied.

"As polite as-" Chris started to yell, but Samuel shushed him and glanced warily towards nearby patrons. Chris ground his teeth, and then hissed, "As polite as when you tried to kill us?"

"That was never my intention, m'boy," the Collector replied. He didn't sound indignant, but rather was patient and understanding, as if it had simply been a misunderstanding that he was ready to clear up. *"I was under orders to capture you, not kill you. If you'd surrendered, things wouldn't've gotten violent."*

Chris and Alycia snorted in disbelief at the same time, and then glanced at each other in surprise.

"Jeeze, you two were made for each other," Ash remarked.

"And you, Mx Patel," the Collector stated, eliciting a look of shock from all three. *"It is a right pleasure to meet you."*

Ash gaped at the screen. "You…you know who I am?"

"Of course! Information is my business. I was rather impressed by your actions at the Magic Asylum and decided to find out everything I could about you."

"But," Ash started, "but they, uh, the feds, they had no idea who I was."

"I'm not the Federal Government, Mx. Your name change hasn't been made official in the government's eyes, so they have no idea who you are, but your identity is spread all over the internet, and that's just for starters."

Looking impressed, Ash commented, "And you're using the proper gender-neutral honorifics for me."

"Naturally. There's no reason not to be polite."

"Except when you're trying to abduct us or kill us," Chris said sourly.

"As I said, I was polite until you resisted. In any case, that's no longer my goal, young'uns. You can consider my service to Nabu officially history."

Eying the monitor suspiciously, Chris thought about the short conversation they'd had with the Collector last spring. "Nnno…no, I don't buy it," he shook his head. "Either you're under Nabu's spell, in which case you still would be…" He almost admitted that only he and Ash could change that, but decided not to tip their hand in that regard. "Or you were willingly working for Nabu, in which case I can't think of any reason for you to stop now."

"M'boy, I have never been loyal to Nabu," the Collector replied, the first hint of indignation in his voice coming through the Bluetooth.

"Then why did you work for them?" Alycia asked.

"Because I'm loyal to Marduk," he replied matter-of-factly.

With a frown, Chris asked, "What's the difference? Nabu is just the embodiment of Marduk."

"Yeah, that's true," the Collector agreed, *"But it's more than that. Nabu is half-human, after all, and has spent four thousand years separated from Marduk's consciousness. She's become her own independent entity. And I suspect she wants to stay that way."*

Tilting his head to one side, Chris considered the Collector's words for a second, and then said, slowly, working it out as he spoke,

"Nabu doesn't want to rejoin Marduk."

"Exactly," the Collector replied pointedly. *"And she sure as heck doesn't want to share the Earth, or the power eight billion human souls can provide, with anyone else, let alone her daddy."*

"Sheesh," Alycia scoffed. "You'd think eight billion souls would be enough to go around."

"Doesn't matter," the Collector pointed out. *"Nabu has grown greedy. Truth be told, she was that way back before the Barrier. She, or rather he back then, tried to grow his own power base in Borsippa, and that's why he had a temple dedicated to himself built there. That was to be his power base, a place from which he could rule his own little slice of humanity from. You see, once Nabu established his own identity, he never intended to let his father be freed. Because the moment Marduk was free and came to Earth, he would force Nabu to reintegrate with him, or so Nabu believed."*

"Marduk never intended to do that?" Chris asked, surprised.

"Point of fact, he did intend to do that, or so legends say," the Collector replied, and Chris imagined that whomever or whatever he was, the Collector shrugged when he replied to Chris's question. *"Either way, Nabu was the one who wanted the Barrier to be created."*

It slammed into Chris's stomach like a hammer. The statement was said ever so casually, but it took long, gut-wrenching seconds to fully set in.

"He *what?!*" Alycia practically screeched, eliciting another warning glare from Samuel.

"Bullshit," Chris shook his head. "No way. Tom told me that when the Barrier cut Nabu off from magic, it drove him insane."

"That it did," the Collector replied. *"Y'see, he was supposed to retain his powers. The deal he made with the Mages was that he would be the custodian core of magic that fueled the Barrier, and that'd give him the power to use magic despite the existence of the Barrier. But the Mages knew he'd be just as bad as his father, and tricked him. They funneled the magic through someone else. A single Mage who would be capable of casting magic when no one else could, but refrained out of fear of cracking the Barrier."*

Chris nodded solemnly. "Tattannu." And then his jaw dropped. "That was why Nabu needed me." He gaped at Alycia, the pieces clicking together all at once. "He didn't know it, exactly, back in the hangar, but if he had used Imhullu on me…"

"Then every single soul linked to the Barrier, and linked to you, m'boy, would have flowed through the dagger. It would have shattered the Barrier just as well

as your touching the Dragonstone did."

Gaping at the screen, Chris found himself rapidly thinking about what might have happened. If Alycia hadn't grown suspicious at the hangar and texted her dad, then Nabu might have succeeded, despite Chris's outburst of magic. In fact, the moment Chris had used magic had probably made him the prime target.

It all revolved around Chris and his family. It should have been Naomi, but Nabu hadn't yet known back then how important she was.

Several minutes of stunned silence passed, the Collector giving them the opportunity to wrangle the revelation.

The real question, he realized, was did it change anything? Other than giving the past six months some extra context, did it give him any insight into Nabu's plans, or how to defeat Nabu and Marduk?

An instant later, a more important question occurred to him. "Why are you helping us?"

"Yeah," Alycia added, "Why help us rescue my dad, or setup drops for enchanted handcuffs for us to practice on? Why give us any of this information?"

"I thought the 'why' would be obvious by now," the Collector replied. *"I serve Marduk, not Nabu. When Nabu and I both wanted the Barrier dismantled, our goals aligned, but now they don't. And Nabu plans to destroy her father."*

Recalling the last dinner he'd had at Sentinel tower, and Babbar's claims that night, Chris said, "I thought you couldn't destroy an infernal."

An enormous pause followed, and Chris thought he may have finally surprised the Collector. *"I suppose I shouldn't be surprised you know about infernals and celestials, what with a gnome and an elf keeping you company."*

"She's not an elf," Alycia growled warningly.

"Sure, and my accent's not southern," the Collector responded indignantly. *"Listen-"*

"So much for politeness," Chris grumbled.

"Do you want to know how to stop Nabu from killing millions of people or not?!"

They had tested the Collector's patience, and found its limits. Chris tried to keep a grin from forming on his lips, but he couldn't help it. Samuel noticed and rolled his eyes.

"Alright," Chris nodded. "Tell us what you've got."

An impatient sigh aired across the link, and the Collector remained silent for several seconds, no doubt collecting his wits. *"As you well know by now, Nabu has orchestrated unrest across the world, especially in Europe and the United States. She also has wormed her way into the graces of the United States President's office."*

"No doubt she's even used her powers to directly influence the President," Chris said. "She'd be a fool not to."

"Agreed," the Collector replied. *"Well, there's more to it. She knows how to destroy Marduk, and she's using a combination of science and magic to do it."*

"She…is?" Chris frowned. "I thought the two were mutually exclusive."

"Oh? I'd have thought you'd realize by now that they are intimately interlinked."

At first he was about to point out the fantastical nature of magic, but then he remembered his comparison of his and Ash's souls as explainable through his poor understanding of quantum physics, and stalled on his retort. "Hmm. I suppose you've got a point."

"He does?" Alycia asked.

Nodding once, Chris said, "I'll explain later. So what's Nabu doing?"

"An enchanter and scientists have been studying Imhullu over the past three months, working to unlock its enchantment and apply it to a weapon. A weapon that could unleash millions of souls in one instant, sending them all to Marduk in an overpowering wave."

Dread filled Chris, souring his stomach. He had just picked up his coffee to take a drink, but now held it just in front of his lips, stunned.

A weapon capable of killing millions all at once.

Gently setting his cup back down, he tried to speak, but his voice caught. After he cleared the block, he whispered, "A nuke."

"I'm afraid so," the Collector replied solemnly. *"Nabu intends to enchant a nuclear weapon and launch it against a highly-populated city. And since she'll need the U.S. President's authorization to launch, she's in position to make it happen."*

"She…she can't," Alycia shook her head, her voice airy with shock. "That…no…"

"Won't that free Marduk?" Chris asked. "Wouldn't that give him the souls necessary to break his bonds in whatever realm he's trapped in and come to Earth?"

"As powerful as Marduk is, he's still a living being with limits." The admission of that was shocking, but Chris felt it wasn't the moment to point out that it meant Marduk wasn't any sort of real god. Then again, given the Collector's intelligence, Chris doubted he was loyal to Marduk out of deific reverence. He really had no idea why the Collector was loyal to Marduk. *"Nabu believes it would destroy Marduk, and while she's stark-raving mad, she could be correct."*

That was the key, and Chris felt every muscle in his body tense upon that revelation. Unleashing millions of souls onto Marduk all at once would overload the infernal, like overloading a capacitor, and would ultimately destroy the Babylonian god.

Frowning, he asked, "Why would you admit that to us? You know we intend to destroy Marduk just as Nabu apparently does, and you've just told us how."

"'Cause I know you're people of moral standards," the Collector responded, as if that were the most obvious thing in the world. *"You'd never sacrifice millions just to defeat him. You wouldn't even sacrifice one person to stop Nabu from destroying the Barrier."*

Chris conceded the point silently.

"You have to stop her," the Collector's voice had returned to its somber tone. *"You* must *stop her. If she succeeds, not only will she destroy my master, but that'll leave her in a position to rule what's left of humanity, and I guarantee you, she won't be kind."*

That was an understatement, and Chris knew it. If she was willing to kill millions just to destroy her dear old dad, what else would she be willing to do? What hellish future awaited them?

Narrowing his eyes, Chris leaned in towards the laptop. "Then tell us."

A pause. *"Tell you what?"*

"Tell us how to destroy Nabu once and for all." He raised his chin. "Tell us now, before it's too late."

"M'boy," the Collector sighed impatiently, *"I've already given you every clue you need to figure it out on your own."*

He had? Chris racked his brain, thinking about everything he'd learned today. He thought they'd destroyed Nabu once, but the demigod's spirit had simply moved into another human's body, subverting and destroying the soul within, no doubt *consuming* the soul within just as sure as if Nabu had used Imhullu…

Imhullu.

Nabu was afraid of being reabsorbed into Marduk's essence.

"We have to use Imhullu on Nabu," Chris whispered. Alycia looked at him wide-eyed, but then she appeared to connect the dots, and realization lit up her face.

"That'll send Nabu back to Marduk," Alycia finished for him.

"Precisely," the Collector spoke triumphantly.

"So where is it?" Ash asked. "If you're this uber-collector of information like Chris said earlier, you must know."

"Of course I know," the Collector replied. *"But you're not going to like it."*

Chris closed his eyes, gritting his teeth. "Where?"

"A well-known, but well-guarded research lab in the deserts of New Mexico."

Opening his eyes, Chris frowned. There was only one place he could think of. "Los Alamos?"

"None-other."

Chris sighed. If he had to guess, on even a good day, getting in there would be a challenge. No doubt with Imhullu there, Nabu would have extra guards, including plenty of magic-powered goons.

"Alright," he nodded once. "Then that's where we'll have to go." He paused, staring at the Skype logo, thinking about what he should say next. Finally, "Thank you."

"You're welcome, m'boy. One last thing before you go. Be on the lookout. Nabu believes the only way to counter the threat that you and the Sentinels pose is to meet you point for point. She has enchanters, shapeshifters, and arcane wielders out there right now scouring for you, right alongside sniffers. And to be frank, with enchanters working for her, they all might have the same abilities as sniffers."

Chris gulped, and looked around the coffee shop suspiciously.

They were exposed, and at that very moment, could be in danger.

"Again, thank you," he nodded.

"Good luck to you all," the Collector said in way of farewell. *"I hope to see you on the other side."*

Without another word, the Skype call ended.

CHAPTER 13

Samuel held out his hand to Chris and the others expectantly, and rather absent-mindedly, they handed the ear pieces over. After packing them and the laptop up, Samuel chugged down his now-cooled coffee, and excused himself before leaving the shop.

Leaving two stunned Sentinels and their friend Ash behind.

Ash took Samuel's chair after that, and the trio stared across the table at one another. It wasn't until a solid minute passed that Chris's thoughts finally turned into words and actions. "We have to tell the others," he stood up, scraping the chair across concrete.

Alycia followed suit, and Ash groaned before also standing.

"What about supplies?" Alycia asked.

"We'll come back for them if we have to," he replied, and headed for the door. "But I get the feeling we need to move fast on this."

Sweeping out of the coffee shop to the sound of baristas wishing them a good day, the trio trudged out into the cold, and adopted a fast walk north-east along Grand Boulevard. The building next to the coffee shop had a white-brick façade, and extended all the way to the corner of the block against the sidewalk. The trio was just about to round the corner when a black cat sauntered into view.

Chris practically skid to a halt, silently thankful the walk had been cleared of ice already, and gaped down at the cat. It had pitch-black fur and striking blue eyes, and pulsed with magic.

"Emmi?!" he frowned down at the new arrival. "What are you doing here?" The cat tilted its head to one side, and he looked around. Two people walked along the northern side of Grand Boulevard, so he held up his hand, "Don't change here. But we've got to get back, something's come up." Skirting around the not-cat, he added, "Come on!"

Alycia and Ash followed, with Ash in particular eying the cat curiously, but then they hastened into a fast walk down Hastings towards the factory.

His imagination ran rampant, with images of a nuclear explosion flashing before his eyes. How soon before Nabu's weapon or, God forbid, *weapons* were ready? What cities did she plan to target? If Marduk was destroyed, would that somehow confer more power onto Nabu?

The terrifying thoughts were dizzying and made Chris sick. He felt his heart racing, his head swimming, and his stomach turning, and it wasn't until Alycia caught up to him that he realized she was calling his name, and she grasped his hand tightly, though she didn't slow him down.

"Hey," she squeezed his hand, "it's gonna be alright, yeah? Nabu hasn't launched yet, so we have time."

He forced down the lump in his throat and nodded, before croaking out, "Yeah." He cleared his throat, and tried again. "Yeah, you're right." But he didn't slow down.

They covered ground almost twice as fast, and made it back to the factory in record time. He glanced back to see the black cat trotting along after them, blue eyes blazing in the snow-reflected sunlight. They found their normal entrance, ducked under the board nailed diagonally across it, and headed into the middle of the factory, towards the dwindling fire and the crowd gathered around it.

"Hey," Chris called out, getting everyone's attention. "Hey guys, we have news!"

"We do too," Tom, who was closest to them, replied. "Abby found exactly what you wanted her to find."

Elation and triumph coursed through Chris, easing his anxiety just a bit. "And we just met the contact," Chris said.

"You're never gonna believe who it was," Alycia added, squeezing his hand again. "It was..."

And then she stopped short, yanking Chris to a stop at the exact same moment that he felt a pulse of magic from behind him. Ash nearly plowed into them, but their powers hadn't been what Chris felt. He frowned at Alycia, and noticed a ghost-white, stunned expression on her face. He followed her gaze, and saw Emmi stand up from the other side of the fire, not as a cat, not shapeshifting from cat form, but just standing up as if she had been there the whole time, shivering even as close as she was to the fire.

"Oh shit," he whispered, dread rushing back into his chest.

Ash noticed Emmi too, and together, the trio whipped around to look for the cat. Chris *knew* he'd felt magic in it, which meant it was a shapeshifter. And since both Shara and Emmi were here...

Ducking under the wooden board covering the door, a tall, lanky man with blazing blue eyes and light brown hair entered the factory, a smartphone already pressed against his ear.

"That's the place," he said into the phone. "I'll hold them as long as I can."

And then he hung up, stowed his phone in a back pocket of blue jeans, and pulled his heavy black parka tightly around him before sauntering further into the factory.

The Sentinels had stared dumbly at him at first, but as soon as the shapeshifter's phone conversation registered on them, a series of profanity and a flurry of movement whirled around Chris. Shara, Tom, and Emmi had sidearms out in a heartbeat, all trained on the shapeshifter, and Alycia raised her gloved arms, enchantments ready.

A gray-green light engulfed the shapeshifter, and before anyone could get a single shot off, he was gone.

Except that Chris could still feel his power. "He's a shapeshifter," Chris told the others, "and he's still here!"

"Babbar," Tom barked. "You know where to take us!"

"Uh," the gnome replied stupidly. "No, not really! I've never been to-"

"Don't!" Shara cut him off. "Don't say it out loud. We don't want the enemy to know where we're going!"

Where they were going next? Chris had thought they'd already settled on another location to escape to, should their present location be compromised. "Can't we fall back on our original plan?" he asked, while turning inward just enough to touch his golden core and send a surge of magic into his body.

"We could," Tom nodded.

"But not until we take care of the shapeshifter," Shara stated. "Either way, we don't want to risk bringing him along."

It was a good point. In Babylon, Emmi had tried to escape Nabu by shapeshifting into a tiny bug, and it had almost worked. Most likely the errant shapeshifter had done the same thing, or changed into a tiny mouse, and could easily slip in close to them just as Nina made her portal to get them away from the danger.

"Spread out," Tom ordered. "Find him, now!"

As the team swept out into the factory, Chris's mind raced, latching onto the fact that Nabu had somehow found Emmi in her bug form back in Babylon. But how?

Then it occurred to him – Nabu had sent out a sort of magical wave, a pulse of insanely powerful magic, like a sort of ping in the ether that allowed Nabu to hone in on every person of power in the area. Could Chris do that?

He knew that he was at least as powerful as Nabu, but the question remained whether he had the same ability. Was that power somehow arcane-based?

The fact was, they didn't have time to search every nook and cranny of a massive factory – the shapeshifter had reinforcements on the way. That meant that now was not the time to try to figure out if he had Nabu's ability or not.

However, he realized in that instant that he could still feel the buzzing pulse of magic from every magic-user present, *including* the shapeshifter's.

"Everyone stop!" he shouted on impulse. Shuffling footsteps halted, and all eyes fell upon him. "Don't move," he added. "Give me a second."

"Chris, we don't have time," Tom started.

"I know! Just let me focus," he insisted.

When no other objections or interruptions presented themselves, Chris drew in a deep breath, and closed his eyes, honing in on his magic core and letting it's radiant pulse act as its own sort of ping. In the soul realm, he could see and feel everyone around him, magic or not, but the trick would be to figure out which one was the shapeshifter, and where in the real world he was.

Breathing slowly, Chris reached out, saw and *felt* every soul. Except, despite knowing that he could feel the shapeshifter's presence, none of the cores surrounding him felt like the gray-green core of the shifter's. How could that be? Unless he had already run away. But if that was the case, why did Chris *feel* something on his peripheral, almost like a feeling of being watched.

Could the shapeshifter mask his soul? Or was it more than that?

Did becoming tiny like a bug shrink his presence in the soul realm? That hardly felt possible.

Until he remembered Shara's words to Emmi back at the training camp. About deriving power from nature. Did that mean if a shapeshifter became a creature, it took on that creature's essence?

Of all of the powers he'd seen, shapeshifting was the one that seemed to violate physics the most, and made the least sense to him. So maybe that's what he had to do, look for a bug's soul with a magic core, rather than a human's soul.

Chris needed a finer degree of control, he needed to be more sensitive to his surroundings. *I should have known it wasn't Emmi,* he thought. *I should have felt it wasn't her.*

When he realized those thoughts were hurting his focus, he banished them, stomped them into the lowest levels of his consciousness. Now wasn't the time for a self-pity party.

Now was the time to prove himself.

Utilizing Shara's breathing techniques, he drew further into himself, into his core, its pulsing warmth a comfort even against the cold of winter. He felt Ash's resonating core, and pushed that sense to the edge of his awareness. Next to Ash's, Shara, Emmi, and Alycia's felt timid, but they were still stronger than most, and he had to push his sense of their souls to the side, along with Mia's. Babbar's was near their level too, and he wondered if the gnome had latent powers he wasn't aware of. Was his ability to see through Nina's cloak a biological feature of his eyes, or magic? Or both?

Nina, Chris thought, and the realization that he didn't sense her powers startled him.

All this time, and he'd never tried to sense her presence. The only time he was aware of her presence was when she used her powers.

Where was she? She should have been on Babbar's shoulder, he'd seen as much when they had arrived, so why couldn't he sense her?

What are you?

Distracted again, he focused his thoughts on the area near Babbar's soul, and peered carefully into the void of the soul realm. She *had* to be there, didn't she?

He tried to increase his ability to sense the smallest of powers. Around him, life flourished, and suddenly he grew aware of the souls of all of the rats infesting the abandoned factory, struggling to survive. It was a side effect of his efforts to find Nina, but it brought him one step closer to sensing the shapeshifter.

If only...

There!

He felt it.

Saw it.

Flying right for him.

Ripping out of himself, he cast a shield of plasma all around him, moments before the shapeshifter transformed from a bug into a much larger bird of prey, intent on ripping his eyes out.

Instead, his talons burned into Chris's shield, eliciting a screeching cry of agony. The scent of ozone mixed with cooked flesh stung Chris's nose, and the massive eagle crashed to the ground next to him, writhing and flapping singed wings.

Dispelling the shield, Chris looked down upon their enemy, uncertain of what to do next.

He didn't have to worry about it. Shara fired her tranq gun, and the dart pierced the shapeshifter right in the neck. After only a few more moments of struggle, the bird fell limp, his chest rising and falling ever-so-slowly.

"Holy shit," Mia breathed. "That happened...*fast.*"

Chris drew in a breath to speak, but a snorting laugh from Ash distracted him. He looked at them curiously, and Ash's cheeks immediately turned a shade darker. "What?" he asked.

"Nothing," Ash shook their head. "It's nothing. Totally inappropriate moment for innuendo..."

Arching a curious eyebrow at Ash, he turned back to the eagle at his feet and knelt down. The shapeshifter was definitely out.

And then he looked up at Babbar, and sure enough, saw Nina on the gnome's shoulder. Yet for the life of him, he still couldn't sense her presence.

What are you?

Nina's scaly head tilted to the side, as if she had heard his thoughts, and he felt the icy grip of shock and fear. Could she read his mind?

"We'd better go," Tom, ever the voice of reason, interrupted his musings. "Babbar, you've always said Nina is intuitive and intelligent."

"Well, aye, she is," the gnome took a step forward.

"Alright, then," Tom stepped closer to them and knelt, so that he came face to face with Nina. Her gaze lingered on Chris for just a second, and then turned to give Tom her full attention. "Nina, we need you to take us to the Sentinel facility in Osaka. Got it?"

Chris blinked, but Alycia asked before he could, "Osaka?!"

"Abby found something in their archives," Shara explained. "Something that just might help us find the answers we need."

Nina's head tilted to one side, curiously dog-like in her expression. She chirped, and curled around to look eye-to-eye with Babbar.

The gnome looked surprised, and then he nodded at Tom. "She says she knows where to go."

"Good," Tom nodded, standing up and gently patting Nina on the head. She purred melodiously. "Everyone gather your things. We're leaving, *now*."

For all of two seconds, everyone stared around, stunned. Then, for most of them anyway, training kicked in, and they sprang into action. They didn't have much in the way of possessions, but what little they'd all managed to keep was either already on their person, or by their sleeping bags.

Chris hastened to his backpack, half-filled with food provisions and one set of extra clothes he'd managed to snag along the way.

But he never reached it.

Explosions rocked the factory.

CHAPTER 14

The first explosion sheered through the corrugated roof and sent a cascade of debris down upon the group. Most everyone scattered and dove for the ground, but Chris and Alycia instinctively cast shields, with Chris's plasma shield inside of Alycia's conjured one.

She cried out against the effort of holding it in place, but as the debris ricocheted off and scattered around the startled Sentinels, a blast of violet arcane energy followed, slamming into her shield and driving her to her knees.

A series of explosions came from ground-level, all around the Sentinels as walls and doors were blown inward with breaching charges. Armed soldiers streamed in, shouting commands to drop weapons, hands up, the usual spiel that Chris had come to expect.

Then, to Chris's shock, the arcane caster that had blasted the ceiling floated down, her hands and feet glowing with energy. She was flying!

Ash, having thrown themselves onto their stomach, gaped up at their new enemy, and then asked Chris, "Can you do that?"

Dispelling his plasma shield to get a better view, Chris shook his head. "Not yet."

There was more to the attacker than he realized, a strange sense about her aura. It was definitely not Nabu, since she didn't have the telltale red hair, but rather a shock of blonde hair tied back in a tight braid, and pale blue eyes. The violet color of her arcane blast likewise was a clue, but there was something else…

The surrounding soldiers commanded attention again by firing upon Alycia's shield, which further weakened her, but also sent ricocheting bullets everywhere outside of the shield. One of the soldiers was tagged by such a ricochet, and stumbled backwards while grasping their wounded arm.

"Cease fire, cease fire!" the arcane caster shouted down at the soldiers. "Unless you wanna kill yourselves, dumbasses." She had a deep alto voice that carried well above the noise of attack, and Chris suspected a trick similar to Nabu's in which she enhanced her voice. *I had no idea that was an arcane power...*

But now that he had a moment to spare, he closed his eyes and looked out within the soul realm. That was when he 'saw' the strange nature of the newcomer's powers – while her core was a distinct shade of violet, it was intermixed with shades of green, swirling around and through the purple sphere.

When he opened his eyes, hers had fallen upon him, while she hovered only a few feet above Alycia's shimmering blue-white shield.

She waited until the soldiers had collected themselves, and then addressed Chris, "Surrender. Now."

Raising his eyebrows at her demand, he asked, "And if we don't?"

Narrowing her eyes, she replied curtly, "I won't ask again."

There was a warning in her voice, an unspoken statement that she would blast Alycia's shield again. Whatever fueled her power was beyond just her soul, he realized. Her power was boosted by enchantments, and she might very well overwhelm Alycia.

But she wasn't as powerful as Chris, and he'd spent months honing his craft in the hours of boredom he'd endured. This would be the first true test of his improved powers.

"Alycia," he looked at her, ignoring the words of protest that came from Tom an instant later. "Give it a one-two."

Her face was screwed in concentration, and sweat beaded her forehead, despite the cold. She was at her limits. After glaring up at the attacker, Alycia's attention wavered, and she frowned at Chris. "A what?"

"Drop the shield," he nodded, and widened his eyes, hoping to convey his intentions without words.

She glanced around at the surrounding soldiers, then back at Chris. "But what about...?"

"Don't!" the violet attacker cautioned. "No plotting or scheming, surrender this instant or I'll..."

"Now!" Chris shouted.

Hoping she didn't hesitate, he gathered every bit of energy he could into a beam of light, and unleashed it double-palm style at the attacker. She barely cast a shield in time, which Chris noted was conjured rather than arcane-based and was a distinct shade of green, and she tumbled end over end along the length of the factory, falling from the air to land with a loud 'whump!' on the ground.

Chris instantly worked to refocus his powers into a renewed plasma shield, trying to control it and surround him and his friends, a much larger sphere than he was used to creating.

The first bullet tore through his shoulder. White-hot pain seared through him. Another bullet pierced his extended left arm. Another through his abdomen.

"CHRIS!!!" Alycia's shriek echoed.

Even as he fell, a terrifying pulse of magic surrounded him, surrounded everyone. He barely noticed a blue shockwave slam into every soldier simultaneously, flinging them like a spoiled child's ragdolls away from the Sentinels.

The bullet wounds felt hot, the pain sharp and shooting, all the forms of agony he knew of and more, all at once. There might have been more gunshot wounds, but he lost all sense of it as a wave of dizziness and disorientation washed over him. He thought he blinked only once, but between blinks he had fallen to the ground, writhing in agony, every nerve seeming to fire at once.

Alycia hovered over him, followed by Tom.

They were shouting. At him? At each other?

Tom barked to the side, and Chris could feel the resonating boom of the commander's voice, but couldn't hear it. Everything hurt.

Everything.

Another blink, and suddenly Babbar stood next to Tom, a copper coin in hand. The gnome flipped it up into the air, and Nina almost missed it, she was so focused on Chris. Moments before it fell too low for her to easily catch, she nipped it out of the air, and chomped hungrily.

"Hold on, Champion!" a woman's voice called out from everywhere and nowhere.

The pulse of magic felt like it ripped violently against his wounds, and he cried out against the white noise, the taste of copper biting at the tip of his tongue.

They appeared somewhere new, the lobby of a business complex somewhere. The semi-hard, frozen dirt transformed into a rock-hard, smooth substance. LED lights inset into a tiled ceiling glared down at him.

Chris blinked again.

Mia had pushed in between Tom and Alycia.

A strange, warm glow washed over her hands as she touched him.

That same warmth washed over him.

Pain subsided.

Darkness enveloped him.

When the light found him again, it was accompanied by a faint, rhythmic beep. *I know that sound.*

Chris blinked his eyes open to a view that reminded him of a hospital room, not unlike the one he first woke up in after the Centennial Airport incident.

Unlike back then, however, someone squeezed his hand. Looking left, he was greeted by a beautiful, warm smile.

"Alycia," he whispered.

"Guys, he's awake!" she called out excitably, nearly bouncing up and down in her chair. Her energy was contagious, and Chris felt like bouncing out of the bed himself. In fact, it felt like he hadn't been there that long. He still wore the same dirty, smelly clothes, so they hadn't stripped him out yet or put on a hospital gown.

The sound of shifting clothes and squeaking feet drew his attention towards the door, where Tom, Shara, and Emmi rushed in. Before they could surround his bed, however, a petite Japanese woman appeared next to him, on the opposite side of Alycia, and she looked intently at his eyes.

"Mister Tatsu," she spoke with a heavy Japanese accent. "Please look at me."

With a deep frown, he felt the urge to sit up, and tried, but the woman pushed him back down, remarkably strong for her size.

"Don't get up yet, please," she stated. "Look at me."

Blinking in surprise, he did as asked, and she flashed a light in his eyes. It stung, and he had to blink away the light. "Hey! What's going on?"

"They shot you," Tom stated matter-of-factly.

The abandoned factory flashed through his memory, along with flashes of gunfire. The searing, shooting, aching pain.

The one that hit his forearm should have shattered bone, and there should have still been pain from that. For that matter, he should have been in surgery. But when he lifted both arms up, other than an I.V., there wasn't a single blemish on his skin. Not even a scar.

"What?" He gaped, and then grasped his chest. He found holes in his shirt, his jacket having been cut off already, but not a single hole in his torso. "How? What's going on?"

"How do you feel?" the woman he assumed was a doctor asked him.

"I, uh," he looked around at the gathered Sentinels, and then at the doctor. "Fine. Better than fine, actually." Something akin to an adrenaline rush coursed through his veins, and he tried to sit up again, this time without protest from the doctor. "In fact I feel like I could run a marathon."

"That'd be a first," Emmi grinned.

"Oye!" Chris protested.

"Are you sure he was shot?" the doctor asked Tom.

"At least six times," the commander nodded.

"Six?!" Chris blurted, and then looked at Alycia. Her smile had dimmed to a look of relief and terror mixed into one. When she nodded confirmation, he gaped again at the others.

"Just look at the blood on his clothes, the holes," Emmi added.

"Well he's fine now," the doctor shrugged, and turned. "Your wife, however…"

As the doctor moved over to a neighboring bed, Chris noticed for the first time that he wasn't the only one being treated. Mia lay in the bed at the other end of the room, hooked up to monitors and an I.V., with a breathing tube shoved down her throat. A nurse tended to her, and the doctor shoved her hands into her pocket.

"Wait, what happened?" he gaped, and swung his legs out from the covers and stood up. All he wanted to do was get out of here, but his curiosity, and his concern for Alycia and her family, kept him at bay. That and the I.V. chord snapped taut. Past Mia's bed and the doctor and nurse, there was a wall of windows, and for the first time in his life, he looked out upon a city from his family's home country – Japan.

Nina had saved them.

But Chris…someone *else* saved him after that.

Mia standing over me, her hands glowing…

"Mia has healing powers," Shara said before anyone else could speak. With his eyes opening wider and wider, Chris gaped at her. "She risked herself to save your life."

"I," he started, stopped. "She…" Turning to look, his view of Mia was blocked by the doctor, so he came around towards the foot of the bed, grabbing his rolling I.V. pole and dragging it with him, and looked upon Mia's face. It was pale, paler than he'd ever seen her. The doctor had obviously considered her life at greater risk, as Mia had been stripped and had a hospital gown hastily thrown over her. Yet there wasn't a sign of a single wound.

"I don't understand," he shook his head.

"I don't either," the doctor replied, and looked expectantly at Shara. The other Sentinels gathered around the foot of the bed, with Alycia coming up beside Chris and clutching onto his hand tightly. "I see no signs of trauma, but she was in shock when she was brought in, and her vitals are weak. Please explain."

Shara's eyes lingered upon Mia for a long moment, and then she addressed the doctor, "Healers are rare on my world, and I imagine anywhere else. Mostly because a lot of them end up accidentally sacrificing themselves to save someone else. Mia used her life force to repair the wounds to Chris's body, but it is an exchange, a trade. The only saving grace is that the pinpoint damage to Chris's body was spread out throughout all of Mia's, but…" Shara paused, and shook her head before settling her gaze upon Tom. "It's going to take some time for her to recover. She traded her health for Chris's."

"So what can we do?" Tom asked, his voice more somber than Chris had ever heard. He turned to the doctor. "How can we help?"

The doctor looked back and forth between Tom and Shara, and then drew in a deep breath before she stared at Mia's vitals monitor. "For now, keep her breathing, keep her hydrated," she nodded at the I.V., "and watch for any change. If the blue-hair is right, there's nothing else to do."

Chris felt a grin stretch across his cheek at the doctor's description of Shara, but it vanished very quickly, and he turned to Alycia, to all of them. "I'm sorry. I tried…"

Alycia's hand squeezed his, a lot tighter than she probably meant to. "Don't," she interrupted him. "You thought fast, you acted fast, and you ensured we all could escape."

He looked around at the others. "Did we all make it? Where's Ash? Where's Tiana and the others?"

"They're fine," Tom assured him without looking away from Mia.

"We couldn't all fit in here, y'know," Emmi remarked with a shrug. "They're getting some much needed rest and a change of clothes."

"Which you should all do," the doctor nodded, and then looked at Chris and the I.V. needle in his hand, before she addressed the nurse in Japanese. The nurse bowed and moved to a counter opposite of the beds, while the doctor looked at Chris. "Please allow the nurse to remove your I.V. Then you can all get a shower and change of clothes."

Chris blinked, and then tried not to be too obvious as he smelled himself. He knew it had been weeks since his last shower, but...

"That bad?" Emmi asked the doctor.

She simply blinked at Emmi, and then pushed past them and out of the room.

The nurse came over with a bandage and needle disposal kit, motioning for him to sit back on his bed.

CHAPTER 15

By the time the nurse finished extracting the needle, to the chagrin of Alycia who had to look away, a familiar face arrived in Chris and Mia's hospital room – Yua Saito.

Barely shorter than Chris, Yua was the second in command of the Japanese Sentinels. She sported a pixie cut, which was now much shorter than Chris's unkempt hair, and carried herself with confidence. Her dark eyes were sharp, and she never missed a thing. He also recalled she was a formidable opponent in combat.

She looked about the room when she entered, pausing briefly upon Chris, before she settled her gaze on Tom.

"Taylor-sama," she spoke while folding into a bow, her voice strong and curt. Tom awkwardly returned the bow. "Let me be the first to officially welcome you to Osaka."

"Thank you," he replied evenly. "I believe you know everyone here."

"Yes," she looked at each member, pausing again upon Chris. Something flashed in her eyes, and he wondered if it had anything to do with their encounter in the mountains of Colorado. But whether the flash in her eyes was hostile or pleasant, he couldn't tell yet. "Doctor Ito tells me you all could use refreshing. Please, follow me."

The nurse finished adhering the bandage to Chris's I.V. site, and then said something in Japanese that Chris assumed was her excusing herself, before she hurried away. Chris pushed off of the bed and stood up next to Emmi and Alycia, and then the trio allowed Shara and Tom to precede them as they followed Yua out.

Walking through the halls, Chris instantly realized they weren't actually in a hospital, but rather a large office-like facility with an emergency medical center in the middle of it. When they left the medical wing, they passed by offices and cubicles, with a flurry of people going about their day, some in business attire, some in casual, overall a strange mix, while the drone of countless conversations in a language entirely foreign to Chris buzzed all around.

Based on the fact that everyone stepped out of Yua's way as she passed through, he guessed they were in a Sentinel facility in Osaka, since he knew Yua to be the second-in-command. But that meant...

"How many Sentinels work here?" he blurted out, and then clamped his hands over his mouth. He probably shouldn't have said Sentinel, not if this wasn't actually a Sentinel facility.

They stopped at a bank of elevators, and Yua pressed the up button before she turned and addressed him. "At least fifty at any one time."

Wide-eyed, he glanced at his friends before he asked, "Isn't that a lot?"

Tom shot him a warning glance, which he took to mean 'stop asking stupid questions,' but he couldn't help it – the continual rush of adrenaline-like energy coursing through his body made it hard for him to keep quiet.

"We are responsible for more than just Japan," Yua replied casually. The elevator doors behind her opened up with a ding, and after allowing two Sentinels to step off, she stepped in and beckoned them forward. The elevator was a little cramped for six people. After she pressed another button, the elevator doors closed and he felt it lurch them upwards. "In fact we are responsible for most of the Pacific Ocean in the northern hemisphere."

Two floors up, the lift stopped, depositing them into what looked, for all intents and purposes, like the hallway of an apartment building. A long corridor stretched ahead, as well as to the left and right, with door after door with numbers in front of them and doorbells affixed next to each one.

"We occupy the top four floors of this building," Yua continued, leading them out and straight ahead. There was a window at the end of the corridor, giving the Sentinels a view down a long avenue that stretched in front of the building. In the distance, he caught the distinct shape of a building that looked like an equilateral triangle, straight out of a geometry book. "And we have smaller facilities in other cities throughout Japan," Yua added.

"I had no idea," Chris frowned. "I mean, I thought each country might have…"

"We're wide-spread, but not that much," Tom countered. "Sentinels are responsible for regions, not just countries. Technically speaking, the U.S. Sentinels are responsible for all of North America. There's a regional office in Panama for Central America, and another office in Brazil for South America."

About halfway down the corridor, Yua stopped the procession and turned to face them. "Indeed. I apologize that Tanaka-sama is not here to greet you. He is currently in a meeting with the Prime Minister, but I am sure he will greet you as soon as he returns from Tokyo."

Tom and Shara exchanged stunned glances. "You're on good terms with the local government?" Tom asked.

Yua hesitated, but nodded after a second. "Yes, we are. Though I would describe our relationship with the Prime Minister as…tenuous. So far our Prime Minister has resisted pressure from the United States to regulate magical persons, but I fear that might not last. However, that is for Tanaka-sama to discuss with you."

Motioning to a door on her right, Yua changed topics, "This apartment suite is yours, and your companions are inside. There is a wall touchscreen you may interact with to communicate with the main desk, should you require anything not already in the apartment." Yua turned to the door, and pressed her thumb on a small sensor beneath the doorbell. A green light blinked on, and the door clicked, allowing her to open the door and motion them in.

"Thank you, Miss Saito," Tom said with an awkward bow, which Yua returned.

The group filed in, with Chris entering last, and Yua closed the door behind them, leaving them to their lavish, immaculate apartment.

It put Shara's old apartment in Denver to shame. The area directly by the door was tiled with smooth, granite tiles, but the rest of the living area in front of them was a wooden floor, or wooden laminate of some kind, Chris wasn't sure. The living room was large enough for two full-sized sofas, with a large kitchen area left of it, resplendent with hanging cookware, granite counter tops, and beyond-modern cooking hardware. In fact, he was surprised there wasn't a Star Trek replicator, but he was sure each device was connected to the building's internal network, the now-ubiquitous 'internet of things' exemplified in this one apartment. There were three doors leading out of the main open area on the right, past the living room, leaving a full bank of floor-to-ceiling windows at the back of the apartment.

The only person present in the living room was Ash, who stood up awkwardly upon their arrival. "Oh, uh, hi everyone," they smiled. "That was fast!" Their eyes fell upon Chris in surprise. "You're okay!"

Trying to smile while taking in the modern, expensive look of the apartment, Chris nodded. "Yeah, I, uh…" He glanced at Tom, and then Alycia. "Thanks to Mia."

While most of the others gawked, Tom looked uncomfortably at Chris, and crossed the threshold into the living room.

"Hey, hold on there," Ash stepped quickly in front of Tom, nearly planting a halting hand on his chest before thinking better of it.

Glowering at Ash, he asked, "What's wrong?"

"Shoes," Ash looked pointedly down. "I mean boots. You forgot to take your boots off."

Furrowing his brow deeper, Tom asked, "Why would I do that?"

Ash motioned towards the entrance, to a spot next to the door, and Chris noticed a large rack for shoes, already full of Ash, Marisol, Tiana, and Babbar's footwear. "It's polite," Ash insisted. "Any weeb knows that."

Almost simultaneously, Chris and Alycia snorted laughter, and Tom glared back at them. "Do I wanna know what a 'weeb' is?"

"Better not to ask," Alycia grinned. "But Ash is right, you're not supposed to walk around a house or apartment in outside shoes."

Scowling, Tom looked ready to ignore the local custom, but apparently decided against it and backtracked. "Fine, whatever."

The front area wasn't exactly large, so it took the five of them some creative maneuvering to get their boots or shoes off and stacked on the racks, and finally they spread out, away from one another.

"The others are getting dressed or showering," Ash motioned to the two bedroom doors. "Thankfully there's two bathrooms."

"Isn't that unusual for inner-city apartments?" Alycia asked.

Waving around at the apartment, Ash said, "I think they can

afford it."

Grinning, Alycia nodded. "Good point."

"Do they have fresh clothes?" Emmi asked.

"Yeah," Ash nodded. "Nothing fancy, though, but I think I'm good in what I'm wearing now. It's the rest of you who've gone without showers and clean clothes for an age or two."

Again, Chris felt self-conscious about his smell and appearance. Especially about the bloody bullet holes in his shirt. Absently, he rubbed inside one of the holes, at unblemished skin. "Well, anyway," he found himself saying, more just to break the awkward silence that had suddenly fallen.

A crash sounded from the kitchen. The adrenaline-like energy in Chris surged, and he charged his hands up with magic, until a familiar, scaly head popped up over the counter top. Nina fixed her eyes on Chris, and chortled, before ducking again.

"Hey!" Ash shouted when another crash racketed the apartment. "I said stop snooping around in there!"

Rushing into the kitchen, Ash bent over and out of sight. "There's no bottle caps in here, okay? Ouch!" They bolted upright and shook their right hand, and then sucked on their finger tip. "That hurt, you little brat!"

Snickering, Chris wandered past the kitchen, towards the broad vista at the back of the apartment. It was late afternoon, perhaps evening in Japan now. Directly below them was what appeared to be an elevated highway traversing over and in line with regular streets, with other streets intersecting beneath it further down in a dizzying crisscross. At the moment, traffic was light, but he assumed that wouldn't last, not in a city this dense.

"We're definitely not in Kansas anymore," he murmured to himself.

Chris was hesitant to sit down on any furniture due to his bloodied and soiled clothing, plus he just felt too energetic. Thankfully, it wasn't a long wait until the bathroom door opened up and Babbar strolled out. He wore the same clothes he'd worn before, but they looked cleaner, as if he'd hand-washed them in the bathtub (which Chris suspected was exactly what he'd done.)

The gnome was as surprised as anyone else by Chris's recovery, but the quick explanation from Shara about Mia's healing powers silenced him.

"I think it would be best if you went first," Tom motioned to Chris's bloodied person.

Since both bedroom doors were closed, and Chris still needed clothes, he asked Ash, "Which bedroom is free?"

"What?" they asked amidst yanking a kitchen utensil away from Nina. Nina appeared to be enjoying playing games with Ash, and Chris wondered if Ash considered it a game or not. "Oh, the one on the right, sorry. Hey, stop it," they turned back to Nina and tugged on a ladle. "That's not a toy!"

"Oye, don't hurt her," Babbar rushed towards them, still scrubbing out his green hair with a towel. "You hurt one scale on her, and I swear, by the goddess…"

Chris didn't hear the rest, and instead he'd slipped into the spare bedroom and closed the door. He still had to go back out into the living room to enter the bathroom that Babbar had vacated, but Chris just wanted a moment of peace.

Peace in my mind would be fantastic, too, he thought grudgingly, finding himself unable to focus or calm down. His hands shook a little, and if he hadn't known any better, he would have sworn he'd eaten a ton of candy. Nothing had made him feel this hyperactive in ages.

The bedroom was almost the same size as the living room, but had no exterior windows, and was lit only by a pair of bed-side lamps. The bed itself was a queen, with silk-smooth white sheets and a light-blue patterned comforter. Against the wall opposite of the bed were two dressers and a genuine, mahogany wardrobe.

"Jeeze, so this is how the one percent live," he remarked as he opened up the wardrobe. The clothes within were divided on two sides, one containing dresses that probably cost more than his education, and the other containing expensive-looking business suits, all of them covered in transparent garment bags.

"Yeah, no," he said to no one, and moved on to the dresser on the same side of the wardrobe where the suits were. The choices weren't particularly pleasing – he preferred blue jeans over any other kinds of pants, but that simply wasn't an option here. So he chose a dark gray pair of slacks, a white tank top, and a black button-up shirt that he was certain was made of silk. After snagging a fresh pair of socks and underwear, of which there were numerous sizes available, he made his way out and then into the bathroom. The rest of the Sentinels had gotten comfortable either in the living room or on barstools against the kitchen island.

Caked in grime, dirt, sweat, and blood, Chris had to practically peel his clothes off. He found garbage bags under the sink (which, of course, had a marble counter top,) and stuffed his old clothes in there, and then gratefully, blissfully, wonderfully stepped into a hot shower.

It wouldn't wash away his problems, and he didn't have a single ache in his body, thanks to Mia's sacrifice, but it felt like the most wonderful thing in the world. Watching the muddy, bloody water swirl down the drain, he imagined his problems going with it, and wished it were that easy in reality.

CHAPTER 16

After finishing showering and shaving for the first time in months, Chris stepped out in his silky, uncomfortable clothes to find that Tiana and Marisol had finished up ahead of him. Emmi and Alycia were taking turns in the master bedroom and bathroom, and that left Tom to take his turn in the second bathroom.

Shara still sat on a bar stool at the kitchen island, while Babbar sat as far away as he could, on the couch, with Nina curled up on Ash's lap next to Babbar, sleeping with a rolling pin clutched in her arms. *That's a new one,* Chris thought with an amused grin.

After a relieved hug from Tiana and Marisol, they joined Shara at the island counter, with Chris sidling up next to her. That was the first time he realized just how bad they must have smelled, since Shara hadn't yet had a turn in the showers and smelled like a combination of a sewer and a gym locker. He tried not to grimace or sniff too obviously.

Glancing to his right, out of the windows at the purpling sky of post-sunset, he asked, "So what'd Abby find? Why are we here?"

Shara looked at Chris, her violet eyes lost in thought. "Hm? Oh, Abby found something. But Tom wants to hold off briefing and debriefing until we're all together again."

"Oh," Chris nodded, disappointed, but unsurprised. Tom hated repeating himself, and did his best to ensure others never had to repeat themselves.

"Plus," she added, "since we're guests here, he wants to bring Yua and, if he returns tonight, Mister Tanaka up to speed."

Nodding again, Chris stared past Tiana and Marisol again,

watching the sky deepen and darken. It was still morning in Detroit, he wagered. This felt strange. "Well, since we all have, um," he paused and frowned, "Jet lag? Portal lag?"

Shara chuckled. "Portal lag, eh?"

"I like it," Marisol smiled. "We get to invent all kinds of new phrases and terms nowadays."

Grinning, Chris stood up and walked around to look out the window again. The scene outside was completely different now, traffic was wall-to-wall cars, and innumerable bicyclists weaved in between them. "Anyway, none of us ate breakfast, right?" His stomach didn't growl, but he knew he should eat, and food would distract them all, especially him, from the pain of waiting.

"Oooh, good idea," Tiana beamed. "Sushi anyone?"

Making a sour face, Marisol asked aghast, "For breakfast?"

"Technically dinner," Tiana shrugged.

"Technically it's raw fish," Marisol gagged.

"Well," Tiana shrugged and looked helplessly at Chris.

"Don't look at me," he shook his head. "I can't stand it myself."

Through an amused chuckle, Shara added, "And I doubt they have California Rolls here."

Chris looked at the TV embedded in the wall in the living room, and remembered Yua's remark about using a wall screen to talk to the main desk. Curious as to just what kind of food could be found around the Sentinel building, he bounced over to it, eliciting a startled and then curious chirp from Nina, who lifted her head groggily and watched Chris's antics.

It wasn't just a normal LED TV, he realized, as he hunted around the sides for a power button, only to find it already glowing green at him. Looking at the screen and frowning, he tentatively touched the surface. After a second, the screen flashed on, and an interface he normally associated with a tablet appeared.

In the top right, a single icon appeared that looked like a wooden desk, and though the written words beneath it weren't English, he reasoned that the shortcut was similar to one he'd seen on the tablets at Sentinel tower, and he tapped on it.

After a moment, the image flickered, and a video conference app launched, showing a middle-aged woman in business attire at a desk, her shoulder-length black hair completely straightened, her dark eyes polite. *"Konbanwa,"* she said, and then asked something else in

Japanese.

"Uh," Chris said stupidly. His ability to speak or understand Japanese hadn't changed in three months.

Ash called out, "Konbanwa," in response, while pushing a complaining Nina over to Babbar and standing up, and then responded in kind to the front desk attendant, speaking fluent Japanese.

Chris stepped aside and let Ash take the lead in the conversation. He didn't understand pretty much any of what they spoke, until he swore he heard the front desk attendant say "McDonald's." That perked up his ears.

Turning to everyone, Ash said, "There's a McDonald's just up the road, and they can have a runner go get us food. Is that 'Murican enough for y'all?" They'd said "'Murican" with a deliberately gruff voice.

Most everyone glanced at one another in stunned silence, except for Chris, who remembered seeing a small McDonald's at the Adelaide airport three months ago.

"Um, okay," Tiana replied with a grin.

"Do you think they serve breakfast all day?" Marisol asked.

After some more back and forth with Ash, the attendant signed off, and Ash found a pad of paper and a pen in a small stationary desk to the left. "They'll have someone pick up our order in a few minutes."

Ash took down everyone's order, writing in Japanese characters that, though he didn't know how to read, he recognized as Kanji.

"How do you know the language?" he asked curiously as Ash wrote down Chris's order for a cheeseburger.

"Oh, I, uh," Ash faltered. "Duolingo." They pressed their lips tight, and then added quietly, "My cousin and I challenged each other."

Feeling color drain from his face, Chris nodded. "Right…sorry."

Shaking their head, Ash cleared their throat and looked at Chris pointedly. He'd almost forgotten that Ash had wanted to hate Chris, wanted to blame him for their cousin's death. "It's…well." Shaking their head again, they managed to say, "We were both kinda anime nerds."

Feeling his face brighten, Chris said, "Hey, Alycia and I are too! Well, her more than me, but still. What's your favorite?"

Giving him an exaggerated double-blink, Ash asked, "How in the world do people actually expect me to answer that? It's like asking me what my favorite oxygen particle to breathe is."

Snorting out a laugh, Chris felt his cheeks warm from the embarrassing noise he'd just made. From over at the bar, Marisol cheered. "Heeeeyyyy, there's that adorable little snort!"

"Shut up," he growled.

"So it's not just Alycia who can get it out of him," Tiana remarked teasingly. "He laughs around other people!"

Shaking his head, he sighed and looked down at the list. "That's almost everyone, right?"

"Hai," Ash nodded. "Just waiting for…"

At that moment, the master bedroom door opened, and a refreshed Emmi and Alycia walked out. Emmi had found a pair of black yoga pants and a tight-fitting black tube top that she wore under a loose-fitting, green button-up shirt, and her hair, still wet, hung loosely around her shoulders. Alycia, on the other hand, wore tan slacks and a black blouse, and like Emmi, hadn't dried her hair. Both, he noticed, had hair bands around their wrists, and recalling countless hours in their apartment, he knew the two were going to help each other braid up their hair.

Shara murmured something that sounded like 'finally' and rushed past them to take her turn at the shower, while Ash called them over to take their orders.

"Seriously, there's a McD's here?!" Alycia's eyes went wide. "That's heaps good!"

Smiling at her use of one of her favorite phrases, Chris let them take down their order, and just in the nick of time, Tom came out of the second bathroom just as there was a knock at the door.

Chris opened the door while Ash rushed to Tom to take his order, and a young boy who was probably only seventeen stood at the door. "Konbanwa," the boy said with a bow.

Returning the bow, Chris motioned for the kid to come in, and looked helplessly at Ash. They finished taking Tom's order, brought the completely-full paper over, ripped it off the pad, and handed it to the boy with a flurry of words that sent the boy running off. Literally.

"Why's he running?" Chris asked while closing the door.

"I told him we hadn't eaten in days and we were starving," Ash said with a shrug.

With all but Shara present and refreshed, the group settled in again. Marisol and Tiana kept to the kitchen and chattered away, and Tom joined them a minute later. Just as Chris expected, Alycia and Emmi sat on one side of the couch facing the TV and took turns braiding one another's hair. Until those two had become friends, he'd thought such activities were relegated to teen girls having sleepovers, but they'd educated him on the matter quite thoroughly. Babbar sat next to them with Nina curled up on his lap, leaving the other couch for Ash and Chris to sit down on. Ash immediately mentioned their conversation with Chris about anime to Alycia, and the two excitedly started exchanging stories of some of their favorite anime, while Emmi rolled her eyes and worked on Alycia's thick brown locks.

It then occurred to him that the apartment didn't have one of those low tables to kneel at, and he wondered about that. Was this apartment specifically designed to accommodate guests from the U.S. or Europe?

By the time Shara emerged from the bedroom, the young boy had returned carrying two large bags of food, and the Sentinels gathered around the island in the kitchen, most of them standing since there were only four chairs, and set to hungrily devouring their breakfast/dinner.

In the midst of eating, another knock at the door called their attention. Chris automatically started for the door, but Ash waved a hand at him and said, "I've got it, weeb."

Great, he thought with a glance at an amused Alycia. *Now they're gonna use anime fandom words to describe everything…*

But when Ash opened the door, it was Yua who stood there, and beside and behind her was an elderly man a head taller than Yua, with silver hair and countless wrinkles – Sato Tanaka, leader of the Japanese Sentinels.

Ash had never met the commander before, but they recognized that he was someone of importance, and immediately dipped into a deep bow before stepping aside, permitting Yua and Sato to enter.

"Ah, excellent," Yua beamed a smile. "You've all already eaten."

Tom stepped away from the counter, quickly wiping his hands on his napkin before clearing his throat. "Commander Tanaka," he said, and hastily bowed. "Welcome home."

Chris recalled that Sato didn't speak English, but never-the-less, he bowed lightly to Tom while Yua translated. Sato responded, and Yua translated back, "Thank you, Taylor-sama. Tanaka-sama wishes to be brought up to speed as soon as possible. Would you and your team come with us?"

Even though almost no one had finished, everyone recognized that it was well past 'normal' business hours, and that by asking them to brief him now, Sato was likely sacrificing his evening. Therefore, no one objected.

"Lead the way," Tom nodded, and led the rest of the Sentinels away from the kitchen counter.

It was only just as Tom, Shara, and Chris followed Yua and Sato into the hallway that they realized they'd forgotten to put shoes back on, and they hurried back inside to do so.

CHAPTER 17

The conference room that Yua and Sato led them to put the Denver Sentinel's conference room to shame. But that was pretty much the case for every aspect of the Japanese Sentinel facility.

Everything was modernized, technologically. In fact, the conference table reminded Chris of the ones from Star Trek The Next Generation – a blackened glass-top with a cherry redwood finished border, and chairs that used a mesh instead of cushions.

And every inch of the walls that wasn't a doorway was covered in some special LED screen technology that Chris had only ever seen demo videos of – basically wallpaper LED screens.

While Alycia and Emmi sat on either side of Chris in the conference room, he leaned back and behind Emmi to ask Shara, "Why don't we have this kind of tech back home?"

Arching a blue eyebrow at him, Shara replied, "'Cause they get more general funding than we do."

With a frown, Chris asked somewhat indignantly, "Why?"

"To put it frankly," Yua interrupted their side conversation, "we have more area to cover. We encounter more magic. Especially so over the past century."

Yua sat to Sato's right, while Sato sat at the head of the table to Chris's right, and Tom sat at the other head of the table on Chris's left. Across from Chris sat Marisol, Tiana, and Babbar, while Ash sat just past Alycia to his right.

Tom nodded his agreement. "Magic was actually *more* commonplace in the Americas for centuries, but over the past three hundred years, North America saw a dramatic decrease in events resulting from cracks in the Barrier."

"Ah," Chris nodded. Then frowned. "What caused such a dramatic down-turn?"

Tom looked uncomfortably around the table. "Basically put, it was wiped out. Violently. And not by Sentinels, either."

Chris's frown deepened, and he looked at Shara, who stared at him with a hollow expression. "Think Salem Witch Trials. Burnings at the stake for any hint of magic. That sort of thing."

"Essentially the European invasion of the Americas," Tom concluded. "There was plenty of that in Europe too, but even the British Empire couldn't stop it from flowing back in from surrounding areas."

Sato spoke a few words, and Yua nodded, "Let us get started, please," she said in a school teacher-like voice.

Feeling his cheeks burn, Chris glanced at Alycia, who grabbed his hand under the table and squeezed it sympathetically.

Sato spoke some more, and Yua nodded. "I've briefed Mister Tanaka on everything I know, and we've received communication from your technical support, Abigail Turner, telling us about the item you wish to examine."

Chris turned expectantly to Tom, while making a point to rest his free hand on the table and drum his finger tips on it. Tom looked at him with a less-than-bemused expression. Looking specifically at Chris, he said, "While you were out getting supplies, Abby told us she found records of an ancient scroll here in Osaka. One which depicted Imhullu and the Dragonstone."

Chris's eyebrows rose up. "That's a big break."

Tom nodded. "Unfortunately, the scroll itself has not been digitally scanned, so we don't know the contents of it. And her image search software only gave it a fifty percent match, low enough that Abby almost didn't bother looking at it. The depiction of the two items on the scroll's outer casing was so badly worn, it was difficult to identify them as such."

Chris ventured a guess, "So we need to examine the scroll physically to see what's written in it."

"Exactly," Tom nodded, and looked at Yua expectantly.

"We know which store house has the item based on our records," Yua nodded. "It will be retrieved from an archive in Kyoto tonight, but it is amongst the oldest relics we have, and finding it will take our people some time.”

Sato said something, and Yua translated, “It is fortunate at all that it was ever photographed.”

Tom nodded. “Any idea how old it is?”

“Until we know exactly where it was stored and by whom, no,” Yua shook her head. “My apologies.”

“No worries,” Tom replied. “It’s not much to go on, but it’s better than nothing.”

“Better than sitting around waiting for Nabu to find us,” Shara agreed. “I think we’ve done enough of that.”

Chris agreed whole heartedly, and in fact found it difficult to sit still even now. He was twisting his chair back and forth, only an inch or so, but as soon as he realized what he was doing, he stopped himself.

And promptly resumed a moment later.

Looking at Chris, the Denver leader said, “Alright, you’re turn.”

Chris blinked, looked at Alycia, and then over at Ash. But Tom’s eyes were settled on Chris, not the others.

Clearing his throat, he nodded and sat up straight, and then launched into a retelling of their encounter with Samuel in the coffee shop, and their conversation with the Collector.

The others listened, with Tom or Shara occasionally interjecting surprised questions for clarity, as Chris explained why the Collector was helping them, and what Nabu’s plans were. And, more importantly, how to defeat Nabu once and for all. Yua helpfully translated the entire time, becoming a sort of background noise as she spoke quietly to Sato, who listened patiently, his fingers interlaced thoughtfully under his chin.

The room was silent for several long moments after Chris finished. He looked around at each and everyone’s face, realizing from their expressions that they were just as shaken as he was by the revelations, especially that Nabu was part of the original plot to create the Barrier, and that she could be killed with Imhullu.

“Son of a bitch,” Tom breathed. “You mean to say we had the means to end her once and for all, and we let it go?”

“Tom,” Shara frowned at him. “It’s not your fault.”

“I hid it,” he shook his head. “We could have used it, and instead I hid it.”

“We didn’t know, Dad,” Alycia soothed. “There was no way we

could know, we just knew that Nabu could use it to free Marduk."

"Isn't that ironic," Tiana sighed. "The one thing Marduk needs to be free of his prison is also the one thing we need to prevent it, or at least end his son…daughter…you know what I mean. One wrong move, and we could bring about the very apocalypse we're trying to avert."

"Yeah, about that," Marisol pitched in. "What if using the dagger on Nabu is enough to free Marduk?"

"They're just one soul," Ash replied. "Even if Nabu is powerful, one soul shouldn't be enough to free Marduk, right?"

Everyone looked at Shara, and when she realized that, her eyes widened. "Why are you all looking at me?"

"You know more about souls and magic than any of us," Emmi replied. "How much energy can a single soul provide?"

Shrugging, Shara replied, "Hell if I know."

So everyone turned their eyes upon Babbar.

"I'm afraid I don't know either," he shrugged, which disturbed Nina, who was curled around his neck on his shoulders, still trying to sleep. "Honestly, the fact that the Collector is loyal to Marduk is news to me, and I'm surprised that a man of his intelligence believes an infernal can actually be destroyed."

Chris nodded, once again recalling the conversation over dinner in Sentinel Tower, when he'd learned all about celestials, the supposed creators of magic, and their nemeses, the infernals. As an infernal, Babbar believed Marduk to be immortal. But according to the Collector, Marduk possibly could be destroyed by a massive infusion of souls all at once.

Sato said something, and Chris didn't need a translation to hear the absolute detest in the Japanese commander's voice. Yua translated, "It is beyond reprehensible that Nabu would consider using a nuclear weapon…" Somehow Chris had the feeling Sato hadn't actually used the word 'reprehensible' based on the fire in his eyes.

"If nothing else, we have to stop that," Tom nodded.

"But at least that goal coincides with another," Emmi added. "We need to get that dagger." Her hands curled into fists, tight enough that her knuckles turned white. "We need to *end* that bitch. Stop her from influencing anyone or anything else on Earth, ever again."

Chris remembered when he'd learned what Nabu had done to her, back in the cabin, with Emmi drunk and delirious with rage.

And he remembered her rage-formed bear.

"Agreed," Tom nodded. "But if the dagger really is in Los Alamos, I can guarantee you Nabu will have it heavily guarded. There would be no hope of sneaking in."

Chris looked at Babbar. At Nina on his shoulder. The gnome stared back with golden eyes. "Oh no you don't," he replied, wagging his finger back and forth. "Nabu almost killed Nina once, I'm not going to put her in harm's way on purpose. Not again."

"Oh?" Chris asked. "I thought you wanted to defeat Marduk as much as we do?"

"I do," he nodded, "and until today, I didn't think we ever could win. Still not sure we can." Absently, he stroked along Nina's velvet-like scaly hide, and she slit an eye open enough to see it was him, and heaved an adorable little breath. "But she was lucky to have survived that gunshot in the tower. She's..." He faltered, his voice cracking. "She's the only family I have left."

Even Shara didn't have anything snarky to say about that. She remained quiet, her eyes growing distant. Chris looked around the table, and all he saw was a respectful, remorseful stare in everyone's eyes.

"I know," he finally said, quietly. "But we might not have a choice."

"Not necessarily," Babbar replied, looking first at Chris, then at Alycia. "That last arcane magic user that attacked us. Did you notice anything strange about her?"

Chris nodded and replied, "Yeah, her powers were intermixed. I think maybe she had enchanted gear helping her out, giving her extra power."

"Exactly," Babbar nodded. "And we've seen that Nabu has displacement abilities. Maybe with Alycia's help, you can..."

"No!" Shara slapped the tabletop. "No way, Babbar. Portals aren't something you can just do willy nilly, and you damn well know that! Even if Alycia could enchant something to give Chris that ability, it'd take decades for him to figure out how to safely make a portal to anywhere, let alone a place he's never been before."

Chris gulped, his head reeling with the idea that he could somehow be given the same powers as Nina or Nabu. "Uh, do I even want to know what would happen if I messed it up? Like, would I end up in orbit or something on accident?"

Shara thought for a second, shrugged, and said, "Part of you might. Another part might end up in the center of the Earth. Another on the surface of the moon. Another…"

"Alright, alright," he held up his hands, his stomach suddenly feeling like it didn't want to keep his cheeseburger down. "I get the picture. Bad idea."

"We'll need Nina," Tom stated, his gaze set upon Babbar. "There's no other way, Babbar, and you know it."

Much to Nina's protest, Babbar clutched at her, dragging her from his shoulders and grasping her tightly. "I won't put her in harm's way again. You can't make me."

Nina looked up at him, squirming in his grip, and nipped at his large nose before purring and cawing at him, somehow managing both at the same time. Babbar's golden eyes opened wide, and he gaped down at her. She chuffed at him indignantly.

"What did she say?" Ash asked.

He gaped up at Ash, and then at Chris. "She says it is her destiny to be with the Champion at the end."

Everyone turned to Chris, and he squirmed uncomfortably. Even Nina looked at him, but unlike everyone else's gaze, hers wasn't expectant or surprised.

They were soothing. Calming. Reassuring.

"Our destinies are interwoven, Champion," a voice spoke. The same voice that had told him to hold on after he was shot. It came from everywhere and nowhere at once, and he frowned at Nina. Had she spoken to him, somehow? He glanced at Babbar, but the gnome made no indication that he'd heard anything from Nina.

He met the tiny dragon's gaze, searching her red, lizard-like eyes, trying desperately to find her soul.

Suddenly a hand waved in front of him, startling him out of his soul search. Alycia asked, "Chris? You awake in there?"

"Wuh?" He blinked, realizing that his eyes felt extremely dry. "What's wrong?"

"You kinda left us there for a second," Emmi said, nudging him in the side. "Only time I've ever seen you become so absorbed in staring is when Alycia-"

Chris jabbed his elbow into her side, shutting her up.

Alycia giggled.

Tom grumbled.

"Sorry," he shook his head, and looked at Nina again, but she was already curling up against Babbar's chest, her eyes groggily closing. "I…Nina…she…"

Somehow he couldn't say it, couldn't convey what had just happened.

So he let his curiosity get the best of him. "Babbar, what is she?"

The gnome looked completely taken aback by his question. "The bloody hell do you mean? She's a dragon, obviously."

"I don't sense a soul in her," he replied.

Babbar looked startled, but recovered and indignantly remarked, "Well that's rather rude of you to say."

"Huh," Ash said, leaning forward with closed eyes. "You're right. I hadn't even noticed, but I can feel everyone else's presence in here." Blinking their eyes open, they added, "But not her. I feel power, but no soul, which…"

Chris nodded. "Makes no sense."

"Even the tiniest insect has a soul," Shara frowned. "Or should."

Chris nodded. "I'm guessing so. I mean, I could even feel all of the rats in the warehouse when I was looking for the shapeshifter."

Shara blinked in surprise. "You…you could?"

"Yeah." He furrowed his brow. "Why, is that strange?"

"Uh," she looked at the others in bewilderment. "You have no idea. It usually takes masters decades to quiet their own thoughts enough to feel the presence of tiny, simple animals."

Though shocked by her statement, Chris tried to brush it off and shrugged. "Well, I mean, it wasn't easy. Dunno if I could do it again…" And then, realizing they had strayed from the topic, he again looked at Babbar. "You didn't answer my question, though. What is she?"

Running a hand through his moss-green hair, Babbar shook his head. "I'm telling you, I really don't know. I found her egg on…" He paused and averted his eyes from everyone for a second. "Well, another world. She hatched, imprinted on me, and we became inseparable. When I found out that she had displacement powers, and that she was able to travel to Earth, we came here to get away from…" He shuddered. "Well, to get away." With a casual shrug, he added, "Other than the fact that her powers were unaffected by the Barrier, I'd no idea there was anything unique about her."

Chris nodded thoughtfully, and stared at Nina, who was breathing steadily now. She was asleep. Again.

Why was she sleeping so much now?

Sato said something that Yua translated, "Tanaka-sama wishes to convene for the night. It seems we still have much planning to do, and we are sure you all could use some rest."

Chris disagreed, but only for himself. He still felt like he could run a marathon.

"Right," Tom rubbed his face. "We should rest up, think about how we might want to tackle an assault on the labs."

"Maybe that scroll will give us some clues, too," Shara added.

"Indeed," Yua nodded and stood up, officially ending the meeting. "I apologize that we didn't have more apartments ready earlier, but we've since prepared two additional ones, so that everyone will have a place to sleep tonight. I will show you which ones are yours."

CHAPTER 18

The two extra apartments were right across the hall from the initial one, which made things easier at first…until it came time to decide who would stay in which apartment.

Because Chris wanted to stay with his best friends, and his girlfriend.

Girlfriend, he thought, grinning. *I've only ever called one other person that in my entire life.*

The grin faltered a second later. Too bad it came at what might be the end of his life. If they couldn't figure out a way to defeat Nabu and Marduk without sacrificing himself.

Trouble was, he was pretty sure he already knew how to defeat Marduk – the Collector had given him the clue. And it wasn't good.

Shaking the thoughts from his head, Chris focused on the gathered crowd outside, and looked specifically at Alycia. Obviously in this situation, as much as they might want…*more,* what he really wanted was to be able to sleep next to her again, hand in hand, maybe cuddled up in each other's arms.

The glower Tom gave him, however, made him gulp.

"Dad," Alycia spoke with a warning tone in her voice.

Tom's glower turned on his daughter.

"I'm an adult," she reminded him. "And I want to spend the evening with Chris and Emmi."

An awkward silence fell upon the group, until Yua quickly excused herself and hurried away. *Smart woman,* Chris thought.

After their host was out of sight, Tom silently turned back to their original apartment, scanned his thumb to unlock the door, and stalked inside.

Shara gently touched Chris and Alycia's shoulders, and said, "I'll talk to him."

Babbar cleared his throat and headed for one of the other apartments, muttering, "I'll just, uh…"

Shara snagged his shirt by the collar and yanked him back. "No way, fungus, you're staying where I can keep an eye on you."

"Hey!" Babbar replied indignantly. The jostling woke Nina up in his arms, and she nipped at Shara's fingers grumpily. Hissing, Shara retracted her hands. "I'll have you know that I'm an adult, too. Respect your elders!"

Sucking on her injured finger, Shara glared at him, and sighed. "Fine, but I swear to the gods, if you ditch us…"

"I'm in this for the long haul, remember?" the gnome grumbled, thumping his chest, much to Nina's chagrin. "Marduk *and* Nabu want me dead. More than that," he curled his free arm around Nina, "they want *her* dead. I'm sticking with all of you for protection."

Scoffing, Shara murmured, "Typical," and followed Tom into the first apartment.

"Well, then," Babbar sniffed. "Whom shall I stay with?"

"Good question," Ash looked down at the ground.

Chris felt a pang in his heart, and before Marisol and Tiana could say anything, he said to Ash, "You can stay with us. Though," he looked at Alycia and Emmi hesitantly. "If it's like the other apartment…"

A combination of surprise and glee crossed Ash's face. "Oh don't worry, I'll take one of the couches!"

Nodding, Babbar turned to Marisol and Tiana. "I guess that means I'm bunking with you two."

Marisol and Tiana looked at one another, shrugged, and then together said, "You get the couch."

As those three, along with the sleeping Nina, headed further down the hall, Chris stepped up to the door right across from the first apartment and unlocked it with his fingerprint. When the door obediently opened, he wondered where the Japanese Sentinels got his fingerprints from, but then remembered that they had access to the databases from Denver, and all of his prints had been scanned before they had left for the training camp.

The apartment was a mirror image of the first one, with the

kitchen on the right as he entered rather than the left, and the windows ahead, over the living room furniture, presented a wide vista of cityscape, the nearest building several stories beneath their view.

Osaka was a bright city, to put it mildly. Building lights, city street lights, and huge digital advertising boards were visible in every direction, and it made for an almost dizzying, and yet simultaneously captivating spectacle.

The four of them took their shoes off, and while Emmi, Alycia, and Ash headed right for the living room couches, Chris sauntered over to the kitchen to find something to drink. He was expecting to find soda, or juice, or something of that caliber.

What he wasn't expecting to find was a dozen different kinds of saké, and at least two brands of plum wine in the fridge.

He hated saké. But plum wine? *That* was a wonderfully, deliciously sweet-tasting wine.

The labels were written in Japanese, but he recognized the design on one – Takara.

"Oooh," he involuntarily said as he pulled the chilled bottle out of the fridge. "Uh, hey," he lifted the bottle up and presented it towards the living room. "Anyone up for something a bit stronger than water?"

The trio in the living room jumped up excitedly and rushed over to see what else was around. Before long, they were back in the living room, with Chris and Emmi nursing overly-fancy, crystalline wine glasses full of plum wine, and Ash and Alycia were pouring shots of warm saké.

Chris was a little hesitant upon seeing Emmi's excitement for alcohol, and felt a little guilty after remembering their last drink together, sort of, in the cabin in the mountains. She had drunk herself silly, and raged out emotions.

Back when Emmi had told him what Nabu had done.

But if Emmi felt any reservations about alcohol again, she didn't show it. He promised himself to keep an eye on her, though, and to make sure she didn't go so far as to warrant a hangover in the morning again.

Before anyone could take their first drink, Chris looked around at the group, especially at Emmi and Alycia, and felt his insides swell.

These were his friends. The two people in the world he cared about more than any others.

So he raised his glass up, just before Ash could knock back their first shot. They paused upon seeing his action, and lowered and waited.

Suddenly he didn't know what to say, he just knew he wanted to say *something*.

Finally, he smiled and said, "To the most powerful mages in the world." He paused, and through a cracking voice, added, "To friendship everlasting."

Warm smiles greeted him back. Wine glasses and shot glasses clinked together, and they took their first drinks. The Takara Plum Wine was as good as he remembered, super sweet without a hint of alcohol taste in it.

Which was dangerous.

An hour of drinking and idle conversation passed, until they inevitably returned to the topic of anime.

Rolling her eyes, Emmi said, "I can't believe you all can watch that crap."

"Hey!" a tipsy Ash scowled. "Now just a damn minute, here."

"Don't let her get you riled up," Alycia advised sagely. "Chris and I have been trying to get her into anime for years, and she just won't give in to the dark side."

"Well, the dark side promised cookies," Emmi remarked sourly. "I'm still waiting on my cookies! Where are my cookies?"

"Oooh, meme war?" Ash perked up.

"Oh, *hell* no," Emmi shook her head in an exaggerated motion. "Those two will kick our asses all up and down this tower with a meme war."

"Hey," Chris held up a defensive hand. "Not me. Aly is the reigning champion." Frowning, he looked at Ash and said, "But speaking of anime, how come when I asked you what your favorite anime was, you lectured me, but when Aly asked…"

"I didn't ask them what their *one* favorite was," Alycia interrupted. "I asked what *some* of Ash's favorites were."

Ash knocked back another shot, and nodded emphatically. "Exactly! That's it exactly."

"Oh," Chris narrowed his eyes. "So you can't choose your favorite oxygen particle to breathe, but you can choose a group of favorite ones?"

Emmi and Alycia chortled and leaned towards one another, while

Ash smiled through bright red cheeks at him. "Yeah. Ones that don't stink."

He opened his mouth to retort their statement, but then paused, and nodded. "Ah. Yeah, good point. Stinky anime stinks, and…I mean…" Alycia burst out laughing, and he felt his already warm cheeks grow hotter. "I mean, I hadn't thought about it that way. I think. I suppose." Shrugging and pouring himself another glass of wine, he said, "That is, I didn't suppose. And supposedly you're supposed to suppose." Tipping the bottle back just shy of a full glass, and happy that there was another bottle in the fridge, he thought about what he'd just said, and realized it sounded like something Jack Sparrow would say. So he added, "Savvy?"

While Emmi and Alycia laughed harder, leaning against one another for support, Ash gave Chris a wry grin and nodded at the bottle. "Damn, kid, you can't hold your liquor at all, can you?"

"Oye," he scowled. "Kid? You're not much older than I am, are you?"

Breathing between laughs, Emmi had to try hard to say, "Chris, I think…I think what they're trying to say…" She gripped her stomach as she laughed harder. "They're more experienced at drinking than you…and you should probably…stop while you're ahead."

Chris had just started to pick up his glass again to take another sip, but stopped and glared at Emmi through narrowed eyes. Looking down at the golden liquid, he sighed in defeat and set it back down. "No, you're right. I'm already thoroughly tipsy…"

Screwing their face up in mock-seriousness, Ash leaned over from the other couch and patted his knee gently. "It's okay, sourpuss. No need to get all pouty…"

"Hey!" he protested as the other two burst into renewed laughter.

With a playful smirk, Ash said to Alycia, "I can see why you like him so much."

"Right?!" She replied between laughs. "He's adorable in his own way."

"And *he* is sitting right here," Chris grumbled, unsure if his sour disposition was enhanced by the wine or not.

But those words immediately shut Ash up, and their face tightened into a grimace. "Right! Right…I…I'm so sorry. I shouldn't have…that was stupid of me…"

Ash's words, and the tone in their voice, was sobering, and Emmi and Alycia's laughter died in a heartbeat. Silence fell upon them like a cold chill, and Chris almost instantly knew he'd hit a nerve with Ash, even if he didn't fully understand why.

"I'm sorry," he said.

Ash shook their head. "No, don't be." The bite of resent in their voice forced Chris to wince. "I just…"

There was a story to their actions, a reason behind it, and he wanted to know.

He wanted to know because he recognized that look. It was one he'd seen in the mirror too many times when he lived with his parents. With his father.

Chris wanted to say something, but somewhere in the back of his mind, he remembered that there are times when silence says more than words ever could. So he waited. It was Ash's choice to tell them about it, or not.

"It's just…family, you know?" Ash kept their eyes averted. "Family sucks."

Chris let out an airy laugh. "You can say that again."

"Family sucks," Ash said, and then looked at him with a glint of mischief.

Slowed by alcohol, his reaction came comically delayed, and he gave Ash an eye roll worthy of Emmi's best. "Smart ass."

"Better that than a dumb ass," Ash quipped. Chris took the sarcasm as a hint that they didn't want to talk further on the subject.

But he wanted to say one more thing. It was funny how alcohol could make him all introspective. "Look, we've all had family trouble at one time or another," he looked at Emmi and Alycia, especially Alycia – the look of worry over her mother twinged at his heart strings. "But if there's one thing I've learned, it's that the *original* version of the old saying holds true." He looked intently at Ash. "The blood of the covenant is thicker than the waters of the womb."

Ash blinked, frowned. "Is *that* how it's really supposed to go?"

He nodded. "Yup."

"Shit, that totally changes the meaning of the saying."

"Exactly." He smiled. "Basically put, bonds of choice mean more than bonds forced upon you."

"Especially," Emmi added, "if I recall, that saying is often applied to bonds formed in the thick of battle. Those who *shed* blood together, by choice. At least, I swear I remember reading about that in a philosophy class at some point."

"That's what I remember, too," Chris nodded at Emmi, and then turned again to Ash. "What I'm trying to say is…we're your friends now. We've fought at least two battles together. As far as I'm concerned, you're one of us, now."

"Yeah," Alycia said with a smile. She reached across Chris to grip Ash's knee firmly and shake it, somewhat drunkenly. "We're here for you now. And damn if this group doesn't go to the ends of the Earth for one another. No talking over you, no ignoring you. You matter to us."

"Agreed," Emmi raised her glass. "To choice. To blood. To chosen kinship."

Without thinking, Chris took up his glass again, while Alycia and Ash held up another shot glass. "To chosen kinship," they echoed, clinked glasses, and drank.

That last shot must have burned going down, because both Ash and Alycia hissed after throwing it back, and each slammed their glasses down on the coffee table. The tears in Ash's eyes might have been from that, but Chris suspected they were from something more.

Clearing his throat, Chris nodded. "So, how 'bout it. If there was one anime you could show Emmi to try to get her into anime-"

"Which I'm not promising will work," Emmi countered, "but I'm willing to give it a go. For Ash's sake."

Nodding acknowledgement of that fact, Chris asked Ash, "Which one would you show her?"

Ash's eyes widened, and they wiped the tears away. "Ooooh, good question. Damn. Umm." They scrunched up their nose in thought, and rubbed their hand through their pixie-cut hair. "Well it can't be a series, we don't have time to binge-watch Full Metal Alchemist. Not even Brotherhood."

Alycia raised her empty shot glass. "An excellent thought, though."

"So it has to be a movie," Ash nodded. "How about a Studio Ghibli film? Oh! I know!" They quickly straightened up, their back popping twice as they went. "How about Howl's Moving Castle?"

A wide grin crossed Chris's face, and he looked at the TV set into the wall. "Think that thing can stream it?"

Standing up abruptly, and then damn near falling over, Ash

steadied themself with Chris's help, and then staggered over to the TV and activated it with a touch. They looked around for a second, tried a few menus, and then clicked something. A prompt came up for voice interaction. Ash spoke in perfectly-slurred Japanese, but the system must have understood it – the Netflix app suddenly launched, and it automatically brought up Howl's Moving Castle.

Ash squealed in delight, and hit play before the annoying auto-play feature started ahead of them. Then Ash plopped down on the couch, lying their head on the headrest closest to Chris. "Oh, I promise, Emmi, you're gonna love it!"

The trio settled in to watch one of the best Hayao Myazaki movies ever to grace the world. Alycia nuzzled closer to Chris, and then Emmi snuggled with her.

Alycia nudged in closer to Chris, and then when he apparently didn't get whatever hint she was giving him, she scrunched up her nose at him, and then forced his arm up and over her, and she nuzzled in underneath, resting her head against his chest.

As the beginning of the movie played, Chris paid little attention at first, and instead looked around him. At Emmi, drawing her feet under her like a pretzel and leaning against Alycia, near-empty glass of plum wine rolling back and forth in her hands. At Ash, practically squirming with delight. At Alycia. The woman he'd crushed on for over four years, now his girlfriend.

His two best friends, and his newest friend.

If this was to be his last night, then it was perfect.

CHAPTER 19

By the time the movie had ended, Alycia had fallen asleep in Chris's arms. Every now and then, he'd glanced over at Emmi or Ash to see their reactions, and was surprised by how enamored Ash was. Emmi, on the other hand, looked only mildly interested, and unlike Ash, hadn't touched her drink since the start of the movie.

Chris tried to stir Alycia, but she mumbled incoherently and drew closer to him, tightening her grip around his torso. Emmi grinned, and said, "You'd better get her to bed."

Chris looked over to Ash, only to find their eyes drooping closed.

As carefully as he could, Chris stood up while allowing Alycia to retain her iron grip on him, and then lifted her into his arms, knees draped over his left forearm. He'd never carried someone before, not like this, and was surprised at how difficult and awkward it was — movies always made it look easy. And Alycia wasn't heavy, either. *Maybe I'm just a wimp and need to lift weights,* he thought.

"Take the master bedroom," Emmi advised. "Ash, do you want the other bed, or...?"

Ash was asleep, evidenced by the sound of a soft snore.

It probably wasn't even evening in the United States yet, but alcohol and an exhausting day had defeated both Alycia and Ash. *There's a joke in there somewhere about A names and alcohol,* Chris grinned to himself. Nodding and saying, "Goodnight," to Emmi, he carefully strode across the apartment and shimmied sideways through the door into the master bedroom. He debated flicking the light on with his elbow, but there was enough glow from a nightlight that he didn't bother.

Chris had expected a California King or similar, given the extravagance of the rest of the apartments, but it was just another Queen bed. While trying to keep a grip on Alycia, Chris carried her over to the far side, and then, while keeping her in his arms, gently lowered her enough that he could drag his elbow across the comforter and sheets and pull them clear enough so that he could finally lower her in, and then began to tuck her in.

After a second of carefully maneuvering the sheets over her, he looked up and saw that she was awake again, beautiful golden brown gazing at him through the soft glow of the nightlight. And then, before he knew what was happening, she leaned up and grasped around his neck, and drew him in for a deep kiss.

They remained that way for an eternity bottled up inside of a second, and just when he thought she might break contact, she kissed deeper, parting his lips, tongue darting inward, searching for his and striking home.

It was like a dream come true, and open bedroom door be damned, he returned the kiss, deeper, stronger, except…

Except for the taste and smell of alcohol. And the fact that mere moments ago, she had been passed out in his arms.

Chris wanted this, he *ached* to be with her. The desire drove him mad, both in his heart and in lower regions. Four years of unrequited attraction, four years of wanting and needing and hoping, and tonight, they could be together. Perhaps the only chance they would ever have.

It could have been the most romantic moment of his life. It should have been. He reasoned that with a deadly battle looming on the horizon, maybe he should just go ahead. Alycia felt eager, pressing their lips together harder, their tongues, her other hand drifting down towards the hem of his shirt…

"Alycia," he broke away, kicking himself mentally with every single syllable of every word he spoke. "We shouldn't."

Eyes that somehow conveyed sleepiness and need at the same time frowned up at him. She barely managed to ask, "Why not?"

The slurring of her words filled him with a sickening confidence that he was right. He hated that he was right, but he knew… "Not like this," he whispered, shaking his head a fraction of an inch back and forth. "Not when you're not entirely in control. Not when it could just as much be…the…alcohol……"

He hadn't even finished his sentence when her eyes drifted close, and her grip around his neck softened. How many shots had she taken? Of saké, no less – not exactly the lowest proofed drink on the market, though neither was it the highest. But two empty bottles of saké on the coffee table, even split between Ash and Alycia, was a lot.

God did he want her. But not like this.

Never without her sober permission.

As gently as he could, he slid her arm off of his neck and lightly laid it on her stomach, and then covered her with the sheets and comforter.

Then, for only a moment, he stared down at her gentle face, beautiful and warm in the pale light. His heart ached, and the sourness of regret crept into him. Not for his decision now, but for the decision still ahead of him.

Clenching his hands into fists, he circled around the bed and left the room, softly closing the door behind him. Emmi was gone, the spare bedroom door closed, and the lights were all off in the apartment, except for a soft orange one glowing above the stove top. He glanced at Ash on the couch, saw that Emmi had covered them with a blanket. Confident that Ash wouldn't wake, he pulled on his shoes and snuck out of the apartment.

He wasn't sleepy, even with two glasses of plum wine in him. But energy still surged through his veins, and two hours of sitting in front of a movie had left him unusually restless.

Across the hall was the door to where Tom and Shara had disappeared into, and he wondered for a moment if they were still awake or not. Should he knock?

Deciding against it, he wandered down the hall to the elevators and summoned one. Without really knowing where he was going, Chris pressed the button for two floors below, and then got out into the business-like section he'd seen earlier.

It looked different at night. There were no people in cubicles or rushing about, and most lights were turned out, leaving only emergency lights permanently lit in the ceiling at regular intervals. Hoping that he remembered where to go, he retraced his earlier steps towards the medical ward. Whether through luck or some strange new superior sense of direction, he found his way, and he peeked into the hospital-like room that he had briefly shared with Alycia's mother.

The lights were dimmed, but Mia's bed was still well-illuminated. As was Shara, sitting in a chair next to her and idly chatting with Mia.

He hadn't made a sound, as far as he knew, but Shara turned to him the moment he peered inside, and smiled. "Chris," she spoke softly.

Mia followed Shara's gaze, and smiled somewhat drunkenly, albeit for reasons entirely different from her daughter. "Sorry," Chris said quickly. "I didn't know you were awake. I just…"

"Please," Mia interrupted softly, her voice scratchy from the now-absent breathing tube. She lazily waved her hand to beckon him. "Come in. We were just talking about you."

"…Oh," he said, and uneasily walked further into the room. "I mean…all good things, I hope?"

Shara laughed and a dreamy smile crossed Mia's face. "Yes," Mia replied with a long, exaggerated nod. "I woke…a few minutes ago. Shara was here. Told me…"

When Mia didn't finish immediately, Shara did so for her, "That everyone made it safely, and that she healed you with magic."

Mia's eyes widened in sleepy glee. "I have powers!" She giggled. "Who would have thought."

Was she on pain killers? Or just so out of it from how far she'd pushed her body?

Inwardly shrugging, Chris stepped up to her bedside opposite of where Shara sat and smiled down at Mia. "Well, I knew you had *some* power, I just didn't know what it was."

She grasped his hand weakly, and then patted it. "I couldn't let my daughter endure watching you die."

A heavy pressure built up in his chest, working its way slowly up into his throat. "Thank you." He nodded, and said it again. "Thank you."

Smiling dreamily, she nodded. "Thank you for bringing me back. For giving me my family back. Or…for giving me back…to…my…"

"To your family," he finished for her, nodding. She agreed by way of patting his hand. "I'm glad I could help. And I promise you." He grasped her hand between both of his. "I promise that I'll watch after Alycia." He added in his thoughts, *For as long as I'm still alive.*

Mia's eyes drifted closed, and her hand slackened in his grip. He set it down, and then looked at Shara. He swore he hadn't said that last bit out loud, but the sharp look she gave him was full of suspicion.

Drawing in a breath, Shara stood up. "Still wide awake?" she whispered.

"Not even remotely tired," he confirmed.

Glancing at Mia, Shara said, "It's a side effect from being magically healed. You'll probably not sleep again for a good twenty four hours. And I slept last night, so I'm good for a few days." She motioned for him to follow her as she headed for the exit. "Come on, keep me company."

Raising an amused eyebrow, he mockingly whispered, "Yes, ma'am."

Shara didn't reply, and together they headed silently back towards the elevator, passing a nurse on their way out. What did Shara have in mind? Would she take them down to the street, and explore Osaka? If they did that, at the very least, Shara would need to hide her ears. Anime-like hair and eyes weren't entirely uncommon in Japan, he reasoned, but the ears would probably raise too much interest, regardless of how few people were still out and about this late at night.

But no, when they entered the elevator, she pressed the button for the top floor. He frowned at that, but once the lift stopped and the doors opened again, he understood – much like the Sentinel tower, they were brought up to a waiting room, with access out onto a rooftop heliport.

Except, like everything else in the building, the waiting room was much nicer. A better description was a lounge, with comfy couches, fancy coffee tables, an automatic coffee/espresso/latte machine, and wraparound windows.

Without hesitation, Shara strode across the burgundy-carpeted floor and opened the doors out onto the pad, but then stopped short, with Chris almost bumping into her. A very chilly, humid breeze greeted them. It was, after all, still winter, even if they were towards the southern end of a Pacific island nation.

"I guess I didn't think that one through," Shara surmised. "I know it's warmer in Osaka than Denver during the winter, but the humidity and cooler temps at night..."

Staring outside for a second, Chris shrugged, and motioned to the empty lounge. "We can just hang out here."

Pursing her lips, Shara nodded and let the door close. "Good idea."

While she strode over to one of the couches, Chris walked up to the coffee station and started surveying the different packets and options. Looking back at Shara as she sat down on the side of a couch furthest from the outside door, he asked, "Coffee?"

"I'm…" She shivered and rubbed her bare arms. "You know what? Yeah. Whatever they have that's sweet."

He wasn't exactly sure how this automated latte machine was with sweetness, but he read over the instructions, or rather looked over the pictures on the instruction, since he couldn't read the written language, and started making what he hoped was a latte. The first packet he selected *looked* like it might be powdered milk or froth…

The silence within the lounge was deafening. The soundproofing was so good that if there was a howling wind out on top of the tower, they couldn't hear it. And somehow, the quiet between them felt unnerving. Keeping his back to her, watching the coffee machine sputter out white liquid into the cup before it opened and awaited a coffee packet, Chris considered why the awkwardness.

The answer came to him moments later – because he was once attracted to her. Still was, if he was being honest with himself, but never-the-less, Shara had known about his crush on her, and she had confronted him about it.

In the end, he had chosen Alycia.

How did Shara feel about that? Did she feel like Chris judged her as being less than Alycia or something?

The coffee machine finished, and he pulled his cup out and sniffed. It smelled like coffee, for sure, and it was hot, but there wasn't a hint of sweetness to it. So he grabbed a sugar packet (he hoped – it was the yellow packet, but he still couldn't read the label) and dumped it in, before tentatively taking a sip.

It scalded the tip of his tongue.

"I don't think there's sugar in it, but we can sweeten it," he informed Shara over his shoulder. "And, uh, I can't read the labels on the different types of coffee, sooo…"

"Surprise me, then," Shara said, her voice surprisingly pleasant. "But bring all of the sugar packets over."

He nodded, and as quickly as the machine would allow, made another latte for her, before taking the cups over to the coffee table, and then going back to retrieve the tray of sweetener packets. He sat down on the couch next to her, so that they both sat in the corner, but there was still ample distance between them that he didn't feel too uncomfortable.

Finally, after dumping three packets of sweetener into her drink, Shara took a sip, sighed contentedly, and leaned back, draping her left arm on the couch arm.

"You don't have to be afraid of me, you know," she arched an eyebrow at him.

Warmth crept into his cheeks. "Uh," he replied ever-so-eloquently, and continued to avert his gaze from her.

"I'm not gonna bite your head off or anything, kid," she said, amusement coloring her voice. "I'm happy for you. For *both* of you."

Biting the inside of his cheek for a moment, he forced himself to look up, into her eyes. Those violet, gorgeous eyes that had first come to him in a magic-induced dream. It'd only been six months ago. It felt like it'd been years ago. Miles ago. *Lightyears* ago.

At a loss for words, he searched her face, thinking about what he could possibly say in response to that. He settled on, "Thanks."

She smiled, and took another sip from her coffee. He tried his again, but it was still too hot to drink. "And I'm glad you're not doll dizzy anymore," she added.

Shara's words took several seconds to register on Chris, and when he realized what she'd said, he frowned and looked at her curiously. "Doll dizzy?"

After returning his stare, Shara's cheeks pinked a little. "Sorry. Old slang folks used to use back in…" She thought about it for a second, her eyebrows creased forward in a way that almost made her look like a blue-haired Vulcan. "You know, I don't remember the last time they used that phrase."

He smiled, but inwardly he had to remind himself that Shara was from another age. Another *world.* And she was well over eighty years old. Hearing Jack Sparrow's voice in his head, he thought, *It would never have worked out between us.*

Another moment of silence passed between them before Shara asked, "So what are you going to do about your problem?"

Furrowing his brow, he asked, "What problem?"

"Oh, you know," Shara shrugged. "The fact that you're still

prepared to die to destroy Marduk." Chris gaped at her, wondering how she knew. "That you're *convinced* you'll have to, even if you tried to *convince* yourself you'd find another way." Holding her coffee in her right hand, she drew up her left and rested her chin in her palm, staring at him. "A person cannot possibly find peace within themselves if they are intent upon following two contradictory paths."

Pressing his lips into a thin line, Chris let out a heavy breath, and nodded. "I know," he said quietly. "I don't know what path to choose. What to think. Hell, I don't even know what to *do*," half-shouted, anger and frustration directed at himself more than anything. "How can I possibly beat Nabu, let alone have a chance to go up against Marduk?"

Shara stared at him evenly, her chin still settled on her hand, but her earlier smile was gone. "There you go again," she said quietly. "Thinking it's all on your shoulders."

"Wh...it is!" He flailed his free hand about, barely restraining the other but still managing to spill a little hot coffee on his knuckles. He hissed, switched the cup to his other hand, and sucked the rapidly-cooling liquid off. "Dammit." Shaking his head, he looked again at Shara, and said, "This is my burden, isn't it? I'm the Champion. That's what Tattannu called me once. I'm the one destined to defeat them both, aren't I?"

"Maybe," Shara conceded. "But why does that mean you can't have help doing it?"

Blinking his eyes in a deliberate motion, he waved downwards, towards the hospitalized Mia. "Because anyone who helps me puts themselves in harm's way."

For the first time that night, Shara gave him an indignant, even furious stare. "Oh, and we're too weak to do that?"

"What?" He flapped his lips for a second. "Uh, no, that's not what I meant, not at all!"

"Because that's what it sounds like," she leaned forward and gruffly set her coffee down, sitting on the edge of the couch. "You make us all feel like we're useless weight, holding you back, keeping you from your damned mission."

"I-"

"When the only reason we've gotten as far as we have is *because* we've been a team," she continued speaking over him.

"Well, I-"

"We've all risked ourselves, all acted to help *each other* through this, because THAT'S WHAT WE DO," she shouted that last part. "We look out for each other, we help each other, that's what it means to be a Sentinel! Haven't you figured that out yet? Haven't you realized that being a Sentinel means you don't have to be alone? That together we're stronger?"

Chris was torn between wanting to apologize and concede and wanting to rebuke her. Her yelling at him hadn't helped, and the repressed rebellious streak he'd nursed throughout his entire childhood and teen years wanted to rear its head like an ugly monster.

So he said it before he thought about his words, "Then show me! Eh? Show me how you can help me."

Raising her eyebrows up, she asked, "Oh? You want me to help you? Fine," she slapped her knees and stood up, and then grappled his forearm in an iron grip. "Come on."

As she tugged him away from the couches and towards the rooftop exit, he asked, "Wait, where? What are you gonna do?"

Shoving one of the doors open, she yanked him out into the frigid cold air, and said, "I'm gonna teach your happy ass how to fly."

CHAPTER 20

"Don't throw me off the roof!"

Shara came up short, and gaped back at Chris. "What?!"

The bite of a cold breeze sent shivers and goose bumps all up and down Chris's chest and arms, and he tried to yank his hand free of her iron grip. The shock and even hurt expression Shara gave him did little to dissuade his line of thought. "I can't fly! If you throw me off…"

Incredulous, Shara released his arm and shook her head, "Gods, Chris, I would never do that! What kind of person do you think I am?"

Rethinking, but glad to have his arm back under his control, he resisted the urge to back up towards the lounge doors. "Well…I've never seen you so pissed off before. I don't know what you do when your temper flares like that."

Shara's frown held for a moment, and then broke down into a laugh. "Then you've never seen Tom and I argue, have you? Wait," she frowned, "Yes you have."

"Well I never saw you drag him out onto a roof and threaten to 'teach him how to fly,'" Chris countered defensively.

Rolling her eyes in Emmi-like fashion, Shara shook her head with a bemused grin. "Chris, I meant it literally. And yes," her grin faltered, fire entering her eyes once more. "I'm still cross with you, and you're still a knucklehead, but I'm going to literally teach you how to fly."

Faltering, Chris barely registered what was happening as Shara grabbed his arm again and dragged him up into the middle of the currently-empty helipad in the middle of the roof. The wind howled again, and he furiously rubbed his chest with his free hand.

"But I can't fly," he protested. "That's not one of my powers."

"Actually it is," Shara replied, halting them in the middle of the pad and turning to face him. "And that's how I'm going to show you how I contribute. I've taught you to use your powers, hone your abilities – you wouldn't be where you are without me. But you've also experimented and learned new things on your own. Tonight, we're going to collaborate to come up with something new to you. You're going to fly, just like that woman in Detroit, and just like Nabu."

"The lady in Detroit had enchantments helping her," Chris continued to object. "I…" He paused, frowned. "I thought that the enchantment was what helped her, but you're saying it's arcane powers that let her fly?"

Releasing his hand again, and drawing her arms in around her chest, Shara nodded. "Exactly. Usually only those who have advanced training and a decade of practice can master the power needed, but," she nodded emphatically at Chris, "you have a leg up on all of the arcane casters on my world." Adding another shrug in, Shara said, "And besides, if you really expect to go toe-to-toe with Nabu again and stab that bitch with Imhullu, you need to be able to fly after her."

Looking around at the city, Chris shuddered at the idea of flying on his own power. Memories of his first flight in a helicopter didn't help, considering how much it had been jostled around by the flood of magic creating wind storms in the mountains.

Flying above razor-sharp, multi-story skyscrapers, with streets hundreds of feet below? That was not Chris's idea of fun.

"Yeah, well even if I can fly after her, Nabu can just portal away, right?" He looked at Shara, hopeful.

"Only if you let her," Shara replied while rubbing her ribs ever faster and harder. "It takes time, at least a few seconds, for her to picture where she wants to go, draw out the power, and form it into a portal. No one is as fast as Nina is at conjuring a portal. *No* one."

Grimacing, Chris looked around again. The tower that the Osaka Sentinels occupied was taller than all of the immediately-surrounding buildings, but not by much, and the glow of white, yellow, and other multi-colored lights and electronic billboards illuminated the chilled, humid night. *At least I'll be able to see where I'm going,* he thought, trying to encourage himself. *But...flying...* He shuddered again.

"Now, tell me," Shara began, pacing around him slowly and looking down at the helipad. "Knowing what your powers are, how could those be applied to help you fly?"

He thought for a second, and shook his head. "I mean, there's hardly any science involved in magic..."

"You know better than that," she lectured, eyes darting to look at him for only a second. He turned on the spot to follow her as she continued pacing. "Science and magic are more interlinked than most people could guess."

Raising an eyebrow, Chris nodded at her, "Except maybe for what you do. I mean, just where the hell does your clothes and anything in your pockets go when you shapeshift?"

With an amused grin, Shara shrugged. "I guess that does seem to fly in the face of conservation of mass, doesn't it?"

"Just a little," he remarked nervously.

"Well, I can't really say how that works either," Shara continued pacing, "But I know that you've already figured out some of your powers by applying your knowledge of physics to it."

Thinking back to when he and Ash's souls interfered with one another, he grudgingly nodded. "True."

"So how would you fly with your powers?"

He rubbed his arms for a second, and then looked at his hands. Creating an electromagnetic field wouldn't work, no matter what X-Men's Magneto would have you believe, even if he had magnets or metal in his shoes.

But the only other option he currently could think of wasn't exactly enticing – propelling energy directly out of his hands and feet, like a rocket or Iron Man. Except, despite what they show in Iron Man, it's not so easy to control and direct the energy necessary to propel one fast enough to fly, let alone hover.

And yet, Chris thought, *the woman in Detroit hovered like it was nothing.* He frowned, and whispered, "If she can do it, I can..."

"Exactly," Shara nodded enthusiastically, her hearing as sharp as ever. "She probably had an enchantment that gave her either extra energy, or helped her refine her control of her power. You have a million souls and an instinctual control over your powers that comes with those souls." She stopped her pacing and turned to face him directly, her back to the lounge doors. "You can do this."

He let out a misty breath, and nodded. "Alright." He decided to try the Iron Man route. It'd worked once before, with the cutting torch from the palm of his hand. If nothing else, it proved that no matter what heat his magic put out, his magic also protected him from his own powers. He wasn't exactly sure how *that* worked, but…

Shaking his head, Chris thought, *Focus!* And Shara echoed his thoughts, "You have to concentrate. Let go of your doubts, and find your center again. This will take a more precise control of your powers than you've ever done before, but I don't think it's too far off from your plasma shield."

Eyes growing wide, he looked at Shara. Plasma. That was the answer. Whenever he launched off a ball of plasma, he felt a recoil-like effect from it. Same with when he expelled a beam of arcane energy.

What if he kept the plasma charge in place? Could he harness and direct the energy?

Closing his eyes, Chris drew in a deep breath, and settled into his routine breathing exercise when he needed to focus or meditate. Breathe in four counts, hold seven, exhale slowly, imagining any stress leaving his body along with his breath, evaporating into the chill night air.

Seeing his golden core in front of him in the soul realm, Chris reached out and touched it, letting its power flow into him, into the very fiber of his being, and he redirected it like he'd done a thousand times. Molded it. Shaped it. Coerced it.

And directed it into balls of plasma energy in the palms of his hands.

Opening his eyes, he looked at those glowing energy spheres, which illuminated Shara and the landing pad immediately around them. The energy from the plasma was excited – like it *wanted* to be released, and like always, it threatened to rip free of his control of its own accord.

But these were smaller than the super-charged ones he'd always summoned in the past. He wasn't looking for an uncontrolled explosion, after all.

So he pointed his hands down, and he pressed that kinetic energy back into himself. The effect was almost immediate, an unexpected –

his arms were yanked up, nearly out of their sockets, wrenching his shoulders up.

But he held onto the energy, held onto the spheres, and dialed back the redirected power as much as he dared. And his feet left the ground for a split second before panic caught up and he terminated the flow of magic from his soul, and the spheres dispelled. His feet landed hard on the helipad, and his arms complained harshly.

"Yes!" Shara pumped her fist into the air. "You almost did it! Damn, you were so close!"

Rubbing one of his shoulders, he glared at her. "Yeah, I almost did it, alright. Almost yanked my arms right out of their sockets!"

"Oh, pshaw," she flipped her hand towards him dismissively. "You didn't know what to expect. You won't let that happen again, will you?" He eyed her through narrowed slits. "And you've had a taste now of what kind of energy can produce the kind of results you want. Like I said, instinct induced by a million souls at your back."

Sighing, Chris switched to rubbing his other shoulder. He was going to feel *that* in the morning…assuming he even slept tonight.

"Besides which," she looked down at his feet, "And don't take this the wrong way," her eyes moved up to his arms, "But I think your arms aren't quite strong enough to hold you up long-term. I mean, how many chin-ups can you do, for instance?"

He regarded Shara's arms, her defined muscles visible in her short-sleeve, silken shirt. Shara was definitely stronger than he was. Looking at his own biceps, however, he knew what she meant then. He didn't exactly lift weights, after all.

Thinking back to their final moments in Detroit, and the attacker that had hovered above them, he nodded. "You think I should direct the energy into my feet."

"I think you should do your feet *and* hands," she corrected. "At least at first, until you gain better control of this ability. Oh, and, uh," she glanced out into the city. "I wouldn't let yourself fly out past the building until you have a feel for it."

Nodding, he lowered his arms, and went back to work on focusing and drawing energy out of the golden core and into the real world. Only this time, he divided the same amount of energy out amongst his four extremities. At first he thought this a good idea, but then realized he probably needed more energy in his feet to lift himself up.

This will be different, he thought, and cringing as he did so, he opened his eyes to look down.

He wasn't sure what to expect. Maybe to see his shoes melting under intense plasma heat? His skin may have been immune to his powers, but were his clothes?

Apparently the answer was 'yes,' though he didn't know how that was possible – golden light surrounded his shoes, as well as his hands. It wasn't just balls of light in his hands this time, it was more like gloves and boots of energy.

He hadn't meant to shape the plasma in that way, but as he lifted his hands up and applied a minute amount of direction to the potential energy this way and that, he felt his hands pushed in the desired directions. The shape gave him more control. Granted both his hands and his feet were irregularly shaped, so it would be awkward at first to control, but with practice...

Looking down at his feet, he drew in a deep breath, and dared to apply the smallest pressure on the soles of his shoes.

And very nearly lost his balance the instant his feet lifted from the ground. He waved his hands about, expelling some energy without thinking about it, which only made him start to lose his balance more.

"Shit," he started, "Shit, shit shit SHIT!" Before he knew what he was doing, he was floating faster and faster towards the edge of the pad.

"Cut power!" Shara shouted.

But it was too late. He shot out over the edge of the roof, and the city streets lay hundreds of feet beneath him.

Chris fell!

There was no turning back, so as he fell faster and faster, he thrust his hands down and rigidly held them in place, easing power into them. The road rushed up at him, the freezing wind whipped around his body, and memories of that last night in Denver flashed into the forefront of his thoughts.

The power in his hands helped turn him upright, and when he had only a half-dozen stories left to spare, he pushed down with the power in his feet. His descent rapidly slowed, and his knees started to buckle under the G forces, but it halted his descent, and he very nearly cheered.

Except he hadn't stopped pushing power into the soles of his shoes, and suddenly he was propelled up, rocketing faster and faster, his legs threatening to give out under the strain. "Crap, dammit, SHIT!" It was only after he roared back up past the top of the roof, a bewildered and relieved Shara sprinting to the side of the building, that he stopped directing the energy out of his feet.

His rapid ascent slowed. Stopped.

And then he started to fall again.

He was headed right for the sharpened spire of a radio antenna atop a neighboring building, the biting-cold air whipping by him with his momentum.

"Aw, hell," he cursed, and thrust his hands forward while pushing energy back into his feet. Which sent him into a backwards thrust, and a few seconds later, he rocketed past and over Shara.

He pushed his hands back to stop his backwards momentum, and then began to ease it off, lowering his hands as his momentum stopped, testing the energy he directed into his feet.

Until, after what felt simultaneously like an age and a nanosecond, he hovered.

Finally.

Somewhere out there, amongst the spires of Osaka, his heart and stomach were trying very hard to catch up to him. But for now, he was okay.

And he was flying!

The mix of elation as he held his altitude, and terror as he looked down at the street far below, sent his heart racing, thumping hard in his chest, as if trying to escape this crazy human form that had nearly committed suicide.

Looking ahead at Shara, he drew in a breath, and knew he needed to get over to her. His hands began to shake, but he controlled them long enough to start easing forward. Without the direct downward thrust from his hands, he started to lose altitude, so he pushed a little more magic into his feet, and brought himself back to eye-level with her.

Slowly, grudgingly, and fighting against intense shivers, he eased back over to the edge of the roof, past Shara, and then slowly, carefully, set himself down on the helipad.

As soon as he cinched off the flow of magic and the glows receded from his hands and feet, his knees gave out, and he collapsed onto them, his hands slapping the concrete pad painfully, his numbing fingers protesting at the sudden sensation.

Shara was at his side in a heartbeat, arms wrapped around him. "Are you okay?" she asked, breathless.

He wanted to say yes. To act all cool and composed. Instead, something built up inside of him, starting in his chest and working its way up, until a fit of laughter just burst out of him. Giddy jitters, shivering against the cold, he just laughed. And laughed. And laughed some more.

"I...can't believe I just did that!" he looked at Shara. "I FLEW!"

Her concerned look softened, and transformed into a smile. "Yeah, you did," she nodded, and then pulled him up onto his feet. "Way to go, Peter Pan."

It was an old one, but none-the-less, Chris smiled at her pop-culture reference.

Then, grasping his arms around his chest, he said through chattering teeth, "Come on, I need to get warm."

She nodded, and while keeping her arms around him, walked them towards the lounge. "Yeah, I'll bet. Maybe next time, you should wear a jacket."

Grinning at her, he asked, "Think they have one in the lounge?"

Arching an eyebrow, she asked, "I don't know...why?"

Looking out at the city, he replied, "Because I'm gonna try again!"

CHAPTER 21

Unfortunately, there weren't any spare jackets in the lounge. Chris and Shara travelled down to the main Sentinel lobby and had to ask the night desk attendant where they might find some, which was an exercise in patience until the attendant used their phone and a translation app to assist with communications.

Once they found jackets that fit, the two of them returned to the roof, and Chris spent the next several hours flying. Every time he took off again, terror seized his chest, and every time he flew out over the streets far below, adrenaline rushed through him and set his extremities tingling.

Higher and higher he flew, faster and further away, before returning each time. His ability to control his flight became more nuanced, and despite wearing no such armor like Iron Man, he started taking chances. Grazing closer and closer to building sides at speed, weaving in and out of radio and cell towers, faster each time. Until he clipped his shoulder and spiraled down onto the roof of a five-story building. If it hadn't been for the thick, warm jacket he'd borrowed, he would have scrapped up his back along the roughened surface.

The scariest part, however, was when he strayed too far from the Sentinel tower, and lost his way back.

The world was a different place from high up, and everything blended together, especially when his only guides were street lights, occasionally lit-up windows, and bright advertisement boards in a language that he didn't understand.

Panic gripped him at first, and he started racing around above, trying desperately to get his bearings. If there were landscape features nearby to orient himself against, he couldn't see them in the night.

At one point, he came across a vast park-like area next to a train yard, and he paused a moment in his panic to stare at an ornate, tiered, pagoda-like structure in the middle, and he thought he remembered reading about that building in some tourist website — Osaka Castle.

Somehow, that sight calmed him, soothed him, and he smiled. He was in Japan, in Osaka, for the first time in his life! There was nothing to panic over.

Recalling that he'd seen a canal-like river near the Sentinel tower, he flew over the castle towards another one just like it, and followed it to his left. The river wound and curved through the city, with some parts joining it and then splitting off again. Letting instincts guide him, Chris kept to the left, even when he came upon a strange, four-way intersection of the canal system. Shortly after that, familiar sights greeted him, and he recognized the tower, so he sped towards it.

Shara wasn't up on the roof, and he wondered if she had grown worried about him in his longer absence, so he gently set down right in front of the doors into the lounge. Surprisingly, not only was Shara inside, but so was Emmi, and they had watched him land, with a wide-eyed look on Emmi's face.

Letting himself in and shivering despite the jacket, he couldn't help but grin at his best friend. "Hey, there," he said brightly. "Couldn't sleep?"

"Uh," was all she managed to say at first. "Um. No. I came up here to just relax and meditate, and saw Shara out on the roof. She just filled me on what you could do, and I couldn't believe it until I saw it!"

He nodded, and then let out a contented sigh. "It's…it's incredible!"

Emmi's shock and awe began to wear off after that, and she gave him a curious look. "So what happened to being afraid to fly?"

"Oh, I still am," he shrugged. "But this…" Looking out the windows at the city, the memories alone filled him with elation. "This is different. No tin can trapping me, and I have full control over my abilities." Turning back to the ladies, his face hurt with how broad his smile was. "I could definitely get used to this."

By now, it was well past midnight in Osaka, but just as Shara predicted, Chris didn't feel the least bit sleepy. Even expending energy into his magic hadn't slowed him down. Emmi likewise was just too anxious about their situation, and since Shara could go days without sleep, the trio stayed up in the lounge for several more hours, enjoying coffee or tea and chatting the night away.

A familiarity had formed between Emmi and Shara, stronger than when they'd bonded at the cabin in the mountains, and it made Chris happy to see Emmi smiling again. The two had a few inside jokes they traded at Chris's expense, but he didn't mind.

When the first glow of dawn appeared in the sky, they decided to head back down to the apartments and see if anyone else was awake. Chris and Emmi returned to their accommodation and found Ash still sprawled out on the couch, their mouth hanging open and light snores escaping them.

Chris peeked in on Alycia and found her snoring a lot louder. He'd never heard her snore in all the time they'd been on the run, so he reasoned it was a response to how drunk she'd gotten. With no one else to talk to, but not wanting to worry either of their roommates when they woke, Emmi and Chris found a spot on the carpet away from Ash, and meditated.

When Naomi greeted him in the soul realm, he was delighted to tell her all about his new abilities, and she grinned from ear to ear over his description.

"My little brother," she mused after he told her about the castle, "Flying around Japan. Doesn't it scare you, though? Nothing beneath you, just magic to keep you aloft?"

"If the Barrier were still here, I'd be nervous about losing my power at the wrong moment," he conceded as they paced around the golden sphere of magic. "But there's something about it…I *do* feel terror each time, but that vanishes when I don't fall. There's more to it, though," he frowned and stopped their walk so that he could face her fully. "It's like whenever I fly, I'm defying death. Naturally I'm supposed to fall to my doom, but when I don't, I feel like I can do anything. *Anything!*"

Her grin faded, but not like it did when he gave her bad news. Her expression morphed into something else entirely – a look of hope. "Including survive the coming battle?"

Cautiously, he nodded. "Maybe. I don't know. Every time I think I know how magic works, how it *should* work, it surprises me again."

A giddy laugh escaped Naomi, and she rushed forward to hug him, clenching tightly. "There! That's the Chris I was looking for. The one who still had hope."

Frowning despite the grin on his face, Chris returned the hug, holding his sister tight. "Well I've not exactly had much reason to hope lately, have I?"

"But now you do," she drew away from him, cupping his cheek in her hand. "So don't let go of that hope. No matter what happens. You keep fighting to stay alive, okay?"

The elation within him faltered, and he remembered Tattannu's last words to him. "I…"

The pressure from her hand increased, and she forced him to look into her deep, dark eyes. "No, don't! Don't go down that path again, Chris. Keep the hope alive, you hear me?"

Clamping his mouth shut, he tried to find the steely resolve he hoped was somewhere inside.

Before he could, something in the real world startled him awake, and he blinked his eyes open, tearing him out of the Soul Realm.

A knock at the door.

Ash stirred, jolting up. "Bwah? Whuzzat?"

Emmi, who likewise was drawn from her meditation, grinned, and together they stood up. Chris plodded over to the door and opened it to find Yua standing before him, a pleasant smile upon her face. There was also an earnestness in her eyes, almost hidden in her show of friendliness, that put Chris on edge.

"Good morning," she said. "The scroll has arrived. Would you like to join your companions for some breakfast before you join us in the conference room?"

Chris blinked, and then turned back in time to see Ash stretch, their mouth wide-open as a loud yawn escaped.

"Uh, sure," he nodded to Yua. "Just give me a minute to rouse Alycia."

The door across the hall opened, and Tom and Shara stepped out. Either they'd heard Yua knocking on their door, or Yua had gone to them first.

"As you wish," Yua bowed, and then headed down the hall

towards Babbar, Marisol, and Tiana's apartment.

Nodding at Tom and Shara, Chris gently closed the door, and returned to the bedroom to rouse Alycia.

She was not happy about it.

Half an hour later, the U.S. Sentinels were finishing up an unusual breakfast in the cafeteria – rice, eggs, fish, and miso soup. Far from what Chris was used to. He could have chosen cereal instead, but he was curious about all but the fish (which seemed too strange to him to eat for breakfast.)

For probably the tenth time since they'd arrived in Osaka, Chris found himself realizing just how little he knew about the world, about other cultures and customs. It made him want to travel more, to see and experience more.

Once everyone was finished, they were led to the same conference room as before, with every square inch of wall covered in LED screens. And in the center of the table lay a sealed, steel-looking cylinder, about four inches in diameter and two feet long, presumably containing the ancient scroll.

Standing beside it was a man that Chris had never met, an elderly Japanese man, his head completely bald, either from age or from shaving, and a strikingly white, long beard and moustache. Beside him stood Sato, who greeted Chris and the others as Yua led them all in.

"Ah, hello," the newcomer spoke in almost perfect English, hardly a hint of an accent.

Yua stepped ahead of the U.S. Sentinels and motioned to the man, "This is Professor Kaito Takahashi. He's an expert on ancient relics and languages."

Bowing deeper than Chris expected, Kaito said, "A pleasure to meet you all."

As Tom stepped ahead of the rest, Yua motioned to him, "This is Commander Thomas Taylor." And from there, she introduced the rest of the U.S. Sentinels, with Kaito bowing each time. He seemed particularly interested and excited to meet Shara and Babbar.

"Now," the professor began as he stooped over the table and collected the steel cylinder, "If you will excuse me, I will take the scroll to the clean room and open it. It has not been opened in quite some time, so we need to ensure a completely controlled environment to preserve it."

"We need to be able to see it," Tom objected, halting Kaito before he could leave.

Nodding at the LED walls, Kaito replied, "You will, I assure you. Together we shall all examine it."

Excusing himself, Saito bustled out, and the Sentinels began to take their seats, with Tom and Sato taking up heads of the table again. "Can we call Abby to be in on this?" Tom asked Yua.

Smiling, Yua replied, "She is already on standby." Depressing a button on the table-top, a panel opened up, allowing Yua to retrieve a tablet and tap in a few commands. A second later, the LED panel to Tom's left, directly in front of Chris, lit up, and Abby's beautiful, smiling face beamed back at them.

"Good afternoon, all you lovely people," Abby popped. *"Oh! I mean, good morning. It is morning over there, isn't it?"*

"It is," Tom nodded.

"It's wonderful to see you again!" Emmi chimed in.

"We missed your charming smile, love," Shara cooed.

"Dawww," Abby visibly blushed, even though she was already wearing blush, and swished back and forth in her chair. *"You guys are too much! I missed you too. Phone and radio conversations just aren't the same, are they?"*

"No, they're not," Shara agreed, almost too eagerly.

"Well then," Tom turned to Yua. "How long until the professor is ready?"

"I would say at least fifteen minutes," Yua replied. "He will need to don a hermetically-sealed suit and ensure the lab checks out on all of its seals before opening the scroll."

"In that case," Tom turned to Chris. "Would you and Shara like to fill everyone else in on your escapades last night?"

Chris's cheeks warmed, and he looked around the room, specifically at Alycia next to him. How much did she remember from when he'd helped her to bed?

But that wasn't what Tom was talking about, and there was no *way* he could know what had almost happened between Chris and Alycia.

Was there?

Clearing his throat, Chris explained to everyone about Shara's insistence that he could fly, and how he learned how to do so. Despite the fact that he had flown for hours, the explanation itself took mere minutes, and he felt he didn't do the topic justice.

The reaction from everyone, however, said otherwise. Tiana was the first to chime in. "Does this mean you won't let me be your pilot anymore?"

"Uh," Chris started. "Well, I mean sure." He felt like he was lying through his teeth, but then decided to opt for honesty. "I mean, depending on what's going on. I feel…that is, flying on my own power is safer…well, that is, you're safe. I mean, you're skilled. You know. I just…don't like being trapped in-"

"A tin can thousands of feet up?" Tiana interrupted him, her tone indignant. "Yes, you've mentioned that before."

"Hey, you're a damn good pilot," he insisted. "And I'll fly with you any day!"

"Uh huh," she grimaced and turned away from him, rubbing at the sides of her head. She usually kept her sides trimmed almost to the skin, but three months on the run meant her hair had grown out considerably, and she kept rubbing it consciously.

"T," he started to object, but she ignored him.

A moment of awkward silence passed, and he didn't know what to say. He had always been terrified of going up in human-made aircraft, it was nothing new. But the look of betrayal in Tiana's eyes took him by surprise.

"Um, what did it feel like?" Alycia asked, no doubt to lighten the mood. "Other than scary, I mean."

"It was…" He thought for a moment, and finished, "Cold. Damn cold. But it also felt freeing, like nothing could hold me back. Nothing could hold me down or keep me from doing anything I wanted."

The smile that plastered Alycia's face warmed him, but did little to overcome the guilt he felt over Tiana.

The screen to the right of Abby (from Chris's perspective) flickered, and a view of Professor Takahashi, donning a fully-sealed, white-colored suit, with a transparent plastic window on the front, appeared. The professor wore a headset similar to a hands-free telephone kit, with the mic just to the side of his mouth, and he nodded.

Without any ceremony, he said, *"I am ready to go. Are you?"*

His question was curt, with a hint of impatience in it.

Sato spoke, and Yua translated for everyone else's benefit, "Yes, Professor. Please proceed."

Further down the wall from the professor's visage, another stream flickered to life, a top-down view of a table, upon which rested the steel-looking cylinder. Kaito's gloved hands entered the viewing area, and he gripped the cylinder tightly and began to unscrew one end of it. The threads on the screw were extremely fine, and it felt like it took an inordinate amount of time to open it.

With each passing moment, Chris grew more and more anxious, adjusting his posture and leaning forward. This was it. This could have all of the answers. The Dragonstone, Imhullu, how to defeat Nabu...

The end finally came loose. The professor very carefully and deliberately set the cap off to one side, out of view of the camera, and then slowly, carefully reached in.

What he pulled out was not at all what Chris was expecting. He had seen images of ancient Japanese scrolls, and they were always made of some paper-like material, rolled up onto or into a ceramic or wooden casing. Sometimes it was a single roll, while sometimes it was two, and only a section of longer scrolls were viewable at a time as they were expanded out and rolled and unrolled.

This scroll was not made of paper. It was still mounted upon and wrapped around a single, tapered center piece, which Chris thought might be called a dowel, but the material that the scroll was made of looked like long, narrow segments of wood, probably bamboo strips, if he had to guess. An inch from the top and bottom, it was obvious that there was something string-like that ran through tiny holes on either side of the strips, linking them together.

"I should say that this is the most unique scroll I have ever seen," the professor stated confidently. *"Scrolls of this age were usually made of early forms of paper that could absorb ink, retaining their writings longer. I do not know if the contents of this scroll will be readable or not."*

Yua translated for Sato, who spoke in return, and Yua translated back, "Thank you, Professor. Please proceed at your discretion."

"Of course," he replied, the barest hint of annoyance in his tone.

Setting the container aside, the professor very carefully spun the scroll so that the line where the scroll ended was visible. Just above the seam were remnants of two symbols, worn so badly that they were almost impossible to discern, but apparently clear enough to have triggered Abby's search algorithm.

Slowly, carefully, the professor began to unroll the scroll vertically.

The writing and artwork were contained on the inside of the scroll, and it became immediately apparent that much of it had been worn away with time. *"More than likely, paint rather than ink was used, due to the nature of the medium,"* the professor explained as he methodically unrolled one segment at a time. *"And it looks as though some form of lacquer was applied after the fact in an attempt to preserve it, but the lacquer eroded over time, exposing the interior."*

The bottom of the scroll was entirely written words, no doubt a form of ancient Japanese, though Chris couldn't begin to guess what it said, and much of it was severely degraded. As the professor continued to unroll it, however, the writing ceased, and artwork became visible.

There was no mistaking what was in the artwork, and Chris immediately suspected that it made this scroll the most unusual in history – an image of a Babylonian ziggurat, and what looked like worn writing in what Chris knew to be cuneiform.

As the top of the scroll was finally unraveled, and the squared temple atop the ziggurat became visible, Chris drew in a surprised breath. "I recognize that structure," he said. "Even as worn as that painting is."

There was no mistaking the golden sphere in the center of the room at the top, even if it was relatively tiny. It was supposed to be the golden core that Chris and Ash shared. The temple from his vision after touching the Dragonstone.

To the left, hovering in the air next to the structure, was a dagger, which even as worn as the depiction was, Chris knew had to be Imhullu. To the right was a circular stone. The Dragonstone.

"I recognize it, too," Ash said, a haunted tone in their voice. "I've been there. In my dreams."

"With Tattannu?" Chris asked. Ash nodded. "Me too. It was where I first learned about our lineage."

He looked at the screen again. At the ziggurat. At the cuneiform above and the Japanese below.

It was all ruined. All so worn that they might be missing vital information.

Was this all a dead end?

A sudden bright light blinked into existence at the top of the scroll, drawing Chris's eye. The golden circle was glowing, a lens flare appearing on the camera. Behind the image of the ziggurat, a new image appeared, one that Chris knew hadn't been there seconds ago.

It was a dragon, serpentine, winged, horned, and ferocious. It's wings moved upon the scroll, opening wide to encompass the entire top half, dwarfing the ziggurat. A ruby-shaped emblem was embedded upon its head, right between and above the eyes, and it flared brightly, a shade of light that Chris was altogether familiar with.

Atop Babbar's shoulder, he heard Nina chirp and chortle.

The red and the gold flared brighter, and merged into a single, blinding white light that extended out of the image on the LED TV and into the room.

Darkness followed.

CHAPTER 22

The soft flicker of yellowed candle light greeted Chris, a warm glow against the cold darkness. It was blinding after being in the dark for so long.

A lantern hung from a rafter, yellowed rice paper surrounding the source of illumination. It grew brighter with every passing moment, but at the same time, Chris's eyes adjusted, and he was able to take in his surroundings. Wood planks creaked beneath his footsteps, the smell of sawdust wafted past his nose, and he drew in the scent, something familiar and alien about it all at once.

Another candle flicker caught his attention, and he turned to find a man in a black and gray kimono sitting cross-legged before a low workbench. Tools such as various-sized and shaped saws and carving implements adorned the wall in neat, tidy rows.

But it wasn't a carved masterpiece that the man stooped over. As Chris slowly walked around to the man's left, he saw the bamboo scroll laid out, and the man carefully wrote beneath the beautiful, pristine painting of the temple with a fine-tipped paint brush.

As the man worked, slowly, carefully writing out calligraphic shapes, his hand and brush glowed a shade of lavender, yet despite the obvious magic involved, Chris could feel nothing.

Now standing ten feet to the man's left, Chris had a better view of his profile. His kimono fit somewhat loosely, and his face was gaunt and bony. His black hair was streaked with strands of white, and there were obvious crows' feet at the corners of his eyes, which had the same spark of lavender glowing in them as his hands did.

"H-hello?" Chris asked. Something was familiar about the man, he realized. Something from a dream.

The man ignored him at first, as he moved from one letter to the next, occasionally dipping his brush tip in a bowl of black paint.

"I'm Christopher Tatsu," he tried again.

The man continued to work. His left hand rose for a moment as he finished a column, and then the glow in his brush and eyes faded, and he let out a sigh. With careful grace, he placed the paint brush horizontally on one edge of the bowl, and then turned to Chris.

Speaking in a quiet, deep voice, he nodded. "That is an unusual name."

Cheeks burning a little, Chris looked down. "Yeah, well. My father didn't exactly want me in his life to begin with, so…"

The man nodded thoughtfully. A second later, he carefully unfolded his legs and stood up. Bowing, he said, "Apologies. My name is Tatsua Akagai."

A frown drew down Chris's face. "Your name is Tatsua?"

The man gave Chris a plaintive look. "Do you really know so little about your own ancestral culture?"

Something burned in Chris's chest, indignation ingrained deep inside of him. The man sounded like his father. "I don't…know what you mean?"

"My surname is Tatsua," he explained. "My 'first name,' as you might say, would be Akagai."

Gritting his teeth, Chris replied, "I know that much. I've watched enough anime to understand how Japanese names work. I was just surprised that your name is Tatsua, not Tatsu."

The man's expression hardened, very subtly, but enough to make Chris's stomach sour. "Nevertheless," he said, his voice growing stronger, "You will call me Sensei, if you wish to address me."

The growing rebellious streak in Chris reared its head. "Oh, really?" Sighing and planting his hands on his hips, Chris shook his head. "I'm not here for a lecture or a review of my failures as a 'son of Japan,' or whatever. In fact," he looked around the workshop, but only half of the walls appeared, the rest were shrouded in blackness. "I don't even know why I'm here."

"You are here because you are the Champion," Akagai said. He unfolded his arms from his wide kimono sleeves and motioned to the scroll. "You are here because you have found my scroll."

Chris looked down at the oddity with a frown. There was no hint of a dragon behind the ziggurat, and the images of Imhullu and the Dragonstone had not yet been painted in. "I don't think I understand," Chris looked back at Akagai.

"That is of no surprise," Akagai replied. It was all Chris could do not to scoff at the old man and walk away. Akagai began to pace back and forth in the confines of the half-rendered workshop. "You see, there was a time when the one known as Nabu almost succeeded in destroying the Barrier. Magic seeped into the world again, resulting in innumerable anomalies everywhere. Among them was that my mother and I discovered our ability to focus our chi into the real world. To use magic, as you call it. That was when my father explained our history, our legacy, passed down through the generations."

Halting his pacing in front of the bench, he looked at Chris with eyes not too dissimilar to his father's. "However, when I asked Grandfather, his rendition of our legacy differed somewhat. I knew then that it was important to find out as much of the truth as I could, and then record it." Motioning to the scroll, he continued, "Thus the scroll before you. By the age you see me as now, my ability to enchant had become almost second nature to me. My father never approved, as he believed it was our duty to protect the Barrier, and heal the cracks. However, I knew that I had to do one thing before I ceased using my powers."

Looking at Chris carefully, he finished, "I must pass on the knowledge to the one who would fulfill our destiny. The one known as the Champion."

Chris nodded thoughtfully, but avoided Akagai's critical gaze. Instead, he focused on the scroll. Then, a thought sparked in his head. "Wait, you're an enchanter?"

"Indeed I am," Akagai said, a condescending smile on his lips. "Good. You recognized that fact and its importance sooner than I anticipated you would."

Scowling at the other's attitude, Chris folded his arms in front of himself. "So those who are descendants from Tattannu aren't just arcane wielders." That title sounded stupid, and Chris decided that, at a later date, he would start to come up with proper names for the different kinds of magic wielders in the world.

"Exactly true," Akagai nodded, and folded his hands inside of his kimono sleeves. "By design, no less, as my scroll will tell you."

Grimacing, Chris shook his head. "Yeah, about that. The scroll is kind of degraded by my time. We can't really read it. Not all of it, anyway."

Akagai didn't look the least bit surprised. When Chris said nothing more, Akagai huffed out an impatient sigh and said, "Thus my enchantments, young one. Once completed, whenever one who is a descendant of Tattannu sees it will come here, and speak with me. Where I may relay the necessary information to him or her."

Chris nodded. "Alright. But then, two such descendants are looking at it right now. Where's Ash?"

"Right here," their familiar voice called. Chris spun around, and Ash appeared from the darkness. "I've been here the whole time. I just...felt like I didn't belong."

Looking at Ash with a critical gaze, Akagai's eyes darted back and forth between them and Chris. "I do not understand. There should be only one Champion. You," he nodded at Chris, "were the one to dismantle the Barrier."

"True," Chris smiled plaintively at Akagai, childishly happy to one-up the old man, "But then you don't know everything, do you? And Ash has as much right to be here as I do."

The forlorn look in Ash's eyes lightened, and a tiny hint of a smile lifted the crook of their mouth.

Scowling, Akagai spun around and faced his scroll. "It matters not," he said at length, while Ash joined him. "I shall relay the knowledge to you both, and let the gods judge you."

"Good," Ash nodded. "So what do you have to say to us?"

For a time, Akagai didn't turn to look at them, but he spoke over his shoulder. "It is the destiny of the Champion to sacrifice everything, in order to become one who can contend with Marduk and finally-"

"Well, we've gotta get through Nabu, first," Chris interrupted.

Akagai reeled on him, his mannerism belying his fury. "That is enough!" he hissed at Chris, and some markings on Akagai's skin briefly flared purple beneath his kimono. "Do not take your responsibilities lightly. Either of you!"

Rebellious streak or not, the fury in Akagai's eyes frightened Chris, and the sarcastic retort he had in mind died before ever leaving his tongue. He nodded silently for Akagai to continue.

At length, the old man began again. "Nabu is only a small part of the larger threat, and will be of little consequence if you accept who you are." Chris frowned at that, but didn't dare interrupt again. "You see, throughout the ages, as Tattannu's descendants have grown in number, so, too, have their abilities diverged. I am an enchanter. My mother was a shapeshifter. Every power imaginable and wieldable by human-kind have touched the core that resides within you," his eyes darted between Chris and Ash. "But to gain those abilities, you must become one with the souls within. You must sacrifice everything."

Chris didn't understand, and he conveyed that as much as he could through his expression. He wanted to say something, to say that Akagai's words were worse than a riddle. But then Ash sucked in a surprised breath. "Oh shit," they whispered. "Are...are you saying we need to go out like the Borg?"

Akagai frowned, but gave no other hint that he had no idea what Ash was talking about.

But Chris did. The Borg. One of the most infamous villains in the Star Trek Universe. Their strength came from their unity of mind and thought, so that their bodies acted as if controlled by one thought, one voice...

One soul.

He gaped at Ash, and they in turn stared wide-eyed at him. Chris was almost afraid to speak the words, but when he did, he turned his gaze back to Akagai. "It isn't enough that the souls within us power our magic. We...*I* have to let the souls become...become one with me?"

Akagai folded his arms into his kimono sleeves again as he considered Chris's words, and then he nodded. "Yes."

"That's what Tattannu meant when he said I must sacrifice everything," Chris whispered. "That's what you mean by it, too. Because once that happens...where will I be? *What* will I be?"

"There will be no you," Akagai spoke quietly. "There will only be us. And as a single collective entity, we can stand against Nabu, and Marduk. However, there is more to tell you." Akagai glanced at his scroll, and then looked back at Chris. Chris, not Ash.

As if he knew that Chris was still meant to be the one to carry out the Champion's destiny.

"What do you know of Marduk's greatest enemy?"

The question caught Chris off guard, his mind still reeling from what he would be required to do, and what it might mean. "Uh, you mean other than Tattannu and the Sentinels?"

Akagai favored Chris with an exasperated stare. "I speak of the one fought in ancient times. Pre-historical."

"Babylonian mythology?" Chris asked. "Are you talking about the dragon that Marduk supposedly vanquished?"

"Not supposedly," Akagai corrected. "Marduk and Mušḫuššu did indeed engage one another in deadly combat. It was Mušḫuššu who imprisoned Marduk in a realm beyond our own, but the battle and the effort of imprisoning Marduk was too much, and Mušḫuššu fell."

Chris nodded, knowing only some of the story from Babylonian mythology that he'd studied while training in the mountains.

Then the pieces clicked into place. "Mušḫuššu was a celestial. And Marduk really is an infernal."

"So you know the truth," Akagai spoke solemnly. "That is good."

"Yeah, Babbar and Shara told us all about it," Chris said. "Over tacos."

Akagai arched an eyebrow at him, which only made Chris grin. He was glad some expressions remained universal throughout the ages.

However, Chris's bemusement faded as more pieces of the puzzle clicked into place. "Wait, wait, wait. So you're saying that despite being imprisoned, Marduk destroyed this…this Mušḫuššu?"

"Defeated," Akagai raised a poignant finger. "Not destroyed."

For a moment, his spirits had been lifted, only in so much that if a celestial could be destroyed, so too could an infernal. Akagai had crushed that hope in one correction. A sullen fear gripped his insides, and he lowered his head. "We can't destroy Marduk, can we?"

After a terrifying pause, Akagai replied, "Yes. We can." Chris's gaze shifted upwards. "That is our destiny. Our purpose. Mušḫuššu was destined to be reborn, and would still be linked to Marduk and his prison. She was meant to be the key. The conduit. The method through which our millions of souls could strike at Marduk, overwhelm him so that his entire essence would scatter into nothingness."

Wide-eyed, Chris looked back and forth between Akagai and Ash. "Wait, so…the dagger. Imhullu." He nodded at the scroll, even though Imhullu wasn't drawn on it yet. "We, I mean I, I don't have to stab myself to channel the souls into Marduk?"

"No," Akagai shook his head. "But Imhullu is essential for one reason, and one reason alone. If you destroy Marduk while Nabu is still separated, Marduk's essence will live on, and like Mušḫuššu, he will be reborn."

Chris blinked in surprise. "I'll bet Nabu doesn't know that."

"He does," Akagai insisted. "Though he may refuse to believe it. Nabu is not the most stable entity in the Universe."

"You can say that again," Chris grumbled.

And then, in the blink of an eye, he understood.

A tingling sensation started in his chest, and grew out into the rest of his body like a giant wave of understanding. Excitement, disbelief, wonder, it filled him as one last piece presented itself, and the whole picture became crystal clear.

Ash must have realized it, too, as they drew in another surprised breath. "Nina?!"

Chris gaped at Ash. "I was just thinking that. Is…" He looked at Akagai. "Is Nina the reincarnation of Mušḫuššu? Uh, Ninazu I think is her full name?"

Akagai arched an eyebrow at them again, and closed his eyes. His features softened for a moment, and he opened his eyes again to smile upon them.

Slowly, deliberately, he stepped closer to them, and then placed a reassuring hand on each of their shoulders.

"Congratulations," he whispered. "You have the answers you need now."

There was no segue, no flash of light. The next thing Chris knew, the workshop was gone, and he was back in the conference room. Alycia's hands gripped his arm and shoulder, shaking him, while everyone stared at either him or Ash.

He looked at the image of the scroll on the screen. There was no dragon behind the temple, no blinding light, and nothing had extended into the room through the screen. It was all normal, and he had the feeling that no one other than he and Ash had seen the psychedelic light show.

But then his eyes fell upon Nina, who sat perched atop Babbar's shoulder. She gazed back at him with cat/lizard eyes gleaming.

Everyone followed his gaze to the tiny dragon, and then flipped back and forth between them.

Chris nodded. "Ninazu," he whispered. "Mušḫuššu."

The dragon couldn't smile, but damn if it didn't look like she did. *"Hello, Champion."* She crawled down off of Babbar's shoulder onto the conference table, and walked closer to Chris. He noticed that she completely ignored Ash.

"It is time to begin," Nina said, without ever moving her mouth. *"The beginning of the end."*

CHAPTER 23

"You can speak!"

Chris's outburst startled the others.

And then he remembered when he first met Nina, in Babbar's videogame-inspired mansion beneath the Colorado mountains. Babbar had pointed out that he could understand Nina, and that she was more intelligent than humans.

"I mean," he corrected, looking around at the others while feeling his cheeks warm, "I know you're more intelligent than an animal, but…" Chris trailed off upon seeing the puzzled looks that everyone gave him. "What?"

"What do you mean, she can speak?" Alycia asked. "When did she say something?"

"You didn't hear it?" Ash asked. "Just now?"

A round of shaking heads met their question.

Chris looked at Nina again, the dragon patiently staring back. She plodded across the tabletop to stand closer to Chris. *They cannot hear me,*" Nina replied, and Chris noted again that her mouth didn't move at all. *"However, you have learned what you needed to understand me at last."*

Exchanging surprised looks with Ash, Chris asked, "You mean, what I learned from the scroll?"

"You can read that thing?" Tom asked.

"No," Chris shook his head, "it was more than that. Didn't…didn't anyone else see what happened? The flash of light, the dragon behind the temple in the scroll?" He looked at the video stream, but the scroll had returned to its normal, degraded, unremarkable state.

Chris looked to Alycia, who shook her head, and then to Emmi, who said, "Nothing unusual happened. We didn't even feel so much as a blip of magic, either."

Looking around the room, he saw similar expressions in everyone's faces. "So it was just us," he said to Ash. "Just Ash and I who saw it?"

"*Yes,*" Nina answered.

"We saw and experienced nothing," Tom replied. "You and Ash both suddenly went stiff for a few seconds."

"A few *seconds?*" Ash whispered. "It felt like five or ten minutes passed."

"*However, it is not that the scroll or Tatsua Akagai taught you to understand me,*" Nina continued, drawing Chris's full attention to her. "*Rather your understanding of your powers has intrinsically allowed you to unlock abilities that were always there. Do you remember when we met?*"

"Of course I do," Chris nodded to Nina, thinking back to that fateful day. "You had supposedly mentioned to Babbar," he nodded at the gnome, who looked perplexed, "that…that I was something special. That you were drawn to me."

"*Exactly true,*" Nina sat down on her haunches and curled her tail around her feet, a very cat-like posture. She tilted her head to one side. "*I knew then that you were the Champion.*"

Eying her suspiciously, Chris asked, "How much of a part of the Barrier's creation were you? I mean, I thought you hadn't been reincarnated yet back then?"

"Reincarnated?" Babbar asked. "What are you blathering on about?"

Nina arched her head around to look at Babbar, and then looked at Chris. Amusement in her mental voice, Nina said, "*Perhaps you had best explain to everyone what you saw in the scroll.*"

Looking around the room again, Chris saw curious, even annoyed looks on everyone's faces, including the Professor's on the camera feed looking at him. Then he noticed Ash, who was staring at the tabletop with a distant look. Guilt and sympathy swirled in his chest, and he realized that, once again, they were being ignored or passed over.

"Ash," he said, wanting them to be included. They looked up at him after a delay, as if they were surprised to hear their own name. "Why don't you tell them about it?"

They stared blankly at Chris for a moment, but this time no hint of a smile appeared, nor did they accede to his request. "It's alright," they said plaintively. "You don't have to patronize me."

"Hey," he frowned, shaking his head. "I'm not being patronizing, I'm trying to include you in the conversation. You're a…a Champion too," he glanced at Nina, but her eyes remained fixed on Chris, not Ash.

"Look, I don't give a damn which of you fills us in," Tom growled, "but one of you better start talking or I'm gonna get pissed off."

"Dad," Alycia spoke in a warning tone. "Be nice."

Tom replied defensively, "I *am* being nice." When Alycia, Shara, Marisol, and Tiana looked at him skeptically, he drew his arms in. "I mean, for me."

Chris stared at Ash expectantly, unwilling to yield. Ash stared back, and then sighed. "Fine," they said. Ash launched into a brief description of what appeared on the scroll from their perspective, and then their conversation with Tatsua Akagai in the old master's workshop. The final revelation was the same as their own, that Nina was the reincarnation of Mušḫuššu, which Ash pronounced exactly like Akagai had, 'mah-shoo-shoo."

"Mushu?" Alycia asked with a frown.

"Wrong movie," Ash replied with a grin.

"Wrong country and culture," Chris added.

The Professor piped in over the video, *"And wrong pronunciation, from all of you."* He paused, and then nodded, *"However, I have heard some in the academic field pronounce it that way, and that is hardly worthy of debate at this moment in time."*

"Indeed," Nina said. *"It is also, as you humans say, a moot point. My name is Ninazu, and I am quite fond of being called Nina."*

Grinning, Ash told everyone what Nina had just said.

After that, Chris and Ash gave everyone a moment to digest what they had learned from Akagai. The longer they waited, the tighter Alycia's grip on Chris's arm grew. He looked into her eyes, trying desperately to convey a sense of confidence that he didn't feel himself. Instead, his heart wrenched, and an overwhelming sense of doom overcame him.

Maybe Chris wasn't meant to die by way of Imhullu, but if he was meant to become one with the millions of souls within him, and those souls were meant to be used to destroy Marduk…how could he possibly survive? His soul would be consumed along with the rest of the Tattannu ancestors' souls.

"So in order to defeat Marduk," Alycia croaked, her voice barely coming out, her jaw constricted. "In order to end all of this. You…" Her grip tightened even more, and Chris grasped her hand as tightly as he dared. "You have to give your soul, and the soul of every single Tattannu descendant, to Marduk."

Chris looked at Nina, whose gaze was still affixed upon him. She nodded ever-so-slightly.

He drew in a deep breath, but before he spoke, Ash interceded, "Not him."

Nina finally broke her gaze, her head snapping to look at Ash. Everyone else did likewise.

"Come again?" Chris asked.

"Not you," Ash said. "Me."

"No," Nina said. *"Chris is the champion, he is the one-"*

"Then why the hell am I here?!" Ash furiously slapped the tabletop. "What the fuck is the point of me having this connection if I'm just useless weight, huh?"

The conference room was deathly silent, and other than Sato's furious glare at their outburst, everyone's reaction was that of shock.

"Your presence and link to the Barrier was not meant to happen," Nina began.

"Oh, great, so I'm just a fucking accident?!"

Nina's eyes flared, and her wings unfurled rapidly, casting a gust of wind through the room that blew everyone's hair. Ash yelped, and Chris felt the familiar push of Nina's magic, the only hint of her power that he ever felt, and usually only when she created portals.

It was a show of power, a sign of her temper, but she did not say anything, not right away. Her glowing red eyes eased, and the rushing wind simmered to a light breeze. Nina folded her wings back in, and resumed her seat. *"I apologize,"* she said, apprehension in her voice. *"I forget sometimes that many humans struggle to believe in themselves. Ash, I am not saying that you have no purpose. If anything, your presence may be a divine providence beyond even my own sight. There was never meant to be a second concurrent Champion, and yet I believe that somehow, you will come to play a significant role in this conflict. However,"* Nina turned her gaze back upon Chris. *"Christopher Tatsu was the one who touched the Dragonstone.*

That forged a link between him and I, and that link will be essential in destroying Marduk. Whatever your role," she again looked upon Ash, *"It must either be separate from that task, or in support of it."*

Chris's mind reeled upon that implication. That fateful decision he had made six months ago had far more consequences than he had ever conceived of back then. Could he have possibly known that by dismantling the Barrier, he was signing his own death certificate? *No, I couldn't have.* He looked at Emmi, remembering why he had done it. *And even if I had...* She in turn looked into his eyes. *I would do it all over again.*

"So, um," Shara said. "I'm guessing Nina is talking to you? Either of you want to fill us in on what's going on?"

Chris looked at Ash to see what they wanted to do, but their eyes were locked with Nina's now, and they weren't saying anything. He decided to tell them what Nina had just said. Alycia gripped his hand tightly again, and he saw redness in her eyes when he finished.

What could he say? What could he do? He wanted to show her all of the love of a lifetime, right then and there. He wanted to *experience* a lifetime of love. But all he would get was a couple of days.

Or less.

"Holy crap-monkeys!" Abby's shocked voice suddenly chimed in. Chris had forgotten she was also in on the conference, virtually. Her bright, usually smiling face was lit up by her computer monitors on a live stream, and that only served to amplify the shock of her face.

"What's wrong, Abby?" Tom asked.

She looked up at the camera, slack-jawed, and then set to work, a torrent of rapid-fire keyboard clacking and mouse clicking. Her image shrank to the top left corner of her video call, and the rest showcased an aerial view of a massive blaze amongst a desert and low-lying shrubs and trees. A large swath of land burned, including the remnants of several buildings.

The aerial view came from a news station local to Santa Fe, New Mexico, and the headline at the bottom of the screen read 'DEADLY BLAZE AT LOS ALAMOS NATIONAL LABORATORY!'

Los Alamos. Where Imhullu was supposed to be.

"Oh shit," Chris found himself murmuring.

Tom and the others turned to him. "Chris?" Tom asked.

He glanced at Nina, who watched the blaze on the screen.

"Guys, there's only one reason Nabu would set the labs on fire," he said.

A resigned grimace drew across Tom's face. "She doesn't need it anymore."

He gave a grim nod. "We're out of time. Her scientists and enchanters have finished their work."

It was Yua who finished putting the pieces together this time. "Nabu and the Americans have a working, enchanted nuclear weapon."

Chris looked at Nina, who turned to face him. He said to her, "That's what you meant by the beginning of the end. You knew that the time was now. That we have to act now."

Nina said nothing, she simply bowed her head in her equivalent of a nod.

Alycia's hand trembled in Chris's, and he gripped it as reassuringly as he could. But there was nothing he could say or do to delay what came next.

"We have to stop Nabu," he said. "Now."

CHAPTER 24

"So what do we do?" Tiana asked the obvious question. "If Nabu has control of the President of the United States, and the President has his finger on the big red button, how do we stop them?"

Chris shook his head, and looked to Tom. So did most everyone else. To his credit, he took it in stride, despite being asked probably the most important question in the world at that moment in time.

He acted without hesitation. "Abby, any idea where the President is now?"

"One sec," she said, her small square of video feed showing her frowning at her screen, the sound of rapid-fire keyboarding filling their ears. *"As a matter of fact, he's giving a press brief right now."*

The video of the blazing fire flickered, and the familiar visage of the President appeared on the screen. Chris felt his stomach sour at the sight – the last time they had watched one of his briefs, he had condemned the Sentinels, marked them as America's Most Wanted, and that was the moment when they saw Nabu in the President's shadow.

While half-listening to the President, Chris scanned the people patiently waiting behind the President. He was mid-speech, *"-and we have made demand after demand of the British government to let us assist in quelling the uprising. These demands have been rebuked at every corner, until yesterday evening, when we stopped receiving any response. As of this moment, the British Prime Minister and all top-level members of their government are suspected to have been captured or killed by the group calling themselves Arcane Dawn, the instigators of the reign of terror in England."*

Chris started upon hearing that. They had been in isolation for months, only getting snippets of news from Abby, and she hadn't mentioned just how bad things had grown in England. Maybe to keep them from worrying about something that was out of their control, but now it came as a shock at a moment when they didn't need surprises.

The President continued, *"More disturbing is that the security of the British nuclear arsenal may have been compromised. Although we evacuated our embassies in Britain some time ago, we had left behind a contingent of troops to help the British military secure their arsenal. They, too, have gone silent."* His face contorted into rage, and he slammed his fist onto the podium that he stood upon, sending a loud bang through the microphones atop it. *"We can no longer sit by idly while these terrorists have their way with our closest ally and threaten the peace and security of the free world! And make no mistakes,"* he raised a finger at the press audience, *"these are terrorists, not freedom fighters. Freedom fighters do not kill police, do not kidnap dignitaries, or destroy buildings. We will do what we must to stop them from spreading any further. Whatever it takes."*

Chris felt his face pale at those words. There was something in the President's eyes, in the tone of his voice.

"It's a cover," he spoke over the President, who continued to prattle on about the need to strike decisively and make an example of the Arcane Dawn. The room turned from the screen to him, their expressions expectant or questioning. "He's giving this conference as a prelude cover for the use of 'all necessary force,'" Chris used his fingers to air-quote. Abby muted the video feed, but put on closed-caption so they could monitor the speech.

"You mean you think he intends to launch on England?" Shara skeptically asked. "Chris, that's insane."

"Under normal circumstances, maybe," he replied, "but I'm sure the President isn't exactly of sound mind and body right now."

"Even still," Shara shook her head. "Nuke the U.S.'s closest ally? They'd be condemned by every power in the world, regardless of his speech."

She had a point, and as Chris thought about it, he was prepared to concede the point.

But Tom had other thoughts. "No," the commander shook his head. "Chris is right. Actually, you're both right. Yes, the United States would be condemned, but it's rather brilliant of Nabu, because that's likely *all* that will happen. Whereas if the U.S. launched against almost any other target, especially if it isn't an ally, there could be a reprisal launch from other nuclear-armed countries."

"Bugger, you're right," Shara hissed. "Nabu doesn't just want to destroy her father, she wants to rule the Earth, and have as many souls as possible under her control. Instigating a third world war would be counterproductive to that goal."

"Aye, and the more souls she has at her disposal after killing her dear old dad," Babbar grumbled, "the more powerful she can become in the long run. So she would use the weapon on the minimum number of people possible while still getting the job done."

Tom turned back to the screens. "Abby, how many people live in London?"

Abby's fingers must have raced across the keyboard, and a Google search result came up on the screen for all to see, but she read it off anyway. *"London proper has about nine million people. The London Metro…"* Her face paled, and she murmured the number, *"Almost fourteen million."*

The number sounded astronomical. Between eight and fourteen million souls, all hitting Marduk at once.

"I do not wish to sound insensitive to the topic," Yua said cautiously. "But would that be enough souls?"

"Oh, aye," Babbar nodded grimly. "I think more than enough. Souls are powerful. They have to be, to fuel such magic as arcana. I don't know how many concurrent sacrifices Marduk was able to arrange before the Barrier, but I am guessing no more than a hundred."

Chris looked at Nina, who stared back at him, seemingly ignoring much of what else was going on around her.

Nina. Whose powers included the ability to teleport.

Chris looked up at the screen with the Google search results. "Abby," he interrupted ongoing musings in the group. Even before he asked, a rushing sensation passed through his entire body, the mere thought of what he was about to propose sending adrenaline surging into his blood, excitement and terror racing through him in equal parts. "Is the President still giving his press brief?"

Abby blinked, typed in a few things, and the video of the press conference reappeared. The President still stood at the podium, his face contorted in rage, his fist pounding the podium again. Closed Captioning hadn't been turned back on yet, so Chris had no idea what ridiculous nonsense was spewing forth now, but it hardly mattered.

"Nina, how rapidly can you teleport again after one time?"

The room fell deathly silent. It felt more oppressive than ever before, as if all eyes, all air, *everything* closed in on him, the shock palpable as it rolled through the group.

Nina's blazing red eyes bore into him, and somehow, he knew she had expected his question.

"Not fast enough," she replied. *"However, I am not the only one in this room capable of creating portals."*

He expected her to look at someone else. Maybe Yua or Sato, the latter of which had remained suspiciously quiet throughout the entire proceeding. Or maybe not suspiciously – maybe wisely. Chris still couldn't really get a read on the Japanese commander, making him the very definition of stoic.

But no. Nina's eyes remained fixed upon Chris.

Until they turned to Ash.

And then back to Chris.

Akagai's words resonated in his head. Within him were the souls of millions, every single one of them having been able to cast magic, even if the Barrier kept most of them from actually exercising their powers.

But still.

But still.

"You can't be serious," Tom choked out. "You...you're suggesting snatching the President of the United States in front of millions of viewers?"

Chris broke his gaze with Nina, and nodded at the commander. "I do."

"That's bloody bonkers, Chris," Alycia chimed in. "Even for us."

"I like bonkers," he nodded.

"But the world already hates magic users," Marisol pointed out, waving at the irate President. "You use magic to abduct him, and you'll just fuel that hatred further."

"Not to mention making us all priority targets," Shara added. "We'd be hunted down-"

"Like we already are?" Emmi defensively asked.

Shara paused, mouth half-open, and then clamped it shut. "Good point," she nodded.

"It's still a bad idea," Tom stated. "Too much could go wrong, and the aftermath would-"

"To hell with the aftermath!" Chris slapped his palm on the table. Silence wound its way into the room again. He let it speak for him for just a moment, before he continued, "I don't think you all understand, this is *it*. We don't have time. The moment the President leaves that podium, I guarantee you, he's going into that famed bunker in the East Wing, and he's going to press that big red button and launch. We don't have *time* to mess around, alright? No more delays, no more thinking about it. It's time to act! And right now, at this very second, we know *exactly* where he is. So all I have to do is..." He looked at Nina. "Is figure out how to portal in and out in the space of a heartbeat."

"You cannot do that," Nina stated. *"Even with your powers, it will take minutes to regain your ability to create a portal."*

Chris arched an eyebrow at her. The implication was obvious, and he looked at Ash, who went from staring at Nina to staring at him. He asked, "Are you thinking what I'm thinking?"

Ash raised an eyebrow at him. They opened their mouth, paused, and then smirked. "Uh, I think so, Brain, but this time, you wear the tutu."

The remark made Chris's brain go blank for a second, but then when he realized what they'd quoted, he let out an airy laugh.

Alycia giggled a second later. In a bemused voice, she said, "Bloody hell, Ash, there's a time and a place for jokes, yeah?"

A sheepish grin stretched across Ash's face, and they looked down. "Sorry, it's just...well, the room was rife with tension. It's how I deal with it."

Chris nodded, still chuckling. "It, uh, I mean," he tried to speak through his laughter. "No, seriously, though," he wiped his hand down his face to try to pull his smile away, "Are you thinking-"

"God, yes!" Ash gave him an exasperated look "I am, alright? I think I am, anyway."

"Well I'm not," Tom grumbled. "Wanna fill the rest of us in?"

Glancing at the screen to make sure the President was still there, Chris replied, "I portal Ash and I in, we snag the President, and Ash portals us out. Any questions?"

"Yeah," Babbar raised a hand. "Since when is 'portal' a verb?"

Great, now everyone wants to tell a joke, Chris thought.

"Now, just give us a second to figure this out," Chris stood up and walked over to Ash, who likewise stood up and met him face-to-face. He nodded at them. "Ready?"

"Indeed," they nodded. "To the soul realm, right?"

"Yup," Chris replied, and closed his eyes. As the days, weeks, and months had passed, centering himself and entering what Ash had termed the soul realm had grown easier and easier for Chris. All it took was a couple of quick, controlled breaths and applying a little focus, and he saw the golden spheres of energy before him, side by side with only a few feet of ethereal air between them.

A second later, the spectral form of Ash stepped up on his left. They drew in a breath, and let it out slowly. "This isn't going to be fun, is it?" they asked.

"I don't know," Chris shrugged, the adrenaline in his system surging again, threatening to pull him out of his focused state. "But we have to try." He looked to his right, and saw the smiling visage of his sister. Beyond her, the gray, blurry figures of other Tattannu descendants milled about vaguely. Somewhere in there, someone had the answers.

Without having to coordinate, he and Ash approached the tandem golden spheres together. He knew what to do, even if he didn't know *how* he knew what to do. At this point, he figured he should just go with it, with whatever his instincts said.

After all, his instincts were fueled by millions of souls, right?

Sucking in a deep breath, he reached out and touched the sphere. Ash did likewise with theirs, and together the duo's fingers touched the surfaces almost simultaneously. The spheres flared, and the inner bolts of electricity playing about inside concentrated on their hands, and in that exact instant, Chris felt a surge of energy. A surge of *life*.

A surge of chatter in his head, of voices of every kind talking all at once, saying a million different things at once, but only on the surface. Only on the edge of his peripheral.

They needed more.

Together, they *pushed* on the surfaces. Pushed and pushed, increasing pressure, tentatively, neither wanting to go deeper, to go further than they had to. And then, finally, like some bizarre overly-strong surface tension, the sphere gave and their hands sank in. The lightning flared brighter, sending tingles all along Chris's spine.

Pressure against his soul, against his very existence.

Light of a million lifetimes.

All right there.

The voices silenced, but the presence of the speakers remained. Grew stronger. Tantalized answers to every question imaginable, and the existence of more questions, beyond his wildest imaginings.

But now was not the time.

Not yet.

"Tell us," he said. "Show us."

He willed it into the ocean of souls, his question echoing and resonating and becoming a deafening cry.

And someone answered.

A man emerged from the distant gray haze, one Chris had seen before. A samurai wearing red-plated armor and a terrifying kabuto over his head, twin swords lashed to his belt. He planted a fist into a palm, and bowed before them.

Then, he stepped in-between the spheres and thrust his arms into each one, the light flaring brighter than ever as the samurai's body dissolved. The bright flare imprinted upon Chris, imparted experience, knowledge, personality.

It threatened to overtake him.

It stole his breath.

Stole his heart.

Seared life into him.

It was only one soul, and the instant that Chris realized what happened, he cried out, yanking back from the sphere, yanking back into the real world, reeling backwards, and falling away from Ash, who nearly fell themself. Chris landed hard on his backside, the word, "No!" escaping his lips.

Alycia tried to catch him, and now awkwardly tried to extract herself from her chair without bumping it into him. "Chris!"

She helped him up, and Tiana helped steady Ash.

"What the bloody hell was that?" Tom gasped. "There was…a light, and lightning ran all across your bodies."

"You convulsed," Alycia whimpered. "I thought…"

"We're okay," Chris breathed, grasping at his chest, feeling his heart hammering a thousand miles per hour, threatening to break free of his rib cage. He looked at Ash, who stared back at him with haunted eyes. "I think we are. Aren't we?"

Pressing their lips into a thin line, Ash nodded. "You and I are, yeah. But, that samurai. He…" Their voice cracked, faltered, and they looked down.

How he felt now, the sudden, constant energy coursing through his veins, reminded him of how he'd felt after Mia's healing magic. He understood then, more than ever, what she had done for him.

What the samurai had done for them.

For the second time that week, Chris's soul and body had consumed the energy of another soul.

"One of our ancestors just sacrificed himself," Chris turned to Alycia. His stomach twisted in a combination of guilt, disgust, and self-hatred. "I…" He glanced at Ash. "We…"

He couldn't finish.

It hurt too much.

But they didn't have time to mourn, to really contemplate the fact that he and Ash had just consumed a soul.

Like Nabu.

Like Marduk.

And more than ever, he feared what it meant he had to do to become one with the remaining millions of souls.

"We have to go," he glanced at Abby's feed, saw the President, looking much calmer now. Was he getting ready to finish his speech?

"What, *now*?" Ash asked, their eyes reddened and wet. "We…after what just…"

Pulling out of Alycia's grip, he stepped closer to Ash. "If we don't go now, his sacrifice will have been in vain. We know how to make portals now, know how to control the radius. We can and *have* to go right now. Are you ready?"

Truth be told, he wasn't. But he couldn't say that now.

There wasn't time.

Sighing, Ash nodded. "I am."

Chris glanced at the others around him, at Alycia, Tiana, Marisol. "You all better backup. And be ready. We'll be back in the blink of an eye, and then," he looked again at Ash. "We have work to do, you and I."

They pursed their lips, nodded. "Yeah. I suppose we do."

He lifted his eyebrows. "You wanted to be a part of this," he reminded them.

"I know, I know," Ash huffed. "Just, come on." They inhaled deeply, and added, "I'll be ready to bring us back."

Chris nodded. And turned inward again. Not to repeat what had just happened, but to draw upon that seemingly endless source of power.

Creating a portal was simple, really. Simple *if you had the power.* And Chris had that power now. He imagined *being* there, behind the President, on that podium in the press room of the White House.

It wasn't a tunnel he created. It wasn't some metaphysical wormhole.

It was a rip in the fabric of reality, requiring immense power.

He slashed that hole open, sending his will forth into the beyond, honing in on that spot behind the President, and he tore another hole. The magic flowed through him like a pressurized hose, blasting into the ether.

White noise.

Blinding pressure.

This time, no copper taste on the tongue.

And they were there.

He opened his eyes, saw the President at the podium a mere five feet to the left of where Chris had appeared. The members of the press stared open-mouthed, while the President slowly turned towards them. Secret Service guards on either end of the room paused for only half a second, and then reached into their jackets.

Chris snagged the President's finely-tailored suit by the scruff and yanked him closer unceremoniously.

"Now!" Chris shouted.

Ash closed their eyes, just as half a dozen guns trained on Chris.

White noise.

Blinding pressure.

And in the space of five seconds, Chris and Ash had succeeded.

They had abducted the President of the United States of America.

CHAPTER 25

In a flurry of waving arms and shocked eyes, the President flailed about, breaking free of Chris's grasp for a second and stumbling over a chair. Tiana caught him easily, and hefted him back on his feet, before she gripped one forearm and wrist and twisted it behind the President.

"Now, now, Mister President," she counseled him. "Easy, *easy!*"

"Get off of me, you traitors!" he roared.

Chris tried to approach him, but there was plenty of fight in the President, and he kicked his feet out, catching Chris in the shins. "Ouch, dammit!" He hopped back, dancing in pain. "Hold on, Mister President! We're not going to hurt you!"

The conference room was exactly as Chris had left it, which considering less than ten seconds had passed, he wasn't surprised.

But the look of horror and rage on Sato's face was almost comical, and Chris had to remind himself that he had probably just forced Japan to break countless international treaties.

Not the best way to ingratiate himself upon one of the elder leaders of the Sentinels.

"Hold him," Tom ordered. The President flailed again, almost breaking free, but Tiana tightened her grip and twisted harder, and a contortion of pain twisted the President's face, taking all fight out of him.

Having experienced one of those arm locks in training, Chris winced in sympathy.

Looking at Ash, he nodded, "Together we can cleanse him faster."

"Right," they stepped up next to Chris, and as one, the duo

reached out and touched the President's temples. He tried to twist out of it, but Tiana applied just a little more pressure.

The connection came easier this time, and energy coursed through Chris's body effortlessly. The soul realm overcame his senses, a darkened infinity surrounded by a million milling figures. Chris and Ash's golden core stood side-by-side.

Only this time, they weren't a few feet or even inches apart. Their spherical edges touched, with sparks flashing in between them.

Soul-Ash was next to him, and gaped, just as the spheres began to spin around one another. "What…what's happening?" they asked.

Chris shook his head. "I don't know."

"You're growing more in-tune with one another," a voice startled them. Spinning around, Chris and Ash saw a familiar figure approach them. Dressed in elaborate white robes with golden and blue trim, and a white turban atop his head, Tattannu stood three feet away from the duo, his arms folded before him.

Heat grew within Chris, fueled by rage, and he took two steps forward before planting a finger in Tattannu's robes. "You! You son of a bitch, where the hell have you been?!"

Tattannu unfolded his arms and glared at Chris, his eyes flashing gold. "How *dare* you speak to me in that way…"

"Don't!" Chris pushed his finger harder, damn near shoving the ancient soul back. "Don't you dare! It's been three *long* months since you told me I had to sacrifice *everything*, and then you disappeared without any further explanation, any guidance, NOTHING!" Chris's voice resonated in the endless void, and in the corner of his eye, he saw that the milling shadows had stopped, and the eyes of millions now watched him.

A warm hand fell upon his shoulder, and squeezed tightly. Ash pried him back from Tattannu. "Chris, don't," they said as soothingly as they could. "This isn't helping."

Blood boiling, eyes seeing red, Chris clenched his fists, and tried to breath. Realizing his tantrum *should* have ripped him out of the soul realm, he looked back, and saw his and Ash's golden core swirling around each other like atoms on-course to collide.

They were stronger now, thanks to the samurai's sacrifice. Staying in the soul realm was easier. But their cores…

Then, despite the bright glow of their dual cores, he saw a smaller, light-gray core off to the left.

The President's.

Looking at Tattannu, he clenched his jaw. So many things he wanted to say. So many questions.

But that would have to wait.

The fate of the planet was literally in the balance.

Turning his back on Tattannu, he stalked towards the President's soul, grabbing Ash's hand as he went, though they came along willingly. He *felt* Tattannu following behind him.

Passing by their whirling cores, Chris and Ash took up positions on either side of the light-gray, diminutive soul, the oily black taint of Nabu's will swirling within. Tattannu took up a position to Chris's left, away from the sphere. Chris's temper threatened to flare again, but he knew that wouldn't help him now. He needed to focus his thoughts elsewhere if he was to clear the taint. So he shoved his anger down, stomping it under heel to keep it away.

He closed his eyes, and pictured Alycia standing beside him, hand in hand-

"I didn't leave you in the dark on purpose," Tattannu said.

Chris grit his teeth. Tried to stomp down on the embers of anger. Focused on Alycia.

"I was pulled away," he continued. "Ripped away by the dissonance that had erupted between your two souls."

"And what caused that dissonance?" Chris asked, losing focus altogether. "What could possibly divide us when we had never met?"

Tattannu turned wise eyes upon him – there was no accusation, no anger. "Your fear."

The burning rage was doused in freezing-cold water. Chris's accusatory stare faltered. The memory of that moment replayed in his mind, in the hospital after being treated for battle wounds. Telling Tattannu that he was beginning to understand. Asking him what Chris would have to sacrifice to defeat Nabu and Marduk.

Everything.

Dreadful terror followed. Fear of his role. Fear of losing everything. Driven deeper by his feelings for Alycia and the hint that maybe, just maybe, she loved him.

Followed by three months of running and hiding for their lives.

His magic, his *soul* was fueled by emotion, or at least directed by it. So when he felt such overwhelming terror at that revelation three months ago, he must have pushed Tattannu away.

Away and to the only other descendant who was unintentionally active.

To Ash.

He stared across at the other Champion, over the dim, tainted soul before them. They had become so heavily involved because of Chris.

However, this wasn't the time for a blame game. Certainly not a self-blame game. Because if Ash hadn't been here, today, then he might not have been able to snag the President. Plus, Chris was certain that Ash's role in all of this was yet to be fully played out.

Maybe it was all for the best.

He knew that time in the soul realm didn't always reflect time in reality, but no matter which way he swung it, he shouldn't be spending this time on the past. Ignoring Tattannu, he set his mind towards cleansing the President's soul again. Tattannu didn't speak on the matter any further.

Reaching inward, he touched on those emotions that he felt towards Alycia. Recalled in perfect clarity the moment they had admitted their feelings to one another, freezing and shivering in the loading area of that abandoned factory. He remembered last night, cuddling with her on the couch, carrying her to the bedroom, that moment of passion...

Without waiting to see if Ash was ready, Chris reached out and touched the surface of the President's soul, and infused that love, that caring, that devotion into his powers. Ash likewise touched, and in a brilliant flash, the darkness writhed and seized, and peeled away like ashes floating off of a burning log.

Until all that was left was the light gray, swirling pulse of a purified soul.

Chris opened his eyes in the real world. The President had stopped struggling, and instead slouched. He and Tiana caught him, and as carefully as they could (he was heavier than he looked,) they eased the President into Tiana's abandoned chair.

Moments after letting go of him, his eyes fluttered open. Groaning, he touched his forehead and massaged for a second. "What...happened?" He looked up at Chris, and his eyes widened. "You. You're one of those Sentinels. But...wait."

Tom pushed past Alycia and Emmi, past Chris and Marisol and Ash, and stood before the President. "President Anderson," Tom nodded and held out a hand. "I am Commander Thomas Taylor of the United States Sentinels."

Tentatively, as if afraid Tom would crush his hand, the President reached out and grasped Tom's hand. Tom pumped it once, and then used his other hand to help pull the President up onto his feet. Releasing his grip, he motioned behind the President, where Sato stood patiently at the head of the table. "This is Commander Sato Tanaka, leader of the Japanese Sentinels."

Sato bowed, and the President, seemingly remembering his diplomatic training, turned fully to face the Japanese commander, and returned the bow. "Mister Sato."

Then, turning to Tom again, President Anderson narrowed his eyes. "I declared you America's Most Wanted."

Tom's jaw clenched. "Yes, sir, you did."

Folding his arms, the President shook his head and stared down at the floor. "This is…wrong. All of it. I was in control of my actions, and yet I wasn't." Then his face paled. "Nabu," he spoke with venom. "It was her!"

When he looked up at Tom, the commander nodded. "It was. She, for lack of a better term, tainted your soul. So that you worshipped her against your own will. It is an old trick." Tom grimaced. "One I fell victim to myself." Blinking fiercely, Tom continued, "You'll be disoriented for a little while, but I'm afraid there's no time to let you recover, Mister President. Nabu intends to use a nuclear weapon on an ally."

Chris didn't think the President's face could grow any whiter. He was wrong. "Oh no," President Anderson croaked out. "The missile. It's already on its way."

A dozen voices cried out, "What?!"

"We loaded it onto a Los Angeles class submarine," the President stated, "and they already have been given the launch codes. They'll fire as soon as they're in position!"

Without missing a beat, and speaking over the horrified gasps and objections in the room, Tom gripped the President's shoulder and asked, "Can you stop them?"

President Anderson pressed his lips into a thin line. "No. They're under orders to maintain communications blackout until completion of their mission."

"And the crew," Tom looked intently. "Do they really know their target? Do you think they would fire upon an ally?"

Grimly, the President nodded. "They would. I chose that ship specifically because the Captain and XO were outspoken supporters of my policies against magic users."

The dread that had started to inch its way into Chris at the outset of the conversation flooded fully in, feeling like a punch to the gut. He stepped back, and looked in horror at Alycia.

She gripped his hand, shaking her head. "Is…is there anything we can do?" she asked.

"A sub-launched nuke isn't very strong," Tom frowned. "And I would think Nabu would need millions of souls."

"She claimed it was enough for her purpose," President Anderson insisted. "But there is one chance. Only one weapon was enchanted with magic, and the sub is under orders to launch only that one missile. Because of the disarray the U.K. is in, we don't anticipate their defenses to be operational. Nothing from that country will be able to shoot down our missile. In fact Nabu insisted she knew for certain that would be the case."

"How does that give us a chance?" Emmi asked with a scowl. "Sounds like we have even *less* of a chance."

Chris looked at Emmi as she asked her question. Looked at the floor. Then looked at Tom, who turned to face Chris. Tom explained, "It's one missile. We won't have to find it and shoot it down amidst a flurry of fakes or un-enchanted weapons. That narrows our target to one. And we might have just the weapon to take it down…"

Nodding, Chris knew then what Tom was thinking. Turning to the President, Chris asked, "Where is the sub going to launch from?"

"Uh," the President stammered, scratched at his head. "I need a map."

"We have one," Yua said, moving back to her spot at the table and picking up the tablet there. She tapped on it for a few seconds, and then the entire wall next to Chris, Tom, and the others blinked on, showing what was clearly a Google Maps view of the United Kingdom.

The President blinked in surprise, though Chris wasn't sure if it was the vid wall tech, or the quality of the image, or something else entirely. He stepped up, and squatted down to peer at the southern part of England. "There," he pointed, "just west of the English

Channel."

"That's awful close," Tom remarked.

President Anderson stood back up and straightened his suit jacket. "Well the Brits aren't exactly at the top of their game right now, and they'd never fire on an American sub. Not yet, anyway." He grimaced, and slowly shook his head. "This is all my fault. I wasn't strong enough…"

"Nabu is at fault, no one else," Tom stepped in front of the President. "She's set us against each other. But now, we have a chance to stop all of this. How long until launch?"

"Minutes," the President replied. "Any minute, and they'll be in position."

Eyes widening, Tom looked at Chris. He nodded, and turned back to everyone else. "That means I have to go. Now."

"What?!" Alycia grabbed his arm. "No, not yet! We're not ready, we have to gear up, we have to…"

"There's no time," he shook his head. "That close range, the missile will take minutes to hit its target. I have to get out there, and I'm the only one both with the power to fly *and* destroy the missile."

"Nabu will come looking once the missile fails to hit its target," Yua pointed out. "We should all get ready and follow."

"Don't go to London," Chris said. "Just in case I fail to stop it. Meet me somewhere on the southern shores."

Pointing at the map, Tom said, "We'll meet up at Plymouth."

Chris glanced at the map, saw the dot representing the city on the southern coast, and tried to imagine where that was in relation to the spot in the sea that the President had pointed at. "Uh, point out again where the sub is supposed to launch from, please."

Looking slightly confused at what was going on, President Anderson bent down and pointed again. Chris burned that location into his mind, pictured what it must be like, above the sea.

Looking around, he realized he needed to be flying when he arrived.

Alycia's hand tugged on him, drawing his gaze back to her.

"Chris," her voice shook. "I…I love you."

For the briefest moment, his determination faltered. He gazed into her golden brown eyes, lost in them for the briefest fraction of a second. Wishing he could stay there forever. He pulled her into an embrace, clutching tightly, as her hands gathered the back of his shirt into her fists and she clenched as tight as she could.

"I love you, too," he whispered into her ear. Pulling back, he looked one more time into her eyes, and then kissed her fiercely.

Pulling away, he stepped past her then, holding her hand, letting it slide, to fingers, to fingertips, until they parted. His heart ached.

"Stay back," he told the others, coming up behind where Tom had previously sat at the head of the table. "And then get your asses to England as soon as I'm gone."

"We'll be there," Tom nodded.

"As will we," Yua added resolutely.

Chris locked eyes ever so briefly with Sato. And for the first time since they'd arrive, he saw the grumpy old bastard smile at him. Brief, fleeting, barely a hint of one, but it was a smile. Maybe an approving one.

Focusing inward to gather power from his golden core, Chris channeled it into his hands and feet, and immediately felt himself lift up off of the floor, until he hovered a good three inches above the ground.

One last time, he looked around the room. At Alycia, his love. Emmi, his best friend. Tom, his newest mentor. Marisol and Tiana, two of the best damn fighters he'd ever known. Babbar, the only one still seated. Nina on the table, who still stared at him, silent now, but somehow approving. And at Shara, once the woman of his dreams, and the one who had taught him all about magic.

My family.

Gracing them with an encouraging smile, he closed his eyes again, and pictured himself hovering above the ocean in the spot where the President had pointed. He didn't want to be too low, so he pictured himself high above.

And he ripped, *punched* a hole through the Universe to that location.

White noise.

Blinding light.

Intense pressure against his soul.

And the frigid cold of the English Channel in winter greeted him.

CHAPTER 26

The blinding light of the golden portal faded, leaving Chris in complete and utter darkness. If he hadn't been floating upright when he arrived, he would have lost all sense of direction, of orientation. Night time. It was night in England.

But there should have been a moon out, shouldn't there?

Shoving down the dread bubbling up in his stomach, he breathed in and out, slowly, methodically, waiting.

Waiting for his eyes to adjust.

A glow from above grew brighter, and he looked up, and *pushed* up, flying skyward, his skin prickling with moisture and freezing cold, made worse by the wind he generated through simple flight.

Finally, almost blissfully, he broke through the top of a layer of clouds, and above him, stretching into infinity, lay a field of glowing stars, the band of the Milky Way visible, and half of the moon visible near the horizon.

Halting his climb, he looked around, saw that there was an almost flat layer of clouds covering the ocean, perhaps even having descended to become a thick, soupy layer of fog. Here, above the clouds, the cold felt colder, the wet felt strangely wetter, and shivers rippled across his skin, prickling in waves like the ocean below.

Would this make it harder for him to see the missile when it launched? What little he knew about military subs, he knew they could launch without ever surfacing, which meant even if the clouds weren't present, he wouldn't see a thing until-

A bright glow to his left. Chris jerked his head that way, and saw a flaring glow moving up, up, and up in the clouds.

The missile.

They'd launched!

And it was miles away from him.

"Shit!" he cursed into the night.

Willing every bit of power he dared into his feet and hands, he angled down, and burst towards the glow, just as the missile passed through the cloud layer and up into the open sky. He kicked in another burst of speed, feeling his legs threatening to buckle under the self-generated G-forces. The wind whipped his face, his arms, and he wished he'd at least stopped for a jacket and goggles, but no, then he would have arrived too late.

His eyes, God his eyes burned from the wind! Without goggles or any sort of protection, they dried out fast, they *hurt*, and it was all he could do to keep them open a slit, enough to see the glow of the rocket trail ahead, rising faster and faster. He angled his pursuit to follow, then realized his mistake and angled higher to try to intercept, but he couldn't deviate too far, or he'd lost sight of the nuke through his squinty eyes.

How close did he have to be to hit it? Chris had never really figured out how his powers worked. Were the beams of energy essentially particle weapons? How fast would they attenuate in the atmosphere? Did he have to be within a mile? Ten miles?

Worse still, would the nuke detonate from his attack?

And how good was his aim?

Glancing below for just a split second, he realized with a start that he had rapidly climbed in altitude. The air *had* to be below freezing this high up, and with every exhale, he swore he felt frost build up around his face.

Looking again at the rocket, he saw that he was gaining, but not fast enough. It had started to angle. Angle to the north-east.

It wouldn't have to achieve orbit or anything like that, London was close enough that it wouldn't be necessary.

But still, his breathing came up shorter and shorter, and he felt like he had to suck in every breath. Before long, altitude sickness would get to him, or worse.

So he halted his ascent, came to a drifting hover, and he charged his hands with golden energy, before he brought them together, palm-to-palm, and unleashed a powerful golden blast of magic. His shot went wide, but he didn't dare stop it, not yet. He adjusted, overshot, adjusted again, missed. The missile was getting further and further away, and his odds of hitting it were dwindling fast!

Finally, feeling utter defeat, he stopped, and squinted, and blinked through dry eyes and squinted again. He could see the faint prick of light that was its exhaust, but soon, too soon, it would be gone.

Chris didn't have a hope in the world of catching it now. Not before suffocating or drying out his eyes. He wasn't *fast* enough, he wasn't...

Wait a second.

Realization dawned on him, and if he had even a split second to spare, he would have smacked himself in the head.

Portals!

He could portal ahead to London, intercept before it detonated, and...

Better still, dumbass, portal up to the missile!

It would be risky. Up that high, he would instantly run out of oxygen. And if he hit the warhead and that detonated the nuke, it would incinerate him on the spot. Unless the safeties on the warhead prevented that.

He looked along its flight path. The glow of London wasn't yet visible from here, and he could see nothing beneath the clouds, so he wasn't even sure if he was over land or not. But the longer he waited, the less chance the missile would splash down in the water after he destroyed or disabled it. The idea of spreading radioactive material all along the south of England made him shudder.

So he drew in a deep breath, exhaled, did so again, recalling somewhere that doing so over and over could help saturate his blood with oxygen.

It had been minutes already since he had made his second portal – long enough. And though it felt harder this time, more tiresome, he tore another hole in the fabric of the Universe, and passed through.

White noise.

Blinding light.

He held his breath, and the light faded.

A nuclear missile bolted past him, the sound strangely muted this high up, though the rumble of the rocket still vibrated him to the core.

He twisted his torso, spun to track it, took aim, ignoring the burning sensation on his skin, the strange pull on his lungs, and he unleashed his blast.

The first lance missed, but he knew that would happen, so he scythed it across, rapidly, back and forth, back and forth, until...

Paydirt! His blast lanced through the missile, and for the briefest second, when the brightest flash he'd seen in recent times blinded him, he thought the warhead had detonated.

But the flash receded, and pieces of a nuclear missile fell from the sky.

It had worked!

Now he was higher than any human was ever meant to be, exposed to low pressure, without enough oxygen to sustain himself.

Lungs burning, Chris powered up his hands again, folded up like a diver mid-jump, and *pushed* towards the Earth far below, the hazy clouds glowing softly with moonlight, a vast carpet beneath him. Vaguely, he saw a glow above him from his perspective, a city or town on the edge of his peripheral. Not likely Plymouth, he had travelled too far east.

Need to breathe!

But I can't.

Not yet.

Not.

Yet.

Further he plummeted, closing his eyes against the burning wind.

But he couldn't help it anymore. Was he low enough?

Chris blew out the air in his lungs, tried to suck more in. The air resisted, or there wasn't much to suck in, but there was *some*. It felt like a weight on his chest, refusing to let anymore air in.

The second breath came easier. The third easier still.

The wind grew stronger, pushed harder, and he knew he had far exceeded terminal velocity.

Since he could breathe at last, he stopped powering his flight, and he spread his arms and legs out, letting himself slow to terminal velocity, when he finally opened his eyes just enough to make sure he wasn't going to slam into ocean or rocks below.

The clouds were *close!* Thrusting energy back into his hands and feet, he pushed against momentum, as hard as he dared, and slowed his descent.

Slower.

Slower still.

Skydiving videos always made it look like they were in the air forever, but the altitude had rushed away incredibly quick, he had fallen *fast*, and the fact was, the membrane of air covering the Earth was paper thin.

Finally, with what looked like a few hundred feet to spare before penetrating the cloud layer, Chris settled into a hover, and he remained that way for a long breath. He righted himself, feet-down, and looked around at the carpet of moonlit clouds.

His heart raced, from adrenaline, from fear, and from trying to catch up on oxygen content.

He was alive.

Chris was *alive!*

Not knowing why, he bellowed out a laugh into the night, the clouds muffling it. He laughed harder, louder, daring the world to echo it back, trying to fill the void with the elation he felt.

"Yeah!" he shouted into nothing. "Yeah, eat your heart out, Superman!"

And then he felt his cheeks burn (despite the frigid chill) and was beyond glad that no one was around to have heard that.

Plymouth. He had to get to Plymouth. Chris tried to rip another tear in the Universe, but it was too much. Too many portals in a short span. He needed to rest before trying again.

Looking north, towards where he'd seen the glow earlier, he set out, slow and steady, ensuring he stayed above the clouds.

First, get to land. Figure out where he was. Then, when he was ready, rip another portal over to Plymouth.

Waves of shivers ran across his skin, and his teeth chattered a million miles a second.

"I....hate...winter!" he shouted at the Universe.

CHAPTER 27

Frosted over, shivering, and wishing he knew how to warm himself up with magic, Chris approached the glowing clouds in a matter of minutes. Slowing down to a relative crawl, he eased down into the clouds, hoping it wasn't a fog, and fearing he'd crash into the waves or, worse, an unlit structure.

The sound of rolling waves grew audible, and he nearly pulled up, until just barely, he saw a distinct light in the haze, which rapidly grew into several lamps on the edge of a wooden pier with a large building at the end.

I just need to land for a minute, he told himself as he slowed even more and prepared to touch down. *Just a minute.*

It was the pitch of night, and not a soul wandered upon the pier as Chris gently landed. As soon as he cut off magic to his hands and feet, he stumbled a little, realizing just how much energy he had spent, and how hard the high-altitude flight had been on him.

He found a picnic table, damp in the foggy eve, and plopped down on it, not caring for the moment that the dew soaked through his silk pants almost instantly. Chris drew in a deep, deep breath, the smell of salt and fish pungent and strangely soothing. His head began to swim, and it felt like the world stuttered for just a second, but after several more deep breaths, everything began to settle.

I'm okay. I'm on dry land… He wiped away some of the dew on the bench. *Sort of. And I'm okay.*

Looking around in the dim, orange light from the lamps, he tried to figure out where he was. There was a children's carousal to the right, painted shades of pink but otherwise shut down, and what looked like a patio for a restaurant in a segregated area closer to shore, the fence made of glass, and tables interspersed evenly with chairs upturned. The fog made anything beyond that invisible to him, and there weren't any helpful signs around to tell him what city he had landed in.

It really didn't matter. Once he could make a portal again, he could just picture his destination in mind, and go there no matter where he was now. He didn't exactly know the layout of England all that well, but he knew he was much further east than Plymouth.

Finally, knowing that Nabu would suspect something was wrong any second, he pushed up from the bench, and lifted off of the pier a few feet. They hadn't settled on a specific meeting point in Plymouth, but he knew he'd given the rest of the team plenty of time, and they should have arrived by now.

Reaching inward, he touched upon his golden core of energy, and ripped a hole through the Universe, drawing himself to a point a good thousand feet above Plymouth.

Strangely enough, the fog hadn't touched the shore here. The open air, though horribly colder, allowed him to see the city spread out beneath him. It was a small city, especially compared to Denver, with only a handful of taller buildings close to the shore in a small concentration. From up here, however, he could see little else, other than a handful of moving lights along roads.

Closing his eyes, Chris reached into the soul realm and searched for Ash's core. He didn't have to look far, because his core felt *drawn* to Ash's now, like a compass pointing north. Spinning in the air, Chris followed that sense, and opened his eyes just as a red flare shot up into the night sky from an open area right along the shore.

That had to be them.

Grinning, Chris eased down into a glide, and headed for the flare at a steady speed. It would feel good to land again, to not have to constantly focus on magic.

A few minutes later, as he drew closer, parking lot lights allowed him to see a large group of dark-clad people waiting, watching.

The Sentinels.

Several stone statues lanced into the sky around them, and Chris had to angle around one with a large sphere atop it, and dropped in low, gently touching down upon the grass.

Half of the group stayed where they were, but the other half rushed forward to greet Chris, headed by a delighted Alycia whose first act was to throw her arms around him.

"I knew you could do it," she beamed. Then, pulling away, she searched his eyes in the dim orange of ambient light. "You did do it, right?"

As the Denver Sentinels, along with Yua, Babbar, and Nina perched on the gnome's shoulder, gathered around Chris, he smiled and nodded. "It wasn't easy, for sure, but I shot it down. I think it might have splashed down in the ocean, but a layer of clouds made it impossible to tell."

"Good," Tom nodded. "Even if it crashes on land, that's still better than the alternative."

Shara stepped forward, unzipping a duffle bag slung over her shoulder and pulling out a black jacket. "Thought you could use this," she said, offering it to him.

"Oh thank you," he snatched it up immediately and threw it on. "Thank you, thank you, thank you! It's freaking cold up there!"

Alycia giggled. "Well duh, mister engineer. You should have grabbed one before leaving."

Shaking his head as he zipped up the jacket, he said, "No, I would have been too late then. They launched seconds after I arrived."

While he explained briefly how he'd brought down the nuclear missile, Shara handed him a cellphone and ear piece to go with his jacket. The phone was already active on a satellite call, and when he placed the earpiece in and tested it, Abby's sing-song voice called back, *"Hello, you wonderful superhero, you!"*

Grinning, Chris sighed contentedly. "Abby! It's good to hear your voice."

"So now what?" Emmi asked. "How will we find and stop Nabu? How do we find the dagger?"

Chris looked out towards the water, towards where he knew a nuclear armed submarine sat. Was that the end of the threat it posed? Would Nabu portal onto the sub to find out what happened? Did she hold any sort of authority in the Navy, or would she-

ROARING PAIN!

It seared through Chris's mind and heart, an overwhelming pulse of magic sizzling through the soul realm, pinging against Chris and Ash's core, and everyone else who was sensitive to it. Chris, Emmi, Alycia, Shara and Ash yelled out in surprised agony, and Chris clutched his head before he fell to his knees.

Moments later, a voice followed.

"Of course it was you!"

The voice came through his mind, through his soul, everywhere and nowhere.

A pulse of nearby magic pressed against Chris's inner being, almost lost in the overwhelming flood of magic that washed over the area. Chris instinctually looked up, and saw Nabu, hovering above them several dozen feet away, past the Japanese Sentinels, next to a red and white lighthouse. She wore the same white-colored clothes she had in the mountains in Denver, loose-fitting shirt and tight pants, her blazing red hair fanning about her head.

Nabu's voice boomed across the open space, magically enhanced, "Do you think you've won? Did you truly believe you could defeat me by destroying a single weapon? I can make more. I can target any major city in the world." She drew nearer, her hands and feet glowing white and keeping her aloft. "Next time I will personally deliver the weapon to ground zero, and you won't be able to stop it!"

The overwhelming flood of magic had finally passed, and Chris climbed to his feet, wondering, *how the hell did she even find us?*

The Japanese Sentinels didn't wait for Nabu's monologue to continue – at Yua's order, they pointed automatic rifles up, and let loose, the roar of machine gun fire echoing across the empty park.

Not one single bullet found its mark. A field of white energy surrounded Nabu, protecting her mortal body from harm.

When the Sentinels ran dry, Nabu, now hovering almost directly above them, sighed plaintively. "Did you really think that would work on me?"

"No," Shara shouted, pulling her pistol from a concealed holster in her jacket. Tom, Alycia, Emmi, Marisol, and Tiana followed suit. "But these will."

As one, they unleashed enchanted rounds from Alycia's handiwork, freezing and flaming and lightning rounds blazing against Nabu's shields, a culmination of three months of practice and hard work.

The pulse of magic skimming off of Nabu's shield was palpable, and Chris and Ash added to the mix, both raising their hands up, wrist-against-wrist, and releasing powerful blasts of golden energy upon the demigod.

It was the most awesome display of magic in a single battle that Chris had yet seen, all concentrated on their nemesis. Chris fueled his powers with rage, with anguish, letting it all out, his golden beam crackling with greater energy.

Nabu just took it all.

Until she couldn't anymore.

In a blur of motion, she launched into the star-studded sky above, enchanted rounds and golden beams piercing the air where she had been.

"Fine!" Nabu's voice boomed as she paused in her ascent, a good thousand feet above. The Sentinels ceased fire and tried to track her, but she was barely visible, even with her glowing appendages. "I'll destroy the city myself!"

And without another word, she rocketed across the sky in a blazing trail of light, heading east by northeast.

Heading for London.

Chris charged his hands and feet with magic, and launched up into the sky as quickly as his body could stand, streaking towards Nabu. If any of his companions objected, their voices were lost in the roar of the wind whipping by.

The air dried his eyes again, and he had to narrow them to slits, wishing upon all things that he could just somehow…

His vision shimmered. The wind suddenly no longer touched his eyes.

Chris blinked, blinked again, and realized why there was a slight hazy glow to the stars above and Nabu's powers ahead. Without knowing exactly how he was doing it, he had shielded his eyes!

In the back of his head, he heard Tattannu's voice, *"We are with you, Champion."*

And then a voice crackled over the earpiece, *"Chris!"* It was Tom. *"Stand down, she's baiting you!"*

No doubt they heard the roar of the wind in his ear, so when he tried to shout out, "I know!" he figured it was lost in the noise.

"I repeat, stand down!" Tom insisted. *"She wants to isolate you, Chris!"*

Nabu was still a long ways away from him, but the glow grew further and further away. He couldn't let her get away! Maybe if he used a portal to get ahead of her, just like he had with the missile…

And then, with a pulse of white light, Nabu was gone in a blink. Her own portal having taken her away.

Taken her to safety.

To cower in fear from the Sentinels.

The more he thought about it, the more that didn't sound like Nabu.

"Shit!" On instinct alone, Chris surrounded himself with a sphere of plasma energy, just as a white energy beam glanced off of it from his left.

He spun through the air, dispelling his shield and redirecting the energy back into his flight, and circled around, searching for Nabu. But the demigod was already gone.

Until she blasted him from behind.

It caught him in the right shoulder, and pain exploded through his body as he felt a distinct POP. The world spun, the stars and the clouds and moonlit land spun, up and down, over and over and over, until he felt ready to vomit.

No matter how hard he tried, Chris couldn't regain control! He tried to move his right arm to help steady and control his spin, but something was horribly, terribly wrong with it. It was near impossible to stop his spin and tumble with his good arm, and he knew he was losing altitude fast!

A blinding flash, and suddenly he thumped into someone's arms, bodies slamming together enough to knock the wind out of him. A shock of red hair in his face told him it was Nabu, that she had caught him.

Whispering in his ear, she said, "Hello, lovely," with a distinctly Scottish accent.

White noise.

Blinding light.

Intense pressure against his soul.

Suddenly he felt warmer. Only by a little, but it was something.

Nabu held him out with her hands under his arm pits, like an adult holding a toddler, and she smiled at him, a show of the strength that Nabu's powers gave her physical body.

And then she dropped him.

Chris had always wanted to believe he would be brave in the face of death. Wanted to believe he would stand (or fall) up to it with composure.

Truth was, he screamed.

Until a split second later, his feet hit concrete, and he collapsed and slammed onto his backside with an "OOF!" and it was all he could do to keep his head from slamming back into a concrete wall behind him.

Blinking in shock and pain, he looked around. To either side were black stone statues of lions facing away. He was in a large concrete square, and directly ahead of him, behind Nabu by several hundred feet, was a large, white stone building, amply lit by countless lights. The square was largely empty and silent, apart from the bubbling of a pair of fountains, each in front of the lion statues.

Chris knew this place. Knew it from video games and photos and movies.

"Trafalgar Square," he commented, both for his own sake, and for the sake of the open communications line still in his ear, hoping the satellite call had reconnected automatically.

"Trafalgar Square?" Tom's voice repeated.

Staring at Nabu, who gently settled onto the concrete, he quietly went, "Mhm," hoping Nabu didn't realize he still was in contact with his team.

"Welcome to dear old Nelson's square," Nabu grinned, her Scottish accent stronger than ever. She motioned above Chris's head, and he craned his neck back as best as he could. A towering pillar stood behind him, he realized. They were inside of the chained-off area around Nelson's statue, and in fact he leaned his back up against the base platform.

Moving just the right way, or rather the wrong way, Chris winced when his right shoulder screamed for attention again. His left hand grasped at it, but that only made it hurt worse, as an incessant, painful pulling sensation made it feel like it would fall off at any second.

"Awww, I'm sorry." Nabu made kissing noises, "Want me to kiss and make it better?"

Then it really dawned on Chris where they were.

London.

"Why the hell did you bring me here?"

She grinned at him, a sickly smile that twisted his stomach and gave him the wrong sort of butterflies. Nabu took one step closer to him. "Because, dear Tatsu." She took another step closer to him. "You've ruined my plans, for a night."

Another step. She was only a few paces away now. "And I was looking forward to my father's death tonight, *and* the destruction of

London."

Another step. "In the name of peace."

One final step, and her boots were next to his feet.

Slowly, almost sensually, she reached behind her, under her loose, white shirt. She tugged. There was a distinctive *shink,* and she pulled a long, slender, ancient dagger into view.

Imhullu.

"I know your secret," she whispered just loud enough for him to hear. "Oh, if I'd known you were Tattannu's Champion back in the hangar, I could have saved us *all* so much bloody trouble. I could have destroyed my father then. Ruled Earth unopposed."

With a kind of slowness that seemed impossible, Nabu stepped over Chris's legs, and crouched low, hovering just above him, her nose inches from his. She pressed the tip of the dagger under his chin, forced him to look up into her eyes. They flashed white.

"Tattannu's Champion," she repeated with a grin.

"You know if you kill Marduk, he'll just come back," Chris grit through clenched teeth, afraid to move his chin too much. "Didn't the mages in Babylon tell you that?"

Nabu's face darkened, soured. All amusement was gone.

"They were cowards," she hissed, and pressed the dagger just enough that it broke the skin under his chin. Something hot dripped down his neck, and he knew it was blood. Could the dagger drain his souls slowly, or would the souls only flow through it and into Marduk upon the death of the host?

Laughing, though trying desperately not to move too much, Chris said, "They defied a demigod. How cowardly could they be?"

A disdainful smirk drew across her face, and she lowered her head so that her eyes stared at him from beneath her brows, a decidedly menacing look. "Bravery and stupidity are not the same thing, my dear Tatsu. You know," she angled her head side to side, looking at Chris from different sides. "You're rather cute. I almost wish I could keep you alive. To enthrall you would be such exquisite revenge."

He sensed it before it happened. Knew it was coming. A mild pulse of magic that he recognized. And he couldn't help but chuckle, and then burst into outright laughter, nearly impaling his own neck upon Imhullu.

Nabu's confidence faltered. "What? What are you laughing at?"

Managing to pause his laughter, he grinned smugly at her. "You, ya big dummy. You're acting like a classic villain, for Christ's sake."

Blinking, she pointed the dagger at his heart, "What are you blathering on about?!"

Opening his eyes wide, as if she should have figured it out, he pointed out, "You're monologuing, dip shit. You know what happens to villains who monologue?"

A blast of golden energy slammed into Nabu, tearing her away from him, sending her sprawling and smashing into the base of the right lion statue, and then sending her careening further out of the square.

"That," he said.

CHAPTER 28

A dozen footsteps running drew Chris's attention to his left, where he saw the Sentinels rushing towards him from the opposite side of the square, weapons drawn, every single one pointing at Nabu.

Their nemesis recovered instantly, jumping up and unleashing a furious blast of white magic at the advancing Sentinels. Alycia expertly raised a blue-white shield, and the blast slammed against it with a deafening crack of thunder, shattering nearby windows and setting off a slew of car alarms.

Given the state of London, Chris cringed – would the infamous Arcane Dawn come barreling down on them? If they were allied with Nabu…

The blast ceased, and Nabu snarled. Legitimately *snarled* at them, as her form was overcome by a white glow, her size growing three times in an instant. Simultaneously, Emmi and Shara pushed to the forefront of the Sentinels and were engulfed by their own, green-shaded glows of magic.

And then monsters faced off against one another. Emmi as a bear, Shara as a gryphon, and Nabu as something new – a long, slender, massive snake's body sporting wings, three rows of fangs that were terrifyingly visible when she hissed, and glowing white eyes. Even at half the height of the house-destroying snakes from Denver, the sight of her new form sent chills of terror through Chris's spine, cave-man fears gripping his heart.

Heedless of the new terror, Shara and Emmi roared a challenge, and attacked above and below, with Shara taking flight and smashing, talons out, into Nabu's head, drawing her face down to the ground, while Emmi swiped chunks out of Nabu's scaly belly.

The Japanese Sentinels established a perimeter around Nelson's statue, while Marisol and Tiana stayed outside of the perimeter, pistols trained on the winged snake, looking for openings to fire upon it. Tom, Alycia, Ash and Babbar, Nina still perched upon his shoulder, gathered around Chris, with Alycia kneeling beside him and shouting, "Chris! Oh my god, your shoulder!"

He thought maybe she referred to how it hung lower than usual, most definitely dislocated or possibly even a broken collar bone. But as Alycia peered behind him at the back of his shoulder, he swore her face turned green. "Oh, God," she whispered, her voice strained, like she had to keep down bile.

Dread washed over the snake-induced terror, along with a cold, cold chill. "What? What's wrong?"

Roars echoed, the ground shook, and the battle raged on. Tiana and Marisol fired off a handful of rounds.

"It's burned, badly," Alycia looked up at Tom. He crouched beside Chris and gently nudged him to lean forward. He hissed in agony when his shoulder shifted.

"Ouch," he managed to say instead of screaming outright.

"Bloody hell, kid," Tom shook his head. "How are you still conscious?"

"Magic," he automatically quipped. "Never mind me, Nabu has the dagger!" Then he remembered the force of Ash's strike against Nabu moments ago. "Or had it," he searched to his right, but Tom and Alycia were both in the way. "Maybe she dropped it, come on!"

Trying to heft himself up, Chris faltered, yelled in pain, fell back. "Chris, don't!" Alycia cautioned, pressing down on his good shoulder.

"We'll look," Tom nodded at Ash. "We've got it, yeah? You're out of this fight, kid."

As Tom and Ash raced towards the statue, Chris shook his head, gripped Alycia's hand with his good one, and stared into her eyes. "I can't be out of this fight," he said. She stared at him, objection in her eyes. "You know it. I know it."

"Chris…"

He glanced at Babbar. At Nina. She stared back at him.

"I can't be out of this fight," he said to them all.

Nina remained silent.

"Help me up," he gripped Alycia's shoulder.

She bit her lip hesitantly, but finally assented and helped, even as she complained, "You're a goddamn idiot, you know that?"

He laughed. "Yeah, but apparently I'm a loveable idiot."

At first, Alycia scowled. But then a smile cracked her lips, and she kissed him on the cheek. "Yeah. You are."

Nabu must have noticed what Tom and Ash were doing. The battle of shapeshifters had taken them up a set of stairs beyond the fountain, but then Nabu suddenly broke off her struggle and, coiling up first, she lunged into the air, twelve-foot-wide wings whipping out into a windy torrent and covering the distance back to the lion's statue in a heartbeat.

Ash yelled in alarm, shoved Tom and themself down, and they rolled underneath Nabu's snapping jaw. Ash came out of their roll and shoved their palms into the air, unleashing a golden blast that clipped Nabu's left wing. The giant snake crashed to the ground, body writhing and sliding, right towards Chris and barreling through Yua's team.

Forcing power into his good arm, Chris whipped it up, thrust his palm out, and projected the largest plasma shield he had ever conjured, stopping Nabu's snake-like body cold, the snake's scales sizzling against his magic.

He dispelled the shield, and Nabu's body glowed white, shrinking back to her human form. Chris and Alycia spotted Yua, who had slid along the square to only half a dozen feet away, and they rushed over to her. "Yua! Are you alright?" Alycia asked.

Groaning, the Japanese XO pushed up onto her elbows. She rubbed her diaphragm, and looked at them plaintively while trying to gasp in air. "Air…knocked out…of me." Similar groans and gasps escaped the lips of the other Japanese Sentinels, none of them looking more than battered.

A blast of magic, and Chris looked up to see that Nabu had narrowly missed hitting gryphon-Shara. Emmi had shifted to some tiny form that he couldn't see, until a second later she shifted into a black panther behind Nabu, and pounced upon the demigod with a furious roar.

Nabu grew in size, turning into her larger-than-normal bear form, and threw Emmi off, just in time for Shara to descend upon her head, talons ripping for Nabu's beady bear eyes.

And then the first violet-colored plasma ball raced into the square, slamming into Shara's flank and sending her tumbling off of bear-Nabu.

The attack had come from a woman out on the street, walking confidently towards them. Confident, no doubt, because of her magic, and the six companions beside her.

All of them magic casters.

Arcane Dawn.

With a furious war cry, the Arcane Dawn members charged upon the square, with the lead woman unleashing another blast of violet plasma towards Emmi, who leapt to the side, barely dodging the attack, which itself exploded above Chris's head on the pillar of Nelson's Statue, gouging a sizeable crater into it and raining chunks and pebbles down upon them.

Another man unleashed a wave of fire towards them, but Ash deflected it with a plasma shield, and then returned fire with a violent golden beam of light that sent the man sprawling.

"Yua, you and your people take on the Arcane Dawn," Chris said to the XO. "We'll handle Nabu."

The Japanese XO had scrambled to her feet, her breathing coming easier, and then she barked orders at her recovering team.

Two of the charging Arcane Dawn members shapeshifted, one into a bear, the other into a great eagle, and they barreled into the ruckus.

Tom yelled a challenge, following Yua into the mess and firing at the lead arcane mage, his enchanted bullets finding their target and instantly freezing the leader solid.

The entire square erupted into chaos, and Chris knew it would only get worse. He searched for Nabu, saw her edging closer and closer to Marisol and Tiana, who were focused on the attacking Arcane Dawn gang.

Imhullu was gripped tightly in her hand.

Cursing, Chris raised his good hand, only to have his line of sight blocked when a pair of eagles tumbled down, talons locked and beaks snapping at one another.

"Aly, check Nabu," Chris shouted.

She saw their nemesis, and just as Nabu brought the dagger down upon Marisol from behind, Alcyia's hand lanced forward, and a shimmering blue-white shield popped up around Marisol, deflecting the blade away and startling both Marisol and Nabu.

Marisol turned, wide-eyed, and unloaded the last three bullets in her magazine into Nabu. They were ice-enchanted, and Nabu's midsection froze instantly, her eyes going wide, and the dagger fell from her fingers as she clutched her wounds.

Chris, Ash, and Alycia rushed forward, passing the eagles-turned-wolves circling one another menacingly. To their astonishment, the solidified core of Nabu's body thawed as fast as it had formed, moments before she fell onto her back.

Running hurt. A lot. But Chris ran anyway, rushing right towards Nabu, who flashed angry eyes upon Marisol. Someone else, maybe one of the attacking gang members, got in Chris's way, but all he could see was Nabu, and all he wanted to do was keep everyone else alive.

So he shunted magic into his feet, leapt, and powered himself into uncontrolled flight. Unleashing a furious, golden beam of energy at Nabu, Chris missed and gouged a burning crevice into the ground, his good arm flailing a moment later when his feet thrust him past and towards the streets beyond.

For the brief instant he flew over, in that moment of terror and anger and hatred, he saw Nabu look up at him. He saw her smirk.

And he saw her point her hands at him.

But Chris wasn't alone. A blue-white shield encased him just as her pure-white blast lanced upwards and splashed harmlessly against the barrier, and then the shield dissipated. Cursing, Nabu raised a white shield just as a golden plasma ball thundered into her, another attack from Ash.

Chris thrust his left hand forward, pulsed magic into it, stopped his forward moment awkwardly, and sought out Nabu.

She bolted up at him, and instead of blazing magic, she collided with him, shoving a fist into his gut as she did, and drove him higher above the streets, away from his friends, away from Ash.

Pulsing magic into his skin, Chris unleashed an electric charge, like the ones he'd accidentally inflicted upon computers in days past, but a thousand times stronger. Nabu yelped, her hair frizzled, and she broke contact, pushing away from Chris.

He tried to bring himself into a hover, but it was impossible with a bad arm, so he realized then that his only choice was to keep moving. Surging magic into his feet, he circled around Nabu, who smugly hovered above the city, and then he turned towards her and blasted forward, unleashing a beam of golden magic at her.

She dodged easily, and turned to attack him, but in that moment, Ash tagged Nabu with another beam of energy. Before Nabu could recover, Shara's gryphon form slammed into the demigod, and she tore into Nabu's back with a razor-sharp beak.

Following Chris's example, the demigod unleashed a crackle of electricity along her skin, and Shara let go in a shriek of agony. Chris had turned around by now, and raced towards Nabu while he unleashed another sizzling golden beam of energy. Distracted by the gryphon, Nabu never saw it coming, and the blast slammed into the demigod, and sent her tumbling from the sky.

For the briefest second, he looked down at the battle below. More Arcane Dawn had manifested from the streets, and the battle was enjoined with gunfire, arcane magic, Earth magic tearing up the square, and more. It was a torrent, a tumult, impossible to keep track of who was who.

Please be alright, he thought when he couldn't find Alycia. Ash yelled his name, and he turned back to Nabu.

Just in time to dodge a plasma ball.

Nabu cursed.

Shara dove in for the kill.

Nabu waved her hand, and a blast of wind surged out, whirled into Shara, tore her from her flight path and sent her spiraling downwards. That same gust of wind blasted into Chris, buffeted him about, but he survived, and pushed on despite renewed pain, thrusting for all he was worth, his legs growing fatigued with having to hold is body up against the G-forces.

We have to end this, he thought. *She'll wear me down, wear all of us down, and then...*

And then a voice called to him over the ear piece. *"Chris!"* It was Tom. *"I have the dagger, get your ass down here!"*

Looking down at the edge of the square, Chris saw Tom waving the dagger in one hand.

Changing course, Chris thrust as hard as he dared, his calves burning, his quads threatening to give out. The ground rushed up at him, and he remembered he had only one good arm. So he flipped around, pointed his feet down, and pushed, pushed for all he was worth.

And his legs gave out.

He slammed into the ground, *hard*, something in his ankle popping awkwardly, his knee, his hip, every joint in his body wailing and crying even as he tucked into a roll and tumbled across the asphalt street, skin scraping on rough concrete, until he flopped to a stop ten feet away from Tom.

Nabu would be right behind him, he knew it, and he tried to stand, but his body simply *wouldn't work* anymore.

Chris had abused it too much that night.

He was mortal. Nothing more.

Tom raced to his side, "Bloody hell, kid, you alright?"

The commander tried to heft Chris up, careful not to hit him with the dagger. "Yeah," Chris said, keeping all weight on his right foot, wincing when anything touched his left, the one where the ankle had popped.

A nice, long stay in a hospital would be wonderful after this. If he survived.

Gaping at the dagger, Chris asked, "Where the hell did you find it?"

The commander never had a chance to answer.

Shara's alarmed voice shouted over the phones, *"Tom, watch out!"*

Tom's eye's darted up behind Chris. Widened.

The commander shoved Chris painfully aside.

A shard of ice six inches thick pierced Tom's chest and tossed him backwards into the ground. The ice shattered. Tom collapsed with a sickening thud. Imhullu clattered down the sidewalk.

And Chris stared in horror.

"TOM!" Shara shrieked.

"Dad?" Alycia's voice followed. *"What's wrong? Shara, what's wrong?"*

Chris glared up into the night sky. At Nabu hovering a hundred feet above and across the street.

Smirking.

Laughing.

"NO!" he roared, and sent a pulse of rage-fueled magic at Nabu.

She dodged, and the attack slammed into the six-story brick and stone building across the street, blasting a fifty foot wide chunk out of it, sending debris raining in every direction.

Gryphon-Shara slammed into Nabu, slammed her into the wall of the building right next to where Chris had obliterated it.

"DAD!"

Alycia's cry tore him away from the battle.

Ash stood beside Alycia at the edge of the square, the latter's features were wide with horror, and she bolted forward and slid to her knees next to Tom, heedless of the concrete tearing up her pants. Ash stayed back to fend off advancing Arcane Dawn thugs.

"No, no, no, no," she shook her head, and gathered up her father's head in her arms. "No, God dammit, NO! Dad, wake up. Wake *up!*"

But Tom didn't stir. Didn't move. Chris rolled up onto his hand and knee, his other hand pulled up as best as he could like a wounded dog, and he crawled on all three towards the love of his life and her fallen father.

She saw him coming, her eyes widening even more. "Chris, oh my God." Her eyes darted between her father and Chris. "No. No, she can't take you all from me. Not like this!"

He crawled to her side, and without looking at Tom, thrust himself into her arms, holding her tight, letting her clutch him, no longer caring about the searing pain, the aches, the razors he felt tearing at his joints.

All Chris wanted to do was hold Alycia.

Hold her back from the pain.

The loss.

Not again, he thought, tears burning his eyes, Alycia's falling onto his shoulder. *Not another parent...*

If only he could have stayed there forever. Comforted her forever.

A thump of something landing hard behind Chris drew their attention away.

Nabu had fallen from the sky, her broken body lying on the blacktop. Above, Shara flourished her wings, shrieked a challenge into the night. It should have been over then.

But you can't kill a demigod that easily.

A white glow engulfed Nabu's body, and she lifted off of the ground. Snaps, cracks, her broken bones mended and jerked back into normal shape, and the gouges in her flesh regenerated fast enough to make Wolverine jealous.

Alycia extracted herself from Chris's arms, stood up. Stalked around her dad's body.

"Why." She started quietly, raising her arms up, pointing her fingers at Nabu, who turned to glower at her. "Won't," Alycia continued, and Chris felt a throng of magic. Strong. Stronger than he'd ever felt from her. "You." Chris remembered Emmi's rage form. Wondered what could happen to Alycia.

"DIE!"

A blue-white shimmering sphere surrounded Nabu, surprising her, surprising Chris. Nabu's head snapped back and forth, up and down, gaping at the containment field. Chris saw something through tears in Alycia's clothes, shimmering blue-white runes glowing brighter and brighter on her skin.

"DIE!" Alycia repeated.

The sphere contracted. Nabu still in it. She wrapped in on herself, wrapped her arms around her torso, drew her knees up.

"Just. Fucking. DIE!"

The sphere contracted again. Bones crunched. Nabu screamed.

She was going to die.

But just her body.

"Alycia, no!" Chris shouted, and tried to stand to go after his love, but his body refused to work, and he fell flat on his face. "We need her alive!"

The sphere constricted again. More bones snapped. Crunched. Twisted.

They needed the dagger. Chris looked over to where it had slid to a stop. "The dagger, we need to use Imhullu!" He hoped someone heard him on the radio, because he couldn't do anything to stop Alycia, his body simply refused to work, even as he stumbled towards the weapon.

The sphere constricted yet again. Nabu's screams sputtered and died.

And then Emmi appeared, flashing into being from whatever smaller form she was a second ago. A giant direwolf came barreling after her, but Ash intercepted it with a plasma blast. Emmi picked up the dagger, looked intently up at Nabu.

"Alycia, get ready," she said into her earpiece.

Did Alycia hear her? Could she hear anything beyond the crunch of Nabu's bones or her own rage?

The blue-white runes on his love's body grew ever brighter. The sphere tightened more.

Emmi transformed into a falcon, but unlike everything else, the dagger didn't disappear into her form, and remained clutched in her claws. As she flew, Chris shouted, "Alycia! Aly...you have to stop. Let go!" Her glowing eyes twinkled, glowed brighter, but for a split second, he saw them look his way.

Emmi soared up above Nabu. Stalled just above the demigod.

"My love," his voice shook, cracked. "Let. Go..." Alycia looked at Chris. The light in her eyes dimmed.

And then Emmi shapeshifted back to her human form, and shouted, "Aly, now!"

The glow around Alycia's body flickered. She blinked in surprise.

The sphere dispelled, just as Emmi's falling form crashed into it, and Imhullu sank hilt-deep into Nabu's shoulder. With a crunch, and a cry of pain, the two smashed into the sidewalk on the other side of the road.

The bulk of Nabu's body was under Emmi, but she still rolled off and tumbled onto the ground, cursing up a storm and grasping at her legs. "Ow, ow, ow," he heard her say, and under any other circumstances, he might have laughed. "Fuck me, shit, that HURTS!"

She was alive!

And Nabu...

A pulse of white light blew out in a wave, running along the ground, washing over Chris and Aycia. His soul felt something push, *shove* against it, and he knew then what was coming. All of that energy, all of that raw *power* contained in Nabu's physical form was about to release in one cosmic blast.

"Emmi!" he shouted. "Aly, we have to get out of here!" Alycia stared at Nabu's fallen body, stared at the energy threatening to release from it.

The marks on her skin still glowed blue.

"Alycia Taylor," he shouted, distantly remembering that using someone's full name was more likely to get their attention. It worked. She turned, looked at him, her eyes glowing blue for only a second before returning to their normal color. "She's going to blow, we have to get out of here!"

Shara must have come to the same conclusion. In her gryphon form, Shara swept down upon Emmi, snatched her up in massive talons, and then took off into the sky.

Alycia, snapping out of her rage-fueled state, gaped at Chris, at her dad's body. Rather than run, she rushed to Chris's side, grasped him in a tight hug, heedless of his injuries, and conjured a blue-white wall between them and Nabu.

Just as an explosion of white light engulfed the street. It was as loud as a spaceship launch, as thunderous as a thousand bombs going off at once. The block-sized building façade, or what was left of it, disintegrated. The street lurched beneath Chris. Heaved. Roiled.

And then the flash was gone.

Chris blinked. Alycia blinked back. They stared at each other. He thought he saw the glimmer of blue within her pupils.

Slowly, afraid of what they might see, they parted and turned to look at where Nabu had been.

Nothing.

Anything within two hundred feet, except for the area behind Alycia's shield, was simply gone. Somehow, she had protected them, the street, Tom's body, all of it.

Half of the building's façade was gone, leaving exposed floors. *Those were homes*, he realized with a sickening feeling. Had anyone been inside?

He should have felt jubilation. They all should have.

Nabu was gone.

But the price was high. Too high.

Silence fell upon Trafalgar Square. The fighting had stopped.

No, he thought. *It's more than that.*

The silence was oppressive. Like a blanket had fallen upon the city, dousing any and all sound. Chris and Alycia should have heard each other's breathing. Looking at her, he frowned, and asked, "Are you okay?" His voice sounded muffled, like a person's voice sounded when one was submerged in a pool.

If it had been from the blast, surely his ears would be ringing, but even that was absent.

There was just…nothing.

Until there was everything. A roar of white noise, louder than the explosion, louder than anything, penetrating not just through his ears, but through his *soul*. Something ripped a hole in the Universe, he felt it, a punch to the chest the likes of which he didn't think was possible.

A blinding light in the distance. White light. All types of magic cascading together at once.

Yet for the sickening, dark sense Chris always felt around Nabu, it was nothing compared to the force that coalesced a mile away. It felt like a frigid darkness wrapping itself up around his soul, sucking warmth and energy straight out of him into a hungry, devouring void.

A tower of light stretched hundreds of feet high a mile away from them, directly down the street from where they stood. A nearby street sign told him that it was a road called Strand.

The light receded, the white noise faded, painfully slowly, but it faded.

In place of the column of light stood a monstrous sight.

A giant of a man, towering over London, skin shimmering in ethereal power. He was the very pinnacle of an old-world god, with a long, curling, translucent beard, and a crown upon a shock of white hair. His skin was translucent, too, as if he were there and not there, and even his clothes, a white shirt and skirt-like lower half, separated by a golden rope, looked only half-real

In the center of his chest, where a human heart would be, a black and orange fire burned.

"Nabu's soul," Chris breathed.

"What?" Alycia asked, breathless.

"Nabu's soul. Four thousand years on Earth. I dunno, but I think…" He looked at the crater where Nabu had perished. "I think Nabu's soul had become more than the sum of its parts." He nodded up at the towering entity a mile away. "I think it was enough."

"Enough for what?" she asked.

The godlike entity's eyes locked on Chris, sending a shiver through his body.

"Enough for Marduk to escape his prison."

CHAPTER 29

Video games and movies had nothing on the vision before Chris. Seeing a giant, vengeful god towering hundreds of feet in real life was far more terrifying than seeing one on a flat screen.

Chris gaped upwards, his broken and battered body forgotten for the moment. Alycia stood next to him, her eyes likewise wide.

The infernal took one step towards them, shaking the ground in a mini-earthquake. That was when Chris realized how precarious their perch was — Nabu's destruction had blasted the ground out all around them, except for a small sliver where Alycia's shield had protected them. That ground began to crumble.

Cursing, Chris gripped Alycia for support, his knees and ankles threatening to give out on him as fresh, shooting pain roared into his nervous system.

"Come on, we've gotta get clear," he tried nudging her back towards the square, just as the road beneath them lurched down at an angle.

Tom's body began sliding down, and Alycia lunged towards it, hand outstretched, "Dad, no!"

Grasping at her, Chris feebly tried to stop her.

Gryphon-Shara came to the rescue. She must have dropped off Emmi already, and now she swooped down upon Tom's body and, with wings flapping so as to keep her weight off of the crumbling street, she gently picked up Tom's form in her talons, and then flew upwards again.

With her father's body safe, Alycia tried to help Chris back towards the square. With a terrifying rumble, the concrete all gave out at once, and Chris and Alycia dove for the edge, just as Yua, Tiana, and Marisol ran to their aid, reaching out hands and catching their arms, yanking them out of the crater just in time.

Chris's knees gave out then, and if it weren't for Tiana's strength and firm grip, he might have fallen face-first onto concrete. As it was, even holding him up by his good arm hurt, and he begged her through gasping breaths, "Put me down, put me down!"

She did as asked, and eased him onto concrete, with Alycia trying to help, but afraid of touching his broken arm. Once he was down, she knelt next to him, and gently caressed his cheek. "Oh, Chris," she said through wet, red eyes. He swore there was still a hint of blue in her irises. "Are you okay?"

DOOM! The thunderous sound of Marduk taking another footstep, covering hundreds of feet in one stride.

Chris looked down Strand, saw the towering form, the glowing white eyes blazing down at him. At *him*.

Marduk had absorbed Nabu and knew who Chris was, knew *what* he was, and was coming for him. At hundreds of feet tall, he'd cover a mile in minutes. The sick, cold, empty feeling grew stronger.

There wasn't time.

"No," he shook his head, finally answering Alycia's question. Tearing his horrified gaze from the god, he looked into Alycia's eyes. "None of us are. Not unless we destroy Marduk."

Even as he said it, he felt his insides twist and turn, an ache welling up within. Alycia knew exactly what he meant, and it broke his heart to see her grow ever more terrified. "No," she shook her head. "No, you can't. No, I…I just lost Dad," she motioned towards her father's body. "I just lost Dad, and I can't lose you too. I can't!"

"Alycia," he said, reaching to caress her face with his good hand.

"No!" she grasped his hand, crushed it tightly. Her voice broke, "I can't. I…I-I can't d-do this without you. I c-can't face it. The emptiness. The l-loneliness. Please, Chris, *please!*"

His throat cinched closed, and for all his effort to talk, he couldn't. There weren't enough words in the world. There wasn't enough time to say what he'd meant to say for so long. Now, more than ever, he regretted waiting so long to tell Alycia how he felt.

All that time they could have been together. And now they had none.

Blinking away tears, he looked around vaguely, until he realized the last place he had seen Imhullu. "Shit, the crater." Looking up, just as Shara shapeshifted into her human form and stared down at them, he said, "I need the dagger."

"NO!" Alycia screeched, gathering up his tattered jacket in her fists. "No, you can't! I can't!"

Shara's lips pressed into thin lines, and with those beautiful, enchanting violet eyes, she stared at him and nodded. She shapeshifted back into her gryphon form then, and glided down into the crater. Hopefully, the dagger wasn't lost.

Chris turned his attention back to his love, his life, his *everything*. And through the tears in her eyes, he saw the heart of her. The soul of her. And he knew then that he would do whatever it took to protect her.

"Alycia," he whispered. "I have to. I have to protect you. Protect everyone," he looked at Emmi as she hobbled over from somewhere near the square. Ash followed, staring forlornly at Chris. The Japanese Sentinels likewise gathered around, Yua joining the inner circle while the others surrounded them and brandished weapons, ready to protect against anything.

DOOM!

Well, almost anything, Chris thought, trying not to look up at the approaching infernal.

The Arcane Dawn must have been defeated, he reasoned. That or they fled when they saw Nabu destroyed, or when they saw a larger-than-life god lumbering towards them.

The distant wail of air raid sirens startled Chris. He knew what that meant. Whatever was left of the government had finally surged into action. A terrifying threat was upon their city, and they were ordering their citizens to do the only thing that made sense – find shelter.

Even if no shelter could ever protect them against Marduk.

He looked then at Tiana. The first pilot he had ever flown with. He looked at Marisol, one of the few survivors from the original Denver Sentinels team that he'd fought along side.

So much death, he thought. *So many losses.* His chest ached at the memory of Grumpy and Grumpier, of Jered, all of the Sentinels who had perished over the past six months. *No more.*

And then he saw Babbar emerging from the darkness, with Nina sauntering along at his side. Chris had to do a double-take on the dragon – she had grown. More than doubled in size, and now stood waist-high next to Babbar. Her appearance startled everyone.

"Kid," Babbar said, his voice remorseful. "As terrified as I am right now..." The gnome glanced at the approaching infernal, just as another thunderous footstep shook the ground with a deafening *DOOM!* "Kid, you can't do this," he looked again at Chris, those strange amber eyes staring thoughtfully.

Chris shook his head. "I don't have a choice. We have to destroy Marduk."

"It can be me," Ash rushed forward to stand next to Chris. Alycia looked up at them, her eyes a mixture of hope and regret. Ash pushed on, "It doesn't have to be you. We're both Tattannu's Champions, right?"

Iron will gripped Chris. "No," he shook his head, and tried to stand up, but his body just *wouldn't work!* "Dammit, no! I did this!" He waved towards Marduk. "This is all *my fault,* okay? I used the Dragonstone, I dismantled the Barrier, this is *my* responsibility."

"You don't understand," Babbar took two steps closer. "Think, Chris! Look at what Nabu's destruction did!"

Chris turned back to the two-hundred-foot-wide crater, just as gryphon-Shara leapt out and soared above them, Imhullu gripped in her beak. And then Chris turned towards Marduk as the god took another step towards them.

DOOM!

The infernal was half a mile away, but he was well within the core of London. He was hundreds of feet tall. And Nabu had only been a portion of the power contained within Marduk.

An infernal.

A literal god.

"Shit," he hissed. "If we destroy Marduk here..."

Babbar nodded. "Then you may as well have let the nuke destroy the city."

"Then, what?" his hands flailed out, and his right shoulder immediately screamed renewed pain. "Agh, dammit! What do we do, huh? How do we stop him without killing millions of innocents?"

He stared at Marduk, as Marduk stared at him, pulling at his soul, draining him of any semblance of warmth. Another footstep.

DOOM!

Shara landed outside of the circle, shapeshifted back into her normal form, and rushed in. "Chris," she said, out of breath, dagger in-hand. "I've got it! But I just thought, we can't destroy Marduk, not while he's in-"

"We know," Babbar interrupted. "We just figured that out."

"Oh," she came up short, standing next to Emmi. Emmi leaned against her for support, all weight off of her right foot. "Oh, so we have a plan then?"

DOOM!

"No," Chris shook his head, sighing.

"Yes," Nina's voice corrected him.

He looked at the dragon, as did Ash. Nina stared back at Chris.

"We do?" he gaped.

No one else had heard her, but as soon as Chris asked, their eyes fell upon the dragon. Somehow, her scales seemed a more vibrant shade of emerald, and he swore she had grown even larger in the last minute.

Her lizard-like eyes gazed into his, and even though he *still* couldn't feel her presence against his soul, he swore she saw him. *Saw* him, for real. His core. His powers.

His ancestors.

The core. The Barrier. All those souls.

DOOM!

Chris understood. "We do."

He turned again to Alycia. "Only, I don't know what will happen. I can get Marduk out of town. I can destroy him. I think," he glanced at Nina before giving Alycia his full attention, "But I don't know what'll happen to me."

Alycia's face was wet with tears, her eyes puffy, and when he finished, her lip trembled. She sucked her lip in, bit down just a little bit, and then nodded. "It's-" Her voice cracked. She cleared it, cleared it again, and drew in a deep, bracing breath. "It's better than..." She looked at the dagger. "That."

He couldn't help but grin. "Yeah, it is." Extracting his hand from hers, Chris reached up and caressed her cheek, brought her gaze back to him. "If it is at all possible, I swear to you, I'll come back." Pausing enough to force down the well of emotions shoving up through his chest, he nodded. "I promise."

Lightly pressing her hands to his, holding it tightly to her face, she managed a weak smile. "You'd better." And then she grabbed his neck, and pulled him in to kiss, tighter, fiercer, *stronger* than they had ever kissed before. He lost himself in that moment, let himself experience it, really *experience* it. *Hold on to this moment,* he thought. *Hold on while you can.*

DOOM!

Their moment was lost. They parted. Chris kept his eyes closed for just a moment. He thought, *When I open them, memorize every facet you can in the seconds you have left.*

And he did. Every freckle. Every nuance. The shape and thinness of her eyebrows. The beautiful swirl of her eyes. The shape of her lips. He took it all in.

One.

Last.

Time.

And then he looked to his best friend in the world. Emmi knelt beside him, tears brimming in her eyes. "You always have to take center stage, don't you?" she asked with forced amusement.

"Hey now," he induced fake hurt into his voice. "Since when have I ever wanted to be the center of attention?"

She laughed. "Yeah. I know, that's not you at all, I just..." Her humor broke, her expression changed in a heartbeat from amused to pained, and she surged forward, wrapping her arms around him as tight as she could, and he hugged back, forcing himself to ignore the pain, the anguish, both in his body, and in his heart.

DOOM!

Something shifted. A change in the air, like a build-up of static. Emmi pulled back, and together they looked up at Marduk. He had stopped, and was raising his hand towards them, a crackling sphere of white energy mired by a black taint growing in his palm.

He meant to destroy them all.

Their time was up.

Chris pushed Emmi away, and then, as fast as his broken body would let him, he closed his eyes and reached inward, visiting the soul realm one last time.

Ash was already there, staring at their resonating souls. The golden spheres spun against one another in a dizzying, blurring circle. He gaped at them, and stepped up next to Ash.

They looked at him then, and smiled. "I was going to try to do this before you could," they said. "Turns out, I have no idea what to do. I...I'm sorry. I wanted to spare you, spare your friends, your family..."

"Ash," he placed a hand on their shoulder, forced them to look into his eyes. "They're your family too, now, remember? So do me a favor?"

Ash reached up, gripped his hand. "Anything."

"Take care of them for me."

They smiled, nodded. "I will. I promise."

Smiling back, Chris squeezed Ash's shoulder, and then let go to face the spheres. Except, something new caught his attention. He looked around, out into the gray haze. The shadows weren't shadows anymore. Every single indistinct figure had coalesced into solid forms. Into the people who had come before him.

All of Tattannu's descendants. And Tattannu himself, who broke away from the crowd and approached. Another person followed, the familiar pale, teenaged form of his sister Naomi.

Together, they stopped between Chris and the golden spheres.

"Champion," Tattannu said. "It is time."

A renewed lump formed in Chris's throat, and he looked at Naomi. At his long-lost sister.

She raced forward and threw her arms around him. "My dear brother," she whispered in his ear. "I am so very proud of you."

The weight of the moment sunk in, and he clutched his sister as tight as he could. "Oh God," he whispered back. "This is it, isn't it? After today, if I...If I somehow..."

She pulled away, but he wouldn't let her go too far. There wasn't time, but he had to make this moment last as long as he could. Because he knew what she was going to say next.

"After this," she nodded, smiling for his benefit. "After tonight. I'll finally be at rest. One way or another."

With a forced gulp, he said in a shuddering breath, "One way or another?"

"There are no guarantees in life," Tattannu said. "You will either succeed or fail, and the fate of all rides upon your next actions. But know this, Christopher Tatsu." Tattannu waved out upon the crowd around them, at the millions of *persons* that were linked to him through a golden sphere of soul energy. "You are not alone in this fight."

Drawing in a shuddering breath, Chris gazed into his sister's endlessly-black eyes. "So you'll be with me, too?"

"I've always been with you," she replied. "And I always will be."

Blinking away tears, he nodded. "Then I know we'll win."

She smiled at that, beautiful, light. It was the smile he remembered. The smile he would always keep with him.

Naomi stepped aside, and before Chris was his soul, still resonating with Ash's. He stepped up to them, and reached out with both of his hands, thankful that his soul avatar wasn't as battered and broken as his real body.

Then, as if on command, the souls stopped their dizzying spin. They hovered before him, side-by-side, but he *knew* which was his. Ash's still touched his, but that hardly mattered now. Because soon, theirs would be reduced to a normal magic-wielders soul. Powerful, but not a million souls powerful.

Chris stepped closer to his core. Touched the outer shell with his hands. The sparking, lancing lightning within coalesced around his hands like a plasma ball. And then he pushed his hands *in,* and the lightning danced all around his fingers, his palms, his hands.

Step.

By.

Step.

He pushed further in. Deeper. Endlessly deeper into the depths of a million souls. Elbow-deep. Shoulder deep. And then his entire body entered.

A tumult of voices. "Champion," they called him. "Chris." "Defender." Innumerable names spoken in innumerable languages.

They all came to him at once. His soul flared. Not *their* soul.

His.

Every single soul drew into his.

All became one.

One became all.

Until all that was left was a single entity millions of souls strong.

The Champion.

CHAPTER 30

There was no Christopher Tatsu. No Naomi Tatsu. No Tattannu. The golden core had turned white, a sign of all powers possible flowing through the veins of a single avatar. Ash's soul had shrunk, diminished, until it remained as a former shadow of itself.

Still powerful.

Still strong.

But not millions strong.

And yet, it still shone bright. Bright enough, perhaps, for two.

The Champion's eyes blazed open in the real world. Their gaze looked out beyond just the physical realm. They saw all. Saw the souls *within* the bodies of every person around them. Persons who were important to one, but to a million, they were nothing more than persons in need of saving.

The Champion's body was broken, but that was easily fixed. Millions of souls fueled their healing powers, and in an instant, the body was mended.

The infernal, Marduk, towered a quarter of a mile away, his house-sized hand outstretched. He unleashed his power, a blazing, crackling white light tainted with darkness.

Exerting the power of thousands, the Champion raised their own hand, and conjured a shimmering white shield above the gathered Sentinels. Marduk's blast smashed into the shield with explosive force, a deafening roar and massive shockwave that swept into the city, shattered windows, and blew radio towers and water tanks off of rooftops.

When the roar subsided and left a distinct ringing in the ears of everyone in London, Marduk smugly shook his head, and lowered his arm.

"CHAMPION." His voice was a roar, penetrating all barriers, resonating against all souls, inducing terror into all. Marduk's white-glowing eyes shifted. His smug face slackened. "MUŠḪUŠŠU…"

The Champion stood up easily. The one known as Alycia backed away, staring in horror at them. "Chris?" she asked.

Without regarding her, the Champion replied, "He is with us." Their voice was a storm of voices.

Alycia paled, and then rushed over to her companions, the one named Emmi and the one named Shara. The Champion felt only a hint of remorse, the souls regretful that so much had to be sacrificed for this, the final battle of a four-thousand-year-old cause.

But Marduk would not sit idly by. And the Champion, though powerful, could not hope to force Marduk from the city alone.

Their gaze fell upon the dragon, now grown to be as tall as Babbar.

With millions of minds and thousands of years of experience, the Champion was able to connect age-old pieces together, and they knew then what they must do. "You are the conduit," they reasoned.

Nina stepped closer. *"Yes. I imprisoned Marduk, and though his shackles are broken, the link still exists."*

"Then that is our path," the Champion replied. They looked at the dagger Imhullu, Marduk's divine weapon. And if Marduk's soul was still tied to Nina's, then so too was the dagger tied to Nina.

Stepping towards Shara and her friends, the Champion held out his hand. There was no friendliness in their action, and they were aware of it, but under the control of so many, it was hard to do more than what was necessary. They felt remorse as a collective when they beheld Shara's response to their heartless motions, but they could do no more. Marduk would attack again, and even as powerful as the Champion was, their shield would not hold forever.

"Please give us Imhullu," the Champion said.

Shara looked down at the weapon hesitantly, then at the Champion's glowing white eyes. "What are you going to do with it?"

"Use it against Marduk," they replied simply.

Alycia accused, "You're gonna stab yourself once you get him out of the city!"

The Champion's eyes darted to her. "No," they replied simply.

Their eyes looked again upon Shara.

Stammering for a second, Alycia said, "You…y-you're lying."

Again, the Champion glanced at Alycia. "No." Back to Shara. "Imhullu. Please. Quickly."

Staring into their million-soul-strong eyes, Shara heaved a defeated sigh, and placed the weapon firmly in their hand. The Champion willed their hand to close about the grip, and felt the connection almost instantly.

A connection to Marduk.

To Nina.

For the first time, they felt Nina's presence. Felt her power.

So much power.

Yet not the power of a soul. Not the strength of a soul.

It was *More*.

In between heartbeats, the Champion understood. Celestials were the source of magic. The source of the power that fueled the souls of all life in the Universe. Yet they themselves did not have souls. They were something else. Something truly alien.

Beyond that, the Champion reasoned that the celestials could not be understood. Not in their present context.

Staring at the dragon, who had now grown so large that they stood eye-to-eye with the Champion, they nodded at the celestial. She nodded back.

Knowing what came next, the Champion knew they must leave the area with Nina. Turning, they marched out of the circle, dispelling the shield that they had forgotten they had left up. Nina followed, with Christopher Tatsu's companions having to hustle out of the way to keep from being pushed aside by the growing dragon.

Once clear of the people, the Champion's pace quickened. First into a fast walk, then into a jog, and then into a run. Nina kept pace easily. And then she leapt into the air. The Champion followed suit, using magic to easily levitate off of the ground and rise higher, higher, and higher still into the air. Nina caught them with her growing paws, wrapped talons around their arms.

And they became one. Nina gave herself over to the Champion, her red-fueled powers coursing and flowing, enhancing the Champion's power. Their white eyes grew a shade red, their souls and their powers. Together, their bodies grew, faster, stronger, larger. Their skin rippled and crackled with energy, growing translucent like Marduk's. Wings sprouted from their back, scaly and emerald. Scales appeared along the Champion's cheeks and neckline, down their arms, talons grew from their fingernails. And within their chest glowed a bright white flame of millions of souls, tinged red by the influence of a goddess.

Imhullu grew with them, morphed, transformed, affected by the energy of both Champion and celestial. It became a sword, curved at the tip, two-handed, the blade easily a hundred feet long.

As one entity, the Champion and Nina hurled forward and smashed into Marduk, who stared dumbly at them until collision. Ensuring the blade did not pierce Marduk yet, the Champion touched down on the street and grappled with the god, charging along Strand, crushing the street and countless cars still parked on it.

Marduk struggled, knocked the Champion off balance. Their shin skinned against a façade of brick and stone buildings five stories tall, sending rubble skittering along the street as citizens, failing to heed the air raid sirens, dove out of the way.

The Champion tripped on a double-decker bus, thankfully abandoned, and they along with Marduk tumbled down, landing atop a large swath of buildings, pulverizing the structures. The Champion felt the sudden release of a dozen souls, and guilt coupled with rage gripped them. More innocent deaths.

Marduk cared not. He blazed his skin with energy, hot enough to ignite into plasma and set their surroundings ablaze. Gripping the Champion, he rolled them over to the south side of Strand, crushing more buildings and slaughtering dozens more, while pinning the Champion beneath them.

Rising up to their knees, and with a roar that shook every building in all of London, Marduk lifted his hands and unleashed a thundering, white-with-black magic assault upon them. The Champion conjured a shield around their physical body, skin-tight, and endured the blast to their face. It blinded them momentarily, and it was enough that Marduk heaved off of them, and then lifted them up until their feet dangled above the rubble of destroyed buildings.

"THIS IS MY WORLD!" Marduk roared, gripped the back of the Champion's head, and then slammed them face-first down into a previously un-harmed building. If not for their shield, the radio tower atop the building would have pierced their eye, but the force of the impact still jarred the Champion. "MINE!" Marduk lifted their head again, and slammed it further down, pulverizing the rubble into a fine powder and driving them past ground level, smashing their face into sewers and tunnels beneath the ancient city. "YOU WILL NOT KEEP ME FROM IT AGAIN. YOU WILL NEVER IMPRISON ME AGAIN!" Marduk lifted again, smashed again. The Champion's shield flickered from the immense kinetic energy rallied against it.

They had to rebound, *now.*

Surging magic throughout their body, the Champion applied the gravity-defying magic to every part of them, and *pushed,* which simultaneously levitated their entire, massive form off of the ground, and shoved Marduk off of them. He stumbled backwards, crushing more buildings under foot, but then he caught the tip of the Champion's right wing at one knuckle, and yanked painfully upon them to steady himself.

Roaring in protest, the Champion extended a hand, and unleashed a furious blast against the infernal. He hadn't prepared himself for such an attack, and it caved in his translucent chest, exposing for a moment his flaming core. The infernal's grip on their wing was torn free, snapping the wing joint, before he lost his footing at the bank of the Thames river and fell backwards into the water, crushing a passing boat underneath and sending up a giant wave that washed ashore on both banks, drowning buildings and washing over bridges both up- and down-river.

Pulsing magic into their back, while simultaneously healing their broken wing, the Champion righted themselves, and levitated higher off of the ground. Marduk sloshed around in the river, and gripped the edge of the river bank to pull himself up. The Thames was not a shallow river, and yet Marduk stood tall enough that even in the middle of the river, it only came up to his knees.

With a roar of rage, the infernal clasped his wrists together, palms-out, and unleashed his most powerful attack yet, a blazing, sun-bright blast that smashed against the Champion's shield and briefly overcame it, sizzling their skin and sending them careening through the sky, up into the clouds and the light of the moon. Their upward momentum stalled, and they fell from the stars in a smoldering, smoking trail, and crashed somewhere far to the north of Trafalgar Square. Their impact crushed countless apartment homes, businesses, and houses, and gouged long troughs through green parks and ripped trees from their roots as they slid a good quarter mile north, extinguishing even more lives.

Half of the Champion's torso was blistered and blackened, and their glowing core was exposed to the outside air for the briefest of moments while their magic raced to heal their body.

Trying to be careful not to crush any more buildings, the Champion rose from the rubble and towered above the smaller, suburban structures. Across the way, lit by the moon breaking through scattered clouds and the glow of city lights, Marduk climbed out of the river and set into a thundering run towards the Champion.

We must end this now. Too many lives lost. Too many souls.

Because the truth was, in proximity to those who died, Marduk consumed the souls as they were released. A fate worse than death, by any measure. The more innocents slaughtered in their battle, the stronger Marduk would become.

So the Champion unfurled their wings and, aided by magic, soared into the night sky. Marduk wasn't content to let that happen, so he leapt high, likewise fueling his ascent with magic.

The Champion watched the infernal's approach, braced themselves for the inevitable. But they didn't expect Marduk's fingers to grow into razor-sharp claws, which he thrust into the Champion's ribs, while smashing into them with his body and sending them end-over-end through the sky, further north.

The physical damage was superficial. The Champion was more than magically-enhanced flesh and bone. But the claws penetrated into the white-hot core tinted red, giving the infernal a direct connection to them.

And he wound his way in, slithered and slunk and inked, the black taint infecting one ancestor after another. Pain beyond agony wracked their very essence. Millions of souls cried out, agonized by the sickness spreading, inch by inch, soul by soul.

"YOU HAVE FAILED, CELESTIAL," Marduk hissed into their ethereal ear. "YOUR CHAMPION WILL SERVE ME, AND YOU WILL BE CHAINED TO THEM FOR ALL ETERNITY."

Thick fear coursed through the Champion's body, and they knew not whether it was Nina's or theirs. It all came down to this, the last moment of their time, the last second of existence. The darkness spread within, and there was no cure for it, not this time.

What could an infernal with a celestial servant do to the Earth?

What hell would be unleashed?   How many souls would be consumed?

The duo sailed through the sky, the ground rushing up at them. More apartments beneath. More houses. More souls.

No more.

With their free, taloned hand, the Champion seized Marduk's face, and *dug* their claws in, gripping tightly to the infernal. He howled, not in pain, but in surprise.

The souls were quickly failing and falling. They wanted to turn on one another, those enthralled ready to revolt against those still fighting. But the Champion wouldn't give in. *Chris* wouldn't give in.

Because something still separated Chris from the others. Something protected him.

And he wouldn't let Marduk harm another soul.

With Nina's help, he ripped, tore, and bashed his way through the Universe. Further outside the city wasn't good enough. There were still too many innocents beyond. And if he was right, Marduk's destruction would not cause a compression wave like a Nuke. No, it would only incinerate anything caught in the implosion.

That left only one option. Even if it mean Chris would not survive.

Marduk knew what was coming. He yanked his claws out of the Champion's chest, tried to push away, but the Champion held on tight, their claws sinking deeper into the infernal's skull.

A hole in the Universe swallowed the two of them.

White noise.

Blinding light.

A torrent of power as millions of souls and a celestial wrenched them from the skin of the Earth, and arrived twenty miles above the city.

And they plunged the blade of the sword into their nemesis, into the very core of Marduk.

The blade pierced his flaming heart, and the remnants of thousands of slain humans from eons passed cried out. Not in terror, but in celebration. In relief.

A flood, an outpour of energy, as the souls of generations of Tattannu descendants connected to Marduk's core, made up entirely of the souls he had consumed throughout his existence, now battered and broken and consumed to mere threads of their former selves.

The descendants rushed in, all at once, through the Champion's hand, through the hilt of the sword, through the enchanted blade, and into the heart of their enemy. An army the likes of which no mortal human could have ever imagined.

The Champion was no more. His hand released the sword, his body falling limp as he fell, fell forever, twenty miles down to his death, while humanity's greatest nemesis writhed and flailed in agony.

CHAPTER 31

Throughout the battle, Ash could still feel a connection to Chris, to the *Champion*. Every blow, every single stab. They felt when Marduk dug his claws into the Champion's body, connected with the souls within, and tried to taint them like the souls Nabu had corrupted.

They watched with the Sentinels as, miles to the north, the two goliaths soared through the air, half-falling, half-floating, further and further away.

And then *his* presence reasserted itself. Ash felt it, recognized it as kinship to their own soul. Felt it within.

"Chris," they said aloud.

Alycia, crouched over her father's body with Emmi beside her, heard Ash. "What?"

In a flash of white light, suddenly the two giants disappeared. A companion flash appeared neck-achingly high in the sky.

It had to have been a portal. Perhaps the largest ever conjured on Earth, Ash guessed. The Sentinels stood riveted, eyes searching the sky for any other sign of them.

Babbar shifted his weight, one foot to another, his hands clenching and unclenching. "Come on, Nina," he said anxiously. "Kick his arse."

In that instant, they all felt it, even those without magic. Thousands of wretched, downtrodden souls cried out in relief. Millions more roared a challenge. The entire *world* rumbled with it. Every person, every animal, every plant and insect and fungus. All life shuddered in response, a collective deep breath.

Waiting.

Watching.

Hoping.

Something slammed into Ash. Something not there, but they still felt it, stumbled, fell over onto their backside.

"Ash!" Alycia's startled shout echoed.

It was as if some great force, stretched taught, had snapped back like a rubber band.

Like a force split between Ash and someone else had just been released from the distant end, and now resided fully within them.

And then a second sun appeared. A bright white flash, bright enough to light up all of the U.K. and Western Europe, flared into existence above their heads, casting noon-shadows upon London, sharper than the sun's shadows.

A cacophony of sound and light that awoke all. It lasted moments, not even a full ten seconds, but it burned its memory into the eyes, souls, and hearts of all who saw it. When it vanished, it left a hazy afterimage in everyone's vision, and a solid twenty seconds later, a booming clap of thunder that rattled windows as far away as Iraq and Greenland echoed through the atmosphere.

A wave of relief washed over everyone. The oppressive, dark, inky pressure of Marduk's presence was gone. As if a weight they hadn't quite noticed or forgotten was there had finally lifted.

The Sentinels erupted into cheers, pumping fists into the air, clasping each other on the back.

It was over!

Marduk was gone! The shadow had passed, and a new dawn approached.

But Ash still sat on the concrete, with Alycia, and then Emmi, kneeling beside them, asking them if they were okay.

Closing their eyes, Ash looked within, into the soul realm. It was eerie now, without all of those hazy figures milling around beyond the edge of their vision. Lonely. Just empty, swirling fog. Ash's soul, still golden, remained, smaller and dim compared to what it once was. Diminished.

And yet.

And yet.

It was brighter than Alycia's and Emmi's, whose souls hovered near Ash's.

Ash blinked at their own soul. At the golden sphere, with a bright point of light inside and bolts of electricity playing within the inner surface.

They blinked again and stepped closer to the soul. Reached out, but didn't dare touch it. Not yet.

They stared at that point of light in the middle. Squinted, peered close, nose a mere centimeter from the surface.

That point of light.

That was more than a point of light.

Two points, impossibly close, impossibly small, spinning around each other in a near-blur.

Two souls.

Ash's, and one linked to and protected by Ash's.

Opening their eyes, they gazed up to the sky where Marduk had finally perished.

"Chris," Ash repeated, and looked at Alycia. "We have to get his body before it…"

Shara gaped down at them, her ears impossibly keen. "Oh my gods," she said, and she, Emmi, and Alycia gaped amongst one another.

"We're running out of time," Ash bolted back up onto their feet. "Shara, I know I have no right to ask this, but…may I? I mean, can I get up onto your back, and…gryphon, I mean. We have to catch Chris, now!"

The other Sentinels had stopped cheering, and Ash had their attention now. Shara looked around, and then nodded. "Alright. Alycia, too, but I can't carry anyone else."

Emmi didn't even hesitate, and simultaneously with Shara, she shapeshifted, this time into a peregrine falcon. Shara's massive, Clydesdale-sized gryphon form, gleaming with white and gold feathers, stood above them a second later.

Ash hefted up onto the gryphon's back, and then held a hand down and helped Alycia onto Shara's back. "What's going on?" Alycia asked, fear and a hint of hope in her voice.

"We can save him," Ash shouted. "Go, Shara, go!"

With a screeching roar, Shara lurched forward, and Ash had to bend forward and clutch at Shara's neck feathers, while Alycia wrapped her arms around Ash's mid-section, and they were off and up in the air in a heartbeat. When they settled into a steep climb, Ash noticed falcon-Emmi flying just beside and behind them, pumping wings rapidly.

Closing their eyes again, Ash looked upon their soul, and then, carefully, afraid, they touched the surface.

They instantly knew where Chris was. And he was lower than they expected.

Pointing just above the horizon, Ash said, "That way!"

Shara adjust course, pumped wings harder. Wind whipped by, stinging Ash's eyes. Alycia held tighter, gathering Ash's jacket into fists.

They kept a hold of their soul, reaching out and searching for Chris. Until...

It's too late.

Ash felt their heart wrench when they knew exactly where Chris was. "Oh no," they whispered. Shara must have heard. She turned her head just enough for one eye to look into Ash's horrified face. Ash pointed down now.

Below them.

Shara followed their finger, and screeched in alarm. With binocular vision, thanks to her gryphon form, Shara probably saw exactly what Ash feared.

Chris had already crashed to the Earth.

Pumping wings hard enough that Ash and Alycia nearly fell off, Shara raced the rising sun, whose predawn glow grew brighter and brighter to their right. Eventually they soared above the rooftops of an endless suburban sprawl, past a hospital, and over a wide swath of green parkland.

Ash and Alycia saw the depression in the grass at the same time, a crater barely visible from a nearby street light. Alycia cried out, "Chris!"

Shara swooped down and landed dozens of feet away at full speed, her four legs pumping beneath them as she rapidly slowed and came to a halt only a few feet away.

Alycia was off of Shara's back before they had fully stopped, and Ash followed a second later, both rushing into the ten-foot-wide crater. Shara shapeshifted and followed, and seconds later, Emmi appeared as well.

Expecting the worst, Ash braced themselves to find the crumpled, flattened, broken remains of Chris. What would a body look like after falling from so high?

But they had forgotten about Nina. As large as a horse, with vast, scaly wings, Nina had wrapped herself around Chris, and held him on her chest and stomach protectively. Nina had been the first to hit, her body absorbing the impact.

The dragon saw the four of them crest the crater, and groaned in relief.

"Chris!" Alycia shrieked.

"What is it?" Abby's voice called over the phones, startling Ash. *"Is he okay? What's going on?"*

As Nina slowly, agonizingly maneuvered Chris to set him down on the bottom of the crater, Shara touched her ear piece and said, "He's here, Nina saved him."

Babbar's worried voice called back, *"Is she okay? Is she alive? Dammit, I should have come with…"*

"She's fine," Shara interrupted. "She's just fine. But I don't know about…"

She fell silent, and the four of them gathered around Chris's limp form. Alycia pressed her ear to his chest, held her breath, but as Ash knelt above Chris's head, they already knew what Alycia would discover.

"He's not breathing," Alycia's voice shook. "Oh God, he's not breathing, his heart isn't going. I," she lifted up, looked down. "Will C.P.R. work?"

"No," Ash said, surprisingly calm even though they didn't exactly know what to do next. "I think his body is fine." They looked questioningly at Nina, who had climbed up out of the crater and slumped down onto her belly.

She looked at Ash, and with a mental voice that was quiet and weary, she said, *"His body is fine. His soul…"*

"His soul is fine, too," Ash declared, and even Nina looked surprised. Looking down at Chris, Ash said, "It just needs to find its way back home."

With that, they bent over Chris, and touched his temples before closing their eyes.

This time, there was no Tattannu to guide them, no millions of collective years of experience. Just Ash and Chris. If they were to find a way to save him, it would have to be on their own.

If Chris's body had any presence in the soul realm, Ash couldn't see it, but maybe that didn't matter. Their souls were in resonance before. Maybe all they had to do was make a connection between Chris's body, which Ash now touched, and their resonant souls.

Stepping closer to the golden sphere, Ash carefully reached out and once again touched the surface.

Nothing happened.

They felt the power, and maybe even felt a second presence, but it wasn't enough.

So they pushed. Their arms passed through the ethereal membrane. Golden lightning danced around their hands. But unlike what Chris had done not a half hour ago, because of how much smaller Ash's soul was now, they didn't have to go so deep.

The membrane passed their elbow, and then their hands were around the two glowing points.

They cupped their hands, and waited, but the second light didn't leave the first. So Ash huffed impatiently. "Really? Come on, Chris. I happen to know that someone who loves you is waiting. Don't keep her waiting any longer." Still nothing. So Ash pressed, "You promised."

Those were the magic words. The two lights stopped spinning around one another, and the second one leapt into Ash's cupped hands. They withdrew it from the center. Further and further out. It became difficult at the outer membrane, as if it protected everything within, but a little coaxing and willpower, and the light came out of Ash's soul.

Immediately it leapt from their hands, and flew over just a few feet before halting suddenly.

A second passed. Two. Three.

And then a bolt of lightning lanced out from it, connecting with a previously-invisible sphere of golden light.

Ash blinked back to reality just as Chris sucked in a breath of air, his eyes shooting open.

Relief washed over Ash, and they released his head as he sat up. At the same time, Shara, Emmi, and Alycia called out his name and surrounded him in the tightest group hug that Ash had ever seen.

A wave of dizziness swept over Ash, and they fell backward onto their butt, gripping their head and trying desperately to stop the world from spinning.

"Woh, there," Emmi saw them falling over and extracted herself from the hug, the others following suit very quickly. Her steadying hand was on Ash's shoulder a second later. "You okay?"

"I," Ash breathed. The world started to stabilize. "Yeah. I think. I just…" They looked down at their hands, and thought, *they look different. I think I look different. I feel different…* "I feel weak. Somehow…less."

As if a giant hole now lived inside of themself. The absence where once there had been so much. Ash had been so much more, and now they were back to just being plain, little old Ash.

Chris stared at them for a long moment, and then he hefted himself up, his broken bones apparently fully healed now. His clothes were a tattered mess, belying the wounds he had endured, but not even scars remained to remind them of his wounds. Shara, Alycia and Emmi stood up with him, and then Chris reached down a hand to help Ash.

They stared at it, hating it. Not Chris, just the need for help. But even with the world no longer tilting or spinning, they didn't feel quite steady enough to stand on their own. So Ash accepted his hand.

And a golden spark arced between them, stinging both.

"Ouch," Ash retracted their hand, shaking the buzzing feeling out of it. In that instant, however, they felt something.

A connection beyond the physical.

A lingering resonance.

They were still more than just 'plain old Ash.' There was still magic in their veins. So they reached up, accepted Chris's hand, and allowed him to help them up.

"Thank you," he said. "Thank you for saving me."

The hint of a smile drew across Ash's face. Then, without even having to look at one another, Chris, Alycia, Emmi, and Shara all encircled Ash and embraced them in a hug.

An overwhelming feeling welled up inside, and Ash didn't know what to do or say. Tears welled in their eyes, fell upon Chris's tattered jacket. All Ash knew was that this, *this* was where they wanted to be. With these people.

With this family.

For the first time since their cousin's murder, they felt wanted.

They felt at peace.

CHAPTER 32

The world is forever changed.

Chris looked down at the dried, dead grass beneath his feet. *No,* he reminded himself. *The grass isn't dead, it's just slumbering.*

He, along with every Denver-based Sentinel, including Ash and Mia, stood on the grounds of Fairmount Cemetery in Denver. Clad in black suits and dresses, they mournfully surrounded a freshly-dug grave, thankful for the warmth that sometimes came during Denver's winters. If there had been any recent snow, it had already melted.

A week had passed since London. He wished he could say that things had returned to normal in that time, but nothing would ever be normal again. Nina had been weak from helping Chris fight Marduk and from saving him from their twenty-mile fall, but once the two teams united, with Tom's body carried between two team members and with remnants of the Arcane Dawn surrounding them, a flip of a copper coin was all the dragon needed, and they were safe back in Osaka.

In the middle of a city street.

Seeing the reaction of ordinary citizens to the appearance of a horse-sized dragon was more than a little amusing, but also terrifying when the police showed up. Still, Sato had the ear of the Japanese Prime Minister, and the situation was resolved quickly.

Then there was the matter of getting back to the United States. The President had immediately issued a pardon for the Sentinels. Not exactly a public pardon, but the hunting squads were ordered to stand down entirely, and the President promised a review of the policies he had enacted over the past three months.

Mia was on her feet by the time they'd returned from London, but she collapsed upon seeing her husband's body, and she and Alycia cried together, with the Sentinels surrounding them with love and support as best they could.

Finally, a private flight was arranged several days later, and for the first time in three months, the Denver Sentinels found themselves looking upon a familiar sight.

They were home.

Cleanup efforts from the fallen Sentinel Tower were still ongoing, and Chris and Emmi didn't dare return to their apartment, not yet. Instead, they, along with Ash, Shara, Babbar and Nina were invited by Alycia and Mia to stay in Tom's old house, down in Englewood. It was tight quarters with so many people, but it was better than living in an abandoned factory. Nina was too large to fit inside of the house, but she happily took up residence in the back yard, remaining invisible so as to not frighten the neighbors or invoke the wrath of the local H.O.A.

The arrangements had been made, and they held a quiet funeral in Fairmount. As far as any graveyard could be, Fairmount was gorgeous, and was a testament to the history of Denver, with stones dating back over a century.

And now, one more would join them.

A hero's grave.

Alycia stood to Chris's right as they watched the procession, until she squeezed his hand, bringing him around from his thoughts. He looked up into her eyes, and she into his, and he knew the moment was at hand.

She would give the Eulogy. She was terrified, and had told him as much last night when they, along with Emmi and Ash, sat around the coffee table in the living room helping her write her speech. So he squeezed her hand back, and smiled, and despite feeling like he was now *less* than he was, diminished, weak, he willed confidence through his eyes and into her soul.

Breaking contact, Alycia stepped forward and stood before Tom's casket. Only the Denver Sentinels, along with Yua and Sato, their former trainer from last month, Benson, and Alycia's brother were present, but that included a not-elf, who no longer hid her ears or violet eyes, a gnome, and an invisible horse-sized dragon.

When Alycia took a moment to collect herself and pulled out her note cards, Emmi scooted closer to Chris's left and took hold of his hand. He smiled weakly at her, and she at him, and together they watched and waited.

Alycia's eyes searched her speech, and then they looked up and met Chris's gaze. They held one another, locked in each other's eyes, for a long time, until she drew in a deep breath, and looked upon the rest of the gathered Sentinels.

"What can I saw about the man who was my father?" she began, and Chris arched an eyebrow. This was already a departure from what she had written last night. "Can words really convey who and what he was? Could I ever do justice for the man who raised me and tried, in his own way, to protect me from the monsters of the world?

"I don't think so. But I'm going to try. Some might see his death…" Her voice shook and broke upon that word, but she cleared her throat and pressed on. "His death as a tragedy. And God knows, I will miss him. Every. Single. Day. But my father died as he lived. Protecting others. Protecting the man that I love," she looked at Chris. "And by doing so, saving every single person on Earth. My father's death *wasn't* a tragedy. It was a triumph! After all, his career was spent protecting the Barrier, protecting *all* of us from Marduk. Now Marduk and Nabu are gone, and…" She turned back and looked upon her father's casket. "Now we have won. We're safe." She rested her hand upon the smooth, polished wood. "So you can rest now, Dad. We'll take it from here."

He heard a whimper, a staunched cry, and looked to Mia. She looked ready to collapse, her breathing coming harder, her lip trembling. Alycia saw it too, and rushed back to her spot next to Chris and her mother and wrapped her arms tightly around Mia.

Tom had died saving Chris. He wanted to feel guilty for that. *I should feel guilty for that.* Chris's body had been broken and bruised, his senses a jumble when Nabu threw that ice spike at him. But he should have known better than to let down his guard.

And now…

Now I am powerless.

Not *really* powerless, but without the countless souls backing his powers, even the simplest magic was near-impossible for him to accomplish. In a life-or-death situation, he wasn't entirely sure he would be of any use.

That was why he wasn't going to stay with the Sentinels.

Chris didn't know exactly what he would do next or where he would go. He just knew that he no longer belonged on an elite team of defenders.

Alycia and her mother parted, but held hands, as Alycia reached out and grasped Chris's hand with her free one. Shara stood next to Emmi, tears falling freely from her eyes, the only time Chris had ever seen her cry, and she likewise took Emmi's hand. And together, they watched as the casket was slowly, gently lowered six feet down. They took turns throwing a single flower on top of the casket then, except for Chris, who felt like he didn't deserve that honor.

Instead, he stood above the hole, stared down at the shadowed casket below, and with trembling lips, said, "Thank you for saving me," before walking back to Alycia and Emmi.

When the funeral ended, the Sentinels were to go back to Alycia's house, but Chris asked if he, Alycia, Shara, Ash, and Emmi could make one quick stop elsewhere in Fairmount first.

It had been two years since his last visit. But he still knew exactly where to find Naomi's grave. He could find it in his sleep, if he needed.

The four of them stood over it then. Other than dried grass from the dead of winter, it was well kept, well-tended. And the plot next to it had been reserved for...

Throat caught up, he saw his mother's name on the gravestone next to his sister's, her death date only three months old.

This was the first time he'd been here since then.

He had lost his mother. Tom was dead because of him. And now, he felt like he had lost Naomi all over again.

But that wasn't why he was here. He was here because Alycia had recently asked him if there was a chance she could ever meet his sister, in the 'fabled soul realm.' That wasn't an option anymore, but Alycia, Ash, and Shara had never seen his sister's grave. Only Emmi had.

"I think I get it now," he told the others while staring at Naomi's stone. "I think I know what Tattannu meant when he said I had to give up everything."

"What do you mean?" Alycia asked, squeezing his hand.

"I know that part of it was because I was meant to become intermingled with the rest of the souls, lost in the cacophony and sacrificed along with them when we destroyed Marduk. But even having survived…" He shook his head. "I had my sister back. For six months, we talked, got to know one another all over again. And now she's gone again."

Alycia stepped in front of him, forced him to look into her eyes. "Hey," she soothed. "She gave her soul to save the world. Sounds a lot like someone else I know, yeah? Like brother, like sister?"

Chris couldn't help but smile, and an airy laugh escaped him. "I suppose you're right."

"No supposing, love," she grinned. "I'm always right, yeah?"

Another laugh, a little louder this time, and he shook his head. "Is this how it's always going to be? Because I-"

And she interrupted him with a quick kiss, killing his retort in a heartbeat.

Pulling away a second later, he stood dumbfounded. He didn't expect this, especially not after her father's funeral. But she still managed a smile, and when he didn't say anything, she asked, "What was that, Hiccup?"

Defaulting to their old form of quoting movies to banter, Chris knew exactly what she meant, and he grinned. "I could get used to it."

It seemed an appropriate movie to quote. Hell, they even had a dragon nearby.

Somehow, despite her fresh loss, Alycia had found a way to cheer him up. Like she always did for everyone. No matter how down she felt, others came first for her.

Maybe that was part of why he loved her. She had the most beautiful soul of all, and that was comparing hers to millions of others.

The five of them looked one last time upon Naomi's grave, and then they found their way back to the vehicles to head for the house.

A wake was held there, with everyone having brought food and drink to contribute to the cause. In the basement, an old 'man cave' turned workout room was re-purposed closer to its original intent, with the bar open and drinks and food spread out across it.

Though Chris wanted to comfort Alycia and Mia for their loss, there came a point when the emptiness welled up so much inside of him that he couldn't stand it anymore, and he went upstairs and out into the backyard. He sat alone on the steps of the paver patio, and buried his face in his hands. The tears flowed freely after that, out of sight of everyone else.

He hated himself. Hated himself because he was more worried about his future than his girlfriend's loss. More worried about the emptiness inside of himself than the emptiness Alycia must feel. Because he felt like he needed as much comfort as she did, and it just wasn't fair, for either of them.

A low rumble and chortle surprised him, and suddenly an invisible shape nuzzled his ear, startling him. Nina coalesced into view, her head stooped low to be level with his.

"I am sorry," she said.

It seemed paltry, yet for all of the pain he felt inside, the words resonated, felt comforting. He smiled and, not thinking about what he was doing, he reached under Nina's chin and scratched, her scales still feeling more like velvet than hard scales. She purred at his action and shook her body, shivering. *"Ooooh, yessss. Don't stop, don't stop!"*

He laughed, despite the emptiness, and bowed his head.

"I think you have a new best friend," Shara's voice startled Chris. He whipped around, saw her coming out, closing the patio door without making a single noise. *How the hell does she do that?*

Huffing out a breath, Chris shook his head, and looked into Nina's red eyes. "No. I mean, yes, but Emmi will always be my best."

A strange chortling chuckle escaped Nina. *"Worry not, my dear Champion. You need not try to earn my respect or friendship. You have it now and forever."*

Not sure what to say to that, Chris simply nodded. Shara sat down next to him, while Nina's head whipped about upon hearing something from a neighbor's backyard. She instantly vanished.

Chris and Shara sat silently together for a moment, before she nudged him with her elbow. "So I hear from Emmi that you don't intend to stay with the Sentinels."

So that's why she had sought him out.

"I don't belong here," he said at length, and looked at his hands, palms up. "I mean, I don't belong on the team anymore."

"Oh?" she asked. "And why's that?"

Because it's my fault Tom is dead. "Because I'm powerless."

He didn't see Shara's reaction. Not until she said, "You're joking, right?" He looked into her beautiful, violet eyes, and was greeted with an incredulous frown. *"That's* what this is about? Because you're suddenly normal like the rest of us?"

It was a strange world they lived in, when an arcane magic user was considered 'normal.' Or maybe just normal to Shara, who had lived with magic before being stranded on Earth.

"Chris, Tom and I, Marisol, Tiana, we all got by without magic. Hells, I got by without it for *eighty years*. Are you trying to tell me I didn't contribute in that time?"

"No," he shook his head, his throat tightening. Looking away, he shook his head again, "No, that's not what I'm saying. But that's just it. You know how to fight without magic. You know how to protect without it. I don't."

"Oh, so Benson's training was for nothing, eh?" Her voice was accusatory, but he allowed it. Maybe he deserved it.

"No," he shook his head. "I'm sure he's good. I was just a shitty pupil."

"Oh, for gods' sake, kid," she huffed and stood up, and began pacing around the patio. "You've handled yourself as well as anyone could expect a fully trained Sentinel to, and by that I mean you handled yourself expertly, alright?"

"People died because of me," he said through a shaking voice.

"People die all the time!" she waved her hands around. "And that's against mere mortals! You went up against a demigod and a *god*, for crying out loud! What more do you expect from yourself?"

He looked down. Opened his mouth to retort. Caught himself, and clamped his mouth shut. "I don't know," he admitted. "I don't know where to go from here."

"Well, after today, maybe join us in celebrating, eh?" Shara stepped closer to him, stooped low, and touched his chin with her fingers, forcing him to look up into her eyes. "We won. We beat the bad guy. We beat him because of *your* sacrifice."

His throat caught again. The emptiness inside resonated. "Not just me," he said. "Naomi's. Tattannu's. All of those souls."

"Hmm," Shara nodded. "Good point. Don't let their sacrifice be in vain."

He frowned up at her. "...What?"

"Don't let their sacrifices be in vain," she repeated. "Stay with us. We might not ever have to fight another infernal…at least, I hope not." Shara shuddered. "But the world is a freaking mess right now. Arcane Dawn still holds London, though we severely weakened their hold over it. Non-magic people still think we're freaks or evil or whatever. And unless I'm mistaken, Nabu's infection will remain in anyone not cleansed, and those people will continue to worship a dead god. Ash wants to join us, but I know that if you two work together, we'll stand a better chance at removing Nabu's influence from the world. Chris," she shook her head, "there's still a lot of work to do. And I need you on my team."

Chris blinked up at her in surprise. "Your team? You mean…?"

Grinning, Shara nodded and stood tall. "Yup. Sato just told me. I'm officially the Commander of the United States Sentinels!"

A broad smile crossed his face, and he stood up and offered her his hand. She gladly accepted it, pumping his arm twice. "Congratulations, Shara. You deserve it."

"Thanks," she beamed.

"But," he frowned, "I thought…you know, with magic working again and all. Don't you want to go home?"

Shara visibly hesitated, her eyes darting around as if she was looking for an answer in the air. "Well, see that's the thing. I can. And I want to. However, I also feel like to do so would leave everyone here with the short end of the stick. Don't get me wrong, Marisol would be my choice to lead in my absence, and that's why I'm going to ask her to be my XO." Chris perked an eyebrow up. "Don't tell her that, though. I want to make it an official request when we get back up and running. What I mean to say, though, is that…"

She sighed, folded her arms in front of her stomach, and stared at Chris. "Tom left us a legacy. I feel like it's my responsibility to make sure that legacy is taken care of. Maybe if the council hadn't offered me the job, I'd be asking Nina to take me home tomorrow, but as it is…I want to stay." She chewed the inside of her cheek, and then made a point to once again stare at Chris. "I want to stay for you, too. And Alycia, and Emmi. Abby, Marisol, Tiana. You're the only group of humans that have ever accepted me, treated me as an equal. So maybe there's hope for your kind after all."

A grin pressed against Chris's cheeks, while simultaneously, her words resonated inside of him. *Tom left us a legacy.* That was too true.

"Chris," she started, and stopped. Then started again, "I need you. *We* need you. Not just your skills and experience, but magic is everywhere now, and we have a dedicated enchanter on our team."

A sly grin drew across her face. "Think of the things you and Alycia could invent, what with your engineering degree and all. The resources of the Sentinels at your back. By the way, the President officially released all of our assets back to us. I know Abby could sure use your help getting a new facility setup."

He nodded. "Good thing we had all those backup servers in Babbar's mansion, but we'll need to setup new equipment at a new place, transfer the data over…"

"Ah," Shara pointed at him, smiling. "You said 'we'll.' So does that mean you're in?"

He hesitated. Thought about what Shara had said.

About those who sacrificed themselves, and why.

Looking Shara in the eye, he finally exhaled and nodded. "Alright. I'm in."

"Good," Another voice startled him from behind. He spun around, and saw Emmi standing at the patio door. *Christ, two sneaky folks on the team,* he grumbled inwardly. "That means I don't have to try to convince you."

Arching an eyebrow, he asked, "What do you mean?"

"If you said no to Shara, it would be my turn to try to convince you," Emmi stepped out, leaving the door open so that Alycia could follow. "And if I failed, Alycia would try."

"Then Ash," Alycia nodded. "Marisol, Tiana, Abby. Eventually we would have worn you down," she caressed his cheek and then kissed it. "But looks like Shara knows how to inspire others." Winking at Shara, Alycia added, "A good trait in a leader."

"Quite," Shara grinned.

"I see," he huffed. "So you all were gonna gang up on me?"

"What can I say," Shara shrugged. "I don't like to lose."

"Ah," he nodded, trying to cover a grin with his hand.

"Now come on," Alycia tugged on his arm. "Let's get back inside. Sorry, Nina," she called over her shoulder. "I wish the house was big enough for you."

Chris relayed her response, "She says it's okay. Just as long as the new Sentinel facility will be large enough to fit her."

"Oh good," Shara beamed. "Sounds like she's staying, too, then."

Chris stopped just before Alycia could pull him inside. He looked out into the seemingly empty back yard. "Are you? Staying, I mean?"

There was a hint of a shimmer nearby, and he *felt* her presence as she contemplated his question. Finally, *"Yes, I think so. Maybe for an age. I wish to see how humanity copes with the return of magic."*

He smiled, and nodded.

"I guess," he looked at Alycia, "as the old saying goes, the more things change…"

"…The more they stay the same," she nodded in return.

CHAPTER 33

Another week passed, and as a temporary measure, the Sentinels utilized Abby's apartment downtown as a centralized location to base operations out of. Some of their gear had been returned to them, recovered from the ruins of Sentinel Tower, and with the exception of things they might need at a moment's notice, the excess was stored in Babbar's mansion. Despite his claim months ago that he only stuck with the Sentinels as protection against Nabu and Marduk, the gnome remained with them.

Nina may or may not have been an influence on his decision.

Shara wanted to keep the Sentinels centralized in downtown Denver in the long run, but it became more and more apparent that being able to buy up and customize the top few floors of an existing building was a difficult order, even with four thousand years of built-up assets funding the Sentinels.

But today was to be Chris and Alycia's first day back 'in office,' so to speak. They could have taken longer bereavement leave, but Alycia insisted that getting back to work would be good for both of them, and Chris agreed.

Still, being in downtown Denver for the first time in over three months, Chris wanted to make one quick stop first. Especially because Alycia had asked him and Emmi to move into her house, with Ash rooming with them until they could get on their feet again.

At seven o'clock in the morning, on a chilly Monday in December, Chris, Emmi and Alycia stood outside of an old ten-story apartment. The façade was tan-colored, but the sidewalk and first floor were heavily covered in graffiti now. Statements about 'blasphemers' and 'evil' and 'thou shalt not suffer a witch to live' tarnished a once-clean building.

Memories of seeing the mob crowded around the building on the news flashed through Chris's memory. How much of this graffiti was three months old? How much was fresh?

Maybe Shara was right to say that there was hope for humanity, but it felt like they still had a long ways to go.

Neither Chris nor Emmi had managed to hold on to their keys, but the apartment office staff was in as early as they used to be, and they grudgingly allowed Chris to borrow a copy of the key to his and Emmi's apartment. They'd come prepared with a paper copy of their pardon, but the office staff didn't bother to look at it. However, he noticed that they were a little happier when Chris told them that he and Emmi would be moving out shortly.

For old time's sake, they trudged up the stairwell rather than take the elevator, all the way up to the eighth floor. There, they found more graffiti scrawled out on their door, and evidence of hastily-patched holes in the walls on either side of their door.

Chris stepped up to the door, drew in a deep breath, and then unlocked and opened up.

And the three of them stepped into the shadows of the past.

Less than seven months since all of it began. Yet it felt like an age had passed, and Chris felt strange, even out of place when he stepped inside.

The apartment was a mess. The police and federal agents had ransacked the place, maybe to look for any clues about where Chris and Emmi might have fled to three months ago. The couch cushions were thrown about and torn open, the coffee table was overturned, the kitchen cabinets were all left ajar.

Cringing, Chris knew his bedroom was likely to look worse. But if he was lucky, there'd still be some clothes left in there that he could recover. The ones he wore now were newly bought - blue jeans and a white t-shirt, but he didn't want to have to buy a whole new wardrobe.

The trio headed down the hallway, towards the two bedrooms and the bathroom.

Lightly smacking Chris's arm, Emmi grinned, "Hey, at least we won't have to share a bathroom anymore."

He smiled at that. Alycia's house had two and a half bathrooms, so that wasn't entirely true yet, but since he and Alycia planned to eventually move into the master bedroom together, they'd soon have the master bathroom all to themselves.

They stood at their bedroom doors then, both ajar, and surveyed the wreckage. The police hadn't been kind.

"Well," Emmi sighed. "I mean…oh hey, my favorite yoga pants!" She disappeared into her room.

Chris and Alycia exchanged amused grins, and then climbed into his room, over clothes, an overturned dresser, and a mattress thrown off the bed. He didn't know why, maybe a force of habit, but Chris started tidying the place up. At least enough that it was no longer treacherous just to walk around. He and Alycia fixed the dresser, the bed, the desk. And then he found a couple of old duffle bags, and started sorting through his old clothes.

At one point, he ducked under his desk to grab his favorite pair of jeans, only to stop short upon spying something peculiar. Alycia sat on his bed, folding shirts for him before putting them in bags, and stopped when he did. Had he made a noise that cued her in on his surprise?

Because under the desk, atop the old wooden floor was a pile of tan-colored sand.

Gaping at the small pile, he shook his head, knowing exactly where that sand had come from.

"Huh."

"What is it?" Alycia asked.

He extracted himself from beneath the desk, looked around, and spotted a small, diamond-shaped plastic container for mechanical pencil lead. He popped the cap off, discarded the pencil lead, and then ducked back under the desk. "Something worth keeping," he said, as he carefully gathered the sand into as big of a pile as he could, and then started pinching it and transferring it into the lead container. Once it was full, he snapped the cap closed, and extracted himself again before sitting next to Alycia.

She scrutinized the sand, and frowned. "Is that what I think it is?"

He smiled and nodded.

The sand that had followed him from his dreams. The sand that had come through his premonitions in the soul realm and scattered across his bedroom floor.

His first legitimate introduction to magic.

"I remember you told me about that," she shook her head and carefully took the container from his hand. "I thought you threw it in the rubbish bin."

"I must have missed a spot," he shrugged.

It was strange to see it. Strange to remember what he was like back then. He had been a conundrum, now that the thought about it. A man of science, who would never believe in magic, and yet he watched anime weekly with Alycia, watched fantasy movies all the time, played fantasy video games.

Maybe that's why he'd ended up accepting it so quickly. Accepting his role and the tasks so vaguely laid out before him.

This sand, it was the stuff that had kicked off his first real adventure.

And had led him to such immense pain and loss.

My own adventure turned out to be quite different, he thought, recalling Frodo's line from Lord of the Rings.

He looked up then, surveyed the bedroom, in a much nicer state than it had been minutes ago. He could actually see the floor, for starters. But he felt an emptiness inside of him. The loss of his sister, again. His mother. His family. Tom.

It all still hurt.

And another Lord of the Rings quote passed through his mind, only this time, he said it aloud. "How do you pick up the threads of an old life?" He looked at Alycia, saw the recognition in her eyes.

She finished the quote for him. "How do you go on, when in your heart, you begin to understand, there is no going back?"

Nodding, Chris sighed heavily, and shook his head.

But when Alycia's hand soothingly rubbed his shoulder, he remembered his answer to that question, the one he'd mumbled quietly the first time he saw the movie.

"You don't," he said simply. "You can't go back. All you can do is move forward. Start again, start fresh. Make the most of what you have left, and build something new with it."

Alycia squeezed his shoulder, and he looked at her as she smiled back at him. "Exactly," she whispered.

Her golden brown eyes. Her beautiful soul. Her love for him.

That was more than enough to start a new life with.

Looking around his room one last time, he clapped his hands on

his knees and stood up. "Well, then, there's only one thing for it."
He held out his hand, and Alycia gave him the container. He looked
at it before he shoved it in his pocket, and then he closed up the bags
and hefted one onto his shoulder, with Alycia hefting the other onto
hers as she stood up.

They met Emmi out in the living room, and he was surprised to
see only one bag packed. It seemed that she, too, didn't want to hold
on to much of the past.

"Ready to go?" she asked.

He nodded, and solemnly whispered, "Yeah."

As they filed out of the apartment, Chris stopped, and looked one
last time around the disheveled apartment.

It was time to let go, he realized. Time to move on.

With a smile, he walked out and asked the two ladies, "The
adventure is just beginning, isn't it?"

Emmi and Alycia returned his smile, and his best friend said,
"Yup. And I can't think of anyone else I'd rather start it with than
you two."

"Yeah. We're stronger together, the three of us," Alycia added.

He smiled at the both of them, and turned back to the apartment
one last time.

With that, Chris closed the door on his old life.

And walked boldly into his new one.

DID YOU LIKE THIS BOOK?

Reader reviews play an important role in a book's success by helping other readers discover stories they might enjoy. Please consider taking a moment to leave a review for *Chronicles of the Sentinels - Champions* on Amazon! You'll be making this author's day :D

ABOUT THE AUTHOR

Jon Wasik has been telling stories since he was a little boy, usually with a cookie and milk at his Great Grandma's kitchen table. It wasn't until 5th grade that he finally put pen to paper, and from that moment on, writing has been his greatest passion.

When he isn't writing, Jon likes to read, play video games, and watch insanely geeky movies with his wife. His Gollum voice impressions are eerie, he quotes Doctor Who like others quote the bible, and he can leap terabytes of data in a single bound!

Want to find out more about Jon, or keep up on the latest news about his books? Check out his website, and while you're there, subscribe to his mailing list! Just go to the following website and click "Join Mailing List" at the top!
http://jonwasik.com/

www.ingramcontent.com/pod-product-compliance
Lightning Source LLC
Chambersburg PA
CBHW021308190726
48288CB00003B/746